KU-187-308

CRASH LANDING

They were now only a kilometer above the surface of the planet, coming in with a rush. Too fast! Han slowed them, using the brake thrusters roughly. G-forces seized him, and he felt as though something were squeezing his chest in a giant vise. He was gasping steadily now, and he dared to look down at his air pak.

Empty! The status indicator was solidly in the red zone.

Hold together, Han, he counseled himself. *Just keep breathing. There's got to be enough air in your suit to support you for a couple of minutes—at least.*

He shook his head, feeling light-headed and dizzy. His breath began to burn in his chest.

He braked again, lightly, and the ship bucked suddenly.

I've lost my forward stabilizer!

The sensational *Star Wars* series published by
Bantam Books and available from all good bookshops

The *Empire* Trilogy by Timothy Zahn
Heir to the Empire • Dark Force Rising
The Last Command

The *Jedi Academy* Trilogy by Kevin J. Anderson
Jedi Search • Dark Apprentice
Champions of the Force

The Truce at Bakura
by Kathy Tyers

The Courtship of Princess Leia
by Dave Wolverton

The *Corellian* Trilogy by Roger MacBride Allen
Ambush at Corellia • Assault at Selonia
Showdown at Centerpoint

The *Cantina* Trilogy edited by Kevin J. Anderson
Tales from the Mos Eisley Cantina
Tales from Jabba's Palace • Tales of the Bounty Hunters

The Crystal Star
by Vonda McIntyre

The *X-Wing* Series by Michael Stackpole
Rogue Squadron • Wedge's Gamble
The Krytos Trap • The Bacta War

The *Black Fleet Crisis* Trilogy by Michael P. Kube-McDowell
Before the Storm • Shield of Lies
Tyrant's Test

Children of the Jedi
by Barbara Hambly

Darksaber
by Kevin J. Anderson

Shadows of the Empire
by Steve Perry

and in hardcover

The Illustrated Star Wars Universe
by Kevin J. Anderson & Ralph McQuarrie

The New Rebellion
by Kristine Kathryn Rusch

Planet of Twilight
by Barbara Hambly

THE PARADISE SNARE

A. C. Crispin

BANTAM BOOKS
TORONTO · NEW YORK · LONDON · SYDNEY · AUCKLAND

THE PARADISE SNARE
A BANTAM BOOK : 0 553 50546 7

First publication in Great Britain

PRINTING HISTORY
Bantam edition published 1997

®, ™, ©, 1997 by Lucasfilm Ltd. All rights reserved. ·
Used under authorization. Cover art by Drew Struzan.
Cover art copyright © 1997 by Lucasfilm Ltd.

The right of A. C. Crispin to be identified as the author of this
work has been asserted in accordance with sections 77 and 78
of the Copyright, Designs and Patents Act 1988.

All the characters in this book are fictitious,
and any resemblance to actual persons, living or dead,
is purely coincidental.

Condition of Sale

This book is sold subject to the condition that it shall not,
by way of trade or otherwise, be lent, re-sold, hired out
or otherwise circulated without the publisher's prior consent
in any form of binding or cover other than that in which
it is published and without a similar condition including
this condition being imposed on the subsequent purchaser.

Bantam Books are published by Transworld Publishers Ltd,
61–63 Uxbridge Road, London W5 5SA,
in Australia by Transworld Publishers (Australia) Pty Ltd,
15–25 Helles Avenue, Moorebank, NSW 2170,
and in New Zealand by Transworld Publishers (NZ) Ltd,
3 William Pickering Drive, Albany, Auckland.

Printed and bound in Great Britain by
Cox & Wyman Ltd, Reading, Berkshire

This book is dedicated to my friend, Thia Rose. When we were twelve, we swore we'd always be best friends . . .

. . . and, more years later than we like to count, we still are.

ACKNOWLEDGMENTS

Writing in the Star Wars universe is like becoming a part of a community—or, even, a family. The writers are encouraged to read each other's books, and there are dozens of nonfiction and technical books devoted to the characters, hardware, planets, and so forth. Writers trade information and tips back and forth, and generally help each other out.

Thus, many, many people helped me with this book. With the caveat that any mistakes readers may find are my own, I would like to thank the following:

Kevin Anderson, who gave me my first chance to write in the Star Wars universe. Kevin and Rebecca Moesta also helped with information about the Star Wars background and characters, as well as hand-holding, encouragement, and sage advice.

Michael Capobianco, fellow writer and significant other, for brainstorming, research help, intelligent advice, and fixing dinner when I was too busy writing to even realize I was hungry. Thanks, dear.

Bill Smith and Peter Schweighofer of West End Games for helping me figure out answers to such odd and esoteric questions as, "What does Han wear for underwear?" They "unstuck" me from quandaries more times than I can count.

Tom Dupree and Evelyn Cainto of Bantam Books for assistance, advice, and encouragement.

Sue Rostoni and Lucy Autrey Wilson of Lucasfilm for the "true facts."

Michael A. Stackpole, for help figuring out how to break a tractor beam, and other advice relating to ships and piloting.

Steve Osmanski, for reading the manuscript and giving sage advice on "techie" stuff.

As always, Kathy O'Malley, friend and writing buddy, for hand-holding and an occasional, well-deserved kick in the pants.

And, of course, George Lucas, who started it all. *Star Wars* blew me away the first time I saw it, and it's been an honor to contribute to the saga in a small way.

Thanks again, and may the Force be with you all.

The Paradise Snare

Chapter One:

TRADER'S LUCK

The ancient troopship, a relic of the Clone Wars, hung in orbit over the planet Corellia, silent and seemingly derelict. Looks were deceiving, however. The old *Liberator*-class vessel, once called *Guardian of the Republic*, now had a new life as *Trader's Luck*. The interior had been gutted and refitted with a motley assortment of living environments, and now contained nearly one hundred sentient beings, many of them humanoid. At the moment, however, only a few of them were awake, since it was the middle of the sleep cycle.

There was a watch on the bridge, of course. *Trader's Luck* spent much of its time in orbit, but it was still capable of hyperspace travel, even though it was slow by modern standards. Garris Shrike, the leader of the loosely allied trading "clan" that lived aboard the *Luck*, was a strict taskmaster, who followed formal ship's protocols. So there was always a watch on the bridge.

Shrike's orders aboard the *Luck* were always obeyed; he was not a man to cross without a good reason and a fully charged blaster. He ruled the clan of traders as a less-than-benevolent despot. A slender man of medium height, Garris was handsome in a hard-edged way. Streaks of silver-white above his temples accentuated his black hair and ice-blue eyes. His mouth was thin-lipped; he seldom smiled— and never with good humor. Garris Shrike was an expert shot and had spent his early years as a professional bounty hunter. He'd given it up, though, due to bad "luck"— meaning that his lack of patience had caused him to lose the richest bounties reserved for live delivery. Dead bodies were frequently worth far less.

Shrike *did* possess a warped sense of humor, especially if the pain of others was involved. When he was gambling and winning, he was subject to bouts of manic gaiety, especially if he was also drunk.

As he was at the moment. Sitting around the table in the former wardroom of the enlisted officers, Shrike was playing sabacc and drinking tankards of potent Alderaanian ale, his favorite beverage.

Shrike peered at his card-chips, mentally calculating. Should he hold pat and hope to complete a pure sabacc? At any moment the dealer could push a button and the values of all the card-chips would shift. If that happened, he'd be busted, unless he took an additional two and tossed most of his hand into the interference field in the center of the table.

One of his fellow players, a hulking Elomin suddenly turned his tusked head to glance behind him. A light on one of the auxiliary "status" panels was blinking. The huge, shaggy-furred Elomin grunted, then said in guttural Basic, "Something funny about the lockout sensor on the weapons cache, Captain."

Shrike insisted on "proper" protocol and chain of command, especially as it applied to himself. Unless engaged in some planetside caper, he always wore a military uniform while aboard the *Luck*—one he'd designed himself, patterned on the dress uniform of a high-ranking Moff. It was hung about with "medals" and "decorations" Shrike had picked up in pawnshops across the galaxy.

Now, hearing the Elomin's warning, he glanced up a little blearily, rubbed his eyes, then straightened up and dropped his card-chips onto the tabletop. "What is it, Brafid?"

The giant being wrinkled his tusked snout. "Not sure, Captain. It's reading normal now, but something flickered, as though the lock shorted out for a second. Probably just a momentary power flux."

Moving with such unusual grace and coordination that even the foppish "uniform" couldn't detract from his presence, the captain rose and walked around the table to study the readouts himself. All signs of intoxication had vanished. "Not a power flux," he decided after a moment. "Something else."

Turning his head, he addressed the tall, heavyset human on his left. "Larrad, look at this. Somebody shorted out the lock and is running a sim to fool us into thinking it's just a power flux. We've got a thief aboard. Is everyone armed?"

The man addressed, who happened to be Shrike's brother, Larrad Shrike, nodded, patting the holster that hung on the outside of his thigh. Brafid the Elomin fingered his "tingler"—an electric prod that was his weapon of choice—though the hairy alien was large enough to pick up most humanoids and break them over his knee.

The other person present, a female Sullustan who was the *Luck*'s navigator, stood up, patting the scaled-down blaster she wore. "Ready for action, Captain!" she squeaked. Despite her diminutive height, flapping jowls, and large, appealing bright eyes, Nooni Dalvo appeared almost as dangerous as the hulking Elomin who was her closest shipboard friend.

"Good," Shrike grunted. "Nooni, go post a guard over the weapons locker, just in case he comes back. Larrad, activate the biosensors, see if you can ID the thief and where he's heading."

Shrike's brother nodded and bent over the auxiliary control board. "Corellian human," he announced after a moment. "Male. Young. Height, 1.8 meters. Dark hair and eyes. Slender build. The bioscanner says it recognizes him. He's heading aft, toward the galley."

Shrike's expression hardened until his eyes were as cold and blue as the glaciers on Hoth. "The Solo kid," he said. "He's the only one cocky enough to try something like this." He flexed his fingers, then hardened them into a fist. The ring he wore, made from a single gem of Devaronian blood-poison, flashed dull silver in the bulkhead lights. "Well, I've gone easy on him so far, 'cause he's a good swoop pilot, and I never lost when I bet on him, but enough is enough. Tonight, I'm going to teach him to respect authority, and he's going to wish he'd never been born."

Shrike's teeth flashed, much brighter than the gem in his ring. "Or that I'd never 'found' him seventeen years ago and brought his sniveling, pants-wetting little behind home to the *Luck*. I'm a patient, tolerant man . . ." he sighed theatrically, "as the galaxy knows, but even I have my limits."

He glanced over at his brother, who was looking rather uncomfortable. Garris wondered if Larrad was remembering the Solo kid's *last* punishment session a year ago. The youth hadn't been able to walk for two days.

Shrike's mouth tightened. He wouldn't tolerate any softness among his subordinates. "Right, Larrad?" he said too softly.

"Right, Captain!"

Han Solo gripped the stolen blaster as he tiptoed along the narrow metal corridor. When he'd wired into the sim and jimmied the lock into the weapons cache, he'd only had a moment to reach in and grab the first weapon that came to hand. There'd been no time to pick and choose.

Nervously, he pushed strands of damp brown hair back from his forehead, realizing he was sweating. The blaster felt heavy and awkward in his hand as he examined it. Han had seldom held one before, and he only knew how to check the charge from the reading he'd done. He'd never actually fired a weapon. Garris Shrike didn't permit anyone but his officers to walk around armed. Squinting in the dim light, the young swoop pilot flipped open a small panel in the thickest part of the barrel and peered down at the read-outs. *Good. Fully charged. Shrike may be a bully and a fool, but he runs a taut ship.*

Not even to himself would the youth admit how much he actually feared and hated the captain of *Trader's Luck.* He'd learned long ago that showing fear of any sort was a swift guarantee of a beating—or worse. The only thing bullies and fools respected was courage—or, at least, bravado. So Han Solo had learned never to allow fear to surface in his mind or heart. There were times when he was dimly aware that it was there, deep down, buried under layers of street toughness, but anytime he recognized it for what it was, Han resolutely buried it even deeper.

Experimentally, he swung the blaster up to eye level and awkwardly closed one brown eye as he sighted along the barrel. The muzzle of the weapon wavered slightly, and Han cursed softly under his breath as he realized his hand was trembling. *Come on,* he told himself, *show some backbone, Solo. Getting off this ship and away from Shrike is worth a little risk.*

Reflexively, he glanced over his shoulder, then turned back just in time to duck under a low-hanging power coupling. He'd chosen this route because it avoided all the living quarters and recreation areas, but it was so narrow and low-ceilinged that he was beginning to feel claustrophobic as he tiptoed forward, resisting the urge to turn and look back over his shoulder.

Ahead of him, the near tunnel widened out, and Han realized he was almost at his destination. *Only a few more minutes,* he told himself, continuing to move with a stealthy grace that made his progress as soundless as that of a wonat's furred toe-pads. He was skirting the hyperdrive modules now, and then a larger corridor intersected. Han turned right, relieved that he could now walk without stooping.

He crept up to the door of the big galley and hesitated outside, his ears and nose busy. Sounds . . . yes, only the ones he'd been expecting to hear. The soft clatter of metal pans, the *sploooch* of dough being punched, and then the faint sounds of it being kneaded.

He could smell the dough, now. Wastril bread, his favorite. Han's mouth tightened. With any luck, he wouldn't be here to eat any of this particular batch.

Sticking the blaster into his belt, he opened the door and stepped into the galley. "Hey . . . Dewlanna . . ." he said softly. "It's me. I've come to say good-bye."

The tall, furred being who had been vigorously kneading the wastril dough swung around to face him with a soft, inquiring growl.

Dewlanna's real name was Dewlannamapia, and she had been Han's closest friend since she'd come to live aboard *Trader's Luck* nearly ten years ago, when Han had been about nine. (The young swoop pilot had no idea of when he'd been born, of course. Or who his parents had been. If it hadn't been for Dewlanna, he wouldn't even have known that his last name was "Solo.")

Han couldn't speak Wookiee—trying to reproduce the growls, barks, roars, and rumbling grunts made his throat sore, and he knew he sounded ridiculous—but he understood it very well. For her part, Dewlanna couldn't speak Basic, but she understood it as well as she did her own language. So communication between the human youth and the elderly Wookiee widow was fluent, but . . . different.

Han had gotten used to it years ago and never thought about it anymore. He and Dewlanna just . . . talked. They understood each other perfectly. Now he hefted the stolen blaster, careful not to point it at his friend. "Yes," he replied, in response to Dewlanna's comment, "tonight's the night. I'm getting off *Trader's Luck* and I'm never coming back."

Dewlanna rumbled at him worriedly as she automatically resumed kneading her dough. Han shook his head, giving her a lopsided grin. "You worry too much, Dewlanna. Of course I've got it all planned. I've got a spacesuit stashed in a locker near the robot freighter docks, and there's a ship docked there now that will be departing as soon as it's unloaded and refueled. A robot freighter, and it's headed where I want to go."

Dewlanna punched her dough, then growled a soft interrogatory.

"I'm heading for Ylesia," Han told her. "Remember I told you all about it? It's a religious colony near Hutt space, and they offer pilgrims sanctuary from the outside universe. I'll be safe from Shrike there. And"—he held up a small holodisk where the Wookiee cook could see it—"look at this! They're advertising for a pilot! I already used up the last of my payout credits from that job we pulled, to send a message, telling them I'm coming to interview for the job."

Dewlanna roared softly.

"Hey, I can't let you do that," Han protested, watching the cook set the loaves into pans and slide them into the thermal grid to bake. "I'll be okay. I'll lift some credits on my way to the robot ship. Don't worry, Dewlanna."

The Wookiee ignored him as she shuffled quickly across the galley, her hairy, slightly stooped form moving rapidly despite her advanced age. Dewlanna was nearly six hundred years old, Han knew. Old even for a Wookiee.

She disappeared into the door of her private living quarters, and then, a moment later, reappeared, clutching a pouch woven of some silky material that might even, from the look of it, be Wookiee fur.

She held it out to him with a soft, insistent whine.

Han shook his head again, and childishly put his hands behind his back. "No," he said firmly. "I'm not taking your savings, Dewlanna. You'll need those credits to buy passage to join me."

The Wookiee cocked her head and made a short, questioning sound.

"Of course you're going to join me!" Han said. "You don't think I'm going to leave you here to rot on this hulk, do you? Shrike gets crazier every year. Nobody's safe aboard the *Luck*. When I get to Ylesia and get settled in, I'm going to send for you to join me. Ylesia's a religious retreat, and they offer their pilgrims sanctuary. Shrike won't be able to touch us there."

Dewlanna reached inside the pouch, her hairy fingers surprisingly dexterous as she sifted through the credit vouchers inside. She handed several to her young friend. With a sigh, Han relented and took them. "Well . . . okay. But this is just a *loan*, okay? I'm going to pay you back. The salary the Ylesian priests are offering is a good one."

She growled her assent, then, without warning, reached out to ruffle his hair with her massive paw, leaving it sticking out in wild disarray. "Hey!" Han yelped. Wookiee head rubs were not to be taken lightly. "I just combed my hair!"

Dewlanna growled, amused, and Han drew himself up indignantly. "I do *not* look better scruffy. I keep telling you, the term 'scruffy' ain't complimentary among humans."

He stared at her, his indignation vanishing as he realized that this was the last time he'd see her beloved furry face, her gentle blue eyes, for a long time. Dewlanna had been his closest—and frequently *only*—friend for so long now. Leaving her was hard, very hard.

Impulsively, the Corellian youth threw himself against her warm, solid bulk, hugging her fiercely. His head reached only to the middle of her chest. Han could remember when he'd barely stood as tall as her waist. "I'm going to miss you," he said, his face muffled against her fur, his eyes stinging. "You take care of yourself, Dewlanna."

She roared softly, and her long, hairy arms came around him as she returned the embrace.

"Well, ain't this a touching sight," said a cold, all-too-familiar voice.

Han and Dewlanna both froze, then wheeled to face the man who'd entered through the Wookiee's quarters. Garris Shrike lounged in the doorway, his handsome features set in a smile that made Han's blood coagulate in his veins. Beside him, he could feel Dewlanna shudder, either with fear or loathing.

Two other crew members—Larrad Shrike and Brafid the

Elomin—were visible over Shrike's shoulder. Han balled his fists with frustration. If it had only been Shrike, he might've chanced jumping the *Luck*'s Captain. With Dewlanna to help him, they might have been able to subdue Garris, but with Larrad and the Elomin also present, they didn't have a chance.

Han was acutely conscious of the stolen blaster shoved into his belt. For a moment he considered going for it, but he abandoned that idea. Shrike was known for being fast on the draw. There was no way he could beat him, and that might get both Dewlanna and himself killed. Shrike was clearly in a rage.

Han licked dry lips. "Listen, Captain," he began. "I can explain—"

Shrike drew himself up, his eyes narrowing. "You can explain *what,* you cowardly little traitor? Stealing from your family? Betraying those who trusted you? Stabbing your benefactor in the back, you sniveling little *thief?*"

"But—"

"I've had it with you, Solo. I've been lenient with you so far, because you're a blasted good swoop pilot and all that prize money came in handy, but my patience is ended." Shrike ceremoniously pushed up the sleeves of his bedizened uniform, then balled his hands into fists. The galley's artificial lighting made the blood-jewel ring glitter dull silver. "Let's see what a few days of fighting off Devaronian blood-poisoning does for your attitude—along with maybe a few broken bones. I'm doing this for your own good, boy. Someday you'll thank me."

Han gulped with terror as Shrike started toward him. He'd lashed out at the trader captain once before, two years ago, when he'd been feeling cocky after winning the gladitorial Free-For-All on Jubilar—and had been instantly sorry. The speed and strength of Garris's returning blow had snapped his head back and split both lips so thoroughly that Dewlanna had had to feed him mush for a week until they healed.

With a snarl, Dewlanna stepped forward. Shrike's hand dropped to his blaster. "You stay out of this, old Wookiee," he snapped in a voice nearly as harsh as Dewlanna's. "Your cooking isn't *that* good."

Han had already grabbed his friend's furry arm and was forcibly holding her back. "Dewlanna, no!"

She shook off his hold as easily as she would have waved off an annoying insect and roared at Shrike. The captain drew his blaster, and chaos erupted.

"Noooo!" Han screamed, and leaped forward, his foot lashing out in an old street-fighting technique. His instep impacted solidly with Shrike's breastbone. The captain's breath went out in a great *houf!* and he went over backward. Han hit the deck and rolled. A tingler bolt sizzled past his ear.

"Larrad!" wheezed the captain as Dewlanna started toward him.

Shrike's brother drew his blaster and pointed it at the Wookiee. "Stop, Dewlanna!"

His words had no more effect than Han's. Dewlanna's blood was up—she was in full Wookiee battle rage. With a roar that deafened the combatants, she grabbed Larrad's wrist and yanked, spinning him around and snapping him in a terrible parody of a child's "snap the whip" game. Han heard a *crunch*, mixed with several *pops* as tendons and ligaments gave way. Larrad Shrike shrieked, a high, shrill noise that carried such pain that the Corellian youth's arm ached in sympathy.

Grabbing the blaster from his belt, Han snapped off a shot at the Elomin who was leaping forward, tingler ready and aimed at Dewlanna's midsection. Brafid howled, dropping his weapon. Han was amazed that he'd managed to hit him, but he didn't have long to wonder about the accuracy of his aim.

Shrike was staggering to his feet, blaster in hand, aimed squarely at Han's head. "Larrad?" he yelled at the writhing heap of agony that was his brother. Larrad did not reply.

Shrike cocked the blaster and stepped even closer to Han. "Stop it, Dewlanna!" the captain snarled at the Wookiee. "Or your buddy Solo dies!"

Han dropped his blaster and put his hands up in a gesture of surrender.

Dewlanna stopped in her tracks, growling softly.

Shrike leveled the blaster, and his finger tightened on the trigger. Pure malevolent hatred was etched upon his features, and then he smiled, pale blue eyes glittering with ruthless joy. "For insubordination and striking your captain," he announced, "I sentence you to death, Solo. May you rot in all the hells there ever were."

As Han froze, expecting the bolt to fry him any moment, Dewlanna roared, shoved Han aside, and leaped for Shrike. The blaster's energy beam caught her full in the chest, and she went down in a heap of charred fur and burned flesh.

"Dewlanna!" Han yelled in anguish. With a quickness he hadn't known he possessed, he dived at Shrike, hitting the captain in a driving tackle around his knees. Shrike went over backward again, and this time his head impacted solidly with the deck. He sagged, out cold.

Han crawled back to his friend, turning her over gently, seeing the great hole the blaster beam had bored into her chest. He knew immediately that the wound was mortal. No medical droid ever constructed could heal this. Dewlanna moaned, gasped, and fought with all her great Wookiee strength to breathe. Han slid his arms beneath her shoulders and tried to ease her struggle. Her blue eyes opened and, after a moment, fixed on his. Lucidity returned, and she rumbled softly.

"No, I won't leave you!" Han replied, clutching her harder. Tears blurred his vision, and she swam below him in a sea of brown fur. "I don't care if I get away! Oh, Dewlanna . . ."

Making a great effort, she raised a huge, furred paw-hand and grasped his arm. Han had to struggle to translate her speech. "I know," he choked, talking aloud so she'd know he understood her. "I know you care about me . . ." she rumbled again, "as much as you do your own children."

Han swallowed, his throat tight and aching. "I . . . I feel the same way, Dewlanna. You're the closest thing to a mother I'll ever have."

A long moan of anguish made her shudder. She rumbled at him again. "No," Han insisted. "I'm not leaving you. I'll stay with you till . . . till . . ." He couldn't finish the sentence.

Dewlanna grabbed his arm with a ghost of her old strength and growled at him urgently. "If I . . ." Han was having trouble comprehending her slurred speech, "if I die . . . nothing? Oh, you're saying that if I don't live, you'll have died for nothing?"

She nodded, her eyes in their nest of hair holding his with all the intensity she could muster. Han shook his head stubbornly. How could he abandon her to die alone?

Dewlanna rumbled softly, faintly. "Yeah, I'm sure you'll be safe, one with the life-power," Han said, trying to sound sincere. He knew some Wookiees believed in a unifying power that bound all of existence together. Personally, he thought this power—he'd never been able to translate the term accurately, the Wookiee word could have meant "strength," or "force," too—that Dewlanna believed in so steadfastly was just superstition.

But if it comforted her to believe in it during her dying moments, Han wasn't going to argue with her. He remembered the words she'd said to him several times. "Dewlanna, may the life-power be with you . . ." For a moment he wished that he, too, could believe . . .

She moaned with pain. Han could see she was going fast. Then Dewlanna rumbled feebly, and again he automatically translated. "Your last request . . ." He choked, barely able to get the words out, "You want me . . . to go . . . to live. And to be . . . happy."

Han struggled not to break down. "Okay," he agreed. "I'll go. I still have time to get aboard that robot ship before it takes off."

Dewlanna whined faintly.

"I *promise*," he agreed, his voice ragged. "I'll go now. And I swear I'll always remember you, Dewlanna."

She was beyond speech now, but he was sure she'd heard him. He laid her gently on the deck, then rose and picked up the blaster. Then, after giving Dewlanna one final look, Han turned and raced out the door.

His running feet resounded through the corridors of *Trader's Luck*; the time was past for stealth. He had to reach the docking bay, and that robot Ylesian freighter! Han had no idea when it was due to blast away from the *Luck,* but the loading schedule posted for the space dock workers had listed it as being ready for blastoff as soon as the droids finished fueling. And when he'd swiped the spacesuit and hidden it, they'd just started that process.

The *Ylesian Dream* might be leaving any moment!

Gasping, Han sprinted for the lock, his feet thudding along the decks that had been his playground ever since he was old enough to remember. In the distance, he could hear sleepy voices, interspersed with shouts and orders.

I can't let them catch me. Shrike will kill me. The certainty lent speed to his flying feet.

He skidded around the final turn and grabbed the spacesuit he'd hidden behind some fueling equipment. The helmet flopped over his arm, banging him in the midsection as he hastily keyed in the code he'd stolen into the airlock door.

Seconds passed. The sounds of pursuit were growing louder. But surely they'd think he was headed for the shuttle deck or even the lifepods. Nobody would guess he'd be crazy enough to try stowing away on a robot freighter—at least that's what he was counting on . . .

The lock hissed open. Han leaped inside, closed the hatch, and began yanking on the spacesuit. He checked the air storage. *Full. Good.* He'd originally planned to bring along some extra air paks, but he didn't dare venture back out. The pak on the suit was good for two days. That should be enough, unless the *Dream* was a really slow vessel. Since it was a robot-drone, he had no way of discovering what course it would be following, or how fast it was scheduled to go.

Han grimaced. Only a desperate man would use this method of escape. He was desperate, all right. He just hoped he wouldn't arrive on Ylesia dead because he'd run out of air.

Let's see . . . food pellets . . . full. Water tank . . . full. Good. That was Captain Shrike again, insisting that all ship's equipment be maintained in perfect working order.

Han dragged the suit up over the arms of his ship's gray jumpsuit and closed the seam running up the front. He picked up the helmet, clumsy because of the gloves, and settled it over his head. It was mostly glassine, and he could see every direction except directly behind him. A bank of holos ran around the bottom rim of the helmet, giving him his vitals, amount of air remaining, and all the other information he needed to survive. Han could "talk" to his suit in a limited fashion by bumping his chin against the communications lever and giving the suit instructions concerning his temperature, air mix, and so forth.

Okay, this is it, the young man thought as he clumped over to the connecting hatch and keyed in the final sequence to equalize pressures between the lock and the *Ylesian Dream.* He could faintly hear a hiss as the air was pumped out of the lock. The *Dream,* being a robot, didn't need air to operate. The ship would be filled only with vacuum.

Finally, the hatch opened, and Han stepped inside.

It was crowded with equipment and cargo, and the corridors were very narrow. The *Dream* wasn't constructed to accommodate a living crew, only for routine maintenance, and Han had to turn sideways to squeeze in. The youth was fleetingly grateful that all standard engineering was designed to function in gravity. Otherwise, he might've had to contend with zero gee, and that would have been a real pain.

He'd been outside the *Trader's Luck* with the welding crew in spacesuits several times since he'd been considered old enough for hazardous ship's duty, hanging in space, tethered to the ship only by a seemingly fragile umbilical. It had been kind of exciting the first couple of times, but Han didn't particularly care for weightlessness, and he'd soon learned *never* to look "down." Seeing nothing but space

beneath his feet for light-years and light-years was enough
to make his head swim.

Han clumped toward the "bridge," figuring that was
where the maximum amount of room would be. He
reached it in only moments—the *Dream* was a small ship.
If her cargo list was correct, she'd brought in a shipment of
top-grade glitterstim spice, and would be leaving with a
cargo of high-quality Corellian electronic components that
could be used in factory maintenance.

Han wondered for a moment whom Garris Shrike had
paid off to be able to receive a shipment of spice. The substance was rigidly controlled by most planetary govern-
ments and also by the Imperial trade commission.

He turned sideways to enter the bridge—and froze.
*What in the name of all the Sons of Barab is an as-
tromech droid doing on the bridge?* Everyone knew a droid
couldn't pilot a ship by itself, so it couldn't be piloting. Han
grimaced behind the glassine helmet. This droid must be
there as a sort of burglar alarm, a sophisticated communications device to help deter portside thieves or space pirates.
Han knew that one of the reasons the Ylesian priests were
eager to hire a pilot—preferably a Corellian, their ad had
read—was that they'd been losing robot ships to piracy.

As he froze, hoping the droid wasn't aware of his presence, the young man felt the *Dream* shudder. *We're un-
docking! I've got to get braced for breakaway thrust!*

Quickly he edged away from the bridge and headed back
toward the cargo area. Finally, he found what he was looking for, and just in time. A small space that he could sit
down in, just the right size to allow him to brace himself
with his arms and legs.

The *Dream* shuddered again, and then again. Mentally,
Han pictured the docking clamps falling away, one by one.
One more to go, then—

The ship shuddered one more time, then lurched violently. Since the *Dream* wasn't supposed to be manned, it
could utilize acceleration patterns that were much rougher
than those used in a vessel with a living crew.

Wham! Han's body jerked, then he braced himself

against the thrust of violent acceleration. The *Dream* was undocked and away!

Mentally, Han pictured them thrusting away from *Trader's Luck,* out of the embrace of Corellia's gravity field. Closing his eyes, he pictured his homeworld turning lazily against the backdrop of stars. Corellia was a pretty planet, with narrow blue seas, green-brown forests, tan deserts, and large cities. On the nightside it glittered like a battle remote studded with lights . . .

The hardest thrust of acceleration hit then, and Han was pinned uncomfortably against the cargo container. *We've made the jump to lightspeed,* he realized.

Moments later, as the ship's speed evened out, he was able to move again. He flexed his arms and legs, wincing as bruises made themselves felt. *From the fight in the galley,* he realized. The thought made him remember Dewlanna with a sudden, visceral sadness. Tears stung his eyes, and he fought them back fiercely. Crying in a spacesuit helmet was a lousy idea, since you couldn't wipe your face.

Han sniffed, trying to blink back the tears. *Dewlanna . . .* he thought. His friend had given her life to give him this chance.

Get hold of yourself, Solo, he ordered himself sternly. His throat ached, but Han gulped, swallowed hard, then bit his lip until the urge to cry receded. He couldn't remember the last time he'd cried, and what was the point? It wouldn't bring Dewlanna back . . .

Han knew Dewlanna believed in an afterlife of the spirit. If she was right about that, then maybe she could hear him now.

"Hey, Dewlanna," Han whispered, "I made it. I'm on my way. I'm going to Ylesia, and I'm going to become the best pilot in the sector. I'll learn enough—and earn enough—to apply for the Academy, the way we always dreamed. I'm free, Dewlanna." His voice broke. *We're safe, Dewlanna. Shrike can't touch either of us, now . . .*

Wedged into his little crevice, the young pilot smiled with grim determination. *I'm free, and I owe it all to you. I'll never forget it, either. If I ever get a chance to pay you back by helping one of your people, I swear to anything that's out there—any god, or life-power, or force—I won't hesitate.*

Han Solo took a long, deep breath of canned spacesuit air. "Thank you, Dewlanna," he whispered.

Wherever she was now, he hoped she could hear him.

Chapter Two:

Ylesian Dreams

When Han awoke from exhausted sleep, he was completely disoriented at first. *Where am I?* he wondered groggily. Memory came rushing back in swift, violent images: his own hand holding a blaster . . . Shrike's face twisted with hatred and rage . . . Dewlanna, gasping, dying alone . . .

He swallowed hard, his throat aching. Dewlanna had been part of his life since he was just a little kid, eight, perhaps, or nine. He remembered the day she'd come aboard with her mate, Isshaddik. Isshaddik had been outlawed from the Wookiee homeworld for some crime that Dewlanna had never referred to. She'd followed her mate into exile, leaving behind all that she'd ever known—her home and their grown cubs.

A year or so later, Isshaddik had been killed during a

smuggling run to Nar Hekka, one of the worlds in the Hutt sector. Shrike had announced to Dewlanna that she could remain aboard *Trader's Luck* as cook, since he'd grown to like the foods she prepared. Dewlanna could have gone back to Kashyyyk—after all, *she'd* committed no crime— but she'd chosen to stay aboard the *Luck*.

Because of me, Han thought as he located the water dispenser nipple inside his helmet and took a cautious sip. Then he tongued up a couple of food pellets and washed them down with another swallow. It wasn't the same as food, but they'd keep him going for the day . . . *She stayed because of me. She wanted to protect me from Shrike . . .*

He sighed, knowing it to be true. Wookiees were among the most steadfast and loyal companions in the galaxy, or so he'd heard. Wookiee loyalty and friendship was not lightly given, but once bestowed, it never wavered.

He leaned back in his alcove, checking the air pak. Three-quarters left. Han wondered how far the *Dream* had traveled while he'd slept. In a little while he'd go to the control room, see if he could decipher the instrumentation on the autopilot.

Han's mind drifted back in time, remembering Dewlanna sadly, then as he relaxed, his mind wandered to even earlier days. His earliest "real" memory—everything else was just meaningless fragments, snatches of images too old and distorted to have any meaning—was of the day Garris Shrike had brought him "home" to *Trader's Luck* . . .

The child huddled in the mouth of the dank, filthy alley, trying not to cry. He was too big to cry, wasn't he? Even if he was cold and hungry and alone. For a moment the child wondered why he was alone, but it was as if a huge metal door slammed down on that thought, shutting everything behind it. Behind the door lay danger, behind that door lay . . . bad things. Pain, and . . . and . . .

The boy shook his head, and his lank, filthy hair fell straggling into his face. He pushed it back with a hand that was so grimed with dirt that his natural skin color barely showed. He wore only a pair of ragged pants and a torn, sleeveless tunic that was too small. His feet were bare. Had he ever had shoes?

The child thought that perhaps he remembered shoes. Good shoes, nice ones, shoes that someone had put on his feet and helped him fasten. Someone who was gentle, who smiled instead of scowled, someone who was clean and smelled good, who wore pretty clothes—

SLAM!!

The door came down again, and little Han (he knew that was his name, but knew of no other that went with it) winced from the pain in his mind. He knew better than to let those thoughts fill his mind. Thoughts and memories like that were bad, they hurt . . . better not to think them.

He sniffled again and wiped futilely at his runny nose. He realized he was standing in a puddle of foulness, and that his feet were so cold he could barely feel them. It was night now, and it promised to be a cold one.

Hunger twisted in Han's stomach like a living thing, a creature that bit painfully. He couldn't remember the last time he'd eaten. Had it been this morning when he'd found that kavasa fruit in a garbage dump, the ripe, juicy one that was only half-eaten? Or had that been last night?

He couldn't keep standing here, the little boy decided. He had to move. Han stepped out of the alley, onto the pathwalk. He knew how to beg . . . who was it that had taught him?

SLAM!

Never mind who'd taught him, they had taught him well. Adjusting his features to their most pitiful, Han shuffled toward the nearest passerby. "Please . . . lady . . ." he whimpered. "Hungry, I'm so hungry . . ." He held out his hand, palm up. The woman he addressed slowed fractionally, then suddenly looked down at his dirty palm and recoiled, holding her skirts back so they wouldn't brush against him.

"Lady . . ." Han breathed, turning with more than professional interest to watch her walk away. She had on a nice dress, soft and shiny, sort of . . . glowing . . . in the harsh streetlights of the Corellian harbor town.

She reminded him of someone, with her big, dark eyes, her smooth skin, her hair—

SLAM!

He began to sob, hopelessly, his small body shaking from cold, hunger, grief, and loneliness.

"Hey, there! Han!" the sharp but not unfriendly voice broke through his wall of misery. Sniffling and gulping, Han looked up to see a tall form bending over him. Black hair, pale blue eyes. He smelled of Alderaanian ale, and the smoke from half a dozen proscribed drugs, but he was steady on his feet, unlike many of the other passersby.

Seeing that Han was looking up at him, the man squatted down onto his heels, which brought him to only a little above Han's eye level. "You're too big to cry in the street, you know that, don't you?"

Han nodded, still sniffling, but trying to control himself. "Y-yeth . . . yes." At first he lisped a little, the way he had when he'd first learned to talk. That was a long, long time ago, Han thought. He'd been talking since the cold season, and it was soon going to be cold season again. He'd been talking since . . .

SLAM!

The child shuddered again as his mind resolutely shut away all his memories of that beforetime. Something else surfaced, something he'd overlooked at first in his misery. Han's eyes widened. This man had called him by name! *How does he know my name?*

"You . . . who are you?" Han whispered. "How do you know my name?"

The man grinned, showing many teeth. It was meant to be a friendly expression, Han could tell, but there was something about it that made him shudder. It reminded him of the packs of canoids that hunted prey in the alleys. "I know lots of things, kid," the man replied. "Call me Captain Shrike. Can you say that?"

"Y-yes. Cap-tain Shrike," Han parroted uncertainly. He hiccuped as his sobbing died away. "But . . . but how did you know my name? Please?"

The man put out a hand as if to ruffle his hair, then

seemed to take in the dirt and scritchies inhabiting his young scalp and think better of it. "You'd be surprised, Han. I know almost everything that goes on here on Corellia. I know who's lost and who's found, who's for sale and who's sold, and where all the bodies are buried. Matter of fact, I've had my eye on you. You seem like a smart lad. Are you smart?"

Han drew himself up, eyed the man levelly. "Yes, Captain," he said, forcing his voice to be steady. "I'm smart." He knew he was, too. Anyone who wasn't didn't last for months on the streets, the way he had.

"Good, that's the lad! Well, I could use a smart lad to work for me. Why don't you come with me? I'll give you a square meal and a warm place to sleep." He grinned again. "And I just bet you'd like to see my ship." He pointed up at the darkening sky.

Han nodded eagerly. Food? A bed? And especially . . .

"A spaceship? Yes, Captain! I want to be a pilot when I grow up!"

The man laughed and held out his hand. "Well come on, then!"

Han let the big hand engulf his, and the two of them walked away together, toward the spaceport . . .

Han stirred and shook his head. *I should never have gone with him that day,* he thought. *If I hadn't gone with him, Dewlanna would still be alive . . .*

But if he hadn't gone with Shrike, he'd probably have awakened some night in the alley to find that vrelts had chewed his ears and nose off, the way they had one of the other "alley urchins" that Garris Shrike had "rescued."

Han smiled grimly. Captain Shrike didn't have an altruistic bone in his body. He collected children and *used* them to turn a profit. Almost every planet the *Luck* visited, Shrike loaded up a group of his "rescuees" and took them down to the streets in the shuttle. There he left them under the supervision of a droid he'd programmed himself, F8GN. Eight-Gee-Enn assigned them to their "territories" and kept track of their proceeds as the children roamed the streets, begging and pickpocketing.

They used the littlest ones, the skinniest ones, the deformed ones for begging. The vrelt-gnawed girl, Danalis, had always done well. Shrike kept her working hard for years by promising her that when she'd earned enough for him, he'd get her face fixed for her, so she'd look human again.

But he never had. When she was about fourteen, Danalis evidently realized that Shrike was never going to make good on his promises. One "night" she went into the *Luck*'s airlock and cycled it—without first putting on a suit.

Han had been on the cleanup crew. He shuddered at the memory.

Poor Danalis. He could still picture her in his mind, handing over a day's begging receipts to Eight-Gee-Enn. The droid was tall and spindly, made from coppery-reddish metal. It had been repaired so many times that it had patches everywhere, as though the droid were wearing a much-mended garment. Copper patches, gold-colored patches, steel-colored patches—and one round, silvery one on the top of its head.

Han could still hear the droid's voice in his mind. Eight-Gee-Enn had had something wrong with its speakers, and its "voice" had alternated between sounding deep and unctuous, to shrill, mechanical squeakiness. But no matter how the droid sounded, they'd all paid attention to what Eight-Gee-Enn said . . .

"Now, dear children, have you all got your territory assignments?" The copper-colored droid swiveled its head a little rustily on its pipe-stem neck, regarding the eight children from Trader's Luck *as they stood ranged before it.*

All of the children, including five-year-old Han, affirmed that they did, indeed, have their territories. "Very well, then, dear children," the droid continued in its deep, then squeaky tones, "let me now give you your job assignments. Padra"—the droid looked down at a small boy only a year or so older than Han—"today we're going to give you your first chance to show us how helpful you can be to these poor citizens who are burdened with credit vouchers, jewelry, and expensive private comlinks." The droid's eyes glittered eerily. They were different colors—one had burned out long ago, and Shrike had replaced it with a lens scavenged from a junked droid, giving F8GN one red "eye" and one green.

"Are you willing to help out these poor, benighted citizens, Padra?" Eight-Gee-Enn asked, cocking its metal head inquiringly, its voice dripping artificial camaraderie.

"Sure am!" the boy cried. He gave Han and the other small children a triumphant glance. "No more baby begging for me!" he whispered excitedly.

Han, who was barely beginning to learn the skills necessary to pick pockets swiftly and undetectably, felt a stir of envy. Picking pockets was easy, once you learned how to do it well. It was far easier to meet Eight-Gee-Enn's quota for a day's "work" picking pockets than it was by begging. Begging required accosting at least three marks, roughly, in order to gain one donation.

But pickpocketing . . . now, that was the best way to earn big money! If you chose the right mark, you could gain enough in one grab to give Eight-Gee-Enn your quota before noon, and then you were free to play. Han wondered whether Eight-Gee-Enn would give him some practice time if he hurried and begged his quota for the day before the others finished.

It was fun to practice with the spindly reddish droid, because Eight-Gee-Enn looked so funny in clothes! The droid would put on street clothes typical to the planet they were on, and then either stand still or stroll past his student. Han had learned to relieve the droid of the concealed chrono, credit vouchers, and even some kinds of jewelry without Eight-Gee-Enn detecting his fingers in the process.

But he couldn't do it one hundred percent of the time. Han scowled a little as he trudged away. Eight-Gee-Enn demanded perfection from its little band, especially from the pickpockets. The droid wouldn't let him start picking pockets until it was sure that Han could do so perfectly, every time.

Absently, he picked up a handful of dirt and rubbed it into his hands, then smeared his already sweating face. What planet was this, anyway? He couldn't recall hearing its name. The native people were greenish-skinned, with small, swively ears and huge dark purple eyes. Han had only learned a few words in their language, but he was a quick study, and he knew that by the time Trader's Luck moved on, he'd be able to understand it well, and speak it— at least the gutter argot—passably.

Wherever this was, it was hot. Hot and humid. Han glanced up at the pale, greenish-blue sky, in which blazed a pale orange sun. The prospect of spending several hours on his appointed street, whining, begging, and cajoling passersby for alms wasn't an attractive one. *I hate begging,* Han thought sourly. *When I get a little older, I'm going to make them let me steal, instead of beg. I'm sure I'll be a good thief, and I'm not that good a beggar.*

He knew his appearance was all right—he'd gotten taller in the past couple of years, but he was still underweight enough to be called skinny. And he knew how to make his voice servile, his manner cringing and cowering, as though only desperation were driving him to plead for alms.

Maybe it was his eyes, Han thought. *Maybe the secret resentment and shame he felt at having to beg showed in them and potential marks could see it.* Nobody respected a beggar, and Han, more than almost anything, had a undeclared desire to be respected.

Not just respected, he wanted to be respectable. He couldn't recall much about his life before Garris Shrike had found him begging on Corellia, but Han somehow knew that once upon a time, things had been different.

Long ago, he'd been taught to believe that begging was shameful. And that stealing . . . stealing was worse. Han bit his lip angrily. He knew that someone, perhaps the parents he couldn't remember, had taught him these things. Once, long ago, he'd been taught different ways . . . different values.

But now—what could he do? Aboard Trader's Luck, there was one cardinal rule. If you didn't work, you begged or stole. If you refused to work, beg, or steal, you didn't eat. Han had no other skills to offer. He was too little to pilot, not strong enough to load smuggled cargo.

But I won't always be! *he reminded himself.* "I'm grow-ing every day! Soon I'm going to be big, in just five more years I'll be ten, and then, maybe, I'll be big enough to pilot!"

Han had discovered that when he made up his mind to accomplish something, he could do it. He was sure that pi-loting would be no exception.

And when I can pilot, that'll be my way off *Trader's Luck, he thought, his mind slipping automatically into an old dream, one that he never told anyone about. Once he'd confided it to one of the other children, and the little vrelt blabbed it to everyone. Shrike and the others laughed at Han for weeks, calling him "Captain Han of the Imperial Navy," until Han wanted to crawl away, hands over his ears. It took all his control to just shrug and pretend not to care . . .*

Yeah, and when I'm the best pilot around, and I've made lots of credits, I'll apply to the Imperial Academy. I'll be-come a Naval officer. Then I'll come back and get Shrike, arrest him, and he'll get sent to the spice mines on Kessel. He'll die there . . . *The thought made Han's mouth curl up in a predatory smile.*

At the far end of his fantasy, Han pictured himself, suc-cessful, respected, the best pilot in the galaxy, with a ship of his own, lots of loyal friends, and plenty of credits. And . . . a family. Yeah, a family of his own. A beautiful wife who adored him, who'd share adventures with him, and kids, maybe. He'd be a good father. He wouldn't aban-don his children, the way he'd been abandoned . . .

At least, Han supposed that he'd been abandoned, though he couldn't remember a thing about it. He didn't even know his last name, so he couldn't try to trace his family. Or maybe . . . maybe his parents hadn't aban-doned him . . .

Maybe they'd been killed, or he'd been kidnapped away from them. Han decided that he preferred that scenario. If he thought of his parents as dead, he wasn't so mad at them, because people couldn't help it if they died, right?

Han decided that from now on, he'd think of his mother and father as dead. It was easier that way . . .

He knew he'd probably never know the real truth. The only person who knew anything about Han's background was Garris Shrike. The captain kept telling Han that if he was good, if he worked and begged hard, if he earned enough credits, someday Shrike would tell him the secrets behind how he'd come to be wandering the streets of Corellia that day.

Han's mouth tightened. Sure, Captain, *he thought.* Just like you were going to get Danalis's face fixed . . .

The child glanced up at the street signs. He couldn't read the ones in the native language, but there was a Basic translation beneath each. Yeah, this was his territory, all right.

Han took a deep breath, then rearranged his features. A green-skinned female clad in a short robe was coming toward him. "Lady . . ." he whined, cringing his way toward her, little hand held out in appeal, "please, beautiful gracious lady, I beg your help . . . alms, just one little credit, I'm so hungreeeeee . . ."

The little cupped green ears swiveled toward him, then she averted her head and swept past.

Under his breath, Han muttered an uncomplimentary term in smuggler's argot, and then turned to wait for the next mark . . .

Han shook his head and forced himself out of his reverie. Time to go and check on the *Ylesian Dream's* progress.

Hauling himself up out of his cubbyhole, the young pilot made his way through the cramped passageways until he reached the bridge. The astromech droid was still there, its lights flashing away as it "thought" its own thoughts. It was a relatively new R2 unit, still shiny-bright silver and green, with a clear dome atop its head. Inside the dome Han could see lights blinking as it worked. It was hooked into the ship's robot controls by means of a cable.

The R2 droid must have been equipped with a motion sensor, because it swiveled its domed "head" toward Han as he clumped boldly onto the bridge in his spacesuit.

The lights flashed frantically as it "talked," but of course the sound waves didn't travel in vacuum. Han turned on his suit's communications unit, and suddenly his helmet was filled with distressed *bleeps, blurps,* and *wheeps.*

"*Whee . . . bleewheeeep . . . wheep-whirr-wheep!*" the R2 astromech announced in evident surprise. Han looked around for its counterpart droid and didn't see one. He sighed. His suit's communicator would transmit what he said to the droid, but how was he supposed to actually *talk* to the consarned R2 without an interpreter? How did whoever had programmed the droid talk to it?

He activated his suit communicator. "Hey, you!"

"*Blurpp . . . wheeep, bleep-whirrr!*" the unit replied helpfully.

Han scowled and cursed at the unit in Rodian, trader argot, and, finally, Basic. "What am I going to do now?" he snarled. "If only you had a Basic-speech module."

"But I do, sir," announced the droid in a matter-of-fact voice. Its words were flat, mechanical, but perfectly understandable.

Han gaped at the machine for a moment, then grinned. "Hey! This is a first! How come you can *talk*?"

"Because there was not room aboard this vessel for both an astromech unit and a counterpart unit, my masters programmed me with a Basic-speech transmissions module so I could communicate more easily," the droid replied.

"All right!" Han cried, feeling a surge of relief. He didn't like droids much, but at least he'd have someone to talk to, and it might actually prove necessary for the two of them to communicate. Space travel was usually routine, and safe . . . but there were exceptions.

"I regret, sir," the R2 added, "that you are guilty of unauthorized entry, sir. You are not supposed to be here."

"I know that," Han said. "I hitched a ride on this ship."

"I-beg-your-pardon, this unit does not understand the term used, sir."

Han called the R2 unit an uncomplimentary name.

"I-beg-your-pardon, this unit does not understand—"

"Shut *up!*" Han bellowed.

The R2 unit was silent.

Han took a very deep breath. "Okay, R2," he said. "I am a stowaway. Is that word in your memory banks?"

"Yes it is, sir."

"Good. I stowed away aboard this ship because I needed a ride to Ylesia. I'm going to take a job piloting for the Ylesian priests, understand?"

"Yes, sir. However, I must inform you that in my capacity as a watch-droid assigned to safeguard this vessel and its contents, I must seal all the exits when we reach Ylesia, then inform my masters that you are aboard, thus expediting your capture by their security staff."

"Hey, little pal," Han said generously, "when we reach Ylesia, you just go right ahead and do that. When the priests see that I fit all their requirements, they won't give a vrelt's ass how I arrived there."

"I-beg-your-pardon, sir, but this unit does not—"

"Shut up."

Han glanced down at his air pak readout, then said, "Okay, R2, I'd like to check on our flight path, speed, and ETA to Ylesia. Please display that information."

"I regret, sir, that I am not authorized to give you that information."

Han was coming to a slow boil; he barely restrained himself from kicking the recalcitrant droid with his heavy space boot. "I need to check our flight path, speed, and ETA because I've got to compute how my air is holding out, R2," he explained with exaggerated patience.

"I-beg-your-pardon, sir, but this unit—"

"*SHUT UP!*"

Han was starting to sweat now, and the suit's refrigeration unit revved up a little faster. He struggled to keep his tones calm. "Listen carefully, R2," he said. "Don't you have some kind of operating systems program that orders you to attempt to preserve the lives of intelligent beings whenever you can?"

"Yes, sir, that programming is included with all astromech droids. For a droid to deliberately harm or fail to prevent harm to a sentient being, its operating system module must be altered."

"Good," Han said. That fit in with what he knew about astromech programming. "Listen to me, R2. If you don't show me our flight path, speed, and ETA, you may be responsible for my death, from lack of air. Do you understand me now?"

"Please elaborate, sir."

Han explained, with exaggerated patience, his situation. When he finished, the droid was silent for a moment, evidently cogitating. Finally, it whirred once, then said, "I will comply with your request, sir, and will display the information requested on the diagnostic interface screen."

Han breathed a long sigh of relief. Since the ship was basically a giant robot drone, it had no controls visible on its control boards, just assorted blinking lights. But, in order to service the ship, there *was* a screen built into the control board. Han stepped carefully around the R2 unit and stared down at the screen.

Information scrolled across it, so rapidly no human could have read it. Han turned to the R2 unit. "Put that data back up, and this time, *leave it there* until I can read it! Get it?"

"Yes, sir." The droid's artificial voice sounded almost meek.

Han studied the figures and diagram that appeared on the screen for several minutes, feeling his uneasiness grow into real fear. He had nothing to write with, and no way to access the navicomputer, but he had a bad feeling about what he was seeing. Biting his lip, he forced himself to concentrate as he ran the figures in his head, over and over.

Ylesian Dream's flight path had been set to take it in a circuitous route to the planet, in order to avoid the worst of the pirate-infested areas of Hutt space. And the little freighter's speed was set far lower than the ship was capable of, slower than even *Trader's Luck* normally traveled through hyperspace.

Not good. Not good at all. If their speed and course weren't altered, Han realized, he'd run out of air about five hours before the *Dream* set down on Ylesian soil. The ship would land with a corpse aboard . . . his.

He turned back to the R2 unit. "Listen, R2, you've got to help me. If I don't alter our course and speed, I won't have sufficient air to make the trip. I'll die, and it will be *your* fault."

The R2 unit's lights flashed as the machine contemplated this revelation. Finally, it said: "But I did not know you were on board, sir. I cannot be held responsible for your death."

"Oh, no." Han shook his head inside his helmet. "It doesn't work that way, R2. If you *know* about this situation and do nothing, then *you will be causing the death of a sentient being.* Is that what you want?"

"No," the droid said. Even its artificial tones sounded faintly strained, and its lights flickered rapidly and erratically.

"Then it follows," Han continued inexorably, "that you must do whatever you can to *prevent my death.* Right?"

"I . . . I . . ." The droid was quivering now in agitation. "Sir, I am constrained from assisting you. My programming is in conflict with my hardware."

"What do you mean?" Han was worried now. If the little droid overloaded and went dead, he'd never be able to access the manual "diagnostic" controls that he knew had to be in these panels somewhere. They'd be tiny, something for the techs to use to test the robot drone's autopilot.

"My programming is constraining me from informing you . . ."

Han took one huge stride over to the little droid and knelt in front of it. "Blast you!" He pounded his fist on top of the droid's clear dome. "I'll *die*! Tell me!"

The droid rocked agitatedly, and Han wondered if it would simply fall apart with the strain. But then it said, "I have been fitted with a restraining bolt, sir! It prevents me from complying with your request!"

A restraining bolt! Han seized on this bit of information with alacrity. *Let's see, where is it?*

After a moment he spotted it, low down on the droid's metal carapace. He reached down, grasped it, and tugged.

Nothing. The bolt didn't move.

Han gripped harder, tried twisting. He grunted with effort, really sweating now, imagining he could feel those molecules of oxygen running out in a steady stream. He'd heard that hypoxia wasn't an especially bad way to die—compared to explosive decompression or being shot, for example—but he had no desire to find out firsthand.

The bolt didn't move. Han tried harder, jerking at it, swearing in half a dozen alien tongues, but the stubborn thing didn't budge.

Got to find something I can hit it with, Han thought, glancing wildly around the control cabin. But there was nothing—not a hydrospanner, a wrench—nothing!

Suddenly he remembered the blaster. He'd left it on the floor in his little cubicle. "Wait right here," Han instructed the R2 unit, and then he was squeezing back through the narrow corridors.

Shooting a blaster inside a spaceship—even an unpressurized spaceship—wasn't a good idea, but he was desperate.

Han returned with the weapon, and examined the settings. *Lowest setting,* he thought. *Narrowest beam.* Clumsy in his spacesuit gloves, he had trouble adjusting the power setting and beam width.

The R2's lights had been flashing frenetically ever since he'd returned, and now it *wheeped* plaintively. "Sir? Sir, may I ask what you're doing?"

"I'm getting rid of that restraining bolt," Han told it grimly. Aiming and narrowing his eyes, he squeezed delicately.

A flash of energy erupted, and the little droid *WHEEEEPPPPED!* so shrilly it sounded like a scream. The restraining bolt fell to the deck, leaving behind a black burn scar on the otherwise shining metal of the R2 unit.

"Gotcha," Han said with satisfaction. "Now, R2, be good enough to point me toward the manual interfaces and controls in your ship here."

The droid obediently extruded a mobile wheeled "leg" and rolled over to the control banks, its interface cable trailing behind it. Han went over and crouched before the instrument panel, awkward in his suit. Following the droid's instructions, he wrenched off the top of one featureless control panel and studied the tiny bank of controls. Cursing at the awkwardness of trying to manipulate the controls while wearing spacesuit gloves, Han began using the manual interface mode to disengage the hyperdrive. Altering course and speed could only be done in realspace.

Once they were back in realspace, Han painstakingly computed a new course, using the R2 unit to perform the more esoteric calculations for the jump that would send them back into hyperspace.

It took the young Corellian a while to lay in their new course and speed, but finally Han triggered the HYPERDRIVE ENGAGE switch again. A second later he felt the lurch as the drive kicked in. Han clung grimly to the instrument panel as the ship hurtled into hyperspace on its new course, at a greatly increased rate of speed.

As the ship steadied around him, Han drew a long, long breath and let it out very slowly. He slumped to the deck and sat there, his legs stuck out before him. *Whew!*

"You realize, sir," said the R2 unit, "that you will now have to land this craft manually. Altering our course and speed has invalidated the existing landing protocols programmed into the ship."

"Yeah, I know," Han said, leaning wearily back against the console. He took another sip of water and then ate two tablets. "But there's no other way. I just hope I can work the controls fast enough to land us." He glanced around him at the nearly featureless control room. "I wish this bucket of bolts came with a viewscreen."

"An autopilot cannot see, sir, so visual data is useless to it," the R2 unit pointed out helpfully.

"No!" Han said, his voice dripping with sarcasm. "I thought droids could see just like we can!"

"No, sir, we cannot," R2 told him. "We recognize our

surroundings by visual relays that translate into electronic data within our—"

"Shut up," Han said, too tired even to enjoy baiting the droid.

Leaning back against the console, he closed his eyes. He'd done all that he could to save his life, by bringing the ship to Ylesia on a much more direct route, at a faster speed.

Han drifted into sleep and dreamed of Dewlanna, as she had been long ago, when they'd first known each other . . .

Han was halfway through the window when he heard the shout behind him. "We've been robbed!"

Clutching his small sack of loot, he kicked, wriggling, trying to squeeze through the narrow enclosure. In the dark outside lay safety. A feminine cry of dismay: "My jewelry!"

Han grunted with effort, realizing he was stuck. He fought back panic. He had to get away! This was a rich house, and when someone summoned the authorities, they were certain to come immediately.

Silently he cursed the new vogue in Corellian architecture that had caused this luxurious home to be built with floor-to-ceiling narrow windows. The windows were advertised as being able to thwart burglars. Well, there might be some truth to that, he decided grimly. He'd sneaked in earlier through one of the doors that led to the gardens, then hidden out until he'd felt safe in believing that all the inhabitants were asleep. Then he'd ventured out to pick and choose among their treasures. He'd been confident that he could wiggle his skinny, nine-year-old self through those windows and make good his escape.

Han grunted with effort again, kicking frantically. It was possible he was wrong about that . . .

A voice behind him. The woman. "There he is! Get him!"

Han turned a little more sideways, wriggled violently, and then suddenly he was through the window and falling. He didn't let go of his sack, though, as he crashed down onto the manicured bed of flowering dorva vines. Breath whooshed out of his lungs, and for a moment he just lay there, gasping, like a drel out of water. His leg hurt, and so did his head.

"Call the security patrol!" The masculine shout came from inside. Han knew he had only seconds to make good his escape. Forcing his leg to bear his weight, he rolled over and staggered to his feet.

Trees ahead in the moonslight . . . big ones. He could lose himself in them, easy.

Han half limped, half ran to the shelter of the trees. He resolved not to let Eight-Gee-Enn know what had happened. The droid might accuse him of slowing down now that he was going on ten.

Han grimaced as he ran. He wasn't slowing down, he just hadn't been feeling well today. He'd had a dull headache ever since he'd awakened, and had been tempted to turn himself in on sick call.

Since Han was almost never ill, he'd probably have been believed, but he didn't like showing weakness in front of other denizens of Trader's Luck. Especially Captain Shrike. The man never missed an opportunity to ride him.

He was in the shelter of the trees, now. What next? He could hear the sound of running footsteps, so he didn't have much time to decide. His muscles made that decision for him. Suddenly the sack was clenched in his teeth, there was bark against his palms, and the soles of his beat-up boots were braced against branches. Han climbed, listened, then climbed again.

Only when he was high in the tree, above the range of a casual glance by pursuers, did he slow down. Han settled back on a limb, against the tree trunk, panting, his head whirling. He felt dizzy, nauseated, and for a moment he was afraid he'd be sick and give himself away. But he bit his lip and forced himself to stay still, and presently he felt a little better.

Judging from the star patterns, it was only a few hours until dawn. Han realized that he was going to have trouble making the rendezvous with the Luck's shuttle. Would Shrike just abandon him, or would he wait?

Far below him, people were searching the wooded area.

Lights strobed the night, and he huddled close to the tree trunk, eyes closed, clinging desperately despite his dizziness. If only his head didn't throb so . . .

Han wondered whether they'd bring in bioscanners, and shivered. His skin felt hot and tight, even though the night was cool and breezy.

Dark waned on toward dawn. Han wondered what Dewlanna was doing, whether she'd miss him if the Luck left orbit without him.

Finally, the lights went out, and the footsteps faded away. Han waited another twenty minutes to make sure his pursuers were truly gone, then, holding the sack gripped in his teeth, he carefully climbed down, moving with exaggerated care because his head hurt so much. Every jar, even walking, made his head swim, and he had to grit his teeth against the pain.

He walked . . . and walked. Several times he realized he'd been dozing while he walked, and a couple of times he fell down and was tempted to just stay there. But something kept him moving, as dawn brightened the streets and houses around him. Corellian dawns were beautiful, Han noticed dazedly. He'd never before noticed how pretty the colors were in the sky. If only the light didn't hurt his eyes so . . .

Dawn turned to day. Cool gave way to warmth, then heat. He was sweating, and his vision was blurred. But finally, there it was. The spaceport. By this time Han was moving like an automaton, one foot in front of the other, wishing he could just lie down and sleep in the road.

Before him, now . . . the Luck's shuttle! With a gasp that was nearly a sob, the boy drove himself forward. He was almost to the ramp when a tall figure emerged. Shrike.

"Where in the blazes have you been?" There was nothing friendly in the captain's grasp upon his arm. Han held up the sack, and Shrike grabbed it. "Well, at least you didn't come back empty-handed," the captain grumbled.

Quickly he sifted through the contents, nodding his satisfaction. Only when he was finished did Shrike seem to notice that Han was swaying on his feet. "What's wrong with you?"

Now beyond coherent speech, Han could only shake his head. Consciousness was fading in and out on him like a jammed transmission.

Shrike shook him a little, then put a hand on the boy's forehead. When he felt the heat, he cursed. "Fever . . . should I leave you here? What if it's contagious?" He frowned, clearly struggling to decide. Finally he hefted the sack of loot again. "Guess you've earned a sick day, kid," he muttered. "C'mon."

Han tried to make it up the ramp, but then he stumbled and everything went dark . . .

He swam up into partial consciousness a long time later, to the sound of voices arguing, one in Wookiee, the other in Basic. Dewlanna and Shrike.

The Wookiee growled insistently. "I can tell he's really sick," Shrike agreed, "but you can't kill one of my kids with a blaster set on full. He'll be okay after a couple of days rest. He doesn't need a medical droid, and I'm not springing for it."

Dewlanna snarled, and Han, automatically translating, was surprised at how insistent the Wookiee was being. He felt a furred paw-hand lay something cold on his forehead. It felt wonderful against the heat.

"I told you no, Dewlanna, and I meant it!" Shrike said, and with that, the captain stomped out, cursing the Wookiee in every language he knew.

Han opened his eyes to see Dewlanna bending over him. The Wookiee rumbled gently at him. Han struggled to speak. "Pretty bad . . ." he conceded, in response to her question. "Thirsty . . ."

Dewlanna held him up and gave him water, sip by slow sip. She told him that he had a high fever, so high that she was afraid for him.

When Han finished the water, she stooped down and scooped the child up into her arms. "Where . . . where're we . . ."

She told him to hush, that she was taking him planetside, to the medical droid. Han's head was swimming, but he made a great effort. "Don't . . . Captain Shrike . . . really mad . . ."

Her answer was short and to the point. Han had never heard her curse before.

He faded in and out as they moved through the corridors, and his next clear memory was of being strapped into the seat of a shuttle. Han had never known Dewlanna could pilot, but she handled the controls competently with her huge, furred hands. The shuttle slipped loose from its moorings, and then accelerated toward Corellia.

The fever was making Han light-headed, and he kept imagining that he heard Shrike's voice, cursing. He tried to say something about it to Dewlanna, but found he didn't have the strength to get the words out . . .

He next regained consciousness in the medical droid's waiting room. Dewlanna was sitting down, with Han's scrawny form still clutched protectively in her arms.

Suddenly a door opened, and the droid appeared. It was a large, elongated droid, equipped with anti-grav units so that it floated around its patient as Dewlanna placed Han on the examining table. Han felt a prick against his skin as the droid took a blood sample.

"Do you understand Basic, madame?" inquired the droid.

For a moment Han was about to answer that of course he understood Basic, and who was Madame?—but then Dewlanna rumbled. Oh, of course. The medical unit was talking to her.

"This young patient has contracted Corellian tanamen fever," the droid told Dewlanna. "His case is quite severe. It is fortunate that you did not wait any longer to bring him to me. I will need to keep him here and observe him until tomorrow. Do you wish to stay with him?"

Dewlanna rumbled her assent.

"Very well, madame. I am going to use bacta immersion therapy to restore his metabolic equilibrium. That will also bring his fever down."

Han took one look at the waiting bacta tank and feebly tried to make a run for the door. Between them, Dewlanna

*and the medical unit restrained him easily. The boy felt
another needle prick his arm, and then the whole universe
tilted sideways and slid into blackness . . .*

Han opened his eyes, realizing his reverie had turned
into sleep, then dreams. He shook his head, remembering
how wobbly he'd been when Dewlanna and the droid
helped him out of the bacta tank. Then Dewlanna paid the
droid out of her own small store of credits and piloted them
back to *Trader's Luck.*

The young pilot grimaced. Boy, Shrike had been mad.
Han was worried that he'd space them both. But Dewlanna
never showed even the slightest sign of fear as she stood
between the captain and Han, insisting that she'd done the
right thing, that otherwise the boy would have died.

In the end, Shrike subsided because one of the pieces of
jewelry Han had stolen that night turned out to be set with
a genuine Krayt dragon pearl. When the captain discovered
what it was worth, he was mollified.

But he didn't pay Dewlanna back for Han's medical
bills . . .

Han sighed and closed his eyes. Dewlanna's loss was like
a knife wound—no matter how he tried, he couldn't get
away from the pain, and the memories. He'd let down his
guard and suddenly find himself thinking of her as still
alive, visualize himself talking to her, telling her about his
troubles with the recalcitrant R2 unit—only to be brought
up short with pain nearly as searing and immediate as he'd
felt yesterday when he'd held her dying body.

Han swallowed another sip of water, trying to ease the
tightness in his throat. He owed Dewlanna . . . owed her
so much. His life—even his true identity—he owed Dewlanna for that, too . . .

Han sighed. Until he was eleven years old, his only name
had been "Han." The boy often wondered and worried
about whether he had a last name. One time he mentioned
his concern to Dewlanna, along with his conviction that if
anyone knew who he really was, it was Shrike.

Very soon after that, Dewlanna learned to play
sabacc . . .

Han heard the soft scratch on the door to his tiny cubicle and woke instantly. Listening, he heard the scratch again, then a soft whine. "Dewlanna?" he whispered, sliding out of bed and sticking his bare feet into his ship's coveralls. "Is that you?"

She rumbled softly from outside the door. Han yanked up his jumpsuit, sealed it, and opened the door. "What do you mean, you have exciting news for me?"

Dewlanna came in, her huge, furred body fairly bouncing with excitement. Han waved her past him, and she sat on the narrow bunk. Since there was no place else to sit, Han settled down beside her. The Wookiee cautioned him to keep his voice low, and glancing at the chrono, Han realized it was the dead of night.

"What are you doing up now?" he asked, puzzled. "Don't tell me you were playing sabacc this late?"

She nodded at him, her blue eyes sparkling with excitement amid her tan and chestnut hair.

"So what's going on, Dewlanna? Why did you need to talk to me?"

She rumbled softly at him. Han sat up straight, suddenly transfixed. "You found out my last name? How?"

Her answer was a single name. "Shrike," Han muttered. "Well, if anyone knows, it's him. What . . . how did it happen? What's my name?"

His name, she told him, was "Solo." Shrike had gotten very, very drunk, and he started bragging about how much the Krayt dragon pearl was worth, what a good deal he'd gotten when he sold it. Dewlanna asked Shrike innocently if Han came from a long line of successful thieves. Shrike, she reported, exploded into laughter at the suggestion. "Maybe some branches of the family, but this Solo?" he sputtered, wheezing with merriment, pausing to gulp more Alderaanian ale, "I'm afraid not, Dewlanna. This kid's folks were . . ."

And at that point, the captain suddenly halted in midword, fixing the Wookiee with a suspicious glare. "So why do you care, anyhow?" he demanded, his momentary good humor gone.

Dewlanna answered only by covering Shrike's bet, and raising.

"Solo," Han whispered softly, trying it on for size. "Han Solo. My full name is Han Solo."

He looked up at Dewlanna, and a wide grin spread across his features. "I like it! It sounds great!"

Dewlanna whined softly and, slinging a long arm around him, gave the boy a hug . . .

Han smiled, remembering, but it was a sad smile. Dewlanna had meant well, but her discovery that his name was "Solo" had led to one of the worst episodes of his young life. The next time the *Luck* was in orbit around Corellia, he'd stolen time away from his pickpocketing and burglary duties and had gone to one of the public archives to do some research.

Shrike didn't like his "rescuees" to spend any time on furthering their education. Each child aboard *Trader's Luck* was given an elementary-level education via the ship's computer, so he, she, or it could learn to read and count money. Beyond that, Shrike discouraged the children from pursuing higher learning.

It was partly because he automatically wanted to flout Shrike's wishes, and partly due to Dewlanna's encouragement, that Han had kept up his studies in secret. He had a tendency to ignore subjects he didn't like—such as history—and to spend all his time on subjects he enjoyed—such as reading adventure stories and solving math equations. Han knew how important math was to anyone who wanted to be a pilot, so he worked hard at mastering as much of it as he could.

Once Dewlanna discovered what he was doing, she monitored his curriculum, making him study subjects that he would otherwise have skipped, leaving gaps in his knowledge. Reluctantly, Han tackled the physical sciences, and history.

He was surprised to discover that some real historical battles were just as exciting as anything he'd read in adventure sagas.

That day in the public archives on Corellia, Han applied

some of his newly learned research skills to learning about his new surname. The results were surprising. When Han looked up the last name "Solo" in the historical records, he was astounded to discover that the name was well known on Corellia. A "Berethron e Solo" had introduced democracy on Han's homeworld three centuries ago. He'd actually been a ruler, a king!

But there'd been another Solo, more recently, who was equally famous—or, to put it more accurately, infamous. About fifty years ago, a descendant of Berethron, Korol Solo, had fathered a son named "Dalla Solo." The young man, taking the alias "Dalla Suul" in an effort to disguise his identity, had made quite a name for himself as a murderer, kidnapper, and pirate. "Dalla the Black" had become a name to make children quake in their beds on lonely outpost colonies or tramp freighters . . .

The child Han wondered whether he was related to these men. Did royal blood run in his veins? Or the blood of a pirate and murderer? He'd probably never know, unless, somehow, he could persuade Shrike to divulge what he knew. He read about Dalla Suul's exploits as a thief, and smiled grimly, wondering if he was actually following some kind of family tradition.

Then he began checking the more recent Corellian news files and society pages in the computer. A search for the surname "Solo" brought up a name. Tiion Sal-Solo. She was a wealthy but reclusive widow with one child, a son. Thrackan Sal-Solo was six or seven years older than Han, in his late teens.

What if I'm related to this Tiion Solo, or she knew my parents? Han wondered. *This could be my best chance yet to get away.*

When he went back to *Trader's Luck*, Han talked it over with Dewlanna. The Wookiee agreed with him that while it was risky, Han had to take the chance of contracting the Solo family.

"Of course," Han said, resting his chin on his fist and looking dejectedly at the table, "once I did that, I couldn't see *you* again, Dewlanna."

The Wookiee growled softly, telling Han that of *course* he'd see her. Just not aboard *Trader's Luck*.

"The last time I ran away, Shrike beat me so hard I couldn't sit down for days," Han said softly. "If Larrad hadn't reminded him that he had something else to do, I really think he might've killed me."

Dewlanna rumbled. "You're right," Han agreed. "If this Solo family takes me in, they're powerful enough and rich enough to protect me from Shrike."

Han even knew something about the rules and manners required of people living in Corellian high society. Every so often, Shrike would run a major scam on rich folks on Corellia. Han had been part of the background during several such con operations.

Shrike would rent a wealthy estate on Corellia, and then set up a "family unit," to provide a respectable backdrop to the scam. Han and the other children detailed to such a "family" would be sent to live on the estate. He'd go to a rich-kids school, and one of his jobs during the scam was to make friends with the children of the wealthy and bring them home to play. Several times, this had resulted in valuable contacts whose parents had been duped into "investing" in Garris Shrike's current scam.

Just a few weeks past, Han had been attending such a school—a school so well known that it had merited a visit from the famous Senator Garm Bel Iblis. Han had raised his hand and asked the Senator two questions that had been insightful and intelligent enough to make the Senator really notice him. After class was over, Bel Iblis had stopped Han, shaken his hand, and asked him his name. Han had glanced around quickly, seeing that nobody else was within earshot, and proudly told the Senator his *real* name. It had felt great to be able to do that . . .

Shrike recruited Han frequently for his scam operations, partly because of the boy's easygoing charm and winning smile, and partly because Han's clandestine studies made him fit into his grade level better than most of the other children. Han had also gained a small reputation as an up-and-coming swoop and speeder pilot—a rich man's sport if there ever was one. He'd met lots of kids from wealthy families while swoop racing, and several times Shrike had managed to lure their parents into whatever scam he was currently running.

In a year, Han would be eligible to race in Corellia's Junior Championship division. That would mean big prize money—if he won.

Han both liked and disliked these assignments. He liked them because he got to live in the lap of luxury for weeks, sometimes months. Swoop and speeder racing was life and breath to him, and he got to practice every day.

He disliked these con operations because he always wound up caring about some of the kids he was ordered to befriend, and all the while he knew they and their families would be irrevocably injured by Shrike's scheme.

Mostly, Han managed to stifle any guilt feelings he felt. He was becoming good at putting himself first. Other people—with the sole exception of Dewlanna—had to come second or not at all. It was self-preservation, and Han was very, very good at that.

I still am, Han thought as he got up from the deck of the *Ylesian Dream* and went to check on their course and speed. The young Corellian smiled and nodded as he read the instrument readings. *Right in the groove,* he thought. *We're going to make it.*

He checked his air pak, seeing it was more than half-gone.

For a moment Han was tempted to explore the *Dream* further, but he resisted the impulse. Moving around would just cause him to use up his oxygen faster, and he was skirting the edge of safety as it was.

So he settled back down, and the memories came back. Aunt Tiion. Poor woman. And *dear* cousin Thrackan. As he remembered, Han's lips pulled back from his teeth in a feral grin that was more like a canoid's snarl . . .

Han swung down off the high stone wall and landed lightly on the balls of his feet. Through the trees he could see a large structure built of the same native stone as the wall, so he headed toward it, staying in the tree-shadow whenever possible.

When he reached the house, he halted, staring at it in amazement. He'd seen a lot of rich mansions, even lived in more than a few, but he'd never seen anything like the Sal-Solo estate.

Towers festooned with creeping vines, four of them, stood at each corner of a large, squarish stone building. An ancient gardener droid moved about arthritically, pruning the bushes that grew down to the edge of a large trench filled with water. Han walked around to the side and saw, to his surprise, that the stretch of water completely surrounded the house. There was no way to enter the place, except to cross a narrow wooden bridge that spanned the water and led up to the front door.

Han had been interested in military tactics ever since he was small, and he'd read up on them. He studied the Sal-Solo mansion, realizing it was built to almost military fortress standards of impregnability. Well, that sort of fit in with what he'd read about the Solo family. They didn't socialize, didn't attend charity events or go to plays or concerts.

In all the times he'd posed as a rich kid, he'd never heard anyone mention the Solo family—and the way those rich people talked about each other, he'd have heard something if they ever mingled with their peers.

Han walked cautiously toward the house. He'd exchanged his ship's gray jumpsuit for a "borrowed" pair of black pants and a pale gray tunic. He didn't want anyone finding out where he'd come from.

When he was nearly to the beginning of the causeway, he stood behind one of the large, ornamental bushes and warily peered across the water to the house. What should he do now? Just walk up and activate the door signal? He bit his lip, undecided. What if they called the authorities on him, reported him as a runaway? Shrike would descend on him so fast—

"Gotcha!"

Han gasped and jumped as a hand closed over his upper arm, hauling him around bodily.

The person who'd grabbed him was head and shoulders taller than the younger boy. He had darker hair than Han, and was stockier as well. But it was his face that made Han stand staring at him in blank amazement.

Han gaped, speechless, at the older boy. If he'd ever doubted that he was really related to the Solo family, those doubts died an instant death. The face of the youth who was holding his arm looked like an older version of the face Han saw in the mirror every morning.

Not that they were twins or anything. But there was too much resemblance in their features to be coincidence. The same shape of the brown eyes, the same kind of lips, the same quirk to the eyebrows . . . the same nose and jaw-line . . .

The other boy was gaping back at Han, having evidently noticed the same thing. "Hey!" He shook Han's arm roughly. "Who are you?"

"My name is Han Solo," Han replied steadily. "You must be Thrackan Sal-Solo."

"So what if I am?" the other said sullenly. Han was beginning to feel uneasy about the way the boy was eyeing him. He'd seen vrelts with more warmth in their eyes. "Han Solo, eh? I never heard of you. Where do you come from? Who's your mother and father?"

"I was hoping you could tell me that," Han said evenly. "I ran away from where I was staying, because I wanted to find my family. I don't know anything about myself except my name."

"Huh . . ." Thrackan was still staring. "Well, I guess you must be one of the family . . ."

"Looks like it," Han agreed, not realizing until he spoke that it was a pun. But Thrackan didn't appear to notice. He seemed mesmerized by Han and, releasing his grip on the other's arm, walked around him, studying him from every angle.

"Where did you run away from?" Thrackan asked. "Will anyone come looking for you?"

"No," Han said shortly. He wasn't about to trust Thrackan with anything that could come back to haunt him. "Listen," he said, "we look alike, so we must be related, right? Could we . . . could we be brothers?" Funny, but after all his dreaming about finding a family that would rescue him from Trader's Luck, Han found himself hoping that wasn't the case.

"Not a chance," Thrackan said with a curl of his lip. "My dad died a year after I was born, and my mom shut herself up here ever since. She's kind of . . . a loner."

That fit with what Han had read about the Sal-Solo family. Tiion Solo had married a man named Randil Sal, some twenty years ago. The public records had carried his obituary.

"Maybe she'd know something about me," Han said. "Could I see her?" He took a deep breath. "Please?"

Thrackan seemed to consider. "Okay," he said finally, "but if she gets . . . upset, you've got to leave, okay? Mom doesn't like people. She's like her grandfather, won't have human servants, just droids. She says humans betray and kill each other and droids never do."

Han followed Thrackan into the huge house, through rooms full of shrouded furniture and paintings draped against dust. The family, Thrackan explained, used only a few rooms, to save the cleaning droids time and effort.

Finally, they came to Thrackan's mother's sitting room. Tiion Solo was a pale, dark-haired woman, plump and unhealthy-looking. She was far from attractive. But, looking at her, studying her face, seeing the bones beneath the puffy flab, Han thought that once, long ago, she might have been beautiful. Seeing her features, a memory stirred within him, so faint . . .

Once, he'd seen features similar to hers, Han thought. Long ago, far away. The "memory," if memory it was, was as fleeting and elusive as a drift of smoke.

"Mother," Thrackan said, "this is Han Solo. He's related to us, isn't he?"

Tiion Sal-Solo's gaze traveled to Han's face, and her eyes widened in distress. She stared at the boy in horror. Her

mouth worked, and a thin, shrill mewling sound emerged.
"No . . . no!" *she cried. Tears gathered in her brown eyes,*
coursed down the flabby cheeks. "No, it isn't possible! He's
gone! They're both gone!"

Burying her face in her hands, she began to weep hyster-
ically.

Thrackan grabbed Han by the arm and dragged him out
of the house. "Now look what you did, you little idiot," *the*
youth said, glancing uneasily up at his mother's window.
"She'll be a mess for days, she always is when she gets like
that."

Han shrugged. "I didn't do anything. She just looked at
me, that's all. What's wrong with her?"

With a muffled curse, Thrackan backhanded Han across
the face so hard it split the younger boy's lip. "Shut up!" *he*
snarled. "You've got no right to talk about her! There's
nothing wrong with her, hear me? Nothing!"

The blow stung, but Han had been hit often, by experts,
and one thing he knew was how to take a punch and stay
on his feet. For a moment he was tempted to fly at the older
boy's throat, but he made himself relax. There had been
genuine pain in Thrackan's eyes as he defended his mother.
Han figured he might have done the same thing, if he'd ever
had a mother. I have to stay here, *he reminded himself.*
Anything is better than Shrike . . .

"Sorry," *he managed to say.*

Thrackan looked a little abashed. "Just watch what you
say about my mom, okay?"

The next six weeks were some of the strangest of Han's
life. Thrackan allowed Han to stay with him in his rooms
(Tiion almost never came into Thrackan's part of the house),
and the two of them spent time talking and getting to know
each other.

Thrackan was a demanding host, Han soon learned. Han
had to agree with him completely, and rush to do his bid-
ding, or he lost his temper and cuffed the younger boy.
Thrackan made Han pilot him around the countryside in an
aging landspeeder, and the two of them even went on a few
expeditions to vacant estates Thrackan knew about, whose

inhabitants were away on vacation. Thrackan would demand that Han pick the locks and disable the security systems, and then the older boy would steal whatever took his fancy.

Han began to wonder whether he'd done himself any favor by running away from Trader's Luck. Two things kept him at the Solo estate: his fear that if he displeased Thrackan, the older boy would turn him over to the authorities—thus allowing Shrike to locate him; and his hope that Thrackan would break down and tell Han everything he knew about who Han really was. He kept hinting that he knew how they might be related.

"All in good time," Thrackan would say when Han tried to pry information out of him. "All in good time, Han. Let's go flying. I want you to teach me to pilot the speeder."

Han tried, but Thrackan wasn't very good at it. The older boy nearly crashed them several times before he mastered even the rudiments of flying the small craft.

I have to get out of here, Han kept telling himself. I'll run away to some other world, where they'll never find me. Maybe I can get adopted or get a job or something. There's got to be some way . . .

But he couldn't think of any way to get free of Thrackan. The older boy was vindictive, sadistic, and just plain mean. Several times Han saw him torture insects or animals, and when he realized that his actions disturbed the younger boy, he did it frequently. Han had never had a pet, but he tended to like furred creatures because of Dewlanna.

He missed her every day.

The situation became more and more explosive, until one day Thrackan really lost his temper with Han. Grabbing the younger boy by the hair, he dragged him to the kitchen, picked up a knife, and held it before Han's eyes. "See this?" he snarled. "If you don't apologize, and don't do exactly what I say, I'm going to cut your ears off. Now apologize!" He shook Han hard. "And you'd better make me believe it!"

Han stared at the shining blade of the knife, and wet his lips. He tried to force out words of apology, but a huge burst of red rage welled up in him. All the insults, all the cuffs and blows and beatings—Shrike's as well as Thrackan's—seemed to come to a head.

With a bellow as loud as a Wookiee's, Han went berserk. He slammed his fist against Thrackan's arm, sending the knife flying, and slammed his other elbow into Thrackan's stomach. The breath whooshed out of the older boy, and before Thrackan could recover himself, Han was all over him.

Kicking, biting, punching, gouging—Han used every dirty trick he'd learned on the streets to beat up Thrackan. Stunned and reeling from Han's fury, Thrackan never did recover, until the fight ended with Han sitting astride Thrackan, holding the knife to the older boy's throat.

"Hey . . ." Thrackan's eyes glittered like a trapped vrelt's. "Hey, Han, stop kidding around. This isn't funny."

"Neither is cutting off my ears," Han said. "Listen, I've had it. You tell me what you know, and you tell me right now, or I swear I'll cut your throat wide open. And then I'm leaving here. I've had it with you."

Thrackan's dark eyes were wide with fear. Something he'd seen on Han's face must have convinced the older boy that Han was so angry he would be wise not to push him. "Okay, okay!"

"Now," Han said. "Talk."

Stammering with fear, Thrackan told the story.

Years ago, Thrackan's grandfather, Denn Solo, and his grandmother, Tira Gama Solo, had lived on the fifth inhabited planet in the Corellian system, a colony world called Tralus. Those were perilous times, and roving bands of raiders and pirates threatened many outlying worlds. The raiders never reached Corellia, but they reached Tralus. A fleet of them landed and devastated the entire colony.

"Grandma Solo was pregnant," Thrackan gasped, because it was hard to breathe with Han sitting on his chest. "And the night their town was attacked, she had her babies. Twins. One of them was later named Tiion. Grandma Solo took her and ran away from the raiders. She managed to hide in a cave in the hills."

"Tiion," Han said. "Your mother."

"Right. The other baby was a boy, Grandma Solo said. Her husband took him. There hadn't even been time to name them. Grandma said it was terrible. Fires everywhere, and people running and screaming. She and Grandpa Denn got separated in the rush to escape."

"And?" Han flexed his hand slightly, and the blade moved against Thrackan's throat.

"Like I said, Grandma Solo and Tiion escaped. But Grandpa Solo and the baby boy vanished. They were never heard from again."

"So who does that make me?" Han said, completely baffled.

"I don't know," Thrackan said. "But if I had to guess, I'd guess that you're my cousin. That somehow Grandpa Solo and his son got away, and that you're the son of his son."

"Doesn't anybody know anything but that?" Han demanded, feeling desperate. This was a total dead end—the disappointment was crushing. "Servants?"

"Grandpa Solo didn't like human servants. He always had droids. And when Grandma Solo made it back to her family on Corellia, Great-grandpa Gama had all the droids' memories erased. He thought it would be easier on her that way. He wanted her to get married again, start a new life." Thrackan struggled to take a deep breath. "But she never did."

"So what happened to your mom?"

"I don't know. She's always been afraid to trust people, and she hates crowds. After my dad died, she just wanted to shut herself away. So she did."

Han's knife hand drooped, and he shook his head. "Okay," he said. "I'm go—"

With a sudden heave, Thrackan threw him off, and then, before Han could counter the move, their positions were reversed. Han gazed up at his cousin, knowing that he'd be lucky to live through this. Thrackan's dark eyes blazed with hate, rage, and sadistic pleasure. "You're going to be very, very sorry, Han," he said quietly.

And Han was.

Thrackan locked him in a bare storeroom for three days,

giving him only bread and water. On the afternoon of the third day, as Han was sitting listlessly in a corner, Thrackan unlocked the door. "I'm afraid this is good-bye, coz," he said cheerfully. "Someone's here to take you home."

Han looked around desperately as Garris and Larrad Shrike followed Thrackan into the room, but as he already knew, there was nowhere to run . . .

Han shook his head and refused to let himself think about the days that had followed. Shrike had been held back in his punishment only by the fact that he hadn't wanted to "damage" Han permanently because of his growing reputation as an expert speeder and swoop pilot. But there had been lots of things he could do that wouldn't cause permanent damage, and he had done most of them . . .

The only time Han had been beaten more severely was after the debacle on Jubilar, when he was seventeen. Han had already been bruised and sore from the gladitorial Free-For-All he'd been forced to fight in, after being caught cheating at cards. That time, Shrike hadn't bothered with a strap, he'd just used his fists—battering the boy's face and body until Larrad and several others had pulled him off Han's unconscious form.

And now he's killed Dewlanna, Han thought bitterly. *If anyone ever needed killing, it's Garris Shrike.*

For a moment he wondered why it had never occurred to him to kill the unconscious Shrike before he'd made his getaway aboard the *Ylesian Dream.* He'd have been doing the inhabitants of *Trader's Luck* a favor. Why hadn't he? He'd had the blaster in his hand . . .

Han shook his head. He'd never shot anyone before yesterday, and killing an unconscious man just wasn't his style.

But Han knew, without being told, that if Garris Shrike ever caught up with him in the future, he was a dead man. The captain never forgot and he never forgave. He specialized in carrying grudges against anyone who had ever wronged him.

Han got up again to check their course, and his air pak.

Only a few hours worth of air left, now. He did some mental calculations, while staring at the display. *Close. It's going to be close. I'd better be ready to pop the cargo door on this crate as soon as we land . . . It's going to be very, very close . . .*

Chapter Three:

CRASH LANDING

Although he'd flown hundreds of hours in swoops and speeders, Han's experience with piloting larger vessels was confined to the times Garris Shrike had permitted him to pilot the *Luck*'s shuttle on easy runs. He'd taken off and landed, but he'd never before tried to land anything as large as the robot freighter. Han hoped he'd be able to handle it. He had confidence in his ability as a pilot—after all, hadn't he been the junior speeder champion of all Corellia three years running? And, last year, hadn't he won the swoop racing championship of the entire Corellian system?

Still, compared to the *Luck*'s shuttle, this freighter was *huge* . . .

Han dozed again, then when he awoke, roved restlessly around the cabin, knowing he should be conserving his energy and his air, but unable to stop himself.

"Sir?" The R2 unit that had been so quiet for so many hours suddenly came back to life. "I must advise you that we have reached the orbit of Ylesia. You must stand ready to make your descent and landing."

"Thanks for telling me," Han said. Going over to the control banks, he scanned the instruments, mentally calculating their descent. This wasn't going to be easy. He had no way to interface with the navicomputer, except via the R2 unit. A pilot had to make split-second decisions, at times, and in cases like that, Han wouldn't be able to wait for the R2 unit to reply.

The ship suddenly shivered, then rocked slightly.

They were hitting atmosphere, Han realized.

He took a deep breath and glanced at his air pak reading, realizing it was going to be close . . . very, very close.

Here we go, he thought, switching to manual control of the *Ylesian Dream.* "Hey, R2," he said tightly, adjusting his course slightly.

"Yes, sir?"

"Wish me luck."

"I-beg-your-pardon, sir, this unit is not—"

Han swore, and the *Ylesian Dream* headed down, for the surface of a planet he couldn't even see. He *could* see the sensor readouts and the infrared scanners, though, and he realized that Ylesia was a world of tempestuous air currents, even in the upper layers of the atmosphere. Mapping sensors created a global portrait of the planet: shallow seas studded with islands, and three small continents. One lay nearly at the north pole, but the other two, the eastern and western continents, lay nearer the equator, in what must be temperate zones.

"Great," he muttered to himself, locating the ship's home-in beacon. He could use it as a guide to plan his landing. The landing field was on the eastern continent. That must be where the Ylesian colony of priests and religious pilgrims was located.

The *Dream* rocked wildly, swooping through the swirling air currents like a child on a rope swing. Han's suit gloves were clumsy on the undersized diagnostic controls as he used his stabilizers to steady their descent. Trying to get the feel of the controls, Han yawed them to port, then overcompensated, sending them skittering to starboard.

On the infrared image, a huge blob of red suddenly loomed up. *That's a huge storm!* Han thought, using his laterals to even out their descent. He allowed the *Dream* to drift a few degrees north, figuring that he'd miss the storm, then swing back south later, when he was beneath the maelstrom.

The ionized particles left in the wake of all that lightning were playing havoc with his instruments, Han realized. He gulped air, felt his chest tighten, and had to fight back panic. Good pilots couldn't afford to let their emotions get in the way, or they'd wind up dead and that would end their trip real quick, wouldn't it?

"R2," Han said tightly, "see if you can chart me those storm areas so I can avoid the ion trails that lightning is leaving. Concentrate on the direct flight path between our present location and the landing field on that eastern continent."

"Yes, sir," the R2 unit said.

Moments later the electrical storm sites appeared before him. "Give me a scaled-down version of that chart in the corner of this screen, R2," Han ordered. Usually it would be the navicomputer's job to "merge" the intended flight path with the geographical features and the storm cells, and to suggest an intended course, which the pilot could then implement and modify as needed.

Han had never missed having a navicomputer at his disposal more than he did at this moment.

He slowed their headlong rush fractionally, then was forced to kick in their thrusters to get them out of the way of yet another wind shear from a storm cell.

Sweat was dripping down his face now as he fought the tiny controls, forcing *Ylesian Dream* into maneuvers only a swoop or a military fighter could reasonably be expected to tackle. Han realized he was still gasping, and wondered for a split second whether it was from stress and adrenaline or whether his air was running out.

He couldn't spare the second it would take to check the air pak.

They were now only a kilometer above the surface of the planet, coming in with a rush. Too fast! Han slowed them, using the braking thrusters roughly. Gee forces seized him, and he felt as though something were squeezing his chest in a giant vise. He was gasping steadily now, and he dared to look down at his air pak.

Empty! The status indicator was solidly in the red zone.

Hold together, Han, he counseled himself. *Just keep breathing. There's got to be enough air in your suit to support you for a couple of minutes—at least.*

He shook his head, feeling light-headed and dizzy. His breath began to burn in his chest.

But they were almost slow enough now to land. He braked again, lightly, and the ship bucked suddenly. *I've lost my forward stabilizer!*

Han fought to compensate. Still too fast, but there was nothing more he could do about that. He flicked on the repulsorlifts and began to set her down, feeling the ship's vibration through his knees and legs as he knelt on the deck.

Hold together, baby! he thought at the *Dream. Hold together—*

With a huge *whooooommpppp!* the forward portside repulsor shorted out. The *Dream* yawed wildly to port, hit the ground, then bounced upward. The starboard repulsor blew, and then its entire starboard side impacted with the ground, nearly flipping the vessel over.

Wham! With a hideous *crunch* that Han could feel through his entire body, the *Ylesian Dream* crashed into the surface of the planet, shuddered once, and was still.

Han was thrown violently across the cabin. His helmet impacted with the bulkhead, and he lay there, arms and legs flung wide, dazed. He fought to stay conscious. If he passed out, he'd never wake up again. Trying to pull himself up into a sitting position, Han grunted with effort. Waves of blackness threatened. He triggered his suit communications channel. "R2 . . . R2 . . . come in!"

"Yes, sir, I am here, sir." The droid's mechanical tones sounded a bit shaken. "If you don't mind my saying so, sir, that appears to have been a most unconventional landing. I am concerned that—"

"Shut *UP* and *OPEN THE CARGO AIRLOCK!*" Han wheezed. He managed to push himself up into a sitting position, but he was afraid he wouldn't be able to stay up. He was swaying like a drunk in a high wind.

"But, sir, I warned you that in the interests of security, all entrances would be sealed pending—"

Han found the blaster he'd stuck into the outside pocket on his suit and, drawing it, leveled the weapon at R2. "*R2, YOU OPEN THAT AIRLOCK NOW, OR I'LL BLAST YOUR METAL HIDE INTO ATOMS!*"

The droid's lights flashed frantically. Han's finger tightened on the trigger as he wondered whether he'd have the strength to crawl to the airlock. Blackness hovered at the edges of his vision.

"Yes, sir," the R2 said. "I am doing as you request."

Moments later Han felt the concussion as air *whoomped* into the *Dream* with near-explosive force. Gasping, he counted to twenty, then, with the last of his remaining strength, wrenched off his helmet. He let himself sink back down onto the deck.

He gasped, found he could breathe, and gulped huge lungfuls of fresh air. Warm air, humid air, air laden with smells he couldn't identify. But it was rich with oxygen, eminently breathable, and that was all he cared about at the moment.

Closing his eyes, Han concentrated on simply breathing, and felt exhaustion overwhelm him. His head throbbed, and he needed just a moment to rest. Just a moment . . .

When Han swam back up to full consciousness and opened his eyes, he found he was staring into a face out of a nightmare. *That is the ugliest critter I've ever seen!* was his first thought. Only years of experience in dealing with nonhumans of all varieties made him able to control his initial reaction.

The face was broad, with two bulbous, protruding eyes, and covered with leathery grayish-tan skin. No visible ears, and only slits for nostrils. Above the nostril slits was a large, blunt horn that was nearly as long as Han's forearm. The mouth was a wide, lipless split in the huge head.

Han shook his own pounding head and managed to sit up, noting from his surroundings that he appeared to be in some type of infirmary. A medical droid hovered across the room, lights flashing.

His host (if that was who the creature was) was big, Han realized. Much bigger even than a Wookiee. It somewhat resembled a Berrite, in that it walked on four tree-trunklike legs, but it was far larger. This creature's head was appended to a short, humped neck that was attached to a massive body. Han figured its back would reach his shoulders when he was standing up. The leathery skin covering its body hung in creases, wrinkles, and loose folds, especially on its short, almost nonexistent neck. The skin shone with an oily gleam.

The four short legs ended in huge, padded feet. A long, whippy tail was carried curled over its back. For a moment Han wondered if the creature had any manipulatory limbs, but then he noticed two undersized arms that were folded against its chest, half-hidden by the loose folds of neck skin. The being's hands were delicate, almost feminine, with four long, supple fingers on each hand.

The being opened its mouth and spoke in accented, but understandable Basic. "Greetings, Mr. Draygo. Allow me to welcome you to Ylesia. Are you a pilgrim?"

"But I'm not . . ." Han muttered, his head spinning. For a moment the name didn't connect, then things snapped into place. Of course. He clamped his mouth shut, thinking that maybe he'd gotten a worse knock on the head than he'd realized. Vykk Draygo was the alias whose ID he'd currently been carrying.

Han had several alter egos, with proper documentation

to back them up. Ironically, he had *nothing* by way of ID under his true name.

"Sorry," he muttered, holding his hand to his head, hoping his slip would be excused as a result of his head injury. "I'm still kind of shaken up, I guess. No, I'm not a pilgrim. I came here to answer a job advertisement for someone—preferably a Corellian—to do the piloting here."

"I see. But how did you happen to be aboard our ship when it crashed?" the creature inquired.

"I wanted to reach Ylesia as quickly as possible, so I took the opportunity to stow away on the *Ylesian Dream*," Han said. "I'd have had to wait a week for a commercial flight, and the ad said a pilot was urgently needed. Did you get my message?"

"Yes, we did," the being said. Han watched it intently, wishing he could read its expression. "We were expecting you—but not in the *Ylesian Dream*."

"See, I brought the ad with me." Han reached for his jumpsuit that was hanging over a chair beside the bed and extracted the holo-cube that featured the Ylesian advertisement he'd replied to. "It says you need someone to start right away."

He handed the cube over. "So . . . Vykk Draygo here, and I'm applying for this job. I'm Corellian, and I fit all your qualifications. I just . . . well, I wanted to say that I'm sorry about crashing the *Dream*. Your ship's a different model than any I ever piloted, but a couple of hours on a simulator will fix that. And I'm afraid that your atmospheric currents came as a surprise."

The being scanned the cube, then placed it on the table. The corners of the massive, lipless mouth turned upward slightly. "I see. Mr. Draygo, I am the Most Exalted High Priest of Ylesia, Teroenza. Welcome to our colony. I am impressed at your initiative, young human. Traveling aboard a robot ship in order to answer our ad so quickly speaks well for you."

Han frowned, wishing his head didn't hurt quite so much. "Well . . . thanks."

"I am impressed that you managed to control and land a

robot craft. Few human pilots have been able to react quickly enough to deal with this world's challenging weather patterns. The damage to our ship is not serious, and repairs are already under way. You landed on soft ground, which was fortunate."

"Does that mean I get the job?" Han asked eagerly. *Great! They're not mad!*

"Would you be willing to sign a year's contract?" Teroenza asked.

"Maybe," Han said, leaning back and relaxing, hands behind his head. "How much?"

The High Priest named a sum that made Han smile inwardly. Even though it was more money than he'd hoped for, he was too much of a trader not to automatically bargain.

"Well, I dunno . . ." he said, rubbing his chin thoughtfully. "I made more than that in my previous position . . ."

A lie, but not one they'd be able to disprove. Vykk Draygo had indeed made more than that—Han had paid well to make sure his alter ego's job record showed that he could command the highest wages. It had taken all of Han's savings, plus the proceeds from two dangerous heists that Garris Shrike hadn't known anything about, to finance those alterations in his alter ego's job record—but Han had wanted Vykk Draygo to be able to command a high salary.

Teroenza pondered that information, then said, "Very well, I can offer you thirty thousand for the year, with a bonus of ten at the end of the first six months, providing you make every assigned flight on schedule."

"Bonus of fifteen," Han said automatically. "And you provide the training sims."

"Twelve," countered Teroenza. "And you pay for the sims."

"Thirteen," Han said. "*You* supply the sims."

"Twelve and a half, and we provide the sims," the High Priest said. "Final offer."

"Okay," Han said, "you got yourself a pilot."

"Excellent!" Teroenza actually chuckled, a deep, booming, oddly melodious sound.

Quickly the contracts were produced, and Han signed them, then allowed a retinal scan as proof of his identity. *Hope they're like everyone else,* he thought, *and just do a general, system-wide check of my retinal patterns.* If the priests ordered a comprehensive—and very expensive—all-systems search to determine whether "Vykk Draygo's" retinal scan was unique, they'd eventually discover that it wasn't. Vykk Draygo, Jenos Idanian, Tallus Bryne, Janil Andrus, and Keil d'Tana all shared the exact same retinal patterns—which wasn't surprising, as all of those individuals were, in fact, Han Solo.

Before Han left *Trader's Luck,* he'd taken the precaution of stashing a small hoard of credits and complete ID sets in two lockboxes on Corellia, in case he ever needed a quick change of identity. Garris Shrike had provided the boy with different sets of ID for each scam Han participated in, and Han had kept each set and updated them as necessary.

The Corellian knew, however, that none of his forged IDs would stand up to Imperial scanners. Before he'd be able to take the Academy entrance exams, Han was well aware that he'd have to pay out a small fortune in bribes on Coruscant to gain ID documentation so genuine that it would pass an Imperial security clearance check.

With all of the business details taken care of, Teroenza then summoned an Under-Priest, or Sacredot, as they were called, and instructed him to take Han on a tour of the complex. Han was left in private to resume his jumpsuit, after being assured that clothing bearing the Ylesian symbol—a huge, wide-open eye and mouth—would be furnished to him.

As he donned the clothes and his boots, he realized that he was sweating heavily. *Hot and humid,* he thought. *Wonderful climate.* But for the money the priests were paying, he was willing to put up with a year's discomfort. By taking this job, he'd get lots of practice flying big ships and access to training sims. That ought to ensure that he could pass the entrance exams to enter the Academy.

The money would mean that he had the proper amount for bribes to make sure his application was processed quickly and actually reached the admissions officers. He knew from his research that without bribes it frequently took a month or more for a cadet candidate to apply, pass all relevant exams, be interviewed, and finally accepted for entrance into the Imperial Academy.

The Sacredot arrived and introduced himself as "Veratil." Han followed him down a corridor, past a large amphitheater, and what appeared to be a registration area. "Our Welcome Center," the priest explained. Veratil led him outside. Han stepped through the door, and even before he could draw a deep breath, he was immediately bathed in sweat. Steaming heat and humidity smote him in the face, almost like a physical blow. The air was rich with smells— heavy perfume from flowers, rotting vegetation—and another odor, one he'd smelled before but couldn't quite identify.

Han stood at the top of the short ramp that led down from the building and looked up at the sky, seeing that it was a translucent blue-gray. The sun overhead was an orangey-red, and looked larger than he was used to. This star must be closer to its planet than Corel was to Corellia. Han glanced at the shadows, seeing it was far past noon, and then glanced at his wrist-chrono. "How long is the day here?" he asked Veratil.

"Ten Standard hours, sir," the Sacredot replied.

No wonder the weather is so stormy, Han thought. *We've got a hot, wet world with a really rapid rotation.*

Han looked out across the cleared area. The permacrete ended abruptly, giving way to the natural ground and vegetation. Pools of water attested to recent torrential rain. Reddish mud made an arresting contrast to lush, blue-green vegetation. The flowers hanging from the vines and trees in the encroaching jungle were huge and multicolored—scarlet, deep purple, and vivid yellow.

"This is Colony One," Veratil explained. "We have also established two new colonies for our pilgrims. Two years ago we founded Colony Two, and last winter we built Colony Three, which is still very small. Colony Two lies about one hundred fifty kilometers north, and Colony Three about seventy kilometers south of here."

"How long has Colony One been here?" Han asked.

"Nearly five Standard years."

Han looked out across Colony One. Directly across from the Welcome Center lay the landing pad. A little freighter lay there, listing on her repulsors. *That must be the* Dream, Han thought, realizing he'd never seen the ship from the outside.

The *Ylesian Dream* was a small vessel, shaped like a fat, somewhat irregular teardrop. On her underside was a bulge where there was a gun well, proving that the ship hadn't always been a robot freighter. Another, larger bulge denoted the location of the primary cargo hold. She was a graceful ship, small enough to be agile. Corellian-built, almost certainly.

Han could see massive shipdock droids working on the *Dream,* beginning to repair her repulsors. The ship, droids, and everything nearby was splashed with reddish mud from the crash landing.

Off to the northeast, high above even the jungle giant trees, Han could make out a glimpse of snowcapped heights. He pointed. "What mountains are those?"

"The Mountains of the Exalted," Veratil told him. "The Altar of Promises where the faithful gather each night to be Exulted lies before them. You shall see it tonight, when you attend devotions."

Oh, great, Han thought. *Do I have to attend services, too?* Then he remembered how much the Ylesians were paying him. Han nodded. "I'll bet it's something to see."

To the pilot's left, he could make out a large expanse of the reddish mud. Several beings of Teroenza's and Veratil's race lolled in mudholes, tended by droids and servants of assorted species. Han recognized a couple of Rodians, several Gamorreans, and at least one human. "Those are the mudflats," Veratil said, waving a dainty hand at the mudbathers and their attendants. "My people relish our mudbaths."

"What *are* your people?" Han asked. "Are you native to Ylesia?"

"No, we are native—or as native as our distant cousins, the Hutts—to Nal Hutta," Veratil replied. "We are the t'landa Til."

Han resolved to learn the t'landa Til's language as soon as he could. *Knowing a language that people didn't know you knew could often prove an asset* . . .

The Sacredot led Han around to the rear of the Welcome Center. Han's eyes widened as he took in the huge cleared area before him. *Clearing that much jungle must have been quite a chore.* The cleared area was roughly rectangular, and at least a kilometer on each side. The mountains were now behind and to his left, and he could see, on his extreme right, the blue-gray glitter of water. "Lake?" he asked, indicating it.

"No, that is Zoma Gawanga, the Western Ocean," Veratil informed him.

Han counted the huge buildings that lay before the mudflats. There were nine of them. Five were three stories high, the other four were only one story. Each was easily the size of a Corellian city block. "Homes for the pilgrims?" he asked, waving at the buildings.

"No, the dormitory for our pilgrims is over there," Veratil said. The priest waved at a massive two-story building on the far left. "The multistory buildings are where we process ryll, andris, and carsunum. The single-story buildings you see extend far underground, a necessity for processing glitterstim, which must be handled in complete darkness."

Andris, ryll, carsunum, and glitterstim . . . Han's nostrils flared. *Of course, that explains the odor! These are factories for processing spice!* He remembered that the *Ylesian Dream* had originally carried a cargo of high-grade glitterstim, the most expensive and exotic variety of spice. The other types were usually cheaper—though they were still one of the most profitable cargoes a smuggler could take on.

"We receive shipments of raw materials from worlds such as Kessel, Ryloth, and Nal Hutta several times a month," Veratil went on. "In the beginning, the robot freighters which supplied us landed here at Colony One, but that practice soon had to be discontinued."

"Why?" Han asked, wondering if he really wanted to know.

"Two ships—most unfortunately—could not negotiate our tricky atmosphere, and crashed. So we built a space station and decided to use living pilots to ferry the raw spice material down to the factories. We used to have three pilots, but now we are down to one, and the unfortunate Sullustan who is currently serving as our pilot has been . . . ill. That is why we need you, Pilot Draygo."

It's so nice to be needed, Han thought sarcastically. "Uh . . . Veratil . . . what happened to those other guys?"

"One crashed, the other simply . . . disappeared. We have also lost a number of robot vessels, which has cut down on our profit margin most grievously," Veratil said sadly. "Spice is a high-credit export, but spaceships are *very* expensive."

"Yeah," Han agreed sourly. "All those crashes would tend to put a crimp in your business." *No wonder they didn't have pilots beating down their doors,* he thought. *Most of the experienced pilots have probably spread the word about how dangerous this planet is for pilots . . .*

Han knew a little bit about the various kinds of spice, mostly from hearing Shrike and the other smugglers discuss their properties.

Glitterstim, mined on Kessel, was by far the most valuable. When exposed to light, then quickly ingested, it gave the user a temporary telepathic ability to sense surface thoughts and emotions. Spies used it, lovers used it, and the Empire used it when interrogating prisoners. Matter of fact, the Empire claimed all the glitterstim mined on Kessel as its rightful property, which was why it was so rare and so lucrative to smuggle.

Ryll came from the Twi'lek world, Ryloth, where it was perfectly legal to mine, and was used for analgesic purposes. There were illegal applications, however, and it could be used to produce several intoxicants and hallucinogens.

Carsunum was a black spice that came from Sevarcos, and it was quite rare and very valuable. Users experienced euphoria, and an increase in their abilities—while under the influence they became stronger, faster, and more intelligent. There was a downside, of course. After the effects wore off, users frequently became listless, depressed, and some even died when the substance had a toxic effect on their metabolisms.

Sevarcos also supplied the galaxy with andris, a white powder that was added to foods to enhance flavor and preserve them. Some users claimed that the drug caused a mild euphoria and increase in sensation.

They're not mining it here, Han thought. *These factories process the raw material to turn it into the finished product.*

"Factories?" Han echoed. "They're huge . . ."

"Yes, and Ylesia has admirable production rates, enabling us to favorably compete with the cost of the spice shipped directly from Kessel, Ryloth, or Sevarcos," Veratil explained. "And we are the only facility that offers such variety of spice. Buyers frequently wish to purchase several different kinds of spice for their customers, and we provide that."

Han saw figures entering and leaving the factory buildings. Many humans, some nonhumans. He recognized Twi'leks, Rodians, Gamorreans, Devaronians, Sullustans . . . and there were others that were unknown to him. All the humans and bipedal aliens wore tan-colored robes that came down below their knees and tan-colored caps that covered their hair.

He gestured at the people. "Factory workers?"

The Sacredot hesitated, then said, "They are the pilgrims that have chosen to serve the Oneness, the All, in our factories."

"Oh," Han murmured. "I see."

He saw a lot of things, now, more and more clearly each instant. And he had a bad feeling about what he was seeing, *These pilgrims come here to attain religious sanctuary, and wind up working in spice factories. I smell a vrelt—a dead one.*

The Ylesian sun was far down in the sky by now, almost to the horizon. Han noticed that throngs of tan-clad workers were streaming northeast, toward the mountains. Veratil beckoned Han with one undersized hand. "It is time for the blessed pilgrims to attend devotions and to be Exulted in the One, render their prayers to the All. Let us take the Path of Oneness to reach the Altar of Promises. Come, Pilot Draygo."

Han obediently followed the priest up a well-worn paved path. Even though they were surrounded by pilgrims, Han noticed that no one ventured very close to them. All of the pilgrims gave Veratil deep bows, hands folded over their hearts. "They offer thanks for the Exultation they are about to receive," Veratil explained to Han as they walked along.

As they moved away from the buildings, the jungle around them closed in, until the path they were walking on was shadowed and overhung with giant branches. Han almost felt as though he were walking in a tunnel.

They passed a huge open area that was evidently some kind of swamp, because it was completely covered in huge blooms that were so beautiful and exotic that Han had never seen anything like them. "The Flowered Plains," Veratil, still playing tour guide, pointed out. "And this is the Forest of Faithfulness."

Han nodded. *I wonder how much more of this I can take,* he thought. *I hope they don't expect* me *to become a convert, because they've got the wrong guy.*

After a twenty-minute walk, the group reached a large, paved area that was fronted with a partially roofed area supported by three monstrous pillars. Veratil indicated that Han should stay with the crowd of pilgrims, then the Sacredot moved on, heading for the pillars. Han saw several of the t'landa Til assembled beneath the pillars, including one that he tentatively identified as Teroenza. They were ranged around a low altar carved from some translucent white stone that seemed to glow with an inner light.

The high, snowcapped mountains made an impressive

backdrop to the scene, as they towered high above the jungle. Han craned his neck, looking up . . . up . . . the tops of the highest peaks were hidden by drifting clouds, stained red from the sunset. The snows on the western sides of the peaks glowed crimson and rose.

Impressive, Han was forced to admit. The simplicity of the natural amphitheater, with its paved floor and pillared altar, made it seem like some vast natural cathedral.

The faithful filed into ranks and stood waiting.

Han stood at the back, shifting impatiently, hoping whatever religious service was about to take place wouldn't last long. He was hungry, his head was throbbing, and the heat was making him sleepy.

The High Priest raised his tiny arms and intoned a phrase in his native language. The Sacredots, including Veratil, echoed him. Then the assembled throng (Han estimated four or five hundred in the crowd) echoed the High Priest's phrase. Han leaned closer to the nearest pilgrim, a Twi'lek. "What are they saying?"

"They said, 'The One is All,'" the Twi'lek, who spoke excellent Basic, translated. "Would you like me to interpret the service for you?"

Since Han was determined to begin learning the t'landa Til's language, he nodded. "If you wouldn't mind."

The High Priest intoned again. Han listened to the ritual phrases repeated by the Sacredots, then droned forth by the faithful pilgrims:

"The All is One."

"We are One. We belong to the All."

"In service to the All, every One is Exulted."

"We sacrifice to achieve the All. We serve the One."

"In work and sacrifice we are All fulfilled. If every One has worked hard, we are All Exulted."

Han stifled a yawn. This was awfully repetitious.

Finally, after nearly fifteen minutes of chanting, Teroenza and all the priests stepped forward. "You have worked well," the High Priest pronounced. "Prepare for the blessing of Exultation!"

The crowd gave forth a sound of such greedy anticipation that Han was taken aback. Moving in a great wave, as though they were truly One, they dropped to the pavement and lay there, arms and legs huddled beneath their bodies, in an attitude of breathless hope and yearning.

All of the priests raised their arms. Han watched as the loose, wrinkled skin that hung below their throats inflated with air and began to pulse. A low, throbbing hum—or was it a vibration?—gradually filled the air.

Han's eyes widened as he *felt* something invade his mind and body. Part vibration, part sound? He wasn't sure. Was it empathy, or telepathy, or did that vibration trigger something in his brain? He couldn't tell. He only knew that it was *strong* . . .

It rolled across him in a great wave. Emotional warmth, physical pleasure, it was all of that and more. Han staggered back, off the permacrete, until he was brought up short by the trunk of one of the forest giants. He braced himself against the tree, his head swimming. He dug his fingernails into the bark, hanging on to the tree. His hands against the bark seemed to be the only thing keeping him from being swept away by that wave of warm feeling and ecstatic pleasure . . .

Han hung on to the tree physically, and himself mentally, refusing to let himself be sucked under with that wave. He wasn't sure where he found the strength, but he fought as hard as he ever had. All his life, he'd been his own person, master of his own mind and body, and *nothing* was going to change that. He was *Han Solo,* and he didn't need aliens invading his mind or his body to make him feel good.

No! he thought. *I'm a free man, not some pilgrim, not your puppet! Free, do you hear?*

Gritting his teeth, Han fought that invasion as he would have fought a physical opponent, and then, as quickly as it had started, the sensation was gone—he was free.

But it was obvious the pilgrims weren't. Their bodies writhed on the stone, and muffled moans of happiness and pleasure made a soft swell of sound.

Sickened, Han looked over at the priests. They obviously

weren't affected as the pilgrims were. *So this is why these poor dupes stay, once they find out they're expected to work in the spice factories,* Han thought, feeling a surge of bitter resentment on behalf of the pilgrims. *They slave all day, then they hike up here and get a jolt of feel-good vibrations that makes even the best spice pale by comparison.*

Han wondered whether he'd be expected to attend these "evening devotionals" every night, and hoped that he wouldn't. It had been hard enough to push away that rush of warmth and pleasure tonight. He was afraid that if he had to be exposed to it every night, he wouldn't have the strength, the resolution, to reject the Ylesian priests' "happy pill."

By this time, the pilgrims were beginning to get up, some of them weaving unsteadily. All of their eyes were glazed, and many looked like addicts Han had seen in spice and oobalah dens on Corellia and other worlds.

"Do they do this every night?" he muttered to the Twi'lek.

The alien's reddish eyes were shining with joy. "Oh, yes. Wasn't it wonderful?"

"Great," Han said, but the Twi'lek was so enraptured he missed the sarcasm.

"Do they ever not hold these 'devotions'?" Han asked, curious.

"They are only canceled if there has been trouble in the factories. One time a worker went mad and took a foreman hostage, then he demanded passage off-planet. Evening devotions and the Exultation were canceled—it was horrible."

"So what happened to the mad worker?" Han asked, reflecting that the "madman" sounded completely sane to him.

"Before morning, we managed to overpower him and turn him over to the guards, thank the One," the Twi'lek said.

Yeah, I'll bet, Han thought. *They couldn't stand being without their little nightly charge.*

The service was evidently over.

Veratil joined Han for the walk back to the central compound. Han was disinclined to talk, and truthfully pleaded fatigue. The Sacredot, saying that he understood perfectly, showed the Corellian pilot back to the infirmary.

"You may eat and sleep here tonight," he said, "and tomorrow we will take you to your permanent quarters in our Administration Building."

"Where's that?" Han asked, pausing halfway through a bite of indifferent—but filling—reedox-stew.

The Sacredot waved his arm roughly northeast. "Not visible from here, but there is a path through the trees. I will meet you back here in, say, six Standard hours? Will that provide you with sufficient sleep?"

Han nodded. He could always try to snatch a nap later. "Fine."

When the priest was gone, Han dragged off his clothes and boots, realizing that he had to get something clean to wear by tomorrow, or he wouldn't be fit for polite society. He considered taking a shower before bed, but he was just too tired.

Han had always been able to set himself to wake up whenever he wished to, so he mentally programmed himself to wake up in five and a half hours. Then, his mind whirling with images and impressions, he lay down on the narrow infirmary bunk and was instantly asleep.

It took him a few minutes the next morning to remember just who he was (*Vykk Draygo, and don't forget it!*) and what he was doing in this sticky-hot place. Han ventured into the shower and was pleased to find the refresher unit contained everything necessary for a human being.

He hummed tunelessly as he soaped himself, but when he lifted a foot to wash it, Han froze in surprise and dismay. Fuzzy, blue-green, mossy stuff was growing between his toes!

Alarmed, Han checked further and was disgusted to find patches starting in his armpits, at the back of his neck, and other, even more personal areas.

Cursing, he scrubbed the disgusting fungus away, leaving

raw skin behind, and then, realizing he was running late, he bolted out of the shower. *What kind of place is this, anyway?*

When he walked back into the sleeping area, he found the medical droid waiting for him, with a new pilot's uniform draped over one arm. The droid held a jar of slimy gray stuff in its other hand. "Pardon me, sir," the droid said. "But may I ask whether you are experiencing any . . . outbreaks of fungus growing on your skin?"

"Yeah," Han snarled. "The climate in this place is miserable. Nobody deserves to live in this dump."

"I quite understand, sir," the droid said, actually managing to sound sympathetic. "May I offer the contents of this jar? It should prevent fungal growths with regular application."

"Thanks," Han said shortly, and retired to treat the affected areas. The stuff smelled horrible, but it soothed the irritation. Then he got dressed, admiring himself in his first real pilot's uniform. The colorful patches looked quite spiffy.

Han refused to let himself worry about the pilgrims he'd seen last night. Nobody had forced the weak-minded fools to come here, so he wasn't going to waste any time imagining their fate. He was going to take care of Han Solo—or, more accurately, he was going to take care of *Vykk Draygo.*

Besides, Han told himself, *I'm going to be piloting for these Ylesians. I'll have access to a ship. If I decide I don't like it, I'll just take my money and . . . vanish. What can they do to stop me, after all?*

Feeling cocky, Han smiled at his reflection in the mirror and gave himself a snappy salute. "Cadet Han Solo reporting for duty, sir!" he whispered, trying it on for size. His dream of the Academy had never seemed so close, so attainable.

When Han stepped out of the infirmary, the first person he saw was Teroenza. Han nodded pleasantly to his employer. "Good morning, sir!"

The High Priest inclined his massive head. "And to you, Pilot Draygo. Allow me to present someone you are going to be spending a lot of time with, during your employment with us." The High Priest beckoned, and Han heard someone behind him. He whirled around, and couldn't stop himself from taking a quick step back.

His first impression was of height, and the second was of sharp teeth and knifelike claws. This being stood nearly three meters tall, taller even than a Wookiee. The creature had a mouthful of needlelike fangs, and claws that looked like they could rip through durasteel. It was furred, but it wore a pair of breeches. A curved knife hung on its belt, and a holstered blaster was strapped to its thigh. Sleek muscles rippled everywhere.

The newcomer grinned, baring even more of those teeth. "Greetings . . ." it said, speaking Basic with a pronounced lisp.

"This is Muuurgh," Teroenza introduced the being. "He's a Togorian, one of the most honorable sentients in this galaxy. The Togorian reputation for honesty and loyalty is unparalleled, did you know that?"

Han looked up at the huge being and swallowed. "Uh, no . . ." he managed.

"We've assigned Muuurgh to be your . . . bodyguard, Pilot Draygo. On planet or off, Muuurgh will accompany you everywhere . . . isn't that correct, Muuurgh?"

"Muuurgh has given word of honor," the Togorian affirmed.

The High Priest folded his undersized arms across his massive body, and his mouth curved up in what almost appeared to be a mocking smile. "Muuurgh is going to make very sure, Pilot Draygo, that no matter where you go, or what you do . . . you will be . . . safe."

Chapter Four:

MUUURGH

Han stared at the huge, black-furred creature, realizing that the jig was definitely up. Teroenza's meaning was unmistakable—step out of line, and Muuurgh will rip you in two. Han eyed the Togorian, realizing that the alien could easily do just that.

He managed to pull himself together and smiled up at the Togorian. "Pleased to meet you, Muuurgh," he said. "It'll be nice to have real company on those long flights."

"Yess . . ." the bodyguard said, stepping closer. Han realized with dismay that the top of his head barely reached the Togorian's breastbone. The alien appeared so feline that Han was surprised to realize he didn't have a tail. "Muuurgh enjoys space travel . . ." the bodyguard said in his strongly accented, lisping Basic. His facial fur was black, but his whiskers and chest fur were white. His eyes were a startling light blue, with brilliant green slitted pupils. "Muuurgh goesss many spaceports, the more the better."

Han had a little trouble understanding the Togorian's Basic, but he could make it out. The young Corellian wondered just how smart this being was. *Have to get to know him,* Han decided. *Just because he can't speak good Basic doesn't mean he's dumb. But if he is . . .*

Han smiled.

"We'd thought we'd give you a day to settle in, Pilot Draygo," Teroenza said. "Move into the quarters we've assigned you, in the Administration Building. Muuurgh will show you where it is. Then, tomorrow, we'd like you to begin ferrying goods and personnel back and forth between the colonies. By the time our next shipment of spice is delivered to our space station, you will be ready to ferry that down for us. After today, I am going to order Jalus Nebl, our other pilot, to take a rest. He has been working too hard."

Han nodded. *I've got to meet up with this Sullustan and compare notes.* "That will be fine. Can I . . . look around a bit? I'd like to check out the lay of the land."

Teroenza inclined his massive head. "Certainly, as long as Muuurgh accompanies you, and you follow all safety regulations while touring the factories."

"Of course," Han agreed.

Teroenza bowed slightly. "If you will excuse me, we are expecting a shipment of pilgrims to come down from our orbiting space station this morning. I have much to do as I prepare to welcome them."

Han nodded, thinking about what lay ahead for those pilgrims. He knew that *mining* spice was considered dangerous, an extremely unpleasant duty—matter of fact, being sent to the spice mines of Kessel was a common punishment for felons—but he knew very little about what happened to the spice once it was mined.

Well, he intended to find out. Maybe there was some way he could turn this situation even more to his advantage. You never knew . . . and it never paid to leave stones unturned. In Han Solo's book, knowledge frequently led to power—or at least to a faster escape . . .

Muuurgh led Han up a paved path through the jungle, until they reached a large, very modern building. "Administration Center," the Togorian said, indicating the building.

The "bodyguard" led Han around to a side entrance, and then down a corridor until he reached a door. "You, Muuurgh, sleep here," he said, opening the door.

Inside was a small suite consisting of a bedroom, refresher unit, and a small sitting room. Han was pleased to see that Teroenza had been mindful of the terms of the contract. In one corner of the bedroom was a fully equipped sim unit. Muuurgh walked to the door of the bedroom and waved a clawed hand at it. "Yours. Pilot sleep here."

"But where will you sleep?" Han asked.

As expected, Muuurgh indicated the sitting room. "Muuurgh here."

Great, Han said. *These priests don't trust me any more than I trust them. With Muuurgh sleeping between me and the door to the outside, I'd be taking a big chance trying to sneak out at night. Just great.*

"That doesn't look very comfortable to me," Han said, doing his best imitation of wide-eyed innocence. Inwardly, he was wondering whether Muuurgh was a sound sleeper. "Maybe you should get a room of your own, so you could sleep comfortably."

"Muuurgh most comfortable when he is keeping word of honor," the Togorian said. Han stared at the catlike being. Had he glimpsed a flash of humor in those blue-green eyes with their slitted pupils? "Muuurgh give word of honor to watch Pilot always, so Muuurgh most comfortable *here.*"

Han nodded. "Right."

He stared for a moment at the blaster in the Togorian's holster. "I had a blaster when I came here, but I don't know where it is, now," he commented. "I guess I'll need to ask about getting it back."

"Pilot not need blaster." Muuurgh flexed his fingers and

the retractable claws popped out. "High Priest say Pilot not need blaster."

"But what if I get attacked by some kind of . . . predator?" Han waved at the omnipresent jungle outside the building. There were probably dozens of predators who might enjoy hunting an off-worlder, either for food or fun.

The giant alien shook his whiskered head. "Never happen. Pilot have Muuurgh, who has blaster."

"Uh . . . that's true," Han said. Mentally, he made a note to ask Teroenza for some kind of weapon. He felt naked without one, even after only having had one for a couple of days.

"So, Muuurgh, shall we go exploring?" Han asked. "I don't have any baggage to unpack, as you can see."

"Explore where?" the Togorian asked.

"I'd like to tour the factories," Han said. "And this Administration Center."

"Fine," the Togorian said. "Come, Pilot."

"Right behind you," Han said, suiting his action to his words.

They walked the corridors of the Administration Center, glanced in at the mess hall, toured the guards' wing, and peeked at the priests' quarters. When Han caught a glimpse of the Armory, he realized that the Ylesian priests must be afraid of a pilgrim uprising, because the percentage of guards to workers was high. The Armory boasted a lot of heavy-duty riot control armament—force pikes and stun gas. The guards they met came from many different worlds. Besides humans, Han saw Rodians, Sullustans, Twi'leks, and porcine Gamorreans.

"So let me get this straight," he said to Muuurgh as they skirted an area in the Administration Center that signs in many languages identified as RESTRICTED ACCESS. "The guards all sleep here most of the time? But why don't they sleep near the pilgrims' dormitory if the priests want to make sure the workers stay under control?"

"Sleep-time not the problem," the Togorian said in his halting Basic. "After pilgrims are Exulted, can barely walk back, go sleep right away. Only time pilgrims get mad, angry at bosses, is before Exultation."

Makes sense, Han thought dourly. *Give the addicts their fix, and then they just sleep it off until the next day.* "Then the guard patro—"

The pilot stopped in midword when he glimpsed something large and grayish gliding far down the corridor in the off-limits area. Han squinted into the dimness. "Hey . . . what was *that*?" he muttered. "That looked just like a—" Han broke off as the object turned the corner. He started after it at a good clip.

Muuurgh made a futile grab for his charge, but Han was quicker than the big alien and dodged. He jogged down the "forbidden" hallway, listening hard for the sound of footsteps, but none came.

When he reached the junction of the corridors, Han turned to stare up the one where he'd glimpsed that flicker of gliding motion. His eyes widened.

Hey, it is a Hutt! What's a Hutt doing here? There was no mistaking the identity of that huge, sluglike form reclining on its repulsorlift sled.

As he hesitated, Muuurgh pounced on him as though he were a vrelt, and picked up the Corellian bodily. Han repressed a yelp of dismay as the Togorian tucked him under one muscled arm and ran back down the corridor, until they were back in the UNRESTRICTED ACCESS section of the Center.

Muuurgh set Han back on his feet and flexed a hand under the Corellian's nose. "My people teach, everyone entitled to ONE mistake," the bodyguard said. "Pilot just have his. No more mistakes, or Muuurgh have to teach Pilot like little cub. Muuurgh has given word of honor, remember. Understood?"

Han eyed the claws that gleamed under his nose, sharp and shiny as razors. "Uh . . . yeah," he managed to say. "I understand, Muuurgh. Humans just get . . . curious, you know?"

"Curiosity fatal sometimes," Muuurgh growled.

"I can see your point," Han said dryly. "Or, rather, your *points*."

Muuurgh stared at the sharp, shining tips of his claws, then his muzzle lifted back from his fangs, and he made a low, mewling sound. For a moment Han froze, then he looked at the Togorian and realized this was the alien's form of laughter. Evidently Muuurgh had caught the joke.

Han managed a weak chuckle. "So, how about we get some food, then check out those factories, eh, pal?" he asked.

"Muuurgh always hungry," the Togorian agreed, leading the way toward the mess hall. "What means this word 'pal'?"

"Oh, a pal is a friend, a buddy, you know. Someone you spend time with that you like," Han explained.

"Yessss . . ." the Togorian said, nodding. "Pilot means 'packmate.' "

"Right."

"Good," the bodyguard said. "Muuurgh misses his packmates."

Han recalled Teroenza saying that his people came from Nal Hutta, the Hutt homeworld, but Han hadn't realized that that meant there were Hutts living on Ylesia. When questioned, Muuurgh confirmed that he had seen several of the "slug masters who ride on air" as he called them.

There's only one reason Hutts are here, Han thought. *They're the real masters of Ylesia. After all, they dominate the contraband spice trade . . .*

Lunch was good, if unimaginative and (to Han's taste) lacking in seasoning. Still, the cook was no slouch. His or her bread was very good, Han thought as he chewed on a bite of Alderaanian flatbread. He realized suddenly, with a pang, that it had been nearly a day since he'd thought of Dewlanna. The thought made him feel vaguely disloyal, but then he took himself in hand. Dewlanna wouldn't want him to mope and grieve over her. She'd always enjoyed life, and she wouldn't expect Han not to, just because she was gone . . .

He came back out of his reverie to find Muuurgh watching him curiously. "Pilot is thinking of someone far away," the Togorian observed, waving the bone he had just finished gnawing. Tiny fragments of raw meat still clung to it, but Muuurgh had cleaned it impressively, Han thought. He had to get every little bit. It required a lot of raw meat to keep that massive body going.

"Yeah," Han agreed with a sigh. "Someone about as far away as anyone can be."

"Pilot have sweetheart?"

Han shook his head. "Well, there've been a few girls here and there," he admitted, "but nobody special. No, I was thinking of the person who more or less raised me."

Muuurgh took a huge gulp of some foamy stuff from a tankard. "Humans raise young much differently than my people do," he said.

"Really? Tell me about your world."

Muuurgh obediently launched into a description of Togoria, a world where males and females, though equal, did not mix their societies. Males lived a nomadic hunting existence, flying over the plains on their huge, domesticated flying reptiles, called "mosgoths." They hunted in packs.

The females, on the other hand, had domesticated animals for meat, so they did not need to hunt. They lived in cities and villages, and it was the female Togorians who had developed all of the planet's technology.

"Well, if your people don't live together, how do you"—Han searched for a polite term—"uh . . . get together, you know, to . . . uh . . . reproduce?"

"We travel to city to stay with our mates once each year," Muuurgh said. "Betweentimes, we think often of each other. Togorians very emotional people, capable of great love," he added earnestly. "Especially males. Great love is why Muuurgh is here. Males of my species rarely leave our world, does Pilot know that?"

"I do now," Han said. "So . . . Muuurgh . . . when

you say great love made you come to Ylesia, what do you
mean? Do you have a mate?"

The Togorian nodded. "Promised mate. Someday be
mated for life, if Muuurgh can but find her." The huge
alien sighed, looking so woeful that Han felt sorry for him.

"What's her name?"

"Mrrov. Beautiful, beautiful Mrrov. As Togorian females
do, she decided to take look at big galaxy. Muuurgh begged
her not to go, but females very stubborn."

The alien looked at Han, who nodded. "Yeah, I've run
into that myself."

"Mrrov gone long time, years. When she not come home
to be mated, Muuurgh so sad that he cannot stay on
Togoria. Must discover what happened to her."

"So . . . did you?" Han took a sip of his Polanis ale.

"Muuurgh traced her, from world to world to world."

"And?" Han prompted when the Togorian paused.

"And Muuurgh lost her. Someone on Ord Mantell said
he saw her board ship at spaceport. Muuurgh check sched-
ules, find out ship had many pilgrims on board. Several
ports of call for ship. Muuurgh take chance, come here,
because so many pilgrims come here." The big felinoid
sighed heavily and nibbled on a meat-dripping bone. "Gamble no good. Muuurgh ask, priests say no Togorians here.
Muuurgh not know where else to go. Muuurgh need credits
to continue search . . ." The alien swallowed a last bite,
and his whiskers actually drooped.

"So you decided to take a job as a guard here, while you
got enough money to go on searching," Han said, guessing
at the logical end of the story.

"Yessss . . ."

Han shook his head. "That's sad, pal. I hope you find
her, I really do. It's tough to lose people that you love."

The bodyguard nodded.

After lunch, they headed down to the factories and
walked around the huge buildings. Han sniffed the air,
smelling the odor of the different spices mingling. His nose
tingled slightly, and he wondered if just smelling the spice
could be intoxicating. He waved at the glitterstim building.

"Let's go inside. I've heard about how they process this spice, and I'd like to see it for myself."

When they walked into the cavernous building, a guard stopped them and conferred with Muuurgh, who explained who Han was. The Rodian guard on duty gave them badges and infrared goggles, then waved them on in.

"Goggles?" Han said in Rodian. He understood the language perfectly, but his pronunciation was a bit laborious. "We have to wear them?"

The guard's purple eyes sparkled at hearing a human speak his language. "Yes, Pilot Draygo," he said. "Below the ground floor, there are no visible lights permitted. You take the turbolift down. Each level down represents a one-grade increase in the quality of the spice. The longest and best fibers are processed far below ground, to eliminate any possibility of their being ruined by light."

"Okay," Han said, beckoning to Muuurgh. The two walked between aisles of supplies, to reach the platform turbolift in the center of the facility. "Let's go all the way down and see the really good stuff," he said to the Togorian. Privately, Han was wondering whether he might be able to light-finger some of those tiny black vials. Selling a little glitterstim on the side in a port city would increase his credit account by leaps and bounds . . .

Han pushed the button for the bottom floor, and the platform, swaying slightly, started down.

Cool air wafted up from the depths as the turbolift went down in pitch-darkness. The draft felt wonderful after the humid heat of the Ylesian jungle.

Within one floor, all light was gone. Han fumbled for his goggles, pulled them up over his eyes. Immediately he could see, though everything was in shades of black and white. The illumination came from small light inserts in the walls. The turbolift plunged downward, and Han could see the workers as they crouched over their workstations. Piles of raw, fibrous threads studded with minuscule crystals lay piled before them.

Finally, six floors down, the turbolift ground to a halt. Han and Muuurgh got off. "Have you ever been here before?" he asked the bodyguard softly. Muuurgh's neck fur was standing on end, and his white whiskers bristled beneath his goggled eyes.

"No . . ." the Togorian whispered back. "My people are plains-dwellers. Not like caves. Not like dark. Muuurgh will be happy when Pilot wishes to leave this place. Only Muuurgh's word of honor keeps him here in wretched darkness."

"Steady," Han said. "We won't be here that long. I just want to get a look around."

He led the way into the factory. The cavernous area was filled with soft swishings, but was otherwise silent. Long tables lined the walls and were ranged in the aisleways. Each table was a workstation, and a worker sat or crouched, according to his, her, or its individual anatomy, before the table. There were many humans, Han realized, sitting on tall stools, hunched over their work.

Few looked up as Han and Muuurgh went up to the level supervisor, a furred Devaronian female, and identified themselves. The supervisor waved a reddish, sharp-nailed hand at the floor. "My workers are the most skilled," she said proudly. "It takes skill to measure and trim the number of fibrous strands so each dose will contain the correct amount of spice. It is essential—but very difficult—to line up the fibers so precisely that they will all activate at the same moment when exposed to visible light."

"Is it a mineral?" Han asked. "I know it's mined."

"It is naturally occurring, but we don't know how it's formed, Pilot. We believe it may have a biological origin, but we're not sure. It's found deep in the tunnels on Kessel, and it must be mined in total darkness, just as you see here."

"And the strands have gotta be put into these casings just right."

"Correct. Improper alignment can cause the tiny crystals to fracture against each other. If that happens, they grind each other into a far less potent—and valuable—powder. It can take a skilled worker an hour to properly align just one or two cylinders of glitterstim."

"I see," Han said, fascinated. "Do you mind if we just wander around? I promise we won't touch anything."

"You may. However, please avoid distracting any of the workers while they are aligning the spice. One inadvertent twist, as I said, could ruin an entire thread."

"I understand," Han said.

The raw glitterstim threads were all black, but Han knew from hearing about it that they would shine blue when they ignited in visible light. Han stopped behind one of the human workers and watched in fascination as the worker separated out threads of ebony-colored spice, aligning them with the utmost care. The threads curled around the worker's fingers, some of them as fine-spun as silk, but the tiny crystals made them incredibly sharp.

The worker positioned one group of incredibly tangled threads in the jaws of a tiny vise, then proceeded to painstakingly separate out the threads, until the crystalline structures were aligned. The worker's fingers moved almost too fast to watch, and Han realized that he was watching a highly skilled craftsman—no, *woman*. He was amazed that these pilgrims could actually accomplish something requiring this much dexterity. After seeing them last night following the "Exultation," he'd more or less assumed that they were dull-witted cretins. They'd certainly *looked* like it . . .

The glitterstim worker took out a minuscule set of pliers to untangle a particularly bad snarl. She wormed the narrow-nosed pliers into the tangle, peering intently to find the place where the sharp little crystals were caught together. The fibrous glitterstim curled around her hands like tiny, living tentacles, the sharp little crystal glimmering. The worker abruptly brought her hand back, tugging, and suddenly the snarl straightened out until all the fibers aligned perfectly.

Except one.

Han watched in distress as one sharp-studded strand cut between the woman's forefinger and thumb. A thin line of blood welled from the deep gash. Han sucked in a breath. A few centimeters deeper, and the tendon in her thumb would have been severed. She hissed with pain, then muttered something in Basic and, freeing her hand, held it to stop the bleeding. Han froze as he heard her accent. This pilgrim was Corellian!

He hadn't even looked at her before, hidden as she was by the shapeless tan robe, her cap pulled down tightly over her goggled head. But now he realized she was young, not old. She grimaced slightly as she examined the cut. Turning her hand over, she twisted in her seat and held her hand over the floor, so the blood wouldn't drip onto her workstation.

Han knew he wasn't supposed to speak to the worker, but she wasn't working at the moment, and he was concerned. She was bleeding profusely. "You're hurt," he said. "Let me call the supervisor so she can fix you up."

The girl—she was his age, possibly younger—started slightly, then looked up at him. Her face was a whitish-green blur beneath her goggles and cap, and seemed deathly pale in the infrared light. *No wonder,* Han thought, *cooped up down here all day long, no exposure to sunlight.*

"No, please don't," she said, speaking Basic with that soft accent that placed her as being from Corellia's southern continent. "If she sends me to the infirmary, I'll miss the Exultation." She shivered at the thought—though it might also have been from the cold. Han himself was beginning to feel chilly, and he hadn't been down here for hours. How did these pilgrims stand it, working down here in the cold darkness all day?

"But that cut looks nasty," Han protested.

She shrugged. "The bleeding is stopping."

Han could see that was true. "But what about—"

She shook her head, halting him in midsentence. "I appreciate your concern, but it's nothing. Happens all the time." With a wry smile, she held out her hands. Han sucked in a breath. Her fingers, wrists, and forearms were crisscrossed with tiny slashes. Some were old and white and healed, but many were dark weals, still fresh and painful.

Han saw small, phosphorescent spots between her fingers and realized they must be the fungus he'd discovered on himself that morning. As he watched, a phosphorescent tendril of the stuff suddenly spread, growing toward the cut between her finger and thumb. She uttered a soft exclamation and pulled it free.

"The fungus loves fresh blood," she said, evidently noticing his distaste. "It can infect a cut and make you sick very easily."

"Disgusting stuff," Han said. "Are you sure you don't need to get that treated?"

She shook her head. "As you can see, it happens all the time. Excuse me, but . . . you're Corellian, aren't you?"

"So are you," Han said. "I'm Vykk Draygo, the new pilot. And you are?"

Her mouth tightened slightly. "I'm . . . not really supposed to be talking. I'd better get back to work."

Muuurgh, who had been watching in silence, suddenly spoke up. "Worker is correct. Pilot must let worker return to work now."

"Okay, pal. I understand," Han said to the Togorian, but then he added to the Corellian woman, "But maybe we could talk some other time. Over supper, maybe."

She shook her head silently and turned back to her work.

Muuurgh motioned for Han to move on.

The Corellian moved one step away, but continued talking. "Okay, but . . . you never know. We're bound to run into each other, this place ain't all that big. So . . . what's your name?"

She shook her head again, not speaking. Muuurgh growled, low in his throat, but Han just stood there, stubbornly.

The woman seemed disturbed by Muuurgh's implied threat. As she fastened a bandage over her cut, she said, "We give up our names when we leave all worldly things for the spiritual sanctuary of Ylesia."

Han was feeling increasingly frustrated. Here was someone who knew this place intimately, and she was the first person from his homeworld he'd discovered here. "Please," he said as Muuurgh pushed him slightly. "There must be some kind of way they refer to you," he said, smiling his most reassuring, charming smile. Muuurgh growled again, more loudly. He showed his fangs.

The woman's eyes opened wide at the display of teeth. "I am Pilgrim 921," she said hastily. Han got the impression that she had spoken up to save him from Muuurgh's ire.

Muuurgh grabbed Han's arm and began walking away, effortlessly dragging the Corellian. "Thank you, Pilgrim 921," Han called back to her, waving jauntily, as though being half carried away by the Togorian was a normal occurrence. "Good luck with those fibers. I'll be seeing you."

She didn't respond. When Muuurgh finally let him go, at the end of the aisle, Han followed the Togorian obediently, half expecting a lecture from the giant being. But Muuurgh seemed satisfied that Han would now obey him, and had relapsed into his former wary silence.

Han glanced back once and saw that the Corellian woman was again intent on her work, as though she'd already forgotten him.

Pilgrim 921, he thought. *I wonder if I'd even be able to recognize her . . .* Between the goggles, the cap, and his impaired vision, he had no real idea of what she looked like, except for the fact that she was young.

Han walked all the way around the facility, watching several other workers as they aligned threads and crystals so they were entirely symmetrical. He didn't attempt to speak to any of them. Finally he came back to the Devaronian supervisor. "So, when they've finished their work, who encases the threads and crystals in the vials?" he asked.

"That is done on the fifth floor," the supervisor told him.

"Maybe I'll just head up there," Han said. "This is fascinating, you know."

"Certainly," she said.

Okay, so they finish up the processing of the really high-grade stuff up here, Han thought as he and Muuurgh ascended into the darkness. The Togorian let out a low yowl of protest when Han only took them up one floor.

"Take it easy, Muuurgh," Han said. "I just want to take a quick look around here."

He wandered the aisles, trying unobtrusively to spot the place where the high-grade glitterstim was enclosed in the tiny black vials that all glitterstim users would recognize. When he reached that area, however, his heart sank. Four armed guards stood by the conveyor belt, watching the little vials as the workers brought their full baskets over and dumped them. Han felt an air current waft past him, realizing that there was a small heating unit down there, warming the chill, evidently for the comfort of the guards.

Four guards? Han peered harder into the dimness. No, hold on a second. He saw a blur of movement, but couldn't discern anything for a long second. Then, as he focused his eyes, he slowly made out oily, pebbled blackness barely visible against the black stone wall. But there were eyes in the midst of that blackness—beady reddish-orange eyes. Four of them. Han squinted, holding still, straining his vision. Then he saw two blasters, each strapped to a warty black thigh.

Aar'aa! he realized. *Skin-changers!*

The Aar'aa were an alien species from a planet on the other side of the galaxy. Denizens of Aar could gradually change color to match the color of the background behind them. This ability made them very difficult to see, especially in darkness.

Han had heard of the Aar'aa before, but he'd never run into any until now. They were reptilian creatures, which explained why this section of the belowground factory was heated. Many reptiles became sluggish and dull-witted when it was cold.

Han peered into the dimness, and slowly, gradually, made out the outlines of the two Aar'aa guards. They had pebbly-textured skin, clawed hands and feet, and a small frill of skin running down their backs. Their heads were large, with overhanging brow ridges, beneath which their eyes seemed doubly small. Their faces had short muzzles, and when one of the creatures opened its mouth, Han glimpsed a narrow, sticky red tongue and sharp white teeth. An upstanding frill of skin ran from between their eyes, back over the tops of their heads, to connect with the frill running down their backs.

Despite their clumsy appearance, they seemed fast on their feet. Han decided that he didn't want to tangle with them. Although shorter than he was, they were broad in the shoulders, and certainly outweighed him by a considerable margin.

Han sighed. *Scratch Plan A.*

The Aar'aa aside, the other guards—two Rodians, a Devaronian male, and a Twi'lek—looked mean, and obviously meant business. They weren't Gamorreans, so there wasn't much chance of being able to bewilder, confuse, distract, or otherwise fast-talk any of them into handing over a fortune in spice. Han grimaced and started back for Muuurgh and the turbolift. *And there is no Plan B,* he thought glumly. *Guess I'll just have to earn all my credits the honest way.*

It never even occurred to him that ferrying spice around the galaxy was, in itself, highly illegal . . .

Pilgrim 921 nibbled on a stale grain-cake and tried to forget the young Corellian she had seen earlier. She was a pilgrim after all, part of the All, one with the One, and worldly concerns such as good-looking young men were behind her forever. She was here to work, so that she might be Exulted and offer her prayers for the blessing of the One as part of the All—and conversations with young men named Vykk had no part in that.

Still, she wondered what he looked like beneath those goggles. What color was his hair? His eyes? That smile of his had made warmth blossom inside her, despite the cold . . .

Shaking her head, Pilgrim 921—*I miss my name!*—tried to exorcise the memory of Vykk Draygo's lopsided, heartstopping smile. She needed to pray, to offer proper devotion. She must do penance for separating herself from the One, lest she be cast out from the All.

Still those sacrilegious thoughts kept intruding.

Thoughts . . . memories, too. He was Corellian . . . and so was she.

Pilgrim 921 thought of her homeworld, and for just an instant allowed herself to remember it, to remember her family. Were her parents still alive? Her brother?

How long had she been here? 921 tried to remember, but the days here were all the same . . . work, a few morsels of unappetizing food, Exultation and prayers, then exhausted sleep. One day flowed into each other, and Ylesia had almost no seasons . . .

For a moment she wondered just how long she'd been here. Months? Years? How old *was* she? Did she have wrinkles? Gray hair?

921's scarred hands flew to her forehead, her cheeks. Bones beneath flesh, prominent bones. Much more prominent than they had ever been before.

But no wrinkles. She was not old. She might have been here months, but not years.

How old had she been when she'd heard of Ylesia and sold all her jewelry to buy passage on a pilgrim ship? Seventeen . . . she'd just finished the last of her undergraduate schooling and had been looking forward to going off-world to attend the university on Coruscant. She'd been going to study . . . archaeology. With an emphasis on ancient art. Yes, that was it. She'd even spent a couple of summers working on a dig, learning to preserve ancient treasures.

She'd wanted to become a museum curator.

As a child, history had always been her favorite subject. She loved learning about the Jedi Knights, and was fascinated by their adventures. She'd grown up in the aftermath of the Clone Wars, and had been interested in that, too. And the birth of the Republic, so very, very long ago . . .

921 sighed as she swallowed a bite of dusty grain-cake. Sometimes it bothered her when she realized that her memories were fading, that her intelligence seemed to be fading, along with her ability to perceive the world outside. She knew that as a pilgrim, she was supposed to eschew all

worldly things, to expunge from her mind and body the appreciation of fleshly pleasures.

In the old days, pleasure and having fun had been the focus of her life. In those days, her life had had little purpose, compared to now. In the old days, she'd drifted from place to place, subject to subject, party to party . . .

And it had all been so *meaningless*.

Life now had *meaning*. Now she was Exulted. Every night, the One conferred blessing upon her, through the priests. Exultation was the way the All communicated with the pilgrims. It was a deeply spiritual experience—and it felt so *good* . . .

921 thought that she'd successfully managed to expunge all memory of Vykk Draygo and his smile from her mind, so she went back to work on her glitterstim pile—only to find herself wondering, minutes later, whether he'd really look for her, try to talk to her again . . .

921 shivered in the ever-present dank chill and tried very hard to forget Vykk Draygo and all he stood for . . .

That night, Han skipped devotionals in favor of spending time with several of the sims. This was his first opportunity to earn an "honest" living, and he didn't want to mess up. Han knew that citizens complained about how hard they had to work, and he figured that was essential for success. It was true that begging, pickpocketing, burglary, and scamming citizens frequently required considerable time and effort, but Han knew that somehow it just wasn't comparable.

Heading for the sim station in his bedroom, Han began skimming through the system, accessing what was available to him. Teroenza had been as good as his promise, and the simulations were there. He scanned what was available, chose the sims he wanted to work on, and ordered the system to prepare several sequences. He was careful to specify "atmospheric turbulence" to be included in each training exercise.

He looked up at Muuurgh, who was standing there,

watching him. "I've got to work for a while," he said. "Why don't you take some time for yourself?"

Muuurgh shook his head slowly. "Muuurgh not leave Pilot alone. Against orders."

"Okay." Han shrugged. "Your choice."

Muuurgh watched nervously as Han put on the visihood, cutting himself off from contact with his real surroundings and plunging himself into a training flight that felt exactly like the real thing. The Togorian was uncomfortable with technology.

Han let himself sink into the sim, and within minutes the sim had accomplished one of its primary purposes—Han quite forgot that it *was* a sim. He was convinced that he was really piloting—really negotiating asteroid fields at high speeds, really piloting through the Ylesian atmosphere, really landing the craft under all sorts of adverse conditions.

The Corellian emerged from the sim two hours later, having successfully landed, flown, taken off, and performed the full range of maneuvers possible with the shuttle he'd be flying to Colony 2 and Colony 3 on the morrow. He'd also reviewed the controls on the transport vessels he'd be flying—the *Ylesian Dream* was being converted to manual piloting—as well as those on Teroenza's private yacht.

By this time, the short Ylesian day was far spent. Muuurgh was dozing on the chair, but awoke instantly when Han stretched. Han eyed the Togorian, regretting that the alien was so alert. It was going to be very difficult to do the nighttime prowling that he had in mind . . .

Muuurgh walked along behind Pilot, pleased that his charge had suggested heading over to the mess hall for a late supper. The Togorian was always hungry. His people were used to hunting and killing, then sharing their kill, so fresh meat was a constant part of their diets. Here, he had to make do with raw meat that had been frozen.

Before Pilot had come into his life, he'd been free at times to enter the jungle and hunt, so he could keep his claws—and his skills—sharpened.

He missed his mosgoth, missed flying through the air on her back, feeling her powerful wing muscles propelling them through the skies of Togoria.

Muuurgh sighed. The skies on Togoria were a vivid blue-green, much different from the washed-out blue-gray color of Ylesia's skies. He missed them. Would he ever see them again, would he ever fly his mosgoth toward a crimson sunset in those vivid skies?

The priests had made him sign a six-month contract for his services as a guard. He'd given his word of honor to fulfill that contract. It would be many ten-days before he could return to his search for Mrrov.

Muuurgh pictured her in his mind, her cream-colored fur, her orange stripes, her vivid yellow eyes. Lovely Mrrov. She'd been part of his life for so long now that not knowing her whereabouts was like an aching wound inside him. Could she have gone back to Togoria? Was she back on their world, waiting for him?

Muuurgh wished he could send a message to his homeworld, ask whether Mrrov had returned, but messages sent over interstellar distances were very expensive, and sending one would add nearly two months to his time here on Ylesia.

Still . . . Muuurgh considered, then thought that perhaps on one of their trips to fly spice to Nal Hutta, Pilot would not mind if Muuurgh sent a message. The Togorian didn't really trust the Ylesian priests enough to send a message from this world.

Pilot seemed like a decent fellow, for a human, Muuurgh mused. Sly, quick, always looking for a way to get around things, but humans were frequently like that. At least Pilot had accepted Muuurgh's dominance as pack leader. That was smart of him. He'd live much longer that way . . .

Muuurgh really hoped that Pilot would continue to be smart. He liked him, and didn't want to have to hurt him.

But if Pilot tried to break the rules, Muuurgh would not hesitate to hurt—even kill—the Corellian. Teroenza had given Muuurgh specific orders, and the Togorian would carry them out to the best of his ability. He'd given his word of honor, and that was the most important thing in the universe to his people.

The Togorian absently groomed his whiskers and facial fur, reflecting that as long as Pilot didn't step out of line, everything was going to be just fine . . .

Chapter Five:

SPICE WARS

The next day Han took the Ylesian shuttle to Colony Two and Colony Three. He discovered that he really enjoyed piloting bigger ships, and his piloting was perfect. He managed to find a few extra minutes on his return run to Colony One to practice low altitude flying, swooping the shuttle so low that the belly nearly brushed the tops of the jungle trees. Beside him in the copilot's seat, Muuurgh alternated between exhilaration and terror as the Togorian experienced swoops, barrel rolls, and even upside-down high-speed flying. Han was in his element, putting the shuttle through maneuvers he'd only done previously during sims. The Corellian found himself whooping joyously at the sheer thrill of it all.

For his last, best bit of precision flying, Han sent the shuttle hurtling down a river-cut canyon, skimming be-

tween the rock walls with so little room to spare that
Muuurgh yowled, shut his eyes, and refused to open them.
Once they were soaring through open skies again, Han had
to shake the Togorian's arm and repeatedly reassure the big
alien that he was finished practicing for the day.

"Muuurgh certain that Pilot is crazy," the Togorian said,
cautiously opening his eyes and straightening up in his seat.
"Muuurgh flies on his mosgoth at home, but not like *that*.
Mosgoths have more sense than to fly like *that*. Muuurgh
have more sense, too. Pilot"—the Togorian gave Han a
plaintive glance—"promise Muuurgh not to fly crazy
again."

"But, Muuurgh," Han said, carefully setting them down
on the landing field at Colony One, "I've got to practice
every chance I get! You see . . ." he hesitated, then decided to trust Muuurgh with part of the truth, "I sort of
stretched the facts a little when I told Teroenza about my
flying experience. I really am a champion pilot, that's the
truth, but . . . I *need* to practice with this shuttle. And
with the bigger ships. Sims are fine, but they can't beat the
real thing."

Muuurgh gave Han a long level look, then nodded.
"Muuurgh understands. Pilot trusts Muuurgh not to say this
to Teroenza?"

"Yeah, something like that," Han said. "Can I? Trust
you, I mean?"

The Togorian groomed his white whiskers thoughtfully.
"As long as Pilot does not crash, Muuurgh does not talk."

"Fair enough, pal," Han said with a grin.

When he and Muuurgh came down the ramp from the
ship, Veratil was there waiting for them in the pouring rain.
By this time Han was growing used to the daily downpours,
though the steamy heat still exhausted him. "The High
Priest wishes to see you at once, Pilot Draygo," Veratil said.

The Sacredot led the Corellian and his bodyguard to the
High Priest's personal quarters, which occupied a large part
of the underground level of the Administration Center.
When Veratil keyed in the security bypass codes and they
walked through the huge double doors into the High

Priest's personal sanctum, Han couldn't repress a low whistle of amazement. "Nice place!"

"This is the High Priest's display room," Veratil said. "He is an avid collector, and very proud of his collection of rarities."

"He deserves to be," Han said sincerely.

The room was easily ten times the size of Han's little apartment on the first floor. Display tables, shelves, and racks showcased treasures and antiquities from around the galaxy. Sculpture from a dozen worlds, paintings, and other art objects were scattered amid ornate antique weapons. Tapestries hung from the walls. Rugs of exquisite beauty were covered by protective force fields that felt squishy underfoot as Han walked on them.

Semiprecious gems adorned the collection of pipes and other musical instruments. Bottles of the rarest liquors in the entire galaxy were suspended in a gold-embossed rack.

Han's fingers literally *itched* for the whole time it took him to traverse the display room. *If I could have five minutes alone in here, I'd be set for life!* he thought wistfully as he slowed down to peer at a *drreelb* carved from living ice. The tiny statue was covered with a layer of dust, which was disturbed by Han's breath. It wafted up into the air, and the pilot sneezed thunderously.

Dust or no dust, this place is worth several fortunes. If only . . .

Sternly, Han reminded himself that he had turned over a new leaf, and was an honest, hardworking citizen these days.

Veratil led them through another security door into the High Priest's personal living quarters. The visitors were ushered into the room by an ancient Zisian majordomo, whom Teroenza addressed as "Ganar Tos." The Zisian was humanoid, but he had wrinkly green skin that hung in flaccid wattles from his receding chinline. His orange eyes were rheumy, and he snuffled constantly, as though he had a sinus infection. *Probably allergic to all that dust,* Han thought.

The High Priest waved Han and Muuurgh to seats and

addressed them. "So good of you to come, Pilot Draygo. I hear good things about your piloting from Colony Two and Three. Today our medical droid placed our other pilot, Jalus Nebl, on indefinite sick leave, so you will be taking his place on interstellar flights from now on."

Han nodded, trying not to betray his excitement. "Fine, sir. I'll keep on schedule. When do I go?"

"The day after tomorrow," Teroenza said. "Muuurgh will, of course, accompany you."

"What's the cargo and destination, sir?" Han asked.

"You will rendezvous with a ship from Nal Hutta at coordinates we will provide you with at the last minute. Security is vital, as I'm sure you can understand. You know that we have had trouble with pirates in the past." Teroenza accepted a small, limp creature from a tray the majordomo held out to him and paused to gulp it. "Have you trained Muuurgh as a gunner, Pilot?"

"Uh, no, not yet, sir."

"See that you do. A good pilot is prepared for all eventualities, correct?"

"Yessir," Han said. "I'll see to it. Uh, sir? What's the cargo?"

"You'll be carrying a load of processed carsunum, and picking up a load of raw ryll transshipped from Ryloth."

"But the ship I'm meeting is from Nal Hutta?"

"Yes." Teroenza did not expand upon this, so Han dropped the subject, resolving to keep his ears open. He sensed that there was more that the High Priest wasn't telling him, but he was hardly in a position to demand to know all the ins and outs.

Teroenza sat back on his massive haunches, small arms waving at the portal through which Muuurgh and Han had entered. "I gather you liked my display room?"

"Liked?" Han was able to speak with complete honesty. "It was *great*, sir! I never saw so many treasures gathered together outside of a museum!"

"My species is long-lived, as are our cousins, the Hutts," Teroenza said. "I have been collecting for hundreds of

Standard years—longer than you, in your youth, can imagine, Pilot."

"I'd really like to get a grand tour sometime," Han said.

"I wish my collection were in condition to be viewed," Teroenza said regretfully. "Ganar Tos, though an excellent cook and an efficient houseboy, hasn't the training to maintain it, much less catalog and arrange everything properly. And I am too busy to indulge myself that way." The giant being gave them a dismissive wave of a tiny hand. "That will be all for now. I shall see you upon your return, Pilot."

"Yessir." Han stood and beckoned to Muuurgh. They left, escorted by Veratil.

Once outside, the Sacredot went off on an errand, leaving them to themselves. Han glanced at his chrono and then at the westering sun. "Tonight I'm going to start training you on gunner's duties," he told the Togorian, "but right now, I think we're owed a break. Matter of fact, we're just in time to visit the refectory where the pilgrims eat. Let's go."

"Why?" Muuurgh asked. "Pilot not want pilgrim food. Pilot and Muuurgh eat in mess hall . . . get decent food, not garbage."

Han shook his head and started walking down the path that led through the jungle to the pilgrims area. "I don't wanna *eat* with the pilgrims, pal," he explained. "I just want to *talk* to some of them. I figure at dinner, they'll all be together, and I can find . . . them . . . easier."

"Them?" Muuurgh echoed. "How many is 'them'?"

"Uh . . . well, you see . . ." Han started, then he stopped, grimacing. "Just one," he admitted. "Pilgrim 921, the one I saw the other day. I'd like to see what she *really* looks like."

Muuurgh nodded. "Ah, yessss . . . Muuurgh understand very well what Pilot wants."

Han felt his face grow hot, and was glad that the Togorian wouldn't recognize that giveaway as a sign of embarrassment.

"Y'know, Muuurgh, old pal," he said, deliberately changing the subject, "you speak pretty good Basic for someone who's been speaking it for less than a year. But there's one part of speech you ain't mastered yet, and that's the pronoun. Never thought I'd find myself playing schoolteacher, but, here goes . . ."

The two walked on down the path together, as Han laboriously covered the grammatical rules governing the use of pronouns . . .

Once in the refectory, Han and Muuurgh roamed the huge dining area. Han glanced from face to face, wondering if he'd manage to recognize her without the goggles, in normal light. Her hair had been covered by the cap, so he didn't even know if it was dark or light.

He walked faster, realizing the meal was nearly over, and he still hadn't found 921. Maybe she wasn't here. Maybe she ate during another shift, the way he heard some of the pilgrims did. But he'd thought most of the humanoids ate during *this* shift—

There she is. That's her! Han wasn't even sure how he knew . . . but he was as positive as if she'd had a sign around her neck that read PILGRIM 921.

Seen in normal light, he could tell that she was tall, and slender—too slender, really. Her cheekbones stood out prominently, and her eyes seemed even larger than they were in her thin, excessively pale, face.

But too thin or not, she was, quite simply, lovely. Not classically beautiful. Her jaw was a little too wide and squarish, her nose a bit too long, for classic beauty. But lovely . . . oh, yes . . .

921 had big blue-green eyes, long, dark lashes, and poreless white skin. Several locks of short, curly hair had escaped from beneath her pilgrim's cap, and Han saw that it was reddish-gold—the color of a Corellian sunset on a clear day.

The refectory hall was usually pretty quiet. The pilgrims didn't talk much, tired as they were from a long day's work in the factories, and the approaching Exultation. But they usually ate in groups.

921 was all alone.

Han saw that she was poking at her dinner, and after one look at the unappetizing mess of gruellike porridge, limp greens, and flatbread on her plate, he didn't blame her. The food smelled bad—almost spoiled. Han's nose wrinkled as he pulled out the seat opposite her and sat down. He was dimly aware of Muuurgh, leaning against the wall, watching him.

921—*I've GOT to get her to tell me her real name!*— looked up, and her turquoise eyes widened as she recognized him. Han was inordinately pleased about that and grinned at her. "Hello. Found you again, see?"

She stared at him, eyes wide, then she looked down at her plate. Han leaned toward her. "So, what's for dinner? Doesn't look great, I gotta admit. But you've got to do more than just push it around your plate, you know."

She shook her head. "Please . . . go away." Her voice was barely above a whisper. "I'm not supposed to be talking to you. You're not of the One."

"Sure I am," Han said. "I'm just a little bit more of an individual One, I guess you'd say."

921's mouth quirked, very slightly. Han found himself wishing he could make her *really* smile. "You don't know what you're talking about, Pilot Draygo," she said softly. "I'm afraid that's obvious."

"Well, proselytize to me, then," Han said. "I've got an open mind. Maybe you can convert me." He smiled, happy that he'd found her, and that she was, at least, talking to him.

921 shook her head. "I'm afraid you're much too much of an unbeliever, Pilot," she said.

Han reached out across the table and took her hand, the one she'd injured. "It's 'Vykk,'" he told her, having to fight a crazy impulse to tell her his *real* name. But he managed to resist. "So, how is your hand? Any ill effects from the other day?"

When he'd first touched her, she'd stiffened, as though to pull away, then when he inquired about the cut, she relaxed. "It's healing," she told him, confirming what his eyes told him. "It will just take a little time."

"It's a tough job, working down there in the dark and the cold all day long," Han said. "Wouldn't you rather do something a little . . . easier?"

"Like what?" she asked.

"I don't know," he said. "What are you good at? What have you studied?"

"Well . . . at one time I wanted to be a curator in a museum," she said, sounding faintly wistful. "I was going to study archaeology. I know quite a bit about that."

"But you came here instead of going on with your studies," Han guessed.

"Yes," 921 answered. "This life is spiritually fulfilling. My old life was empty and meaningless."

Han hesitated. "How do you *know* that the doctrine they teach here is the right one? There are a lot of religions in the galaxy."

She considered his question carefully, then, finally, replied, "Because when we are Exulted, I feel very close to the One. It's a mystical moment. I feel One with the All. I'm sure the priests must be Divinely Gifted to be able to offer the pilgrims the chance to be Exulted."

"Hmmmm," Han said. "Sounds like maybe I should give it a try." *Over my dead body,* he thought, but was careful to conceal his true feelings.

"Perhaps you should," she said. "It's time to head for the Altar of Promises, now. Perhaps you'll be blessed by receiving the Exultation, too."

"You never know," Han said. "Can I walk you there?"

She smiled a little, eyes downcast. "All right."

They walked together up the jungle path, side by side amid the pilgrims, with Muuurgh trailing behind. Han tried to make conversation, but 921 was silent and unresponsive. When they reached the Altar, Han did not withdraw to the back, but instead stood beside 921 in the midst of the group of believers.

"You shouldn't be here," she whispered. "It's obvious you're not a pilgrim."

"If anyone complains, just tell them I'm a pilgrim candidate," Han said, trying to gently tease her, but 921 wasn't having it. She scowled and turned away from him, concentrating on the ceremony.

Teroenza and the other priests treated the crowd of faithful to a devotion that was identical to the one Han had attended before. This time, Han had little trouble resisting the effects of the Exultation—he remained clearheaded throughout. Instead, he watched 921, saw her rapt face, and inwardly shook his head. *How can she be taken in by this ridiculous bilge?* he wondered. *She's obviously intelligent. Why can't she see that however these priests do what they do, it's some kind of trick, not a Divine Gift?*

Han watched in distress as 921 sank to the ground to receive the Exultation, then he crouched beside her as she writhed on the ground. *It's a miracle their hearts don't just stop,* he thought. Later, when the moment of Exultation was over, and the priests were gone, he helped her to sit up. She was smiling, though very weak.

"You okay?" he asked, concerned. The Exultation, whatever its other physical and emotional effects, seemed to leave the pilgrims drained. "You don't look so good."

"I'm fine," she said, still trembling, and tried to get up. Han was quick to catch her and offer a steadying hand.

"Thank you," she whispered, her breath still ragged. "I'll be fine, now."

"I'll walk you back to the dorm," he said. "Just in case. You look kinda shaky."

She didn't argue as he took her arm, and they started back along the path. It was growing quite dark by now, and Ylesia had no moon. Han could barely make out the path ahead, but 921 produced her goggles from the pocket of her robe and put them on. She led the way, but he kept hold of her arm to steady her.

"So, do you ever miss Corellia?" he asked.

"No," she said, but he could tell it was a lie. "Do you?"

"I don't miss the people, but I miss the planet," Han said honestly. "Corellia's a nice place. I always wanted to go to the ocean, but I never got the chance. Ever been to the ocean?"

"Yes . . ." she said slowly, as if his question brought back memories she'd rather not think about.

"You got a family there?"

"Yes . . ." she hesitated, then added, "at least, I think so. I haven't talked with them in almost a year."

"Is that how long you've been here?" Han asked.

"Yes."

They picked their way through the hot, wet darkness in silence. Han was very conscious of holding her arm beneath the wide sleeve of her robe. Her bones were too close to the skin, but her flesh itself was warm and soft and very female.

"So, you planning to stay here for good?" Han asked as a small clot of shambling pilgrims passed them in the darkness. "Or is this just kind of temporary?"

"Temporary?" He could barely see the light blur of her face, with the dark line of the goggles running across it, as she turned toward him. "How could it be temporary? I want to serve the One, be part of the All, forever."

"Oh," Han said. "Well, uh . . . what about stuff like . . . falling in love, traveling, maybe settling down someday and having kids?"

"We give up those kinds of attachments when we become part of the All," she said, but there was a hint of regret in her voice.

"Too bad," he said.

Without warning, it began to rain steadily. Han could feel 921 shiver slightly, despite the warmth. He pulled a rain poncho out of his pocket and spread it over both their heads. They walked along, huddled beneath it, bodies touching. Han was conscious of Muuurgh following at a discreet distance. *Poor guy. He hates to get wet . . .*

The pilot raised his voice to be heard above the spatter of the rain. "You know, I can't just go on calling you 921. If we're gonna be friends, you've gotta tell me your name."

"Who says we're going to be friends?" she asked.

"I just know it," Han told her. He grinned, knowing she

could see him in the darkness. "I'm *irresistible* when I put my mind to it."

"You're conceited, that's what you are," she said, sounding half-vexed, half-amused. "Conceited, cocky, arrogant . . . insufferable . . ." she broke off, chuckling. Han realized it was the first time he'd heard her laugh.

"Oh, go on, please!" the pilot mock-protested, laughing himself. "I love it when women compliment me. Music to my ears." He was delighted to hear her sounding so *alive.*

"I'm tired," she said, her momentary good humor vanishing like morning mist. "And here we are at the dorm. Thanks for walking me back . . . Pilot Draygo."

There was a faint circle of light emanating from the windows in the dormitory, and Han stopped them right on the edge of it, so he could see her, but they wouldn't be fully illuminated to any onlooker.

"Not 'Pilot,' " he reminded her. "It's Vykk."

She tried to step back, away from him, but Han tightened his grip on her arm, careful to be gentle, but not letting her pull away. "Vykk, okay?"

"Vykk . . . right," she said. "Now, please . . . let me go. And . . . don't come back. Please."

"Why not?" Han was hurt.

"Because . . . you're not good for me. For my spiritual essence."

He smiled in the hot darkness. "Admit it. You like me."

"No, I don't."

"Yes, you do. Admit it." He stepped closer to her, looking down into her face. She was tall, only half a head shorter than he was. Gently Han reached up to push the concealing goggles up, off her eyes. His fingers lingered on her cheek as he did it. "There," he said softly, "that's better. It's wrong . . . totally wrong . . . to cover this face, these eyes . . ."

"You're . . . you're being blasphemous," she said, sounding breathless, but she didn't jerk away.

"No, I'm not," he said. "Tell me your name."

She shook her head miserably, and her eyes were haunted. "Vykk . . . I can't . . ."

"All right." *I can wait*, Han thought. "But I will see you again, right?"

She hesitated for so long that he found himself holding his breath. Then she ducked her head, mumbled, "Yes," and pulled away. This time, Han let her go.

921 ran away, into the dormitory, without looking back.

Han leaned forward in the pilot's seat, glancing at the figures rolling by on the screen of the navicomputer. "Ready to enter realspace, at rendezvous coordinates," he said aloud. "Three . . . two . . . one . . ."

He pulled back the lever, and the stars around the *Ylesian Dream* suddenly elongated into thin streaks of light all reaching toward a central point—a point toward which the ship plunged. The engines roared, then throttled down, and then—with a suddenness that took some getting used to—they were back in realspace.

"Right on course, Muuurgh," Han said triumphantly. "I'm getting this interstellar flying stuff down pat lately, ain't I?"

"Aren't," the Togorian corrected. "I have been reading book Pilot gave Muur—" he stopped himself, "uh, *me*, and 'ain't' is not correct way to talk Basic."

"Remind me to teach you about articles sometime," Han muttered. "Don't I even get a gold star for bringing us to the rendezvous right on the money?"

"Much better than first time," Muuurgh commented, referring to their first interstellar trip, three weeks ago. Han had made a tiny error in programming the navicomputer on exactly *where* to bring them out of hyperspace, and the *Dream* had wound up three parsecs from where they were supposed to emerge.

Han had had to make an extra hyperspace jump to bring them into correct position.

"Hey," Han protested, "that was just my first time! And it wasn't my fault that screen is so old that an eight looked like a six."

"Pilot has done better since then," Muuurgh acknowledged. "Second and third trips went okay."

"You bet they did," Han muttered. "I'm *good,* Muuurgh . . . I really am. I'll bet that I could almost pass the exams to get into the Imperial Academy now. A few more months practice, and I'll really be set."

"Muuurgh will miss . . ." the Togorian paused. "Correction. *I* will miss Pilot when he goes."

"I'll miss you, too, pal," Han said, meaning it. "But don't worry, we can—"

The *Ylesian Dream* shuddered violently as a loud *whang!* reverberated through her hull. "What the—" Han pushed buttons, turning on the rear viewscreen. "Muuurgh, something hit us!"

"Asteroid?" the Togorian suggested.

Whangggg!

"No!" Han yelled, staring incredulously at the viewscreen. "Two ships! They've gotta be pirates! Get to the gunner's well!"

As he stared at the screen, the rightmost vessel launched another shot. "Brace yourself!"

Muuurgh, who had unstrapped himself and gotten up to head for the gunner's mount, yowled as another shot *whanged* against the hull, sending him back into his seat with bruising force.

Cursing, Han yanked the *Dream* hard to port. Who were these guys? Pirates usually fired warning shots and demanded that the attacked vessel surrender. Their goal was to steal the cargo, commandeer the ship, and keep the crew alive so they could be sold as slaves. Destroying or crippling the ship and killing the crew wasn't cost-effective.

"Muuurgh! Get below! They're gonna blast us into atoms! We've lost a shield!"

As the Togorian propelled himself out of the copilot's seat and lurched out of the control room, two more shots grazed the *Ylesian Dream. They're aiming at the hyperdrive engines! They're out to cripple us!*

Han sent the ship into a desperate roll, flipping her up on her side, just in time to avoid another blast that nearly singed his underside and would have blown out his Quadex power core.

He put on a burst of speed, trying to get far enough ahead of the pursuing pirates to double back and shoot at them. He had little confidence in Muuurgh's ability to actually hit anything while manning the gun well. The Togorian was quick and able, but he'd never actually *shot* at a live— much less moving—target.

As he sent the ship hurtling recklessly along, straining her speed to the utmost, Han flipped open his communications channel. He had to let someone know what was happening, in case the *Dream* was crippled and they got a chance to get to a lifepod.

"Ylesia Colony One, this is *Ylesian Dream*. Colony One, this is the *Dream*. We are under attack, repeat, under attack. Two vessels jumped us just after we emerged from hyperspace!" Han's voice cracked from the strain. "Honest, it wasn't my fault! They're chasing us, and I'm taking evasive maneuvers—Pilot Draygo out!"

Han glanced at the viewscreen with the sensor readouts below, saw that they'd gained on their pursuers—he still hadn't gotten a good look at the pirate ships—and then sent the *Dream* spiraling down, beneath the oncoming ships. As they whooshed by overhead, he flipped his vessel up into a tight turn. "Muuurgh! *Now!*" he yelled into the intercom.

A Togorian roar and a splat of energy rewarded his command—but Muuurgh missed his quarry completely. One of the pirates had turned, and was firing again—

Wham!!

The *Ylesian Dream* shook violently as the ship sustained a major hit. Han's stomach lurched as he heard a yowl of sheer agony float up from the gun well. "Muuurgh? Muuurgh? Are you hit?" he yelled, but there was no answer.

A quick status check told him that they'd suffered a tiny drop in pressure, but that the leak had been automatically sealed by the ship's systems.

"All right, you creeps . . ." Han muttered, homing in

with his Arakyd concussion missiles, centering the rightmost pirate in the cross-sights . . . "take *that!*"

The *Dream* lurched violently as the missile shot away. Han grimaced as the pirate managed to evade at the last second. He tried again . . . if he could just get him moving more to his portside . . .

"Yes!" Han muttered savagely as he launched another missile right into the path of the pirate, anticipating his evasive maneuver. "Gotcha!"

A second later a bright yellow-white light splashed out in all directions, expanding into a fireball of incandescent beauty. Han had to look away, and when he looked back, the other pirate was hightailing it in the opposite direction at full throttle.

"No you don't," Han growled. "I'll get you, too—" With a fierce stab of his finger, he tracked and launched again.

The concussion missile followed its target, but then the pirate ship vanished in a burst of striated light. They had jumped to hyperspace and safety. Han cursed under his breath as he put the *Dream* on autopilot and bolted for the gun well. Was Muuurgh okay?

Seconds later Han was standing in the ruins of the gun mount, seeing the pressure sealant that the *Dream*'s systems had automatically triggered to squirt out and mend the pressure leak. There was a strong ozone smell and scorch marks where the blast had hit them.

Muuurgh was still strapped in the movable seat, but the Togorian was slumped, unconscious, and he didn't stir as Han unstrapped him and managed to half carry, half drag him up the ladder to the control room.

The Togorian was breathing, but there was a burn mark along one side of his head, just below his right ear. Han looked further, running his fingers through the black fur, and discovered a swelling lump just back of the ear. The Togorian had obviously taken a nasty blow to the head. Han wasn't sure what to do—he knew first aid for humans, and a few species of aliens, but Muuurgh's people were rare in the galaxy.

Got to get him to a medical facility, he thought, covering the unconscious alien with a blanket and going forward to check his navicomputer. *Where's the nearest system?*

Han scanned star charts, then his finger stabbed down. "Okay," he whispered. "Here we go." He glanced over at the Togorian. "Hang on, Muuurgh!"

Han programmed the ship for the short hyperspace hop, then, before giving the command, went to check the engines. The nose-wrinkling smell of a burned connection made him grimace. *Wonder whether I should use the backup hyperdrive unit instead?*

But the backup was much slower, and he had no way of knowing how serious Muuurgh's condition was. Han decided to chance using the main hyperdrive engine. He held his breath as he initiated the jump to hyperspace. From the way the ship hesitated, and the laboring sound of the engine, he started to sweat.

The *Dream* strained, shuddered, but the stars suddenly blazed at him in streaks, and they *jumped.*

Han came out of hyperspace a short time later, thanking his lucky stars that the *Ylesian Dream* had held together for that hop. The ship's lightspeed engines definitely needed repairs . . .

The Corellian headed into the star system he'd chosen, toward the sole inhabited world. While he was still fairly far out, he placed the *Dream* on autopilot and went back to check the box of glitterstim. The world he'd chosen was known to have customs and spice checks, so he opened up the secret compartment the priests had had built into the cargo deck and removed the boxes of Doreenian ambergris perfume that he carried as a "cover" cargo. Grunting with effort, Han lugged the heavy containers of perfume into the cargo bay and put them down. Then he placed the much smaller container of glitterstim vials in the concealed compartment, making sure it sealed shut. Unless someone knew it was there, he'd never spot it, and the hatch was designed to be scanner-proof.

By the time Han returned to his pilot's seat, the world he'd chosen was growing in his viewscreens. As he approached, he saw it was a lovely world, hanging blue and white and tan against the night-blackness of space.

As he swooped toward it, Han suddenly remembered that he'd shut down his communications system after sending off the message to Ylesia. *Better turn it back on,* he thought, *check in with the spaceport authority and get clearance to land.* He glanced back at Muuurgh, who hadn't stirred or made a sound. *And arrange for transport to the nearest hospital* . . .

As his fingers clicked on the comm unit, the vid-screen filled with an image of a kindly looking man with a little, dark haired girl sitting on his lap. Han was startled, then realized that this message was prerecorded, and played to every ship on an approach vector.

A voice-over identified the man: "His Majesty, Bail Prestor Organa, Viceroy and First Chairman."

The man smiled into the screen. "Greetings. On behalf of myself and my people, I bid you welcome to Alderaan."

Chapter Six

ALDERAAN AND BACK AGAIN

Han listened with half his attention as the man—King somebody or other, did they say?—continued with the vid-message. "As many of our visitors are already aware, Alderaan is a peaceful world, a world where we have eschewed weapons and their use. While you are our guest, we ask that you respect our traditions and our laws, by leaving your weapons with the Port Authority during your stay here.

"You will find that Alderaan has much to offer a visitor. We have almost no crime . . ."

Right, Han thought. *I'll just bet . . .*

"And no pollution. Our lakes are clear, our air is pure, and our people are happy. We have wonderful museums, and we invite you to visit them. Be sure not to miss our grass paintings as you fly over them on your landing ap-

proach. Our grass painters are among the greatest artists in
the galaxy. We welcome visitors to our beautiful world, and
we ask only that you come in peace, and that you obey
our—"

With a muttered curse, Han leaned over and snapped
the audio portion of the broadcast off. He made a rude
gesture at the screen. *A whole planet full of honest citizens?
I'll believe it when I see it* . . .

Minutes later, Bail Organa's canned message was replaced by a live traffic controller from the Port Authority.
Han snapped the audio back on. "Captain Draygo, piloting
the *Ylesian Dream*," he said crisply. "Request permission to
land. I was attacked by pirates, my ship is damaged, and
I've got an injured gunner. Can you arrange for med-lift to
meet my ship as soon as I land?"

"Certainly, Captain Draygo. I've assigned you a priority
approach vector. We're slotting you in at Docking Bay 422.
Just follow the landing beacon to your site. We'll have a
transport and med droid standing by."

"Thanks."

Han's approach vector did indeed take him over the
grass paintings, and distracted as he was, he couldn't help
but be impressed. The huge plain of windblown, flowing
grass boasted a kilometers-wide abstract design picked out
in multicolored wildflowers. *Neat trick,* he thought. *Wonder
how they do it? And why they bother? It's not like you
could sell art like that and make money off it* . . .

The capital city of Alderaan, Aldera, was located on an
island in the middle of a lake. The site of the lake was
actually a meteor crater that had filled with water from underground springs. The remains of the huge, relatively "recent" (in geological terms, at least) crater surrounded the
lake in a series of low, jagged foothills whose sides were
splashed with green fields and forests. The water filling the
millennia-old crater sparkled brilliant ice-blue in the early
morning rays of the sun.

The spaceport was on the far side of the island, and Han
swooped low over the city on his assigned approach vector.
In just minutes he was bringing the *Ylesian Dream* down

for a perfect landing. He'd now had so much experience landing despite massive storms and vicious air currents that landing a ship on a normal planet seemed like child's play.

The medical unit was waiting, as promised. Han quickly unbuckled Muuurgh's blaster and stowed it away, then he brought the med droid with the anti-grav stretcher on board, and helped load Muuurgh onto it. "Do you think he'll be okay?" he asked the attending droid.

"My preliminary scan indicates that there is no life-threatening trauma as a result of the head injury," the droid replied. "However, we will need to run further tests. I would anticipate that your crew member will require an overnight stay in our facility."

"Okay," Han said. *I've got to figure out some way to pay for Muuurgh's treatment,* he thought as he watched the stretcher bearing the Togorian vanish inside the transport, which promptly lifted off and headed south.

Seeing a technician going by, Han waved the woman over. "Listen, I've sustained some damage," he said. "Can I get a repair crew in here right away?"

"Let me see how bad it is," she said. Han guided her into the gunner's mount, then into the engine room to check out the hyperdrive. "Both jobs will require at least six hours work to fix," she told him. "But we can start on it today."

"Good," Han said. He had done minor swoop and speeder repairs while he was a racer, but he'd never tackled anything as big as this, and he wanted to make sure the job was done right.

As the repair crew came aboard the *Dream,* Han wondered what he should do next. Call Ylesia, he decided. The priests were going to have to arrange for payment for the repairs and Muuurgh's treatment.

Han headed for the control cabin, intending to place the call immediately. His hand was actually on the switch when he suddenly froze.

Waaaaiiittt a minute . . . he thought. *What am I doing? I'm sitting here with a load of glitterstim, the most valuable spice of all, and I'm just going to take it back to Ylesia so they can sell it again?*

Han checked back in his automatic log recordings, listened to what he'd said during his transmission. He grinned to himself. *This is a piece of cake. All I have to do is tell the priests that I was boarded and the pirates took the glitterstim. Muuurgh was out cold, he doesn't know what happened. I can sell this spice here on Alderaan, stash the money in an account here, then send for it later. They'll never know . . .*

But if he wanted to keep his job as a pilot for the Ylesian priests, he'd have to make the deal *fast.* He'd reported himself at the rendezvous coordinates, and the priests weren't stupid. They could check on how long it would take a ship to get from where he'd been attacked to Alderaan. He could account for a few extra hours by pointing to the damage the *Dream* had sustained and pleading the slowness of the journey, the need to nurse the ship along . . .

Okay, Han thought. *I've got about five hours I can fudge here . . . no more. By that time I've got to call in and let them know I'm alive, that their ship is damaged, and that they have to arrange for payment. Any more time than that, and they'll get suspicious . . .*

Pulling his battered brown lizard-hide jacket out of his locker, Han straightened his worn pilot's coverall as best he could. Then he combed his hair. *Don't want to look scruffy,* he thought wryly, thinking of Dewlanna and how the Wookiee had always told him he looked good with his hair standing straight up, like one of her people.

Pulling on the jacket over the gray uniform, he stared regretfully at Muuurgh's blaster, wishing he could strap it on. *Stupid planet. Whoever heard of a world with no weapons allowed?* With a sigh and a shake of his head, Han left the *Ylesian Dream* to the repair crews.

He walked quickly to the entrance to the spaceport, then caught one of the free shuttles that led into the capital city of Aldera. The metropolis glittered white in the sunshine, as clean and luxurious as a city in a dream. Han stared out the windows of the shuttle, taking in the ultra-modern towers, domes, and layered buildings, their white shapes interspersed with green terraces. The island was hilly, and the city architects had followed the natural lines of the place rather than leveling it. The result was pleasant and varied to the eyes . . . beautiful and modern, without seeming harsh or artificial.

The automated shuttle's canned program indicated points of interest as they passed. Han saw museums, gigantic enclosed gallerias, office and government buildings, and finally, as they approached the heart of the city, he saw the tall, sharp spires and shallow domes of the royal palace gleaming white and gold in the sun. Han smiled wryly, wondering if the child princess he'd seen was somewhere on those grounds, living her rich, perfect life. *With any luck, I'll soon be rich, too . . .*

Han stayed aboard the transport as it glided along its route, and he continued scoping out the city. They were out of the big buildings, now, and heading through the residential suburbs.

Han had to admit that it looked like a nice place to live, as he gazed at the many fountained plazas and courtyards, the affluent homes, clean streets, and the well-dressed people they passed. *But this isn't the area I want . . . I'd better do some exploring on my own. They don't want tourists to see the places I want to go . . .*

After the shuttle let him off, Han walked around the central part of the city, checking out the lay of the land. Instinctively, he headed for an area where the houses were smaller and not as well maintained. Finally, in a neighborhood that was definitely lower-income, and boasted more than one tavern and hock shop, he realized he'd come to the right place.

Han scanned the streets as he walked, looking for a particular type of individual. Finally, he spotted what he was looking for. A boy dressed in clothes that were borderline too small, ragged, and not very clean was sauntering along the street, glancing oh-so-casually at each passerby. Han recognized the child, though he'd never seen him before.

A pickpocket. Ten years ago, *he'd* been that child.

Han increased the length of his strides until he caught up with the boy. As expected, the lad shifted his weight and altered stride to brush against Han as the Corellian walked past him. Also expected were the lightning-fast fingers that delved deep into the pilot's jacket pocket. The fingers came away empty; Han's ID and the few credits he was carrying were sealed into the inside pocket of his coverall.

Han lengthened his strides until he was ahead of the boy, then, without warning, he spun on his heel and confronted the child. "Hey, there," he said, smiling pleasantly and holding up the boy's identdisk and money. "Lose something?"

The boy's mouth dropped open in amazement, then he recovered himself and glared at Han, his black eyes smoldering.

Han leaned casually against a storefront. "Careless of you to lose these things . . ."

The boy swelled up like a poisoned mrelfa lizard, then launched into a furious and detailed description of Han's ancestry, personal habits, and probable destination. Han listened patiently until the urchin began to sputter and repeat himself, then he waved for silence. "I'll give 'em back," he said genially, "in exchange for some information."

The boy glared sullenly, tossing his overlong hair back out of his eyes. "What kind of information, you son of a diseased pervert?"

Han tossed one of the credit coins into the air, caught it effortlessly, without looking. "Watch your mouth, junior. I just want to know where in this town people go to make deals."

"What kind of deals?"

"You know what kind of deals. Deals they don't want the law to know about. Deals for substances you can't buy legally."

"Spice?" the boy frowned. "What kind?"

"Glitterstim."

The boy's brow creased even farther. "What's that?"

Just my luck, Han thought. *I run into the only dumb pickpocket in Aldera. Great.*

"Glitterstim," Han said. "It's . . . well, it's really valuable. Even more so than carsunum or andris."

The boy shook his head again. "Never heard of them, either."

I don't believe this! "What about andris? You got andris here? Used to flavor food, preserve it?"

The kid nodded. "Yeah. Andris. We got that. Expensive stuff."

"Right," Han said. "When you buy andris, who do you buy it from?"

"I don't buy it, creep," the boy said. "Now gimmee back my money and ID."

"Just a second, be patient," Han said, holding the items up, safely out of the boy's reach. "So, okay, you don't buy andris personally. But if you or your friends wanted some, how would they get it? Buy it in a store? Or a government agency?"

The boy's expression was eloquent as he shook his head. "No, man. We'd buy it from Darak Lyll."

At last! A name! "That's what I wanted. Darak Lyll. What's he look like?"

"Taller than you. Long hair, beard. Fat around his middle."

"Old or young?"

"Old. Gray hair."

"Where's he hang out?" Han asked.

"Do I look like his keeper?" the pickpocket demanded scornfully.

Han took a deep breath. "Just tell me the names of any places where he might go on a typical day. Don't lie, or I'll swear out a complaint that you tried to rob me."

The boy named six taverns, telling Han that they were all within a five-minute walk. Han straightened up and flipped the boy his ID and money. "Next time keep it *inside* your clothes, junior," he said. "Next to your skin." He patted his own money and gave the lad a smug smile.

The lad snarled at Han and walked away, cursing.

Alderaanian taverns were much too clean and well lit, Han decided, an hour later. He'd been to three of the six so far, and none of them appeared seamy enough for his purposes. No sign of Darak Lyll, either.

At one place he'd glimpsed a man in the back slide something to another under cover of his arm, and then receive a credit disk slipped to him just as clandestinely. Han had waited until the first man had gotten up to use the refresher unit, then he'd followed him. When the man came out, Han was waiting for him in the dim hallway.

"Like a word with you, pal," he said.

The dealer, a small, sharp-faced man who reminded Han of a ranat, eyed the Corellian suspiciously, then evidently decided Han offered no threat. "Yeah? What about?"

"You deal in spice?"

The man hesitated for a long moment. "How much you want?"

"No, pal, I'm selling, not buying. You interested?"

"What you got?"

"Glitterstim. A hundred vials."

"Glitterstim!" The man's voice scaled up, then he hastily lowered it and stepped closer. "Where'd you get *that*, son?"

"I'm not your son, and it's none of your business where I got it. You interested?"

"On any other world than this one, better believe I'd be interested, but . . ." The man shook his head. "No. No channels to unload it. I'd have to try and smuggle it off-world, and that's too risky. They'd send me to the mines on Kessel to dig out the infernal stuff. Glitterstim can be dangerous, y'know. Make you blind, if you take too much. Drives Biths mad, y'know."

"I know all that," Han said impatiently. "Thanks for nothing, pal."

Scowling, he stalked out of the tavern.

He finally ran down Darak Lyll in the fifth tavern he visited. Han recognized the man from the pickpocket's description. Lyll was playing sabacc, and when he saw Han standing there, watching the game, he cordially waved the young Corellian over. "Care to sit in for a hand?"

Han had played sabacc before, but that wasn't what he'd come here for. He stared directly at Darak Lyll and raised his eyebrows. "All depends on what you'll accept for a stake, Lyll."

The man's expression didn't change a whit as he glanced casually up. "You got something good, Pilot?"

"Might."

"Well, the ante is twenty credits."

Han shook his head. "Changed my mind. Going out to get some fresh air."

He stood outside, leaning against the alley wall, for about five minutes. When he heard someone approaching, Han said, without looking, "Took you long enough. Must've been winning."

"Idiot's array," Lyll said, using the sabacc player's term for a top-notch winning hand. "So, what've you got?"

Han turned to look at the man. "Glitterstim. One hundred vials."

"Whooo!" Darak Lyll whistled in amazement. "Where'd you come by *that*?"

"None of your business," Han said. "Want it? Give you a good price . . ."

"Wish I could, young fellow, wish I could," Lyll said, sounding regretful. "But I'd be a fool to take it. Just no market here on Alderaan."

Han cursed under his breath and turned away. *What am I going to do?* he wondered. His time was definitely running out. Maybe he should hop an intercontinental shuttle to some other city. Maybe it was only Aldera that was so preternaturally clean on this world . . .

Han sighed. *I don't have time. I either sell that stuff in an hour, or I—*

A hand fell on his shoulder. It took every bit of self-control Han possessed not to yell and bolt, he was so keyed up. Instead he just turned and glared at the middle-aged, dark-skinned man who'd fallen into step with him. "I think you've mistaken me for someone else," he said evenly.

"I don't think so, Vykk," the man said. "Pilot Vykk Draygo, out of Ylesia, right?"

"So what?" Han said. "I don't know you."

"Marsden Latham," the man said, flashing a holo-ID

badge under Han's nose. "Alderaanian internal security force."

Oh, no . . .

"We've been keeping an eye on you, Pilot Draygo, ever since you limped in here this morning. We're happy we can help you out with repairs and fix up your partner. You saw that message when you first came within frequency range of Alderaan?"

"I saw it."

"Well, it's meant to be taken seriously. We don't like trouble here." The man smiled suddenly, showing very even, very white teeth. "You wouldn't be out to cause us any trouble, would you, Pilot?"

Han strove to keep his face impassive. *They know that I've been trying to cut a deal . . . must've been watching me all morning . . .* Silently, he cursed the official. Aloud, he said, "Course not, sir. I'm a peace-loving kinda guy."

"I told my chief that, and I'm glad to have my impression confirmed. Nice talking to you, Pilot Draygo. Enjoy your stay on Alderaan."

The man's strides came faster and longer, then, and he walked away from Han, up the street.

The Corellian forced himself to keep walking slowly, forced himself not to glance behind him. They were there, no doubt, shadowing him. The game was over, and he was busted. Scowling, Han shook his head, half in disgust, half in admiration. Those security operatives must be good. He'd had no idea they'd been tailing him.

Obviously, the man's "talk" had been a not-so-veiled warning to stop trying to sell his cargo. He'd have to take it back to Ylesia. There weren't any other planets close enough to reach so he could make the sale.

He checked the time, discovered he just had time to get out to check on Muuurgh before he'd have to call back to Ylesia. Han's strides came faster as he headed for the nearest public transport station.

The University medical facility where the Togorian had been taken was attached to the University of Alderaan campus. Han swung down from the repulsorlift public transport and stood looking around for a moment. *Nice . . .* he thought, *real nice . . .* For a moment he wondered if the Academy would look anything like this. *Probably not,* he concluded. *It's a military establishment. It'll look more like a base, I'll bet . . . but this . . . this is real classy . . .*

Green and blue lawns stretched across the central quadrangle. Flower beds made bright splashes of color and surrounded the huge central fountain. At the center of the fountain was a massive sculpture carved from living ice of a young Alderaanian man and woman standing with linked hands, reaching for the skies. *Hey, that's got to be worth a barrel of credits,* Han thought, eyeing the sculpture and realizing it must be a priceless work of art.

Definitely a classy joint, Han decided as he walked past the huge fountain and continued up the impressive white-stone stairs to the medical facility.

The info-droid at the front desk gave him the number of the Togorian's room. Han hurried down the corridors, then, outside, paused to speak to the medical droid. "Your friend sustained a severe blow to the cranium," the droid said. "It would probably have killed a humanoid. Fortunately, Togorians have very dense bone matter, and so he is relatively uninjured. We have been quick-healing him since he came here, and he should be ready to leave by tomorrow morning."

"Thanks," Han said, opening the door and going in.

Muuurgh lay curled on a large, round pallet. The Togorian was covered with tiny sensor units that reported on his condition. As Han entered, the blue eyes opened. Muuurgh raised himself partly up. "Pilot!"

"Hey, how're you doing, pal?" Han was surprised to feel a huge wash of relief when he saw the Togorian conscious and lucid again. He hadn't realized he'd gotten so fond of the big felinoid. "They treating you all right?"

"Pilot . . ." Muuurgh seemed utterly amazed to find Han here.

"You look surprised to see me," Han said. That was a

huge understatement. Muuurgh didn't look surprised—he looked flabbergasted.

"Muuurgh is . . ." The big alien shook his furry head a little dizzily. "I mean, I am. I never thought I would see you again."

Han drew himself up. "Why not? Did you think I'd just dump you here and swipe the cargo?"

"Yes," replied Muuurgh simply.

"Well, I'm here, ain't I? If it wasn't for me hauling us into Alderaanian space by the skin of our noses, you'd be dead meat by now. I suggest you remember that, pal. You owe me."

Muuurgh nodded dazedly. "Yes, Pilot . . . I owe you."

Han scowled at him and sat down on the edge of the pallet. "And skip that 'pilot' formality. I'm Vykk from now on, okay?"

Muuurgh put out a paw, laid it gently over Han's arm, the huge clawed fingers with their now-retracted claws dwarfing the human's limb. "Okay, Vykk . . ."

After Han left Muuurgh to the tender ministrations of the medical droids, he went back to the *Dream* and called Ylesia. Teroenza was not available, so he asked to speak to Veratil. When the Ylesian's horned, bloated visage appeared on the screen, Han gave him an abbreviated account of their adventures, promising to start back to Ylesia the following day. Veratil, in his turn, promised to arrange payment for the ship repairs and Muuurgh's treatment.

When he'd finished with his call, Han found that he was hungry, so after checking his small hoard of credits, he headed over to a combination tavern and eatery on the campus of the University of Alderaan. It was set into a secluded courtyard, and a rainbow-colored fountain sent showers of crystal drops into the air before the entrance.

Han pulled the door open and went in.

The tavern was filled with fashionably dressed young people . . . talking, laughing, drinking, and eating. Han hesitated, feeling suddenly self-conscious, but his natural bravado came to his rescue. *I'm just as good as they are,* he thought defiantly, following the serving droid to a small table. Despite his brave front, the young Corellian was uncomfortably conscious of the way his sweat-stained coverall and battered jacket contrasted with the elegant, trendy garb of the students who chattered and laughed at the tables.

Once seated, Han ordered an Alderaanian ale. Studying the menu, he noticed that the place featured "nerf cubes and tubers in wine sauce" for a special. It was a little pricey, but he ordered it anyway, knowing that nerf was said to be a delicacy. The stew came with a plate of flatbread, which made him think of Pilgrim 921. *Wish she were here,* he thought. *It'd be nice to have someone to talk to* . . . Dipping a square of flatbread into the dish, he tasted, chewed, then smiled. *This is really good!* It had been a long, long time since he'd had really good food . . . denizens of *Trader's Luck* frequently existed on space rations during their voyages. The only times Han had really eaten well was when he'd been playing his part in one of Garris Shrike's scams. He remembered one barbecue he'd gone to on Corellia. Traladon ribs with special sauce . . .

But even barbecued traladon ribs couldn't equal nerf, he decided. Hungrily, Han dug into his meal. When he was about halfway through, a pretty girl with long, curly chestnut hair and bright blue eyes walked up onto the tiny stage, carrying a mandoviol. Seating herself on a stool, she began to strum it, then, a moment later, her voice rang out, clear and true, in what was evidently a traditional Alderaanian ballad.

It was the usual stuff, about a girl who lost her lover to the lure of the space lanes, and how she waited but he never came home—but the singer's voice was so pure, so unaffected, that she lent the clichéd words true emotion and dignity.

When she'd finished, Han, along with the other patrons, clapped enthusiastically. The girl sang another song, then stepped down off the stage and walked straight toward Han. For a moment he thought—hoped!—that she was coming over to sit with him, but no such luck. She slid into a seat at the next table.

Since the tavern was evidently a popular hangout, the tables were crowded close together; the girl wound up sitting within arm's length of Han. The other person at the table was a round-faced young man a year or two older than the pilot. *Probably her boyfriend,* Han thought, covertly eyeing the young man. He had light brown hair and pale, hazel-green eyes. Unlike the girl, who wore a simple, ankle-length blue dress and sandals, her escort was a tribute to modern fashion.

His purple tunic was belted with a wide, orange belt that clashed with his knee-high red boots. His yellow britches clung to his legs like a second skin. Han, in his worn, gray coverall, felt like a house-warbler next to a paradise bird.

As the singer shook back her hair and smiled triumphantly, Han managed to catch her eye. He mimed clapping, and she grinned and bowed. "You were great!" he told her.

"Thank you!" she said. "That was the first time I've gotten up my nerve to sing in front of a crowd!" The girl was flushed, breathless, and very charming. Han smiled back at her. *I wouldn't mind spending the evening—and the night—with her . . .*

Aloud, he said, "We're a very lucky audience, then. Witnessing the beginning of a great career."

"Thank you!" She held out her hand. "I'm Aryn Dro, and this is Bornan Thul."

Han took her hand and, instead of shaking it, bowed over it, as though she were Corellian nobility. His lips didn't touch the back of her hand, but he came close enough so she could feel the warmth of his breath on her skin. "I'm honored, Aryn," he said. "Vykk Draygo."

When he released her hand and turned to greet her escort, Han could tell the young man was irked, and making no effort to hide it. "Greetings . . . ." Han said, since he wasn't sure what honorific, if any, was proper on Alderaan.

"Greetings," Thul said. "Aryn, you were magnificent.

Would you care to go somewhere else to celebrate your triumph?"

Can't stand competition . . . Han thought, smothering a mischievous grin. He, too, had seen Aryn's blue eyes light up when he'd introduced himself.

"Listen, I won't intrude," he said, flashing his most charming smile at the singer. "I just had to tell you how much I enjoyed your singing. But I won't take up any more of your time."

Thul looked as though he'd have liked to say "Good!" but didn't quite dare.

Aryn shook her head and put a reassuring hand on Han's arm. "Oh, no! Of course you're not intruding . . . Vykk." She eyed his coverall. "I was going to ask you if you went to school here, but you don't, do you?"

Han shook his head. "No, I'm only here for tonight. Flew in this morning for repairs. Got in a fight with some pirates and damaged my ship."

The wide blue eyes grew even wider. "Flew? Pirates? Are you a star pilot?"

Han shrugged modestly. "Yeah."

Bornan Thul was getting hot under the collar, the Corellian noted. *Doesn't like the idea of his girl talking to a working-class guy like me, the stuck-up so-and-so . . . well, tough, brother Bornan . . .*

"Oh, my . . ." Aryn breathed. "That's so . . . exciting. Real pirates? What happened?"

Han shrugged again. "Came out of hyperspace, and they were on me quicker than stink on a Skeeg. Two of 'em. Blasted one, but between them, they damaged my hyperdrive. So I came on to Alderaan for repairs."

"You blasted one?" Bornan demanded sharply, raising a skeptical eyebrow. "With what?"

"With an Arakyd missile, pal," Han said evenly. "I blew his butt into little bitty pieces."

Aryn shivered, half with excitement, half with distress. "That sounds . . . really scary."

Han took a swallow of ale. "All in a day's work," he said, deliberately laconic.

By this time Bornan had had just about enough. His face reddened, and he grabbed Aryn's arm. "Sweetheart, let's go. I'm taking you out to the best place in town. If you'll excuse us . . . Pilot Draygo."

The girl hesitated for long moment. *I could get her,* Han thought. *I know I could. That'd really stick in this upper-class jerk's craw, too, to have me walk out of here with his girl . . .*

For a moment Han was tempted, then he made himself relax and relinquish the contest. He sensed that Aryn was a really *nice* girl, someone who didn't deserve to be treated like a gaming piece so he could score points off her snotty boyfriend. One of the reasons he found her attractive, Han realized, was that she reminded him a little of 921, with her wide blue eyes and sweet smile.

Besides, he thought, *those security guys are probably still tailing me. Old Bornan here might just be man enough to pick a fight, and if they're still around, that could get messy . . .*

So Han stood, respectfully, and gave Aryn a formal bow. "Been a real pleasure," he said. "Enjoy your celebration."

"Thank you . . ." she said, and gave him a last, quick smile before she allowed Bornan to lead her out.

Han sat back down to his cooling food, reflecting that this incident had reminded him of just how much he detested stuck-up rich people. He'd encountered lots of them on Corellia, while working Shrike's scams, and the fact that most of them weren't worth a blaster bolt to blow them to atoms was the only thing that had made him able to act his part during the swindles.

By the time Han returned to the *Ylesian Dream,* and the tiny bunk that had been installed in part of the cargo area for him, he was slightly the worse for the Alderaanian ale. Thoughts of 921 kept running through his mind, and he cursed aloud in the silence, wishing he could *stop* thinking about her. Han had never before encountered a woman that he'd spent time thinking about when she wasn't with him . . .

The knowledge that 921 had wormed her way that deep

into his mind unsettled Han, made him uncomfortable. *She's just a girl, Solo. You don't even know her blasted name. Quit mooning around like this. You going soft in the head or something?*

Han flung himself down on his bunk and groaned aloud, remembering the events of the day. *What a world,* he thought muzzily. *So goody-goody that a guy can't even sell a perfectly good cargo of spice . . .*

The trip back to Ylesia was uneventful. Han piloted the *Dream* down through the clouds without a single mishap, and hardly even shook the ship as he did it. Even Muuurgh, who was still nursing a headache, couldn't complain. It was becoming second nature to Han to see, analyze, and avoid the paths of the planet's massive storm systems.

The moment the ship was down on the landing pad, Han's communicator came to life, summoning him to meet with Teroenza immediately. Han had been expecting this. He sent Muuurgh off to the infirmary to get some treatment for his headache, and walked up to the Administration Building alone.

This time he was met by Ganar Tos and escorted into the High Priest's inner sanctum, where he'd been before. Teroenza was resting in a most unusual piece of furniture—a sort of sling or hammock that allowed the High Priest to lean back on his massive haunches and take his weight off his back legs. His thick forelegs were supported by a movable padded leg rest that could swing in and out to allow him to get into the contraption.

The minute the High Priest saw Han, his expression (which Han was beginning to be able to read) turned positively benevolent. "Pilot Draygo!" he boomed. "I understand you are a hero! Your bravery and courage are beyond price, but I have ordered a bonus to be placed in your account."

Han blinked, then smiled. "Thanks, sir."

"We have lost two ships that failed to return from their rendezvous points over the past year and a half," Teroenza continued. "You are the first pilot to get a look at your attackers and return to tell us who they were. What did you see?"

Han shrugged. "Well, it all happened real fast, and I was kinda busy, sir. But I'm pretty sure that the ship I destroyed was a Drell-built ship. Looked like it. That chisel-shaped prow and stubby stern are pretty distinctive."

"Did they communicate with you? Give you a chance to surrender before attacking?"

"No, they shot first, and just kept on shooting. They weren't trying to destroy the *Dream,* because if they had been, they'd have done it. But they had no interest in the ship, which was strange—most pirates would try to disable the ship enough to take it, while leaving it easy to repair so they could use it or sell it. These guys were out to cripple the *Dream,* and kill me and Muuurgh."

"How did they attack?"

"From behind. They could've nailed us before we even knew they were there. They had at least two clear shots, and the shielding on the *Dream* isn't that good." As he remembered the battle, Han took a deep breath. "I think we need to strengthen the shielding, sir."

"I will order that to be done, Pilot," Teroenza agreed. The huge t'landa Til folded his tiny arms, and his massive forehead wrinkled as he considered what Han had told him. "Interesting that they attacked first, without engaging a tractor beam and attempting to gain your surrender."

"Yeah . . . that's what I thought."

Han had known several traders aboard the *Luck* that had spent time on pirate crews, and had listened to them bragging about their adventures. A straight-out attack wasn't the usual pirate style; it would have been more typical for a deep-space pirate to fire a warning shot, then, after the pilot had surrendered, board the ship. "It's funny, it's like they planned to disable the *Dream,* probably killing me and Muuurgh in the process, and *then* board her when she was dead in space."

"No communication or demand for surrender at all."

"None," Han affirmed.

Teroenza smoothed the loose folds of flesh beneath his chin thoughtfully. "Almost as though they were willing to risk destroying the *Dream* and her cargo rather than communicate with you . . ."

"Yeah, I'd say so."

"How close were you to the rendezvous point when you were attacked?"

"We'd come out of hyperspace less than five minutes before. No doubt, sir, they were waiting for us. They knew we were coming."

"Had you made any transmissions referring to your course or coordinates, Pilot Draygo?"

"No, sir. As instructed, I maintained strict silence on all frequencies."

Teroenza rumbled thoughtfully, deep in his chest, then nodded his massive horned head. "Again, I commend your bravery. How is Muuurgh?"

"He'll be okay. Took a hard blow to the head, though."

"I will want to speak to him when he is well enough. Very well, Pilot, you are dismissed."

Han stood his ground. "Sir . . . I'd like to ask a favor."

"Yes?"

"My blaster was taken from me when I arrived on Ylesia. I'd like it returned. If there's any chance I might be boarded by pirates sometime in the future, I want to be able to shoot back."

Teroenza considered for a moment, then nodded agreement. "I will order your weapon returned to you, Pilot. You have certainly demonstrated your loyalty and earned our trust by your actions these last few days." The huge being waved a small hand. "Tell me, Pilot Draygo, did it never occur to you to attempt to sell your cargo and tell us it had been stolen by the pirates?"

Han shook his head. "Nossir, it didn't," he said earnestly.

"Very good. I am . . . impressed." Teroenza's wide, lipless mouth curved up in what was evidently meant as a smile of approval. "Most impressed . . ."

Han walked out of the Administration Building, thankful that he'd been able to lie convincingly since he was seven.

He was especially proud of his ability to fabricate on a moment's notice.

His footsteps took him down the path toward the infirmary. Time to check up on Muuurgh, see how the Togorian was doing. Also . . . it was time to meet Jalus Nebl, the Sullustan pilot who'd been placed on sick leave.

Han had a few questions to ask the Sullustan . . .

Chapter Seven:

BRIA

Muuurgh was lying curled up on one of the large pallets his species used as beds. Han walked over to the Togorian and sat down beside him. "How's the head?"

"My head still hurts," Muuurgh said. "The medical droid says I must stay here tonight. But I told him no, I could not do that, because Vykk might need me."

"No, I'm fine," Han assured the big felinoid. "I'm going to visit the Sullustan, eat dinner, do a few sims, and engage in a little target practice. Then I'm gonna turn in early. It's been a long day."

"Did Vykk tell Teroenza about the pirates?"

"Yeah, I did. He's gonna want to talk to you when you're up to it. And . . . good news. Teroenza's giving me my blaster back."

"Good," Muuurgh said. "Vykk needs to protect himself from pirates."

"That's what I pointed out, pal." Han stood up. "Listen, I'm going next door, talk to the other pilot. I'll check back on you tomorrow morning, okay?"

Muuurgh stretched luxuriously, then curled up on his pallet, looking almost like a huge black, furry circle. "Okay, Vykk."

Han walked down the corridor until he found the medical droid, then he asked to be guided to the Sullustan pilot's room.

Once he reached it, Han signaled the door chime and, a moment later, heard a voice say in Sullustan, "Enter."

Han opened the door, only to be met by a wall of forced air that covered the doorway like a curtain. Han had to step through the doorway, into cool, refreshing air. The door sealed shut behind him with a hiss. *Canned air,* Han realized. *They've got the Sullustan on a recirculating air system, so he's not breathing Ylesian air. Wonder why?*

Jalus Nebl was sitting before an entertainment vid-unit, where a galactic news documentary was in progress. Han walked over and offered his hand to the big-eyed, droopy-jowled being. "Hi, I'm Vykk Draygo, the new pilot. Pleased to meet you."

He spoke in Basic, hoping the alien understood it. The jowly alien nodded at Han and said, in his own rapid-fire shrill language, "Do you understand the tongue of my people, or shall we require a translator to converse?"

"I understand it," Han said in extremely halting Sullustan, "but speak it only bad. Understand Basic you okay?"

"Yes," the Sullustan said. "I understand Basic quite well."

"Good," Han said, reverting back to his own tongue. "Mind if I sit down?"

"Please, do so," the pilot answered. "I have been wishing to speak with you for some time, but I have been quite ill and, as you can see, confined to these few rooms where the air is specially filtered for me."

Han sat down on a low bench and looked closely at the alien. He couldn't see any outward damage. "That's too bad, pal. What happened? Overwork?"

The Sullustan's small, wet mouth pursed unhappily. "Too many missions, yes. Too many storms, I flew through. Too many almost crashes, my friend. One day I awoke, and my hands"—the Sullustan held out his small, delicate hands with their narrow oval claw-nails—"my hands would not stop trembling. I could no longer handle the controls of my ship." The alien's already mournful expression grew even sadder. Han almost expected to see tears well up in those big, already wet eyes.

Han looked at the alien's hands and saw that they were, indeed, shaking uncontrollably. He felt a mixture of dismay and pity. *Poor guy! That'd be awful!* "That's a bum deal, pal," he said. "Was it just, y'know, your nerve being shot, or what?"

"Pressure, yes," the Sullustan agreed. "Too many missions, little rest, over and over. Too many storms. But also . . . too much hauling of glitterstim. Medical droid says I have bad reaction to it. Makes Jalus Nebl very sick indeed."

Han shifted uncomfortably on the bench. "You mean you're allergic to glitterstim?"

"Yes. Discovered this as soon as I began hauling it, and tried to stay away from it, but it is in the very air of this world. Even locked in those vials, tiny traces escape to the air. When Jalus Nebl breathes it in, over days, weeks, more than a planet year . . . causes bad effects. Muscle tremors. Slowed reflexes. Stomach is upset, breathing grows hard . . ."

"So *that's* why they've got you confined to the infirmary, with these filters running," Han said. "Trying to get it out of your system."

"Correct. I *want* to fly again, friend and fellow pilot Draygo. You are one of few who can understand this, correct?"

Han thought of how he'd feel if he couldn't fly any-more—if he'd been so overworked and poisoned by spice exposure that his hands shook all the time—and he nodded. "Hey, pal," he said sincerely, "I'm really sorry. I hope you'll be better soon." He lowered his voice, and switched to trader's argot. "Understand you trader-talk, friend?"

The Sullustan nodded. "Not speak," he replied, equally softly, "but understand fine."

Han glanced up at the ceiling. Were the Ylesians or their security monitoring this room? No way to be sure. But he hadn't met too many droids who could translate trader's argot, because it was a bastardized mix of a dozen or more tongues and several dialects, with no fixed syntax. He waved up the volume on the newscast higher . . . higher, then mouthed, barely making any sound, "Friend-pilot, when hands grow steady, then if me you, not say farewell, just fly off bad spice world, quick quick. Understand?"

The Sullustan nodded.

Han lowered the volume slightly, then went on, as if nothing had happened, "I got attacked by pirates the other day."

The Sullustan leaned forward. "What happened?"

"They shot up my ship, damaged the hyperdrive engines, but I managed to get one of them with a missile," Han said, gesturing "boom" with his hands. "Had to put into Alderaan for repairs. Ever been there?"

"Nice world," the Sullustan commented dryly. "Too nice, for some things."

"Tell me about it," Han said with feeling. "Anyway, when I came back here, Teroenza had a hundred questions about what kinds of ships the pirates were in, why they didn't fire warning shots or try to commandeer the *Dream*, stuff like that. I got the distinct impression that there was more to this attack than just a random pirate raid. For one thing, they were waiting for me at the rendezvous point. How'd they find out those coordinates?"

"Ah," said Jalus Nebl. "There may indeed be much behind this attack, Pilot."

"Please . . . call me Vykk. Us pilots gotta stick together."

"You call me Nebl, then. My nest-name."

"Thanks. So what do you think is going on?"

"I believe that the t'landa Til are worried that these 'pirate' vessels may instead be from Nal Hutta. Hutt-dispatched ships, masquerading as pirates."

Han whistled softly. "By all the Minions of Xendor . . . that takes the cake. The Hutts are fighting against each other?"

"Is not hard to believe if you have ever spent time among Hutts," Nebl said dryly. "Hutt alliances are made and broken on the spin of a credit-coin. Hutt loyalty melts away in the face of loss of profit or power, you know?"

"I'm beginning to see a pattern, here," Han said, shifting uneasily on the hard bench, thinking of how close he'd come to being cosmic dust. "There are factions of Hutts on Nal Hutta?"

"Oh, yes. One family or clan will gain power and wealth, only to fall when another family plots their demise. It is no wonder that Hutts are the most distrustful of sentients—being a food-taster for a Hutt is most likely a job of short duration, Vykk. It is very difficult to poison a Hutt, but that does not stop assassins from trying it—and, occasionally, succeeding. And the clans are not above using missiles, assassins, or ground troops to accomplish their goals."

"But the Hutts are the ones who are really running this place," Han pointed out.

"Ah! You saw Zavval, then?"

"If that's the bloated sonofagun who rides around on that repulsor sled, I sure did. Haven't had the honor yet of meeting him face-to-face."

"Pray you never do, Vykk. Zavval, like most Hutts, is not easy to please. The priests can be hard masters to satisfy, but compared to the Hutts, *their* masters, they are nothing."

"So, what's going on with this world? You've got Hutts running this world, who're clashing with other clans of Hutts on Nal Hutta—why?" Han thought for a moment, then answered his own question. "Oh. Of course. For the spice."

"Naturally. The Hutts and the t'landa Til, their caretakers, profit in two ways from Ylesia. First, there is the processed spice. But the Ylesian Hutts must *buy* their spice from other Hutt families who provide the raw materials. Have you ever heard of Jiliac or of Jabba?"

"Jabba?" Han frowned. "Jabba the Hutt? I think I've heard of him. Isn't he supposed to be the guy who pretty much controls Nar Shaddaa, the smugglers' moon that orbits Nal Hutta?"

"That's right. He divides his time between his home on Nal Hutta and a spice transshipping operation he runs through a back-of-beyond planet called Tatooine."

"Tatooine? Never heard of it."

Nebl shuddered. "Trust me, you don't want to go there. It's a dump."

"I'll keep that in mind. So this Jabba and Jiliac get the raw spice and ship it here for processing, right?"

"Yes. But lately, I believe, they may be trying to increase their profit by sending out ships to masquerade as pirates, and having them hijack the Ylesian spice ships. That way, Jabba and Jiliac get the processed spice for nothing—something that would please them greatly."

Han pursed his lips in a silent whistle. "Talk about biting the hand that feeds you . . ."

"Indeed. Yet I have no difficulty believing them capable of doing it."

Han ran a hand through his hair and sighed. It had been a *very* long day. "Yeah, from what I've heard, a Hutt would sell his own grandmother—assuming they have such things—for a credit's profit."

"So you must be very, very cautious, young Vykk. Tell Teroenza you need increased shielding."

"I have."

"Good. Greater firepower would not be amiss, either."

"Yeah, you're right." Han fixed the Sullustan with a steady gaze. "Nebl, since we're talkin' frankly here, tell me something. There ain't nothin' to this religion thing the priests are pushing at these pilgrims, is there?"

"I do not believe so, Vykk. But I do not understand exactly what the Exultation is. I am not a believer, so I have never felt it, but judging by the way the pilgrims react, it has a more intoxicating effect than any dose of spice."

"Yeah, it packs a wallop, all right," Han agreed. "What I'm figuring is that this whole setup on Ylesia is just one big scam to get their lousy spice processed cheap."

"That is not their only motive, Vykk. Do you remember that I said there were two ways that the priests and the Hutts profit from these colonies?"

"Yeah," Han said. "So go on, what's the second way?"

"Slaves," Nebl said bluntly. "Trained, compliant slaves. The Ylesians export the pilgrims from the spice factories when they consider them fully trained, all will to resist removed. They are taken to other worlds and sold. Their places in the factories are taken by fresh shipments of pilgrims."

"And the slaves are too cowed and brainwashed to complain or tell the truth about Ylesia and what's waiting for the pilgrims here?" Han asked.

"Certainly. And even if they *did* talk, who listens to a slave? And if the slave gets too noisy . . ." Nebl made a sudden, unmistakable hand across throat gesture. "Silencing a slave is easy."

Han was thinking about 921. She said she'd been on Ylesia nearly a year . . .

"How long do they keep 'em before they ship the slaves out? And where do they send them?"

"A year is standard. They send many of the strong ones to Kessel, to work in the spice mines. Nobody ever gets off Kessel alive, you know. And the pretty ones . . . they are the lucky few. They go for dancing girls or boys, or to the barracks pleasure-houses. An undignified life, perhaps, but far easier than slaving and dying in the mines."

Nebl was watching Han intently out of his wet, luminous eyes. "Why do you ask? Is there a particular slave that matters to you?"

"Well . . . kinda," Han admitted. "She works in the glitterstim factory, down on the deepest level. She's been here close to a year."

"If you care for her, you should get her out of there, Vykk," the Sullustan said. "The death rates for the glitterstim workers are very high. The spice cuts them, and then the fungi get into their bloodstreams, and . . ." He made a tossing-away gesture with his fingers. "Get her out of there. Being shipped off-world as a slave is her only hope."

"Off-world?" Han fought back a stab of fear at the thought that he might never see Pilgrim 921 again. "What, I'm supposed to *hope* that she gets shipped out to some barracks pleasure-house, to be a plaything for bored Imperial troops?"

"Better that than a miserable death from slow blood-poisoning."

Han was thinking fast, and he didn't like what he was thinking. "Listen, Nebl, I'm glad we got to talk. I'll come back and visit again sometime. Right now . . . there's something I've gotta do."

The alien nodded kindly. "I quite understand, Vykk."

Once outside, Han realized that the short Ylesian day was definitely waning. The pilgrims would be at evening devotions. If he hurried, he might be able to catch up with 921 and have a few words with her. He had to figure out some way to get her out of that factory and yet keep her here on Ylesia.

Despite the wet heat and the fine drizzle that was falling, Han began to jog through the jungle, up the familiar path. His breath burned in his chest after the first five minutes or so, but he refused to slow down. He just had to see 921's face, reassure himself she was still here, on Ylesia.

What if she'd been shipped off-world? He'd never find her . . . never! Han felt panic nibble at the edge of his mind and cursed himself in every language he knew. *What has gotten into you, Solo? You've got to get hold of yourself! Things are going good for you here on Ylesia. At the end of the year, you'll have a stack of credits waiting in an account on Coruscant. Now is no time to lose your head over some crazy religious fanatic. Get over it!*

But his body and heart would not listen to his mind. Han's strides came longer and faster until he was running full tilt. He rounded a turn near the Plain of Flowers, and nearly ran headlong into the first of the pilgrims on their way back from evening devotions. They were staggering or shambling along, that drugged, ecstatic look in their glazed eyes.

Han began elbowing his way through the throng, feeling like a fish swimming upstream. He squinted at faces in the gathering darkness, peered beneath caps, searching, searching . . .

Where was she?

Increasingly worried, Han began grabbing pilgrims' arms and demanding to know if anyone had seen Pilgrim 921. Most ignored him or stared stupidly, slack-jawed, but finally an old Corellian woman jerked her thumb behind her. Han turned to find 921 some distance behind the others. Relief flooded through him. He hurried up to her, still panting, sweaty, and disheveled from his run.

"Hi," he wheezed, hoping the greeting didn't sound as lame to her as it did to him.

She looked up at him in the twilight. "Hi," she said uncertainly. "You've been gone for a while."

"Off-world," Han said, taking her arm and falling into step with her. "Had some cargo to transport."

"Oh."

"So, how's it been going?" he asked.

"Fine," she said. "The Exultation was wonderful tonight."

"Yeah," he agreed grimly. "I'm sure it was."

"How was your voyage, Vykk?" she asked after a minute or so of silence. Han was pleased by her question; it was the first time she'd betrayed any curiosity about him and his life.

"It turned out okay," he said, picking his way down the muddy path, trying not to get his boots any worse than they already were. He was splashed to the knees with all that running. "Pirates shot at me, though."

"Oh, no!" She looked distressed. "Pirates! You could have been hurt!"

He smiled at her and shifted his grip so they were walking hand in hand. "How nice to know you care," he said with a touch of his old cockiness. For a moment he thought she might pull away, but she let him hold her hand.

By the time they'd reached the dorm, it was dark. Han walked her over to their same spot, halfway between the light and the darkness. He took off her infrared goggles. "What are you doing?" she asked nervously.

"I want to see you," Han said. "You know those goggles hide your eyes." He took her hand and raised it to his lips, then kissed the back of it. "I missed you while I was away," he murmured.

"You did?" He couldn't tell whether the thought pleased or distressed her. Maybe both.

"Yeah. I thought about you," he continued softly. It occurred to him that this was the first time he'd ever been this honest about his feelings with a girl. For once in his life he wasn't putting on an act. "I didn't want to," he added honestly, "but I did. You *do* care, don't you? Just a little?"

"I . . . I . . ." she stammered. "I don't know . . ." She tried to pull her hand away, but Han wouldn't let it go. He began to kiss her fingers, her scarred, lacerated fingers. The touch of her skin against his mouth intoxicated him as much as the Alderaanian ale. He rained soft, tender little kisses over her knuckles, her fingertips.

"Stop that . . ." she whispered. "Please . . ."

"Why?" he asked, turning her hand over, so he could kiss her wrist. Han gloried in the jump of her pulse against his mouth. He pressed his lips against her palm, feeling the ridges of scars old and new. "Don't you like it?"

"Yes . . . no . . . I don't know!" she burst out, sounding on the verge of tears. She yanked her hand back, and this time Han let it go, but stepped forward to catch her sleeve.

"Please . . ." he said, holding her with his eyes as much as with his hand. "Please . . . don't go. Can't you tell that I care about you? I worry about you, I think about you . . . I *care* about you." He swallowed, and it hurt. "A lot."

She caught her breath, and it sounded like a sob. "I don't want you to care," she said, her voice ragged. "Because I'm not supposed to care . . ."

"You won't even tell me your name," Han finished, and he couldn't hide the touch of bitterness in his voice.

She stood poised for flight, like a bird, her eyes wide and tormented. "I care about you, too," she whispered, finally. Her voice trembled. "But I shouldn't. I'm only supposed to care about the One, and the All! You want me to break my vows, Vykk! How can I give up everything I believe in?"

Hearing her admit that she had feelings for him made Han's heart turn over. "Tell me your name," he pleaded. "Please . . ."

She stared at him, eyes bright with tears, then she whispered, "It's Bria. Bria Tharen."

Then, without another word, she picked up the skirts of her robe and ran away, through the door, into the dorm.

Han stood in the darkness and felt a slow, wide grin spread across his face. All his exhaustion fell away, and his feet felt as though he were wearing repulsorlift boots. He walked away from the dorm, still smiling, and barely noticed when the skies opened up and it began to pour.

She does *care* . . . he thought, slogging through the ubiquitous mud. *Bria . . . that's nice. Sounds like music or something. Bria . . .*

The next day, after long hours of thinking and planning during a mostly sleepless night, Han went in search of Teroenza. He found the High Priest and Veratil relaxing in the mudflats that lay about a kilometer inland from the shallow Ylesian ocean. Both priests lounged at their ease, immersed in warm red mud up to their massive flanks. Occasionally one or the other would roll over and thrash a bit, to cover an area that had dried out.

The two Gamorreans on guard duty looked positively envious of their masters. Han, on the other hand, came close enough to the mud wallow to catch a whiff, and grimaced. *Ugh! Smells like something died last week!*

The Corellian stood balancing precariously on the bank and waved to get Teroenza's attention. "Uh, sir? I'd like a word with you, if possible."

The High Priest was in a good mood, relaxed from the mud. He waved an undersized arm. "Our heroic pilot! Please, join us!"

Climb into that muck? On purpose? Han thought, repressing a grimace. But he understood that the t'landa Til were offering him a great honor. He sighed.

When Teroenza beckoned to him again, Han grinned and waved back genially. He unfastened his gunbelt, letting his newly reclaimed blaster in its holster slip to the ground. After yanking off his boots, he unsealed his pilot's coverall and stepped out of it, leaving him clad only in his shorts. Carefully, he placed his belt-pouch atop the pile, with the open end facing the mudhole.

Then, with a grimace that he tried to turn into a smile, the Corellian stepped off the bank. Red mud oozed up his legs, and for a second Han nearly panicked, picturing himself sinking completely out of sight. But there was solid ground beneath the mud. Waving and smiling at the two t'landa Til, Han grimly waded out until he was slithering in mud up to his thighs.

"Isn't this wonderful?" Veratil asked, generously catching up a huge blob of mud and slathering Han's back. "Nothing in this galaxy beats a good mud bath!"

Han nodded vigorously. "Yeah! Great!"

"I suggest you go for a roll," Teroenza boomed. "That always refreshes me after the stresses of everyday life. Try it!"

"Sure!" Han agreed, smiling through clenched teeth. "A good roll sounds like just the thing!" Gingerly, he lowered himself into the mud, and with a great slosh and *splat!* he rolled completely over in the slimy, oozing stuff. It didn't help his mood to notice that there were long white worms inhabiting the mud. Han assumed they weren't carnivorous, or the priests wouldn't be having such a wonderful time.

Bria, honey, I hope you appreciate this . . . he thought as he completed his roll and sat back up, coated now from the neck down. "Wonderful!" he said loudly. "So . . . squishy!"

"So, Pilot Draygo . . . why did you wish to speak with

me?" Teroenza asked as the High Priest languidly settled deeper into the wallow.

"Well, I think I may have solved your problem, sir. The problem of how to take care of your collection, that is."

Teroenza's massive head swiveled on his almost nonexistent neck. "Really? How?"

"I've made friends with one of the pilgrims, a young woman from my homeworld. Before she came here to be a pilgrim, she was studying to be a museum curator, and she knows a lot about caring for rare things. Antiquities, collectibles, stuff like that. I'll bet she could properly catalog and care for the stuff in your collection."

Teroenza listened intently, then the High Priest sat back on his haunches, mud squishing up around him. "I had no idea any of our pilgrims had such training. Perhaps I will interview this one. What is her designation?"

"She's Pilgrim 921, sir."

"And where does she work?"

"In the glitterstim factory, sir."

"How long has she been here on Ylesia?"

"Almost a year, sir."

Teroenza turned to Veratil, and the two priests began talking in their own language.

I gotta learn their lingo for myself, Han thought. He'd found a language program to teach elementary Huttese, and been studying that for the past month. But he'd been unable to locate any translation guides or programs for learning the t'landa Til language. He strained his ears, hoping to be able to decipher what the priests were saying, but t'landa Til was apparently sufficiently different from Huttese to make it impossible for him to understand anything.

Turning back to Han, Veratil said, "This Pilgrim 921 . . . would you say she's attractive, as your species measures attractiveness? For example, do you find her appealing as a potential sexual partner?"

Deep in the mud, Han crossed his fingers. "921? Oh, nossir, she's . . . well, to be frank, sir, she's so ugly that if I had a pet with a face that homely, I'd make it walk backward."

When they heard Han's words, both priests guffawed and slapped their arms across their chests, which was apparently their species' way of paying tribute to a witty turn of phrase.

"Very good, Pilot Draygo," Teroenza boomed. "You are indeed a sharp fellow, and I shall investigate this young woman." He sloshed around a bit, letting the mud slop up around his huge flanks. "Ahhhhhhh . . ." he sighed with pleasure.

"So, Veratil." Han squirmed around in the mud until he was facing the Sacredot. "I've got something I'm curious about. Mind if I ask you a question?"

"Not at all," the younger priest said.

"How do you guys do that thing you do with the pilgrims each night at the devotion? What they call the Exultation? It sure packs a wallop, whatever it is."

"The Exultation?" Veratil chuckled, a low, booming sound. "That moment of rapture the pilgrims regard as a Divine Gift?"

"Right," Han said. "I've never been able to experience it," he admitted. *Because I've fought it as hard as I can,* he added silently. *Because the last thing I want is some critter as ugly as you giving me jolts in my pleasure neurons . . .*

"That is because you are a strong-minded individual, Pilot Draygo," Veratil said. "Our pilgrims come to us because they are *not* strong-minded, they are weak, and looking for guidance. And their diets are designed to make them even more . . . malleable."

Teroenza spoke up, "The Exultation is a refinement of a ability we males of the t'landa Til use to attract the females of our species during mating season. We create a frequency resonance within the recipient's brain that stimulates the pleasure centers. The humming vibration is produced by air flowing over the cilia in our neck pouches when we inflate them. Our females find it irresistible."

"We males also have a low-grade empathic projection ability," Veratil said. "By concentrating on feeling good, we can project those feelings at the crowd of pilgrims. Both effects, taken together, produce the Exultation."

"Neat trick!" Han said admiringly. "Is it difficult?"

"Not at all," Teroenza said. "What we find difficult is having to lead the pilgrims in those endless services and prayers. At times, I've been so bored that I nearly fell asleep, waiting for my turn to lead the devotions."

"Last year, one of the Sacredots *did* fall asleep," Veratil said, booming with his species's version of laughter. "Palazidar fell right over. The pilgrims were *most* upset."

Both priests enjoyed the memory. Han laughed, too, but inside he was simmering with anger, thinking of the pilgrims staggering down the path, religious faith and devotion shining in their eyes. *This place makes any of Garris Shrike's scams look like nothing*, he thought disgustedly. *Someone should shut these greedy vermin down . . .*

For a moment he wished he could be the one to do it. Then Han reminded himself that sticking one's neck out for others was a good way to get one's head and shoulders permanently separated. *So why are you doing all this for Bria?* his treacherous mind asked sarcastically.

Because, his heart answered, *Bria's safety has become as important to me as my own. I can't help it, it's just the way things are . . .*

Now that he'd accomplished what he'd come here to do, Han began to think about how to gracefully (metaphorically speaking) extract himself from the mud and the company of the priests.

He was rescued by the arrival of a Hutt, who came gliding over the mudflat on his repulsorlift sled. A small squad of guards trotted vigorously alongside, panting in the humid heat as they struggled to keep up.

"Zavval!" Teroenza hailed his Hutt overlord, standing respectfully. Feeling like a fool, Han did likewise.

This was the Corellian's first close-up encounter with a Hutt, and he tried not to stare at the creature's huge, recumbent form, the enormous, pouchy eyes amid the leathery tan skin, and the green slime that oozed from the corners of the being's mouth. *Ugh . . . they're even uglier than Teroenza and his crew*, Han thought. He reminded himself that Hutts had been civilized for probably longer than his own species—but he still couldn't quite eliminate the revulsion their appearance caused.

Or maybe it was just the knowledge that it was the Hutts who'd dreamed up the idea of running a religion on Ylesia as a cheap way to enslave innocent sapients that repulsed him.

The Hutt leaned toward Teroenza and said in Huttese, "I've received a message from home. Jabba and Jiliac deny everything, and we have no proof. The clan council has refused to . . ." Han couldn't catch the word, "so we have no other way to . . ." and he finished with a phrase that Han couldn't translate.

"Regrettable," replied Teroenza in Huttese. "What about my requisition for more troops, armament, and shielding for our ships, Your Excellency?"

"Approved," Zavval said. "Should be arriving any day."

"Good."

Teroenza continued, in Basic, "Zavval, I would like you to meet our brave pilot, Vykk Draygo, who saved our shipment of glitterstim."

The huge Hutt chuckled, a "heh, heh, heh" sound that was so deep and resonant that Han could feel it as well as hear it. "Greetings, Pilot Draygo. You have our lasting gratitude."

"Thank you, sir . . ."

Teroenza waved an undersized arm. "The correct form of address is 'Your Excellency,' Pilot Draygo."

"Okay, then. Thank you, Your Excellency. I'm honored to be able to serve you."

The Hutt chuckled again, and said to Teroenza in Huttese, "A most polite and perceptive young man—for a human. Have you arranged for a bonus? We want to keep him happy."

"Yes, I have, Your Excellency," Teroenza replied.

Han, of course, did not let on that he'd understood any of the exchanges in Huttese.

"Good, good," Zavval said.

Han stood watching as the alien turned his repulsorlift sled and glided away. Teroenza and Veratil began slogging their way out of the mud with grunts of effort. The High Priest addressed Han in Basic. "His Excellency is pleased with your performance, Pilot. Has the factory foreman informed you as to when the next shipment will be ready for transport?"

Han, too, was squishing his way toward the bank. "He said at the end of the week, sir. In the meantime, there are two shipments of pilgrims due in at the space station, one tomorrow, one the day after."

"Good. We don't want to be shorthanded in the factories."

Once back on the bank, Han scooped up his clothes, then turned east and gestured in the direction of the ocean, a kilometer away. "I think I'll walk over and rinse off," he said, "before I get dressed."

"Ah, yes," said Veratil, "we use the mud as a cleansing agent, but it does not cling to our skins the way it appears to cling to yours. Once dry, all we need to do is shake"—he gave a pronounced shudder, and dust rose in clouds—"and it all flakes away, as you can see."

"Yes, I see that," Han said. "But I'll have to use water to rinse."

"Be careful not to go too far into the ocean, Pilot Draygo," Teroenza cautioned. "Some of the denizens of the Ylesian oceans are quite large, and very hungry."

"Yessir," Han said.

Holding his clothes and boots away from his red, mud-covered body, Han began picking his way barefoot toward the ocean. He couldn't see it yet, because of a ridge of sand dunes, but he could smell the warm, brackish water.

When he reached it a short time later, he cautiously ventured out, knee-deep, and then squatted down to let the pounding surf sluice over him. Again and again the waves washed over the Corellian, rinsing away all trace of the red muck.

Then Han went over to the sandy shore, found a smooth patch, and stretched out to dry. He felt the dim Ylesian sun beating down on him, drying him, leaving his hair salt-stiffened and tousled. *But anything's better than that mud,* he thought drowsily.

He was almost asleep when Han jerked awake, remembering something he'd forgotten. He got to his feet, walked over to his clothes, then fumbled with his belt pouch. Looking carefully around before he did so, he withdrew the tiny audio-log recording device he'd "borrowed" from the *Ylesian Dream* and, seeing that it was still running, turned it off with a decisive *snap.*

Satisfied that he'd successfully recorded the entire exchange between himself and the Ylesian priests, Han walked back to his spot, lay down on the warm sand, and took a well-deserved nap.

Chapter Eight:
REVELATIONS

Han flew many missions for the Ylesians during the next three months. Several times he was able, with Muuurgh's complicity, to make small "side runs" to hone his piloting skills and to allow Muuurgh to practice with the weaponry. Han successfully landed vessels on airless moons, on ice moons, even on a small asteroid, barely bigger than his ship. He learned to dock with a space station, matching airlocks perfectly on the first try.

As a result of Han's run-in with the "pirates," the Ylesian Hutts increased the weaponry and equipped their ships with better shielding. They also tightened the security surrounding the dates and locations of their shipments, and refused to agree to any more off-planet rendezvous points. Instead, Han was ordered to fly his cargo to a planet and exchange the processed spice for the raw materials planetside. In a populated area, there was less chance of a double cross that might lead to an ambush.

Teroenza made it clear to Muuurgh that Vykk Draygo had passed muster as a trustworthy employee, so Muuurgh no longer felt compelled to spend every waking moment with the Corellian. The big Togorian was still bound by his promise to guard the pilot, however, and Muuurgh never forgot that.

True to his promise, Teroenza interviewed Bria and gave the Corellian woman the job of maintaining and cataloging his collection. Han was able to see her every day he was on Ylesia. Once she began getting better food in the mess hall, and healthy exposure to fresh air and sunlight, that pale, wan, too-thin look vanished, and her eyes grew bright, her step lighter, and her smile came more readily.

She liked her new job, both because she enjoyed caring for the antiquities and because she felt that serving the High Priest was a sacred honor. Bria continued to attend prayer times every morning and devotions every evening. When Han was on Ylesia, he usually walked her to and from the service.

Bria was offered a room in the Administration Center, but told Teroenza that she preferred to stay in the pilgrims' dormitory. Not only did she enjoy the company of her fellow pilgrims at prayer time, but she found she was uneasy at the thought of occupying an apartment in the same building as Vykk Draygo. Bria Tharen was still wary of the Corellian, still unwilling to respond to the feelings he awakened in her. She was a pilgrim, she reminded herself constantly. Her loyalty, her duty, her spiritual self, was reserved for the One and the All.

Still, there was no doubt that she enjoyed Vykk's company. He was so alive, so full of energy, so charming and attractive . . . Bria had never met anyone like him.

During the hour before evening devotions, when her daily work with the High Priest's collection was done, Bria developed the habit of searching out Vykk and Muuurgh (they were almost always together) and then the three of

them would go to the mess hall for a cup of stim-tea together . . .

Bria walked through the jungle, enjoying the small re-
spite from the heat that the lowering sun brought. A breeze
was blowing in off the ocean, which was where she was
headed. She walked quickly, feeling the skirts of her tan
pilgrim's robe brushing the plants that grew along the edges
of the path. Brilliant flowers hung from drooping vines . . .
scarlet, purple, and green-yellow. Their sharp, slightly as-
tringent scent made her nostrils flare as she passed them.

The Exalted One, Teroenza, had told Bria that she was
free to put on regular clothing, in place of her bulky pilgrim
garb, pointing out that it would make it easier to tend his
collection . . . but so far the girl clung to her robes, as she
clung to her vows.

The young Corellian woman reached the mudflats and
paused to make an obeisance before the mud wallow where
two priests lounged. Both ignored her, but Bria was used to
that. Priests paid little attention to pilgrims, unless they
needed to direct them in their work. That was natural . . .
their minds were on higher things, soaring on spiritual
planes that humanoids like Bria could not hope to
reach . . .

The first time Bria had seen the priests wallowing in the
red stinking mud, she'd been shocked. It was unsettling to
see them indulging in such a . . . secular . . . activity.
But over the past three months, ever since she'd come to
work for His Exaltedness, Teroenza, Bria had gotten used
to seeing them.

She was glad that she no longer had to work in the darkness of the glitterstim factory. Working in the Administration Building was much nicer. Climate-controlled, with
good lighting and the food . . . the food was *much* better.
It had taken Bria nearly a full month to be able to eat a
regular meal. At first she'd been so listless, so drained of
energy, she'd just picked at her food, as she'd been doing
for months. The medical droid had had to treat her for

malnutrition, as well as traces of fungi-induced blood-sickness.

But now she was fine.

Things were much better for her, she had to admit, since Vykk had come into her life. If only . . .

Bria frowned, and sighed. If only Vykk were a pilgrim, too. Then they could worship together, attend prayer times together, and receive the sacrament of Exultation together. But Vykk . . . she couldn't escape the fact that he was an unbeliever, even though he'd never admitted to it. Vykk believed in nothing but himself.

When they attended devotions together, he would hold her arm or her hand to steady her on the way back to her dorm. The touch of his hand made her question her devotion to the One, the All, and Bria didn't like that. She wanted nothing to shake her faith or make her question her vows.

By now she'd reached the sand dunes. As she'd half expected, she heard the sound of a blaster bolt whine and sizzle. "Vykk!" she called, not wanting to sneak up on a man who was doing target practice. "Vykk, it's me!"

As she climbed to the top of the dune, the wind grabbed her robes and whipped them about her legs. She had to hold onto her cap, lest it be blown off by the ocean wind.

Below her, on the beach, she could see Vykk, legs braced in a shooter's stance, his blaster in its holster, which he wore slung low, far down his thigh. Muuurgh was some distance from the Corellian, holding several black ceramic target pieces. Without warning, the big Togorian flung two of the targets into the air, one high and to his left, the other low and to his right.

Vykk's hand was a blur of motion so fast that Bria's eyes could barely follow it. A blaster bolt shattered first the rightmost, then the left target piece. Tiny droplets of slagged ceramic rained into the restless Ylesian surf.

Muuurgh yowled his approval. Vykk turned, ready to practice distance shooting at the stationary target they'd set up, then he spotted Bria at the top of the dune. With a wave and grin, he holstered his blaster and loped toward her.

Bria was struck, as she always was, by how good-looking he was, with his regular features, brown hair and eyes, and lean build. Taken all together, he wasn't actually a classically handsome man—but any woman who'd ever been on the receiving end of his smile wouldn't notice that.

"Hi!" he yelled, running up to her.

Before Bria could fend him off, he dropped a kiss on her forehead. Breathless, she pushed him away. "No, Vykk. That's against my vows."

"I know," he said unrepentantly, "but someday, honey, you're gonna kiss me back."

"I wondered if you wanted to go for stim-tea before devotions," she said.

"Not today," he said, suddenly serious, looking down into her face. "There's something we need to talk about, Bria. I've waited until you were . . . better, because I'm afraid it's gonna be a shock. But you gotta find out sometime."

Bria looked up at him, wondering what was going on. "What are you talking about, Vykk?"

"Let's go and sit down," he said. "Over here, on the beach, okay?"

He led her over to a smooth spot in the sand, and when Muuurgh came up to see if they were going back, Vykk shook his head. "Give us a little privacy for a while, pal, okay?"

The Togorian walked away, up the dune. Bria watched as his inky form vanished behind the hill of sand.

Her heart began to race as Vykk took a small device out of his pocket. "This is the audio-log recorder I pulled out of the *Dream*'s control panel," he told her. "I'm going to play a recording I made a couple of months ago, before Teroenza asked you to look after his collection. Just be patient and listen, okay?"

"I don't know . . . I can tell I'm not going to like this," she muttered. "I've got a bad feeling about that recording."

"Please," he said. "For me. Just listen."

Bria nodded, her hands twisting in her lap. Suddenly the ocean breeze, instead of seeming pleasant, made her shiver despite the sun dipping toward the west.

Vykk turned on the recorder. Bria listened to the conference that ensued . . . heard Vykk greet the priests and heard them invite him to take a mud bath. Bria recognized Exalted Teroenza's and Sacredot Veratil's voices talking to the pilot. Mud baths. They were saying how relaxing mud baths were. Bria stirred restlessly, and Vykk held up a warning finger and mouthed, "Wait."

She forced herself to sit still, though she was becoming increasingly uncomfortable. Surely the priests had not known that Vykk was recording their conversation—his actions were worse than eavesdropping, more like outright spying!

Then—Bria caught her breath in dismay—she heard Veratil and Teroenza laughing and talking about the Exultation—they were saying it was *not* a Divine Gift, they were saying it had nothing at all to do with the One or the All!

Bria's eyes widened, then narrowed in fury, and she shot to her feet. The wind whipped her pilgrim's cap off, allowing her golden-red curls to spring free, but she paid no attention. She was trembling with anger as she faced Vykk. Seeing her reaction, he shut off the recorder and stood to face her.

"How *could* you?" Bria demanded, her voice low and shaking. "I thought you were my friend."

He stepped toward her, hands raised placatingly. "Bria, sweetheart, I *am* your friend. I did it for you . . . you need to know the truth. I'm sorry you're—"

Bria's hand and arm seemed to move of their own volition, coming up in a roundhouse *slap!* that connected solidly with his cheek. Vykk staggered back, hand pressed to his face. "You're lying!" she cried. "Lying! You faked that to make me break my vows! Admit it!"

He dropped his hand and stood staring at her, and his eyes were full of sadness and pity. Slowly, Vykk shook his head. "I'm sorry, babe," he said. "Sorrier than I can say. But I didn't fake it. What you heard is the truth, and gettin' mad at me won't change that. Teroenza and his crew don't have any Divine Gifts. They invented this whole scam just to get factory workers and slaves to sell."

The print of her hand was darkening on his cheek, dull red where she'd struck him. Bria could see the marks of her fingers. She fought the impulse to throw herself at him, babbling apologies. How could she have hurt him like that?

At the same time, though, she was angry clear through. Bria could feel her face working. Her chin trembled as she tried to control herself. "No!" She clenched her hands. "No! That's not true! You faked it. What are you . . . telepathic? How did you know about Sacredot Palazidar? You weren't even *here* then!"

He shook his head. "I didn't know, Bria. I didn't know, and I didn't fake this recording. I'm gonna prove that to you." Digging into his pocket, he held out a small black vial.

Bria knew only too well what it was. "Glitterstim? Where did you get it?"

"Light-fingered it during a delivery," Vykk said. "You know what it can do, right?"

Slowly Bria nodded.

"This is the only way I can prove to you I'm not lying. If you open it, expose it to light, then swallow it, it'll give you temporary telepathic abilities. You'll be able to read my mind, and you'll *know* that I'm not lying about the Exultation—and that I didn't fake that recording. Here"—he reached out and dropped it into her hand—"take it."

Bria looked down at the tube. "I . . . I need to think about this, Vykk. I need to decide what to do."

"I'm not lyin', honey, I swear." He came closer to her, reached out to take her hands. "Trust me."

She backed away from him. "Just . . . leave me alone for now, Vykk. I'll . . . see you later. After the devotion. Right now, I have to go."

He looked at her. "You could skip it, this once. It's not like anyone takes roll call."

Skip the Exultation? Bria felt physically sick at the thought, and her reaction terrified her. What if Vykk was right? What if the Exultation was nothing more than a combination physical and mental vibration from an alien species? If no Divine Gift was present, then the pilgrims were no better than addicts getting a fix.

Bria gazed into Vykk's eyes and had a queasy feeling that he *was* telling the truth. Her fingers tightened over the small black cylinder of glitterstim. Here lay her answer. With this, she could find out the truth . . .

She turned and began walking away, leaving him there on the beach. Bria heard Vykk call out to her, but she waved him away and kept moving. She didn't have much time if she was going to make it to the devotion on schedule.

Half an hour later she stood amid the hordes of pilgrims, watching the sun set in bloody splendor behind the Altar of Promises. It was almost time for the Exultation. She glanced around her, thinking that if she was going to do this, it had better be soon. Surreptitiously her fingers withdrew the black cylinder from the pocket of her robe. Light . . . she needed light to activate the glitterstim. And yet . . . she couldn't do it while anyone would see . . .

Finally, the moment came that she was waiting for—the signal to the faithful that the Exultation was about to begin.

Bria had stationed herself in the crowd so that she had a clear view of the High Priest and the Sacredots as they led the pilgrims in the devotion. But she was far back in the crowd, far enough back that she ought to be able to shield the glitterstim with her wide sleeve, so its activation wouldn't be noticed by the t'landa Til. And the other pilgrims would be so busy with the Exultation that they'd probably barely notice a blaster bolt.

All around her, pilgrims were falling to their knees. Bria let herself follow them, and as she did so, she flipped open the top of the vial of glitterstim. Under the cover of her body as she bent forward from the waist, she pulled free the fibrous dose of the drug—and wondered, for an insane second, whether this was a dose she herself had prepared.

As the pilgrims prostrated themselves, the priests' throat pouches began to distend. As the beginnings of the vibrating hum resounded through the air, Bria held the glitter-stim before her, full in the last rays of the setting sun.

Within seconds it activated, sparking blue, but none of the pilgrims noticed, and the effect was hidden from the High Priest. Even though she'd never taken glitterstim before, Bria knew exactly how many seconds to wait. A moment later she shoved it into her mouth and allowed her saliva to quench the sparking substance.

As she mouthed the drug, then swallowed it, the Exultation began.

Bria shuddered as though she'd been blaster-shot. The effects of the glitterstim were immediate. Blood rushed through her body like a ship going into hyperspace. Her head pounded.

But the physical effects were as nothing to the mental ones. Her mind *opened* in a way she'd never afterward be able to describe. As the waves of the Exultation took her, she experienced the pleasure of all the other pilgrims in the crowd.

The sensation was so overwhelming that she almost passed out. Only the anger that had been simmering inside her ever since Vykk had played that recording kept her sane—and focused.

Got to . . . open . . . my eyes . . . she thought. *Focus . . .*

Gagging, gasping, Bria opened her eyes, shuddering as the waves of pleasure wracked her with such intensity they were nearly transformed into pain. She stared at Teroenza, forcing herself not to look away, to narrow her mind to only encompass his.

Images, alien images, flooded Bria's mind, stamping themselves indelibly into her consciousness. No matter how much she wished to forget, she knew she never, ever would. Teroenza's mind, like that of every sentient, was full of surface trivia—wondering what he'd have for dinner, boredom with the ceremony, thoughts of the new security measures the Hutts had ordered him to implement, a minor gastrointestinal churn in his middle . . .

There was not a hint of divinity in the High Priest's

mind. He did not believe in the One or the All. As a matter
of fact, Teroenza was proud of himself for *inventing* the
One and the All, so these credulous pilgrims could have
something to believe in.

Bria gagged, her mouth filled with the bitter aftertaste of
the glitterstim. It was hard to think with the Exultation going on, but she forced herself to stay attuned to the High
Priest's mind . . . sifting, making absolutely *certain* that
what he was doing was purely a physical and mental *trick*—
something that all males of his species could do on demand.

Suddenly Teroenza jerked, looking around him wildly.
His mind filled with suspicion, then certainty—he knew he
was being telepathically probed!

The Exultation wavered, then lessened abruptly as the
High Priest stopped humming. The Sacredots continued in
a ragged chorus, but without their leader, the Exultation
stopped dead. Pilgrims cried out with shock, and some even
fainted.

Bria pulled her mind free from Teroenza's and joined
the crowd of pilgrims who were moaning in distress, crying,
and stumbling back and forth, disoriented. Some stood
shivering and whining as they gazed beseechingly at the
priests.

Teroenza lumbered off the dais by the Altar and began
thrusting his way into the crowd. The t'landa Til peered
down into faces, distractedly muttering blessings, as he
tried to cover up the fact that he was desperately searching
for the pilgrim who had just scanned his mind.

Luckily, Bria was far back in the crowd, quite near the
end of the amphitheater. She let herself be shoved backward, off the permacrete, until her feet encountered gooey
jungle loam. With a single quick, decisive movement, Bria
dug her toe into a lump of trampled leaves and mud and
lifted it. Her fingers released the glitterstim cylinder, and it
fell, landing in the center of the hole.

Bria turned, and as she did so, her foot pressed the lump
of mud back down into the jungle floor. The entire sequence of events had taken only a second.

She began edging her way along the back of the crowd,

toward the path, allowing herself to be carried along with the tide of incoherent, querulous, confused, and dissatisfied pilgrims.

A cautious glance behind her assured her that Teroenza had abandoned his search, apparently having realized how hopeless it was, and how much his atypical behavior was upsetting the pilgrims. Bria hoped that he'd put the entire experience down to some relative newcomer deciding to experiment with a stolen vial of glitterstim.

She moved numbly down the path, her footsteps slow and unsteady. The effects of the glitterstim had faded so much that she was barely aware of the thoughts and emotions of those immediately around her.

She wasn't surprised when Vykk fell into step beside her. As usual, he took her arm to help support her. Bria leaned against him, grateful for his support, and felt his arm go around her waist, until he was half holding her up.

The swift equatorial dark was all around them, now. Bria could barely see Vykk. He led her down the path, avoiding the worst of the mud puddles. Then, when they reached the dorm, she stopped. "I'm . . . not going in there just yet," she mumbled. "I need . . . I need to talk to you, Vykk."

He nodded, his features barely visible in the light cast from the open doors. "Okay. I don't think anyone will mind if we go up to the mess hall for a cup of stim-tea. You look like you could use it."

Together, they turned away, into the darkness. Bria leaned on Vykk as they went up the path. She had never felt so weary. A droid would have moved with more animation.

When they reached the mess hall, Vykk sat her down and fetched them cups of stim-tea, plus a sugared pastry, which he pushed at Bria. "Here," he said. "Eat this. You look like you need it."

Obediently she sipped her tea and nibbled on the pastry. She hadn't had dinner, and the food seemed to steady her, bring the world back into focus.

She leaned toward Vykk, ready to talk, but even as she

opened her mouth, he shook his head warningly. "Guess I'd better get you back to your dorm," he said loudly. "That'll teach you to skip meals, 921. I thought you were going to pass out on me back there."

Taking the hint, Bria got to her feet in silence and followed him out.

When they reached the outside of the Administration Building, Vykk pulled out a pair of infrared goggles and pulled them on. "You got yours?"

Nodding, Bria located them and pulled them into place. The night suddenly resolved itself into ghostly black and greenish-white images. She could see Vykk's face now, half-hidden as it was by the goggles.

His arm came around her again as they started down the jungle path together. "You took the glitterstim," he said quietly.

"Yes," she said, feeling as numb as if she'd been beaten into unconsciousness. "You were right. Forgive me for doubting you . . ."

"Hey," he said, trying to sound cheerful and failing utterly, "I'd have wanted to check out my story, too, in your place. Was it . . . was it rough?"

She nodded, and suddenly feeling rushed back, in a black tide, leaving her shaking and gasping. "Oh, Vykk!" she babbled. "I was in his *mind*, Teroenza's *mind*, and it was terrible! No Divine Gift, just a bored, selfish sentient who wants to get richer so he can add to his collection!"

"Take it easy," he said, holding her shoulders to steady her. "You've had an awful shock."

"I feel . . . I feel . . . so . . . betrayed," Bria got out, between chattering teeth. "It was . . . terrible . . ."

"Hey, there, sweetheart . . ." His arms went around her, and the expression of sympathy was her undoing. Bria began to sob, huge, gulping, wracking sobs that *hurt*. Vykk helped her take her goggles off, then he just held her, stroking her hair, patting her back, murmuring soothing reassurances and endearments.

She held on to the front of his coverall with both hands, twisting and wringing the fabric, and weeping so hard she scared herself. Bria had never cried like this before. The sense of desolation was terrible.

"I . . . don't . . . have anything left," she choked out between spasms of crying. "Nothing . . . nothing . . ."

"Of course you do," Vykk murmured, kissing her cheek gently. "You've got us, right?"

"Uh . . . us?" she whispered.

"Sure. We're gonna be together, sweetheart. We're gonna get off this hellish planet, and we're gonna be happy."

She raised her head, staring blindly into the darkness; her night-sight could barely make out the lighter blur of his face. "But they never let pilgrims go," Bria mumbled. "I read that in Teroenza's mind."

"We won't *ask* 'em, honey. We'll just up and *go*."

"Escape?" she whispered.

"You got it," he said. "As soon as I can figure out a way to do it, we're gonna get out of here. I've already begun thinkin' about it." He gave her a quick kiss on her cheek. "Trust me. I've had experience at this kind of thing. I'll figure it out."

"But . . . but your money," she said. "You're under contract, and you can't break it. If you run away, you'll lose your money. You told me you needed those credits they're paying you to try and get into the Academy. How can you give that up?"

He shrugged. "One credit is as good as another. I'll just have to get it outta Teroenza another way."

Bria's mind was fogged with exhaustion and the grief of betrayal. It took her a full minute to realize what Vykk was talking about. "The collection . . ." she whispered. "You're planning to steal Teroenza's collection and escape."

"Pretty good," he said approvingly. "You sure you're not still having some of those glitterstim insights?"

"I don't think so," Bria said wearily. "I just know that you've asked me about it a lot of times, asked me what items are the most valuable. You really think you can break the security locks and steal the collection?"

"Not the whole thing," he said. "It'd take a bigger cargo

ship than any on Ylesia to haul it all away. I'm just gonna take the small stuff—the really valuable small stuff." He looked at her intently. "And you're gonna help me, right?"

She hesitated. Stealing antiquities was contrary to everything she'd ever believed in. But Teroenza's antiquities weren't in a museum, where the public could see them. They were being hoarded by a greedy private collector. If Vykk stole them, they'd be put back into circulation, and there was a good chance that at least some of them *would* wind up on public display in some store or gallery.

"Okay," Bria said. She drew a long, shaky breath. "I'll help you, Vykk."

"Good. You and me, we're gonna swipe a ship, and we're getting ourselves off this planet. I'm sick of the heat, sick of the humidity, and sick to death of these priests and their hokey religion."

Bria took a deep breath. *Leave here? Never attend devotion and receive the Exultation again? How can I live without it?*

Resolutely, she put the question out of her mind. She'd manage somehow. Maybe she could wean herself away from it over the next week or so, until they left.

"There's just one more thing, Vykk," she said uncertainly.

"What, sweetheart?"

"Muuurgh. What about Muuurgh? You told me that he'd given his word to guard you—that he's as much your guard as your protector. What will you do about him?"

Vykk drew a long breath, and she saw the blur of his face move as he shook his head. "That's the vrelt in the kitchen," he said, using an old Corellian phrase for "bad luck" or "disaster." "I don't know what I'm going to do about him. I really like the big guy, but he's told me about this word of honor code of his people. I'm afraid he'll be loyal to Teroenza no matter what."

"You mean if he finds out what we're planning, he'll turn us in?"

"Good chance of it."

"Oh, Vykk . . ." There was a catch in her voice. "What are we going to do? What if we can't get away?"

"Don't worry, honey. Leave that to me." Vykk sighed. "If I have to, I'll deal with Muuurgh. I'm a better shot than he is, and much faster on the draw."

"You'd *shoot* him?"

"If it's a choice between you and me, or Muuurgh, yeah, I will. I just wish I could convince him to throw in with us. If he did, I'd take him wherever he wanted to go. And give him enough credits to continue his search."

"Search?"

"Yeah. He's looking for his mate, and he came here thinking she came to Ylesia. But he guessed wrong. Togorians are rare, so rare that I'd never even heard of 'em till I got here. If a female Togorian was here, she'd stick out like a sore thumb."

Bria drew in her breath, startled. "But . . . Vykk! There *was* another Togorian here! I remember seeing one—oh, six, maybe eight months back. I just caught the one glimpse, but I'm sure of the species."

"Really? Was it a male or female? What'd it look like?"

"I have no idea what sex," she said. "I don't think this Togorian was as big as Muuurgh. It was white, with orange stripes . . . I think. I saw it one evening, just after devotions, and it was getting dark."

"I'll have to tell Muuurgh," Vykk said. "Those priests lie for a living. It's entirely possible Mrrov—I think that's her name—has been here on Ylesia the whole time. Maybe at Colony Two or Three."

He fell silent. Bria stood there, mulling over what he'd just said, and finally, she couldn't stand it any longer. "Please, Vykk," she pleaded, "tell me you didn't mean that about shooting Muuurgh if he tries to prevent us from stealing Teroenza's collection! There's got to be a way to avoid that!" Bria *liked* Muuurgh. Over the past couple of months she'd gotten to know him a little, and she admired the big felinoid.

"I'll take care of him, whatever it takes. If I have to, I'll shoot him." Vykk's voice was grim. "But maybe I can just . . . stun him, or give him a knock on that thick skull of his, leave him tied up, so the priests won't blame him when we make our getaway."

"Oh, Vykk . . ." Bria's eyes filled with tears again. "Please try to figure out something, so Muuurgh doesn't get hurt. You're good at that."

"I will, sweetheart," he said, "I will . . ."

He leaned forward to drop a quick kiss on her forehead, and this time she did not remind him of her vows. *I have no vows,* Bria thought dully as they began walking back toward her dorm. *No vows, no religion . . . nothing at all . . .*

She glanced sideways in the darkness.

Nothing except Vykk . . .

Muuurgh glided soundlessly out of the jungle and stepped onto the path. The Togorian's night-vision was far better than a human's; he could easily make out the distant pair walking down the path. They were almost to the dorm.

The felinoid had been creeping through the jungle with exaggerated care for the past couple of minutes, determined to get close enough to overhear their whispered conversation. The Togorian had only managed to get close enough to catch the tail end of what they'd been discussing—but he'd heard enough.

Pilot and Bria were planning to escape. They were planning to steal from his masters. Pilot was planning to "take care" of Muuurgh.

The Togorian shook his massive head unhappily. Muuurgh had given his word of honor to his masters—his course *should* be clear. But it wasn't.

He knew well enough what he *should* do. He should go to Teroenza tomorrow morning and tell him what he'd overheard. Or perhaps he, Muuurgh, should kill Pilot himself and tell the priest why after the deed was done.

But he stood there, hesitating. It was obvious that Pilot was desperate enough to shoot him to get away. Muuurgh had given his word of honor to guard Pilot.

But Pilot was also Vykk . . . and Muuurgh had come to

think of Vykk as a friend. Vykk was determined to protect his female. Muuurgh could understand that. He'd do almost anything to protect Mrrov . . . if he could only find her . . .

Muuurgh growled, low in his throat. Perhaps he should pretend to be friendly, so that Pilot would allow him to get close enough to use his teeth and claws. Muuurgh was an expert hunter. Once he'd gotten hold of his prey, there was no escape.

Could he kill Vykk to keep his word of honor?

Muuurgh growled again and turned back into the jungle. Tonight he would hunt, and he would kill. He would tear open and consume his fresh prey. Perhaps that would clear his mind, and then he would be able to decide what to do . . .

Muuurgh glided beneath the giant trees, as silent and invisible as a wraith . . .

Chapter Nine:
Lost and Found

The next morning Han whistled cheerfully as he showered, and even rubbing the nasty-smelling anti-fungal gray goo over himself couldn't depress him. He and Bria were getting off this world, and they'd have plenty of credits once they sold the stolen items from Teroenza's collection. Han would be able to pay for his new ID, food, and lodging while he took the exams to get into the Academy.

And when we got out, he'd be an officer, a respected man, and Bria would be waiting for him . . .

Rubbing his wet hair with a towel, he headed for his clothes, which were lying across the foot of his bunk.

He had no warning, none at all. One moment he was walking, the next something had grabbed him and flung him to the floor so hard it knocked the wind out of him. Han gasped like a beached whaladon and spots danced before his eyes.

But there was something else, there, too . . . holding him down, something that had one gigantic hand pressing his chest. Instinctively, Han lay still, gasping and finding breath, realizing that hand could crush him like a dilga-nut.

Blackness swam before his eyes—no, the blackness was real. Real and furry, with a white spot in the middle of its chest and bristling white whiskers. Han managed to focus his eyes. "Muuurgh . . . ?" he gasped feebly. "Wha's goin' on . . . ?"

Muuurgh snarled into Han's face, his huge fangs so close that Han could see them gleam with saliva. "Pilot planning to escape, take Bria," he growled. "Vykk planning to *steal* from Ylesian masters. Vykk planning to *take care* of Muuurgh . . ."

"But—" The hand pressed down, slightly, and Han subsided, eyes bulging.

Muuurgh raised a massive paw-hand and flexed it slightly. Scimitarlike claws extruded. "Now treacherous Pilot will die," the Togorian snarled.

"No!" Han put up his hands in a gesture of appeal. "Please! Just listen!"

"Muuurgh listened last night. Muuurgh heard plenty," the Togorian said grimly.

"Hey, pal!" Han babbled, imagining what those claws would do to his exposed throat. "I thought we were friends!"

"Muuurgh liked Pilot. Muuurgh is sorry to have to kill Pilot. But word of honor was given. No choice for Muuurgh."

The hand started down. Han squeezed his eyes shut and waited for the end.

He felt the breeze of the Togorian's swing graze his cheek, his throat, but nothing touched him. After several eternities, Han opened his eyes again. Muuurgh was staring down at him, plainly torn.

Finally, he grabbed Han by the shoulder and hair, jerked him to his feet, and pushed him in the direction of the Corellian's clothes. "Get dressed! Muuurgh not want Pilot's blood on his claws. We go to tell Teroenza what Pilot and

girl are planning. Priest will tell other guards to kill trai-
tors."

Han hastened over to the bunk, and began dragging on
his clothes. At least he wouldn't die naked and wet. "Listen,
Muuurgh," he said, "you've gotta listen to me. Please! What
can it hurt?"

"Pilot lies. Muuurgh knows he lies. Muuurgh—*I will not
listen.*"

That's a good sign that he's regaining his cool, Han
thought. *The grammar I taught him is coming back.*

Sealing the front of his coverall, Han sat down on the
edge of the bunk to pull on his boots. "Your people have a
code of honor, right?" he said, thinking as fast as he'd ever
thought in his life.

"Yes."

"If you give your word of honor to someone who's em-
ploying you, you've got to keep it, right?"

"Yes. Pilot can move faster than that. Put on those
boots."

Han slowly inserted his right foot, toes pointed down,
and began to pull the boot on. "Well, pal, suppose you gave
your word of honor to someone and found that everything
he told you was a lie on his part of the contract. What does
that do to your agreement? Do you have to keep your word
to someone who's lied to you and made a fool out of you?"

Muuurgh eyed Han suspiciously, but said nothing.

"C'mon, pal, what's your code of honor say about making
agreements with liars, eh?"

Muuurgh shook his massive head, then his ears flattened
in anger. "If a Togorian makes a word of honor with a liar,
contract is void. There is no honor to be had dealing with a
liar."

"All right," Han said with a surge of satisfaction. He
picked up his left boot. "Listen to me, pal. I think Mrrov is
here, on Ylesia. I think Teroenza lied to you."

Muuurgh stared at Han, then his blue eyes narrowed.
"You would lie to stay alive, Vykk."

"Yeah, I would, pal," Han said honestly. "But I swear to
you I ain't lying about this."

"Swear? What is this 'swear'?"

"It's . . . like a word of honor, sort of," Han said. "My people swear by the most important thing in the world to them. It's like . . . sacred, I guess you'd say."

"So what does Vykk swear by?"

Han thought for a moment. "I swear," he said, slowly and distinctly, "by Bria's life. You know I care for her . . . a lot. Don't you?"

Muuurgh considered for a moment, then nodded.

"Okay, then, I swear to you, on Bria's life, that last night she told me she saw a Togorian here, six months or more ago. That would tie in with the time you were searching for Mrrov, wouldn't it?"

Silently the Togorian nodded again.

"She saw a Togorian, Muuurgh. Ask her yourself. Teroenza and his goons lied to you when they said she never came here. She's probably still here, on Ylesia. Probably not here at Colony One, 'cause that's too risky. But there's a good chance she's at Colony Two . . . or maybe even Three. But Colony Two has been there longer, they've got a lot more pilgrims there than at Colony Three. So I'm betting she's at Colony Two. It's worth checking out, isn't it?"

"What did she look like?" Muuurgh asked slowly.

For a moment Han was tempted to lie, say he didn't know, because what if he was wrong about the Togorian being Mrrov, and Muuurgh got mad and killed him right here and now? He took a deep breath. "Bria said she was white and some other color. Striped. She thought they might be orange stripes, but she said it was almost dark, so she's not sure."

I sure hope Mrrov wasn't solid-colored or spotted!

Muuurgh's ears flattened, and he hissed like a leaky valve, teeth bared ferociously. Han desperately looked around for something to brain the Togorian with, but there wasn't a thing in reach. Silently he resigned himself to being ripped in two.

Then Muuurgh's furious hiss mutated into a pain-filled yowl of anguish. The big alien sank to the floor, clutching his head and yowling in an ululating keen. "You have described her!" he growled, finally. "By all the gods of my fathers, can she have been here all these days, while I *believed* those liars? I will go now to tear their throats out and *eat* their hearts!"

"Whew," Han muttered softly. *I'm glad that worked!*

Muuurgh leaped to his feet, obviously ready to make good on his threat.

"Wait!" Han leaped up and grabbed one huge arm, hung on as he was dragged across the floor, through the living room, almost to the door. He dug his heels in and refused to let go. "Muuurgh, if you want her back, *stop!*"

Muuurgh slowed, then stopped. "Good," Han said, panting. "Now let's talk about this like rational sentients, okay? Sit down."

Muuurgh sank down onto his pallet. Han switched on some music, then pulled his beat-up chair so close to the Togorian that they were nearly touching. "Talk low," he whispered, and Muuurgh nodded.

"I've got a plan," Han said. "I think I know how to get her, if she's still here on Ylesia." *I just hope they haven't shipped her off to the spice mines,* he thought, but he didn't say it aloud. Muuurgh knew what happened to the slaves as well as he did, by now.

"Okay, Vykk," Muuurgh said, equally softly, "tell me the plan."

Han thought a moment. "I'm going to need your help for some of this. I've got some preparations to make, and I'll try to get everything possible set up before I leave."

"Leave? Vykk is leaving?"

"Yes, but I'm not talking about our final escape. In a couple of days I've got to deliver a message and a gift from Zavval to a Hutt named Jiliac on Nal Hutta. I'm supposed to stay there and wait for a reply. I've never been to Nal Hutta, and I don't know the drill there, but Jalus Nebl has."

Muuurgh nodded to show he was listening, and nervously began to groom his white whiskers.

"So, okay. The *Dream* is really too small for three. I'm gonna point that out to Teroenza and tell him Nebl wants to get back into flying again as my copilot. I'm pretty sure he'll agree to let me and Nebl fly this mission together. I'm gonna suggest that you stay here, 'cause there won't be room for you."

Han got up and began pacing back and forth as he thought. "The priests know you like to hunt, right? So when I get permission to take Nebl with me, you should request to spend a couple of days hunting. You can move fast over rough ground, right?"

"Very fast," agreed the Togorian. "Fast enough to track and kill prey."

"Do you think you could make it on foot to Colony Two?"

"Yes." Muuurgh sounded positive.

"Well, it's our best shot. If Mrrov is still here on Ylesia, there's a better than fifty–fifty chance that she's at Colony Two. You should go there and scout it out, find out if she's there."

"And rescue her!" Muuurgh leaped to his feet.

"*No!*" Han snapped. "Sit *down*. That would be the worst thing to do. They'd start a planet-wide search for the two of you. They'd use sensors tuned to Togorian readings to pinpoint you. Then you'd be captured and probably killed. Or sent to the mines of Kessel, which amounts to the same thing."

"You want Muuurgh to see Mrrov, and not let her see him?"

"Exactly. Just find her, scout out where she sleeps, eats, stuff like that. Then, when we make our getaway, you and me will hop over to Colony Two and break her outta there. I've been doing some late-night scouting around this place, in case you haven't noticed."

"Muuurgh noticed," the Togorian said dryly. "Everywhere Vykk went, Muuurgh was behind him, watching. Why do you think I knew to listen when you walked Bria back to her dorm?"

"Well, anyway, I've figured out how to create a diversion that'll keep the guards busy while we get the best stuff out of the collection. And I know where the communications center is. I'll make sure that communications between the colonies are down by the time we get outta here. We'll hop over to Colony Two, and before they know what's happening, we'll grab Mrrov and be hightailing it off this planet. Then I'll take you both back to Togoria, okay?"

Muuurgh looked at Han, his blue eyes narrowing, whiskers twitching with emotion. "You would do this for Muuurgh and Mrrov?"

"Yes. I swear it. If you help me and Bria break into and steal Teroenza's stuff, I swear to you we won't leave without Mrrov."

The big Togorian thought about that for a long time, then his eyes met Han's. "I will do it," he said. "Word of honor."

Han nodded. "It's a deal, pal."

That same evening, Han went over to Teroenza's treasure room to find Bria. He was wondering if she'd be attending devotions now that she knew they were faked. Standing outside, he knocked on the heavy, metal-sheathed door. "It's me," he called in response to her voice from inside.

The door opened, and Bria stepped out. Han's eyes widened. "Hey! You look *great*!"

For the first time since he'd known her, she'd doffed her bulky tan robes and concealing cap. Instead, she was wearing a simple pale blue tunic and trousers. Although modest in style, they revealed a figure that was slender but definitely female.

"Exalted Teroenza told me I could dispense with my pilgrim robes while I was working on the collection," she told him. When she saw the warmth in his eyes, she blushed a little, but smiled. "He was afraid that I'd catch my robes on some valuable artifact and knock it off a shelf."

"Well, I approve," Han said. "Want to get a cup of tea?"

"Sure."

When they were seated in the mess hall, with cups of stim-tea before them, Bria smiled shyly at Han. "So . . . you really like the way I look?"

"You bet," he said. "You're the prettiest girl on this planet, no kidding."

She smiled, then the smile faded, and she looked troubled. "You're apparently not the only one who thinks so, Vykk . . ."

"What do you mean?"

"I had the strangest exchange with Ganar Tos, Teroenza's majordomo, this morning. He'd apparently never seen beyond the pilgrim robes, but when I put these clothes on, he really noticed me. He followed me around for about an hour while I was trying to get some rearranging done, making conversation—or trying to. Those orangy-red eyes of his gave me chills. He's old, but it's obvious he still has . . . um . . . plenty of life in him, if you get my meaning. *Male* life."

Han sat back. "You mean, that old creep was coming on to you?"

She shivered. "I'm afraid so. He wanted to know how old I was, whether I was ever married, whether I had any children. He asked me why I'd wound up coming to Ylesia to be a pilgrim. *Very* personal questions! He had a lot of nerve."

Han leaned forward. "So why *did* you come here? Or do you consider that too personal to tell me, too?"

She smiled wanly at him. "Of course not, Vykk. Why'd I come here? It seems so long ago, it's hard to even remember. I was going through a bad time. I'd just finished kid's school, and was kind of scared at the idea of going to the university. I'd never been on my own before.

"My mother always kept a tight rein and made me feel as though I could never do anything right. Studying hard and behaving myself weren't enough for her." She smiled, but it was not a nice smile. "My father encouraged me to have a career, but all Mother could think about was my making a 'brilliant match.' She thought her dreams had come true when I started seeing Dael."

Han felt a stab of jealousy, but reminded himself that there had been other girls in his past. More than a few, matter of fact . . .

"We were on the verge of getting engaged when I caught him sneaking around with another girl. So I told him it was over. My mother was furious with me for breaking up with Dael. He came from one of the richest families on Corellia, and she'd already begun planning the wedding." She sighed. "She ordered me to go to him and apologize, get him to take me back. For the first time in my life, I told her 'no.'"

"She sounds like a very . . . determined . . . woman," Han said cautiously.

"Determined isn't the word. Mother had pushed me at Dael ever since we were in school together, and I didn't have the courage to tell her that I didn't like him that much. It's funny"—her blue-green eyes grew misty—"I didn't much want Dael, but when I knew he'd been sneaking around with someone else, I felt betrayed and heartbroken. People are strange, aren't they?"

Han nodded. "Go on," he said encouragingly.

"Well, just about that time, I heard about a revival that was being held by a Ylesian missionary. I was feeling pretty down on myself, because I just knew I couldn't do anything right. Uprooted, you know? Cut off from everyone.

"So I went to the revival. The Ylesian priest finished his service with just a few seconds of Exultation—and it made me feel so *good*. Like I *belonged* with those people. So I sold my jewelry, ran away, and caught the next ship for Ylesia."

She smiled wistfully. "So that's my story. And to return to the subject at hand, what do you think I should do to keep poor old Ganar Tos at arm's length?"

"Well, if he bugs you too much, mention it to Teroenza. I'm sure he doesn't want anything to interfere with your work, and if Ganar Tos is doing that, then he'll put a stop to it."

"Okay," she said, cheering up. "That's a good idea."

"Are you going to devotions?" Han asked, giving her a significant glance.

She shook her head. "No. I don't want to."

"Won't they notice when you don't go?"

"I can always say I had a headache or was working late. Most of the pilgrims can't *wait* to go, so they don't keep tabs on who's there."

"That's true. How about a walk, then?"

"Sure."

When they were outside, Han walked them clear to the Flowered Plains before he broached the subject on his mind. Quickly he summarized that morning's interaction with Muuurgh. Bria was alarmed to realize that the Togorian had been listening to them last night, and said so.

"Yeah, me, too," Han replied. "That big guy can be real quiet when he wants to be. No wonder he says he's the best hunter on this planet. He's apparently been following me the whole time I was scouting out the lay of this place, and figuring out the best way to get us out of here."

"We'd better be careful where we are when we're discussing escape plans," she said, glancing nervously around.

"Why do you think I walked us clear out here before I even brought up the subject? The trees have ears around here. We've gotta be real careful. Last night it was only Muuurgh, so we're okay, but it coulda been one of the skin-changers they've got as guards down in the glitterstim factory."

She shivered at the thought. "So what did you have to tell me?"

"Muuurgh's going to ask to go on a hunting trip while Jalus Nebl and I make the run to Nal Hutta. We've got it all set up. Teroenza approved me taking Nebl with me today. Nal Hutta's two systems away, and it'll take us four days, maybe five. I promised Muuurgh he'd have that long to find out if Mrrov is still here, and that, if she is, we'll take her with us."

"That would be good," Bria said. "I hated the idea of leaving Muuurgh behind. If Teroenza got angry enough, he'd probably kill him for letting us escape, whether Muuurgh was responsible or not."

"Right." Han sighed. "I just wish I could figure out a way to break into Teroenza's living quarters and search the place until I found where he keeps those ship access codes

and the security lock codes for the collection. So far, I'm
stumped. I've figured out a way to keep the guards busy,
but if I can't get those codes, I may have to change my
plans. I might have to set the Welcome Center on fire or
something."

"Security codes?" Bria frowned and closed her eyes.
"Security codes . . ." She drew a deep breath, then began
reciting a string of numbers, symbols, and letters.

"That sounds like it!" Han grabbed her arm in excitement. "How'd you get them?"

She gave him a tremulous smile. "They were in Teroenza's mind. I'm afraid they're burned into mine, along
with everything else. I wish I *could* forget them—and all
that other stuff—but I can't."

He grabbed her shoulders and gave them an ecstatic little shake. "Well, don't wish that till we're off this mudhole.
Bria, honey, this is great! You've saved me a lotta trouble!"

She smiled at him shakily. "I paid an awful price for it,
but if it helps us . . . I guess it was worth it."

"It will be," Han promised. "Trust me. I swear it will
be."

She nodded.

"So all we have to do is avoid arousing suspicion until
we're ready to make the break. That's gonna be easy for
me—Nebl and I will be off-world. Think you can manage
to just do business as usual here till we get back?"

"I think so," she said. "But . . . hurry back!"

"I will, sweetheart," he said.

Bria gave Han a pleading look. "After we're free, could
we go to Corellia, Vykk? I want to see my folks again. I
want to let them know I'm all right."

Han gave her a reassuring smile. "Sure, sweetheart. I've
got some business to take care of on Corellia, so that'll be
one of our first stops, okay?"

She gave him a radiant answering smile. "Okay."

When Vykk left her at the door to her dorm, Bria told
herself that she'd just go upstairs and take a nap until it was

time to go to dinner. If anyone asked, she'd plead a head-ache as an excuse for missing devotions.

But when she reached her room, she picked up her pilgrim's robe and cap and stood holding them. *Tomorrow,* she thought. *I'll start tomorrow. After all, I've had a rough couple of days. Nobody could expect me to miss the Exultation just like that. I need a day to work myself up to it . . .*

And before she knew what she was doing, Bria found herself back in her robes and cap, hurrying down the Path of Immortality, toward the Altar of Promises . . .

Two days later a jittery Han and a placid Jalus Nebl stood waiting outside Jiliac the Hutt's audience room in his Winter Palace. A small holo-recording device rested at Han's feet; it was designed to project a visual and audio simulacrum of the sender. Nebl was steadying a large, elaborate box on an anti-grav lifter. The box contained the gift Zavval the Hutt had sent to his business associate, and sometime rival, Jiliac.

"Wonder how much longer we'll have to wait?" Han muttered nervously, pacing a bit. "It's been almost an hour."

"For an audience with a clan leader, this is nothing," Jalus Nebl said. "Once I waited two days to even reach the antechamber. And don't forget, we've got to wait for a reply. Once I waited a week."

"Don't tell me that," Han grumbled. "I don't want to hear about everything that can go wrong. I'm still skeptical that we're gonna walk out of this place alive. Hutts are notoriously bad-tempered, y'know."

"I already told you, we're perfectly safe," the Sullustan replied.

"Forgive me if I'm being dense, by *why* can you be so sure of that?" Han snapped.

"Long ago, in the early days of their coming to Nal Hutta, Hutts lost so many messengers that communications between the clans completely broke down, and everyone lost profit because of it," Nebl explained. "So all the clans made a sworn pact—a messenger from one Hutt to another is sacrosanct. While we're delivering Zavval's message, and taking back his reply, we cannot be touched or interfered with in any way."

"Yeah, I sure hope you're right," Han mumbled. He looked over at the big box. "I thought Zavval was mad at Jiliac," he whispered. "So how come he's sending him a gift?"

Nebl shook his head. "Gifts are traditional. To gain a Hutt's attention, you must either present him with a gift or threaten him or her. Sometimes Hutts do both at the same time."

Han grimaced. "Weird. You sure you don't have any idea what's in there? That box is big enough to hold most anything. Even a body, if you folded it up. I'd feel better if I knew."

"The box is sealed," Nebl pointed out. "If we open it, His Excellency Jiliac will know. We don't want any trouble."

"Yeah . . . I know." Han grimaced and, to distract himself from his worries, looked around.

The antechamber was high-ceilinged, with skylights. It was built of light-colored stone, and the pale walls were hung with tapestries woven (it was said) by Jiliac's enemies while they languished in his dungeons, waiting for the mercy of execution. One depicted the original Hutt homeworld, the desolate and barren planet Varl, and another the great cataclysm that destroyed it long, long ago. Still another showed the great Hutt diaspora to Nal Hutta in the Y'Toub system. Nal Hutta, Han knew, meant "glorious jewel" in Huttese.

The last tapestry was a full-sized portrait of Jiliac himself, reclining in state upon his lavishly appointed but tasteful dais.

Han hadn't seen much of Nal Hutta, since he and Nebl had been whisked into a droid-chauffeured landspeeder and taken south, to Jiliac's remote Winter Palace. The Hutt Lord's retreat was located on a small island near the equator. Jalus Nebl had informed Han that he was lucky, that this island was, by comparison with the rest of Nal Hutta, a virtual "garden spot" on this dank and noisome world.

This island reminded him of Ylesia—hot, humid, and full of giant trees choked with huge vines.

Han's attention jerked back to the here and now when he realized that Dorzo, Jiliac's Rodian majordomo, was beckoning to them. "His Supreme Excellency Jiliac, clan leader and protector of the righteous, will see you now."

Hastily Han picked up his recorder, and then he and Nebl walked into the audience chamber.

It was huge. Han paced up the central aisle toward the dais, feeling the luxurious pile of an expensive carpet beneath his boots. The chamber was filled with fawning sycophants of all races, tastefully garbed dancing girls and boys, and an orchestra off in one corner. A massive buffet table heaped with food from a dozen worlds made his nostrils twitch as Han suddenly recalled that he'd forgotten to eat lunch.

Jiliac reclined at his ease on an audience dais, smoking something that Han couldn't identify, but which he wanted no part of. Even the faint whiff he got of the expelled smoke made his head swim.

Jalus Nebl nudged Han, and he nervously stepped forward. "Almighty Jiliac," he said in Huttese, recalling the speech Zavval had rehearsed with him, "we come from our Ylesian master Zavval the Hutt to bring you a message and a gift. First, the gift . . ." He beckoned to Nebl, and the Sullustan, as agreed, stepped forward.

Jiliac peered down at them, then ordered, in Huttese, "Open it. I wish to see what Zavval deems worthy of me."

"Yes, Your Excellency," squeaked the Sullustan, who set about slitting all the seals and releasing all the catches.

Han watched in fascination as the Sullustan raised the lid on the box and withdrew two crystalline globes with bronze supports, which he balanced one upon the other, and then placed the entire contraption upon a sturdy, curved bronze stand.

All of the metal was chased with gold and silver designs. There was a small housing on the back of the bottom globe that contained some kind of battery, Han thought. The Corellian stared at the thing in perplexity. He had no idea what the device was.

Jiliac did, however. "A combination hookah and snack-quarium!" he boomed, speaking, of course, in Huttese, which Han by this time understood very well. "And one almost worthy of our greatness! Just what I wanted! How did he know?" He turned his attention back to the two messengers and continued, more formally, "Messengers, Zavval's gift pleases me. Let us hope his message does, as well. Activate it, human."

Han bowed low, set the recorder on a low table, and switched it on. Immediately a holo-simulacrum of Zavval appeared, filling the space before Jiliac's dais. "My dear Jiliac," Zavval said, stretching out a hand toward Jiliac, as though he could see the other and were really present. "Over the past year, some unfortunate occurrences have plagued our shipping operations out of Ylesia. Ships have disappeared, and one ship was attacked. As one of the heads of our Kajidier, it was my duty to trace down these despicable incursions."

Jiliac's pleased expression had faded. Han cast a nervous glance at the Sullustan. *I sure hope he's right about us being safe!*

"We have traced these so-called 'pirates' to Nar Shaddaa, and recently my operatives have captured and questioned one of the captains of these vessels. This unfortunate individual revealed—before succumbing to a weak heart—that he was recruited and sent upon his villainous missions by *you* and your great-nephew, Jabba. Your enmity wounds us deeply—and what is more important, cuts into our profit margin. Be warned, Jiliac. Leave our shipments alone. Any more attacks will meet with swift reprisal upon you and your clan. We have assembled a great fleet, which will surely vanquish your paltry forces."

We have? thought Han wildly. *There's just me and Nebl! Zavval's bluffing. Or did he recently hire more pilots?*

Zavval's message continued, inexorably, "Accept our gift as a peace offering, or meet with grim consequences—

among which your own death will be the least. Jiliac, I appeal to you in the name of Hutt brotherhood to cease hijacking and terrorizing our vessels. We can make a much better profit if we work together, instead of contending with each other."

By this time, Han and the Sullustan were backing away in terror, because Jiliac was swelling up like a poisoned wound.

"Heed my warning, Jiliac. Cease your—"

"*AiiiiiieeeeeeeaaaaaaaarrrrrrrRRGGGGGGGGGGGGGHHH-HHHHHHHHHH!!!*"

Jiliac's scream of fury made Han and Nebl leap behind the buffet table. The Hutt Lord's tail lashed out in a giant sweep to strike the recording device, sending it flying. Zavval's image vanished.

Jiliac slid forward. Han watched in horrified fascination. It was the first time he'd seen a Hutt Lord move under his own power.

"Messengers!" Jiliac screamed. "Come forth!"

Slowly, reluctantly, Han and Nebl crawled around the edge of the table and got shakily to their feet. "Yes, Almighty Jiliac?" Nebl quavered. Han was incapable of speech.

"I send you back to that worm-ridden parasitical infestation who calls himself Zavval," Jiliac raged, tail lashing, as he moved back and forth. "Tell him he has maligned me and my kin, Jabba. Tell him this lack-witted attempt to incite me into a precipitous attack has failed utterly. I will bide my time. He is a dead Hutt, but for the moment, by my grace, he may pretend to be among the living. *I* alone will decide when he is to die—and it will be at my convenience. Do you understand, messengers?"

"Yes, Almighty One!" Han said, having recovered his voice. It was obvious that Jiliac was letting them go, and he wanted nothing more than to get off this world. He bowed, then bowed again. "I'll tell him *exactly* what you said!"

"Good! You may go. Take my message to Zavval—immediately!"

Bowing, Han and Nebl backed from the audience room.

Once outside, they hastily leaped into their transport and ordered the droid driver to return them to the spaceport immediately.

Han had never been so glad to see the *Ylesian Dream* waiting for him. He and Jalus Nebl ran across the landing field, scrambled up the ramp, and threw themselves into the control cabin.

Only when they were out in space, and Han was pulling the lever to send them streaking into hyperspace, did enough of his sense of humor return that he was able to grin feebly at the Sullustan. "Well, Nebl," he said, "that went well, didn't it?"

The Sullustan rolled his large, wet eyes. "You still don't understand, Vykk," he said. "When one is dealing with Hutts, there are wheels within wheels within wheels. It's entirely possible that Zavval sent that message because we *are* vulnerable, to keep Jiliac from attacking more openly. We're just underlings. We only see part of the picture. All you can do is pray to any gods you believe in that you never anger a Hutt. One would be better off dead, and that is no understatement."

Han nodded. "I believe you. Still, if I were Zavval, I wouldn't rest too easily at night. He may not have long to live . . ."

Muuurgh glided through the jungle in the dimness of the short Ylesian twilight. It had taken him a day and a half to travel the 147 kilometers to Colony Two. Part of his slowness had come from the perilous crossing of the Gachoogai River. He'd been so exhausted by struggling through the rapid current that he'd had to take two hours out of his trip to hunt and then another hour to sleep. He was still tired from his ordeal . . . but he was finally here.

He listened for the sounds of chanting voices as he skirted the perimeter of the compound. Colony Two followed, as far as he knew, the same schedule as Colony One, so the pilgrims should be at the evening devotions.

His nostrils flared as he tested the wind, constantly sniff-

ing for any Togorian spoor. Several times, Muuurgh got
down on his hands and knees and moved forward, sniffing,
drinking in the scents left by the pilgrims who had recently
passed this way.

Five minutes later he jerked as if he'd been hit with a
stun-prod. *Mrrov! Mrrov came this way, no more than a
day ago!* Wandering cautiously around the outskirts of the
buildings, he located first the dorm she slept in, then the
factory where she worked.

Lastly, he followed the freshest scent trail to a path that
he was sure must lead to the Altar of Promises. Apparently
Colony Two was laid out on a nearly identical plan to Colony One.

Without checking farther, the Togorian melted back into
the jungle and moved as quickly as he could toward the site
of the devotions. For a moment he wondered whether
Mrrov might scent *his* trail, but it was unlikely. He'd been
thoroughly soaked in that river, and had deliberately
avoided the instinct to rub against anything and leave scent
markers. He didn't want Mrrov to try following him back to
Colony One, and possibly becoming lost in the jungle when
his trail was interrupted by the river.

The Togorian arrived just in time to automatically resist
the mental and physical waves of the Exultation. Narrowing
his eyes, Muuurgh scanned the writhing forms in front of
him—

—and found Mrrov. She was twitching, but not really
writhing . . . and there was something false about the way
she moved that allowed him to pick her out easily.

She is faking, Muuurgh thought. *I knew Mrrov was too
strong-minded to be fooled by these liars for long!*

He strained his eyes to make out every line of her beneath her pilgrim's robe. But all he could see clearly was
her head, orange stripes contrasting vividly with the white.
He longed to see her lovely yellow eyes, but he was behind
her and to her right. She could not see him.

For a second, Muuurgh nearly threw caution and his
vow to Vykk to the winds—it was everything he could do

not to race into the crowd of pilgrims, grab his mate-to-be, and carry her off into the jungle.

But he had given Vykk his word of honor. Mrrov must not know he was here.

As the pilgrims staggered to their feet, the Exultation over, Muuurgh's eyes widened as he saw that Mrrov was wearing a blue sash—as were about fifty of the hundred or so pilgrims at the devotion.

That sash! That's the sash of the Chosen Ones! Oh, no! He could have hissed aloud in his frustration and fear. Muuurgh had been on Ylesia for many months. He'd seen those sashes before.

Sure enough, as the pilgrims began shuffling into the night, the High Priest stepped up to call out to them in his booming voice. "All pilgrims who were issued blue sashes today, please remain behind! Your High Priest has an announcement to make!"

Obediently, the pilgrims with blue sashes stopped walking toward the path and instead shuffled forward. Mrrov looked as though she was thinking of yanking off her sash and making a run for it, but she didn't. Muuurgh yowled inwardly. *Does she know what those sashes mean?*

"Those of you who have received these blue sashes are being honored as Chosen Ones. Your piety and devotion to the One and the All have caused us to select you for a singular honor. Tomorrow night will be your last devotion here at this Altar. At dawn on the following morning, you will be taken by spaceship to meet with our missionaries, and each of you will be selected by one of our missionaries to accompany him out to spread the word of the One and the All."

Muuurgh heard excited, greedy murmurings from the crowd, and knew the true pilgrims were ecstatic over the implication that they would be able to receive Exultations without sharing it with hundreds of other pilgrims.

Stupid . . . was the Togorian's first thought. *They are no better than* bist *or* etelo, *worthy only of being hunted and eaten. Those spaceships will take them only to the mines of Kessel or the pleasure-houses of the Imperial* soldiers. *They will receive no more Exultations, they will live in degradation and misery, and most of them will die within a year* . . .

His second thought raised the fur along his neck and spine. *Only a day and a half until they ship her out of here! Since the Imperial soldiers want only humanoids in their pleasure-houses, that must mean that Mrrov is destined for the mines on Kessel. They figure that since she is Togorian, and strong, she will last a long time in the mines* . . .

Muuurgh slammed a hand against a tree bole. *Curse them, I have little time! The Ylesian overlords will undoubtedly call upon Vykk or the Sullustan to ferry these pilgrims to the space station to await the Kessel transport that is coming. I must be back at Colony One to help Vykk, so we can all escape together!*

Muuurgh leaped to his feet and loped off through the jungle, feeling fear drive the fatigue from his body. He turned his face southeast, heading back for Colony One. There was no time to lose . . . Mrrov's very life hung in the balance.

The Togorian ran, leaping over logs and streams, ducking through low-lying bushes. His breath came easily, but he knew that would not last long. He was already travel-weary—but that could not be allowed to matter.

Like a black shadow in the blacker night, the Togorian ran . . .

Bria had just finished devotions and was heading for the path leading back to her dorm when Ganar Tos fell into step beside her. She stiffened, keeping her head down, and refused to look up. *I wish Vykk were back! He's been gone three days, now* . . . *Ganar Tos wouldn't be following me around like this if Vykk were here* . . .

The elderly Zisian reached out to grasp her arm, but Bria yanked it away. The majordomo smiled as he stepped forward, barring her path. "The Exalted One, Teroenza, wishes to speak with you, Pilgrim 921," he said.

Oh, no! she thought, feeling her heart seem to stop, then

slam in her chest so hard she was afraid Ganar Tos would actually hear it. *Teroenza has figured out that I was the one who telepathically probed his mind!*

"Wh-what does he want?" she managed to say, through stiff lips, wondering if she should just try to make a run for it. Perhaps she could hide out in the jungle for a day or so until Vykk returned . . .

"He has something to discuss with you," Tos said, smiling at her. Bria cringed from that smile, but she decided there was no point in running. The guards would only track her down and kill her . . .

So she turned and headed back toward the Altar of Promises.

When she reached Teroenza, the High Priest peered down at her as she made the proper obeisance. Bria's heart pounded, and she was so frightened she felt light-headed, dizzy.

"Pilgrim 921," Teroenza addressed her in his booming voice, "you have served us faithfully, and I am pleased with you. I am also pleased with my loyal servant, Ganar Tos. I wish to reward both of you."

Bria glanced sideways at the Zisian, whose orange eyes were practically glowing with happiness. *Oh, no. I have a bad feeling about this* . . .

Teroenza indicated the majordomo. "Ganar Tos has asked me for your hand in marriage, and I am pleased to grant his request. Stand before me, and I will pronounce the words to make you his wife."

Bria gasped and wondered if she should let herself faint. She felt as though she might be able to do it—black spots swam before her eyes, and her ears rang. Then she felt a wash of pleasure engulf her, such exquisite pleasure that she almost passed out from that. The pleasure was so intense, so warm, so loving, that she might almost have agreed to anything, just to have it continue.

But just as she was about to nod like a pliant zombie, Vykk's face swam before her eyes. Bria's spine stiffened, and her chin came up. She didn't dare faint—if she did, she'd likely wake up married to Ganar Tos and being carried back to their nuptial bed. The thought made her gag, and the priest's pleasure-vibes lost their power over her. Bria experienced a sudden, vivid image of herself sharing a bed with Ganar Tos, and for an awful second she was afraid she might be sick.

Control yourself! she commanded. *Think!*

"But, Exalted One," she murmured timidly, forcing herself to keep her eyes modestly downcast, "I have taken vows of chastity. I cannot marry anyone."

"Your piety does you credit, Pilgrim," Teroenza boomed. "And yet, the One and All bless fruitful unions, just as much as they bless the celibate state. I am granting you a special dispensation so that you may marry Ganar Tos and raise your children to be faithful to the One and the All."

Clever old monster, Bria thought, hating Teroenza as she'd never hated anyone before in her life. *There's no way around his argument without my committing blasphemy.*

She took a long, deep breath, to give herself time to think. "Very well, Exalted One," she said meekly. "If you say this is the will of the One and the All, I must bow to it. I will be a good wife to Ganar Tos." Gritting her teeth inwardly, she forced herself to lay her hand on his warty green arm.

"Good, Pilgrim," Teroenza said, raising his arms to begin the ceremony.

"*But,* Exalted One," Bria raised her voice slightly, "I must follow the customs of my own people before I can consider myself legally married." Before the priest could refuse her, she hurried on, "They are simple, and easily fulfilled, Exalted One. I ask for but a day to purify myself and meditate upon the sacred state of marriage. Also, on Corellia, it is traditional for a woman to wear a green gown to her wedding. I can easily ask the tailor droid to prepare one for me by tomorrow evening."

Bria held her breath as Teroenza hesitated. Finally, the High Priest must have decided that she wasn't asking for that much. "Very well, Pilgrim 921," he boomed. Ganar Tos's face fell. "Tomorrow evening, before the entire assembly, you and Ganar Tos shall be joined. May the blessing of the One and the All be upon you."

Teroenza sketched a quick sign in the air, and then turned and lumbered away.

Ganar Tos headed purposefully for Bria. "I will walk you back to your dorm," he said.

"Very well," she agreed, but she pulled away when he tried to put an arm around her. "The groom must not touch the bride during the last day before the ceremony," she cooed, lying through her teeth. "Another Corellian tradition. Surely you can wait one short day, my groom-to-be?"

He nodded shortly. "Very well, wife-to-be. I swear to you, I will be a good husband. It is my fondest wish that we will be blessed with many children."

"That is my fondest wish, too," Bria said sweetly. Within the voluminous sleeves of her robes, she crossed all the fingers of both hands.

Please, Vykk, she thought frantically, *hurry back! Please!*

Chapter Ten:

FAREWELL TO PARADISE?

Han and Nebl made good time on their return trip, and Han guided the *Ylesian Dream* down through the clouds on the nightside. They saw several spectacular storm cells lit up from within by lightning, but when they landed at Colony One an hour or so past midnight in the short Ylesian night, it was not, for a miracle, raining. Jalus Nebl turned to Han and commented, "Nice landing. I can't say I've ever done better."

Han smiled at the praise and was still grinning happily as they came down the ramp and onto the landing field. Both he and the Sullustan had to hastily don their infrared goggles—the night was dead-black, and not a single star was visible.

"Well, I'm off to get a few hours of sleep, lad," the Sullustan said as he turned to head for the infirmary, where he was still under treatment, though he was no longer having to breathe filtered air. "Good night."

"Night, Nebl," Han answered, and he turned, yawning, toward the path that led to the Administration Center. *My bunk's gonna feel awful good,* he thought. *Think I'll sleep in and—*

Without warning, something large grabbed him from behind, and a furred paw-hand clamped over his mouth to stifle his yell of surprise. Han gasped as he was lifted clean off the path and carried a few steps into the jungle. Then a familiar voice breathed into his ear, "Muuurgh is sorry to have to do that, but Vykk was going to yell. We must be quiet."

The Togorian set the Corellian on his feet again, and Han took a deep breath, preparatory to giving the giant alien a good scolding about not scaring people on dark nights. Muuurgh shook his furry head, and something about his expression, as seen through the infrared goggles, stopped Han in midword. Instead he asked quietly, "What's wrong?"

"I found Mrrov," Muuurgh said. "Pilot will be roused at dawn to fly to Colony Two and take her and other shipload of pilgrims to space station to meet an incoming ship. Ship coming from Kessel, must be—so no time to lose. Must escape. *Now.* Or Mrrov will be gone."

Han shook his head. He was tired—he'd been sleeping in short shifts for the past four nights, and it was catching up with him. "Escape? Tonight?"

"Yesssss!" Muuurgh's anxiety was catching. Han could feel adrenaline beginning to course through his body. "Must escape! Tell Muuurgh what to do! Almost two hours before dawn. By sunrise Mrrov will be waiting with others at Altar place, and Vykk and Muuurgh must be ready with ship!"

"Okay, okay, pal. Calm down." Han tried to think what had to be done first. "You've caught me by surprise here, and I need a second to unscramble my brain. First things first. We'll need some blasters. Five or six of 'em. You used to live in the guards' barracks. Think you can sneak in and get 'em?"

Muuurgh nodded. "Yessss . . . I will get five or six blasters."

"If I were you, I'd swipe 'em from the Gamorreans. They're dumb as a box of rocks, and they sleep like logs."

Muuurgh's whiskers twitched with amusement. "Yessss . . ."

"Okay, then. Meet me in front of the Administration Center in half an hour."

With a final nod, Muuurgh melted into the underbrush.

Han headed for the Administration Center. First item on his agenda was to knock out the Colony's comm units. He didn't want anyone summoning reinforcements from the other colonies, or warning them that there was trouble afoot.

When the Corellian reached the comm center, he dug in his pocket for the scrap of flimsy that Bria had given him containing all of the security codes she'd gained from her foray into Teroenza's mind. There was the code for Teroenza's personal yacht, *Talisman*, the ship Han planned to use for their getaway. There was the code for Teroenza's private living quarters, and the code for the collection room. And there was also the code for the operations center that contained the Colony's generators, the base security viewscreens, the droid repair shop, the weapons lockers, and the comm unit.

Han tiptoed through the quiet hallways, wondering if he'd catch a glimpse of Muuurgh on his errand, but he saw not a flicker of motion. By now he knew enough about the security layout of Colony One to automatically avoid the bored night guards—who were, most likely, from what he'd seen on his previous forays, asleep at their posts.

It seemed an eternity before he reached the operations center, but finally he was there, entering Bria's code. With a soft electronic hum, the door swung open. "That's my girl," Han muttered as he crept inside.

There was a guard stationed there, as Han had known there would be. A Twi'lek, asleep in the chair, feet propped up on the comm-unit console, head-tails dangling behind him like two ropes of pallid flesh. Resounding snores vibrated through the still air.

Han drew his blaster, changed the setting to STUN, and squeezed the trigger. A blue, circular burst erupted, enveloping the guard. The Twi'lek jerked once, then collapsed bonelessly into the chair, looking exactly the same—except the snores had stopped. "That's a definite plus," Han muttered, holstering his gun.

Stepping over to the comm unit, he pulled out the small multitool most pilots automatically carried in their pockets, and set to work loosening the casing. He intended to disable the comm unit, then replace the casing, so whoever tried to use it wouldn't realize for a while that it had been sabotaged.

Moments later he lifted the outer shell off and put it on the floor. His eyes widened at the myriads of wires, circuits, transponders, cables, and row after row of identical unlabeled compartments. Han groaned aloud. "How'm I supposed to know which of these carries the line to the power generators?"

Selecting a wire at random, he cut it with the multitool's small laser torch. The power indicator remained ON. Han cut another wire. Then another. With growing frustration, he grabbed a handful of the circuits and yanked them loose.

Still no visible result.

Swearing under his breath, he ripped and tore and lasered ruthlessly, until he was breathing hard with the effort—and the power was still on!

Over five minutes had passed.

"Stupid board . . ." Han snarled and, drawing his blaster, thumbed it up to full intensity and discharged it right into the middle of the stubborn console's innards. Flames shot up, the smell of singed insulation tickled his nostrils, sparks erupted—

—and the power indicator went out.

"That's better," Han muttered grimly. For good measure, he stunned the Twi'lek again, then he turned and left.

Once outside the Administration Center, he pulled on

his goggles and headed down the jungle path at a trot. His strides came faster and faster, until he was nearly running full-out, and only a headlong fall into a mud puddle slowed him down. Dripping and cursing, he climbed back to his feet and headed off again.

The other buildings were ahead of him, now, including Bria's dorm. Han had checked out the dorms long ago and determined that unlike the Administration Center and the spice factories, they were not guarded at night. After all, the t'landa Til didn't care whether anyone harmed their slaves—slaves were easily replaceable.

Bria's little bunk was on the second floor. A dim nightlight glowed in the stair landing. Han tiptoed up the stairs, blaster set on STUN at the ready, but he met no one. The pilgrims were so euphoric after the Exultation each night that they slept like the dead.

Han wasn't sure exactly which bunk Bria occupied. Peering through his goggles, he padded quietly down the central aisle, glancing at the sleeping faces in the various types of sleeping couches, pallets, and bunks favored by various species.

A board creaked beneath his foot, and Han paused, holding his breath. A figure sat up in a human-style bunk, clad in a sleeveless white nightshirt. "Vykk?" she whispered.

Han nodded and beckoned urgently. "Fast!" he hissed.

To his surprise, she was already wearing her pants. Grabbing her overtunic and her sandals, she tiptoed toward him, automatically avoiding the squeaky floorboard.

Together, in silence, they made a cautious way down the stairs, through the hall, and out into the blackness of the night. Bria pulled on her goggles.

"C'mon," Han said, catching her hand before she had time to say a word. "We've gotta hurry!"

He broke into a run, and she pounded gamely alongside him. Soon, though, her strides shortened, and he could tell that she was fighting a stitch in her side. Slowing to a rapid walk, he towed her along the jungle path. She was breathing too hard to speak, but Han, who was in better shape, caught his breath quickly.

"Tonight's the night," he told her. "I need you and Muuurgh to start in on Teroenza's collection, while I get the guards off our backs. Think you can do it?"

She nodded breathlessly. "Ganar Tos . . ." she gasped.

"Forget him," Han said curtly. "You'll never see him again, with any luck."

"But he . . . and Teroenza . . ." She yielded to his urgent tug and began jogging again. "Going to make . . . me . . . marry . . . him . . ."

Han's eyes widened. "Ganar Tos wanted to *marry* you? Minions of Xendor! Good thing we're gettin' outta here!"

Unable to speak again, she just nodded.

By the time they reached the Administration Center, Bria had her second wind. She followed Han as he led the way down the darkened corridors to the door of Teroenza's collection room. Muuurgh was waiting for them. At his feet lay a pile of blasters. Bria's eyes widened. "What are those for?"

"Diversion," Han said. "Okay, now . . . here's this bypass code . . ." Quickly he entered the code, and as before, the door opened. The three of them tiptoed into the huge, dimly lit room. Han reached into Bria's desk and removed a powerful glowrod and flicked the bright light around the room. "Think we dare turn on the lights?"

She nodded. "It's well sealed. I checked that last week. No way to see it from Teroenza's apartment."

Han switched on the overhead lights, and the room was suddenly fully illuminated.

Since Bria had taken over the maintenance of the collection, she'd rearranged the entire room. The collection cases gleamed, the shelves were far less cluttered, and the colors on the tapestries were vivid, freed from their film of dust. The room's three white central support pillars had been freshly painted.

"All right," Han whispered. "You and Muuurgh get started and begin picking out the items you selected. I'll be back in about fifteen minutes, okay?"

She nodded. "But what'll I carry them in?"

"Last week I hid a knapsack behind the backsides of the

two sprites on the white jade fountain," Han said, pointing to the huge artifact. "That'll get you started. I'll try to bring something else back with me if I see anything that'll work."

"Okay," she whispered.

Muuurgh was some distance away, examining a collection of jeweled daggers. Bria hesitated, her expression anguished. Han put his hands on her shoulders. "What is it, honey?"

"Vykk . . . I've never done anything like this before!" She bit her lip and gestured at the blasters Muuurgh had brought. "Guns, and stealing! People could get *hurt*—even *killed*! You could get killed, or me!" She was shivering all over.

Han put his arms around her, pulled her to him. "Bria, we have to go tonight," he said, though it was an effort to keep his voice gentle and hide his impatience. "Tomorrow they're shipping Mrrov to the mines of Kessel. The ship's probably going to arrive in orbit anytime now to take her away! It's now or never, sweetheart."

"And . . . and . . ." She was clinging to the front of his coverall with both hands. "I'm afraid of what will happen to me when I leave here. Without the Exultation . . . how can I live without it?"

"You'll have me," he reminded her. "We'll be together. I'll be with you . . . every minute. You'll be okay . . ."

She gulped and nodded, but two tears ran down her cheeks. Han gave her an encouraging grin. "Hey . . ." he said. "I'm better than Ganar Tos, right?"

Bria managed a choked laugh, and then gave him a watery smile.

Han grabbed the blasters and headed out the door, making sure it was closed behind him, then down the corridor.

Carrying six guns in one's arms, he discovered, wasn't easy. He finally wound up shoving them into the front of his coverall and into his belt. They impeded his motion somewhat, but that was better than juggling them in his arms and fearing that one or more would fall to the floor with a crash.

The night was as dark as ever, but Han knew that dawn

couldn't be more than an hour away now. He managed an awkward lope down the muddy path, blasters whacking into his legs and bouncing against his chest.

It took him nearly seven minutes to reach the first glitterstim factory, and another two to creep up close enough to the guard, a huge Gamorrean, to stun the alien at close range. Seeing the creature's huge, porcine bulk, Han gave him an extra shot to keep him quiet for as long as this was going to take him.

Then he turned and walked into the factory, straight to the turbolift, the extra blasters nearly tripping him as he squeezed through the mesh door. Setting the turbolift for the bottom floor, he endured the ride down, down, into the night-black chill and the darkness beyond darkness.

When Han reached the bottom level, the one where Bria had worked, he turned right to where he'd caught a glimpse of the containers of raw glitterstim waiting to be apportioned to the workers.

Yanking the five blasters out of his belt (he kept the sixth as a spare, since he hadn't known to make sure his own was fully charged for tonight's escapade) Han arranged them atop the glitterstim in a tasteful "rayed sun" design. Then he quickly opened each one up and, peering through his goggles, set the powerful weapon to OVERLOAD. A thin whining filled the air, growing louder, echoing in the cavernous space, as more and more whines joined the first in the dank depths of the factory.

"That oughta do it," Han whispered to himself, and knowing he had only minutes to get free before the whole place went *boom,* he bolted for the turbolift.

The rush of wind across his sweating face felt good. Han leaped out, ran down the first floor of the factory, leaped over the recumbent Gamorrean, who was just beginning to snort and stir, and ran off, into the night.

He was halfway back to the Administration Center when Han felt the ground shake and turned to see a gout of yellow flame reaching into the night. Moments later the blue sparks of glitterstim fizzed up like fireworks, sending sparkling streamers high into the air.

Han could barely guess how many credits he was watching go up in smoke. It was a sobering sight.

Ahead of him, he heard a commotion from the Administration Center, and moments later he had to jump off the path and continue through the jungle as a gaggle of yelling guards nearly ran him over.

Slipping in the muck of the forest floor, Han managed to keep to a good pace as he ran the rest of the way. His boots left muddy footprints on the steps of the Administration Center as he pounded up them, then down the corridors toward Teroenza's treasure room.

There were guards all over now, shouting and yelling questions, but none stopped or questioned Han. He made it to the door of the collection room, looked both ways, and then slipped inside.

Bria and Muuurgh looked up, saw him, then relaxed visibly. "How's it going?" Han whispered.

"Okay," Bria replied softly. "We've almost finished the A list."

"Great."

"What did Vykk do?" Muuurgh asked.

"Vykk blew up the glitterstim factory," Han said with satisfaction. "A whole bunch of pilgrims are now out of a job."

"Oh, Vykk! If we get caught—" Bria's face was chalky.

"We won't," Han said. "I've got everything under control."

He reached for a hand-sized sculpture of a torsk from Alzoc III, carved from lapis, and when it proved heavier than he'd realized, yanked hard to pull it toward him.

The sculpture tilted up, to reveal a snarl of wires and transponders. Somewhere, next door, in Teroenza's personal apartments, an alarm began to buzz stridently.

Han stared at the sculpture, then at his fellow thieves. "Uh-oh . . ."

Chapter Eleven:
ESCAPE VELOCITY

B ria stared at Han, terrified and furious. "Oh, *great*! *Now* what are we going to do?"

Han thought quickly. "We're getting out of here. The A list is good enough. Bria, you take the knapsack, okay? And here, take this." Pulling the spare blaster out of his belt, he handed it to her, showed her how to aim it, and where the trigger was. "We may have to fight our way outta here."

"Wonderful," she said bitterly. "Under control, right, Vykk? Nothing to worry about!"

Han could only shrug helplessly. This time, it definitely *was* his fault.

"Which way?" Muuurgh, the practical one, wanted to know. "Through priest's door or main door?"

Han considered for a second, but was saved from having to make a decision—both doors simultaneously burst open.

Teroenza stood framed in the door to his apartments, snorting with rage. Zavval and a squad of guards filled the big double doors.

Han grabbed Bria and dived behind the huge white jade fountain, while Muuurgh took refuge behind the room's central support pillar. "Get them!" shrilled Zavval, moving forward on his repulsorlift sled. Teroenza charged like a mad beast, head down, horn ready.

Han snapped off a shot, saw the blue stun bolt, and cursed as he thumbed the weapon's intensity up to FULL. The stun beam didn't even slow Teroenza down. Muuurgh aimed, fired, and brought down a Sullustan guard.

Han squeezed the trigger again, but the blaster bolt ricocheted off Zavval's sled and struck the support pillar nearest the door, burning it half-through. The pillar sagged, but held.

As Teroenza headed for Muuurgh, the big Togorian leaped out and grabbed the High Priest, clutching him around the neck and by his horn. Digging his heels into the carpet, Muuurgh braced himself against the High Priest's forward motion. The t'landa Til's momentum caused him to "crack the whip" and his massive hindquarters swung around and slammed into the middle pillar with a huge *thump!*

The floor quivered, and dust sifted downward from the ceiling. Teroenza's rear feet skidded, and the High Priest went down. The ground shook again.

Han aimed and snapped off a shot, and a Gamorrean screamed and fell back into the hallway. Bria edged around the fountain, blaster ready, but before she could fire, one of the guards did. She screamed and ducked as a blaster bolt blew out a chunk of the fountain, sending jade fragments flying into the air. Teroenza, struggling back to his feet, let out an anguished howl of protest.

Another blaster bolt sizzled past Han, so close that the Corellian felt it singe his hair. He dropped to the floor, rolled, and snapped off two more shots at the underside of Zavval's sled. As he'd intended, the blaster bolts hit the housing for the repulsorlift unit. But, instead of sinking to the floor, the sled's speed and directional controls went wild.

With Zavval vainly trying to control it, the big sled hurtled forward at top speed. Seconds later it slammed into the far wall and bounced off. Mowing down everything in its path, the sled caromed around the collections room, with Zavval a helpless passenger.

A Rodian guard who was concentrating on trying to shoot Han didn't see it coming and was struck down in a spray of blood. The sled hurtled through a display case, and Teroenza screamed as he saw his precious collection of antique vases reduced to powder.

The Hutt crashed into the opposite wall, and the entire room shook. Dust and debris rained from the ceiling. Han and Bria threw themselves flat as the hurtling sled whanged into one of the jade nymphs and shattered her.

Zavval was yelling, and most of the guards by now had wisely made a quick exit.

Then the sled, with Zavval's massive weight atop it, plowed directly into the room's central pillar. The support column buckled and groaned, then bent in two and snapped off—and then the one Han had partially vaporized followed suit.

With a last, agonized groan, the repulsorlift sled settled to the floor and died.

Han stared in frozen horror as, seemingly in slow motion, half of the ceiling rumbled, bulged, cracked, then broke into huge chunks and plummeted down. He recovered himself just in time to grab Bria and yank her out of the way as a huge chunk of stone flooring hurtled at them from the upper level. Throwing her to the floor beneath the bowl of the stone fountain, Han fell on top of her, shielding her.

Zavval screamed shrilly as massive chunks rained down on him, pinning him to the shattered remains of his sled. Dust rose in a choking cloud. Coughing and gagging, Han crawled off Bria as soon as he was sure the ceiling fall had ceased. He stared at the spot where Zavval had been, but all he could see of the buried Hutt overlord was his spasmodically jerking tail.

Teroenza had thrown himself flat beneath the protection of a massive antique table and remained relatively unscathed. When the debris stopped falling, he crawled out from under the dust and rubble of his now-cracked table. Staggering toward Han, Bria, and Muuurgh—the Togorian was sheltering in the doorway to the priest's apartment—Teroenza howled, slavering with rage. Obviously still intent on revenge, the t'landa Til lowered his head, horn pointed, and charged.

Han aimed and fired a bolt into his right flank, sending him crashing to the floor with a scream. The sickening smell of burned meat filled the air. A blaster bolt from one of the guards struck the fountain again, and tiny shards of sizzling stone whipped by Han's face. One buried itself in his neck, and when he yanked it free, his fingers came away slick with blood.

Han sighted along the barrel of his blaster, fired, and the last guard went down in a heap.

"Come on!" he yelled, grabbing Bria and the knapsack and gesturing to Muuurgh. "We're gettin' outta here!"

Slipping in the rubble and stumbling over bodies, the three thieves headed for the double doors. When they reached them, Han motioned his comrades back and cautiously slid his head around the edge of the door, only to be rewarded by a blaster bolt that nearly took his ear off.

"Muuurgh, take Bria out the other way!" he ordered. "Go through Teroenza's door, and we'll catch them in a cross fire. On the count of fifty!"

The Togorian nodded, and he and Bria slithered and slipped back through the ruins of the treasure room, past the moaning Teroenza, through the door of the priest's apartment.

Silently, Han counted. At fifteen, he stuck his hand around the edge of the door and snapped off four quick shots, and was rewarded with a howl of agony.

One more down . . .

He waited, breathing hard, trying not to cough on the dust that still filled the air.

Forty-five, forty-six, forty-seven, forty-eight, forty-nine . . . fifty!

Han dived out the door, hit the corridor rolling, and fired. Red blaster bolts zinged past his legs and where his head would be, but he got another guard, a Whiphid. As they'd planned, Bria and Muuurgh were firing from behind the guards, and two more fell.

The remaining two guards, a Devaronian and a Gamorrean, took to their heels and pounded away from Muuurgh and Bria, leaping over Han's still-recumbent body as they did so.

Han got shakily to his feet, just in time to hear Muuurgh let out a huge battle roar and grapple with—who? Han couldn't see anyone!

Has he gone crazy? Han wondered, but then he glimpsed a reddish-orange eye, a mouth full of teeth, and heard a loud hiss. He saw a blaster wave, seemingly in mid-air, then suddenly he could make out the pale-skinned, warty, scaled being. *A skin-changer!*

Muuurgh growled and snarled as he savagely attacked the Aar'aa. The Togorian was so much taller than his opponent that Muuurgh was bent over nearly double. Han winced as the Togorian fell to his knees, grasping his foe. The reptilian creature was the exact color of the neutral walls and flooring in the dimly lit corridor. With a motion like a striking gral-viper, the Togorian buried his fangs in the being's throat and ripped. Reddish-orange blood spurted into the air.

Muuurgh jumped back, and Han watched, fascinated, as the Aar'aa sagged, then fell, with ponderous slowness, to the floor. As the being lay there, it slowly reverted from its pale color to its own natural skin tone, a grayish-tan. Han didn't have to look twice to know that it was dead.

Bria was staring in horror at the spot where the dead Aar'aa lay. "He almost had me," she whispered. "If it hadn't been for Muuurgh . . ."

"How'd you see him, pal?" Han said, holstering his blaster. "I couldn't see a thing!"

"I did not *see* him, I *smelled* him," Muuurgh said matter-of-factly. "Togorians hunt by sight and smell. Muuurgh is a *hunter*, remember?"

"Thanks, pal," Han said, and put an arm around Bria. "I owe you one. Now we'd better—"

"Look out!" Bria yelled, and Han instinctively ducked. Bria's blaster went off in stun mode just over his head, making his ears ring. He straightened up in time to see Ganar Tos slowly crumpling to the floor as a blaster slipped from his green fingers.

Han walked over to the old majordomo and, picking up the blaster, slipped it into his belt. Bria came to stand beside him. "All I can think is that if you hadn't come back today, tonight I'd have been his wife," she murmured, and shuddered so deeply that Han hugged her reassuringly.

"I'm glad you only stunned him," Han said. "He may have been a lecherous old creep, but how can I blame him for being attracted to you?" He smiled at her, his eyes very intent.

She glanced down, and her color rose. "I didn't want to marry him, but I'm glad he's not dead."

"Well," Han said, "I owe you one, honey."

"No, you don't," she said. "We're even. If it hadn't been for you, I'd be buried under that ceiling back there, like that Hutt."

"Yeah, I'm afraid old Zavval's no longer with us," Han said. "And I suppose the Hutts will blame me for it."

For a moment Han remembered Teroenza, who was still alive, only wounded. Should he go back and finish off the t'landa Til? The thought of walking up to a helpless sentient and coldly shooting the creature in cold blood didn't appeal to him.

"Let's get out of here," he said, beckoning to Muuurgh, who was licking Aar'aa blood off his paws with fastidious distaste. "C'mon, Muuurgh, you can finish grooming your whiskers later. Don't forget—Mrrov is waiting."

As they jogged out of the Administration Center, they

could see the glitterstim factory still shooting up blue
sparks into the air—but the sky was no longer black, but
lighter, almost blue.

"Dawn's not far off!" Han said. "C'mon!"

The three broke into a run down the jungle path. When
they neared the end, Han motioned them to stay back as
he cautiously scanned the landing field. He saw no
guards . . . apparently all of them were still fighting the
fire or in the Administration Center.

Still, they went cautiously, blasters ready, every sense
alert for movement or sound.

When Han reached the *Talisman,* he quickly coded
Bria's access code into the lock, then the three went up the
ramp.

The *Talisman* was a little larger than the *Ylesian Dream,*
teardrop-shaped, bulging along its keel. But instead of
cargo space, most of its interior was given over to lavish
passenger quarters and amenities. It was proportioned and
laid out for the t'landa Til, so only the pilot's cabin contained human-style seats. There was one small, human-
sized bunk in a guard's cabin, but the rest of the passenger
cabins were outfitted with the sleeping "hammocks" the
t'landa Til favored.

Once inside, Han motioned Bria to the copilot's seat and
instructed Muuurgh to strap himself into one of the passenger berths.

He'd never flown this particular ship during his time
here—Teroenza had been too worried by the pirate attacks
to risk traveling before the weapons and shield upgrades
had been completed.

Quickly Han familiarized himself with the controls. The
Talisman didn't have as much weaponry or shielding as the
Dream, but for a private yacht, it was now heavily armed
and well shielded.

"Preflight checks completed, we're good to go. Strap in,
folks . . . we are outta here!" Han cried, and raised ship.
The *Talisman* responded well to his touch and seemed a
willing—though rather slow—craft.

"Now for Mrrov," Muuurgh called excitedly. "Right, Vykk?"

"Right, pal," Han said. "We should be there just at sunrise. Where are they assembling the pilgrims destined for the Kessel ship?"

"The Altar of Promises," Muuurgh replied.

"The Altar of *Broken* Promises," Bria amended, a bitter tone in her voice. "I wonder whether Teroenza will survive?"

"I didn't wound him that bad," Han said. "I'll bet even now he's on his way to the infirmary and the medical droid."

As he flew, he kept an eye on the map. "Oh, and by the way, there's something I'd better tell you two."

"What?" asked Bria and Muuurgh together.

"My name's not Vykk Draygo. My real name is Han Solo. It'd be good if you started calling me that."

"Han?" Bria said. "Why didn't you tell me before?"

"I was afraid if I did, you might slip and give me away to Teroenza or one of his goons," Han said matter-of-factly. "But I wanted you to know, so I told you as soon as I could."

"Vykk was an alias?"

"Yeah. One of several, actually."

"Muuurgh will have to get used to this," the Togorian said. "How close are we now . . . Han?"

"We should be there in less than five minutes," Han replied.

"How are we going to do this?" Bria asked. "I mean, there will be guards there, too."

"I don't know," Han said. "But I'll think of something."

He concentrated on his piloting, and then, when they reached Colony Two, he flew the *Talisman* over the camp from south to north, skimming low over the treetops. "You said the pilgrims were supposed to assemble at the Altar, right?" Han asked Muuurgh.

"Yesssss."

"Okay, then, I wonder if we'll have enough room to do what I'm thinkin' about . . ." he muttered, peering at the viewscreen that showed the actual area, and also at the schematic that showed the topographical features and camp buildings. Colony Two was over the Mountains of Faith from Colony One, set on the northeastern edge of the Zoma Gawanga, the shallow ocean that enclosed the entire eastern continent.

"I think we can do it," he muttered. "I just hope the repulsorlifts on this baby are in prime working condition. We'll need to hover and lower a wire. I don't think I'll have room to actually *land*. Muuurgh, go back to the middle air-lock and see if there's a wire we can let down. I think most of these ships are equipped with emergency gear, and a wire and hoist should be part of it."

Muuurgh disappeared, and Han concentrated on flying a slow circuit of the Colony. Bria peered out the viewscreen. "I see them!" she said excitedly. "There's a big crowd assembling at the Altar!"

"Good," Han said abstractedly.

Muuurgh reappeared. "Yes, we have a wire. There is a harness that can be attached to it."

"Okay, pal. Here's what we'll do. I'm going to bring this crate down over the amphitheater, real slow. Then I'm gonna set her to hover on her repulsorlifts. Mrrov has no reason to know who we are, so she's gonna have to get a look at you in order to run over to the ship, right?"

"Yesssss."

"You're gonna have to go down in the harness and let Mrrov see you. Bria, you control the wire, okay?"

"All right . . . Han," she said.

"Both of you stay sharp. There may be shooting. The ship's deflectors should protect us against small-arms, but once you're outside, that won't count, Muuurgh."

"I understand."

"If the guards get too aggressive, I can give 'em a burst from the ship's light laser cannon," Han said. "I'll aim over their heads, so I won't hit the pilgrims, but that should make the point."

"Muuurgh is ready, Han."

"Okay. Here goes."

Carefully Han brought the *Talisman* in over the amphitheater, wishing he'd had more time to get used to the "feel" of these controls. He circled the amphitheater, belly holocams on, so he could get a good look at the layout. Han was conscious of all the pilgrims looking up and pointing, as he dropped lower and lower with each pass. Finally, he was close enough to engage the repulsorlifts and hover, about twelve or thirteen meters above the permacrete.

Han could see several priests and a bevy of guards behind the milling crowd of pilgrims. He knew the Sacredots must be wondering why the High Priest's personal yacht was being used to ferry pilgrims to the Kessel slave ship.

"That's as low as I can get and hover safely!" Han yelled. "Lower Muuurgh!"

He kept a finger poised over the controls that would lower the light laser cannon, but he didn't want to make an aggressive move first. Han could hear Bria and Muuurgh talking, their voices muffled by distance. He glanced over at the belly holocam screen just in time to see Muuurgh descending, his blaster still holstered.

The cam didn't provide audio, but he watched as Muuurgh's mouth opened, and knew he must be calling to Mrrov.

Guards milled, still uncertain, but clearly uneasy. This whole scenario was highly irregular, and they were getting suspicious. One of the guards shoved his way through the crowd of pilgrims. When the human guard reached the forefront of the crowd, he had his blaster drawn and was clearly calling to Muuurgh to identify himself and state what he was doing.

"Bria," Han yelled, turning his head, careful not to jostle the controls on the hovering vessel, "stand by! Looks like they're gonna—"

Two things happened simultaneously: a tall figure in a pilgrim's robe suddenly broke and raced toward Muuurgh's dangling figure—and the guard aimed his blaster.

Han had only a glimpse of orange stripes on white fur and knew the running figure must be Mrrov. He saw a spurt of blaster fire from the guard's weapon, and it was answered twice in rapid succession, by Bria and Muuurgh.

Two more guards drew their weapons and fired. The crowd of pilgrims panicked and scattered, trampling each other and the guards.

Han lowered the light laser cannon, grateful for the pirate attacks that had made Teroenza decide to beef up the ship's shielding and weapons capability. He fired a burst, careful to aim over the heads of the running, screaming crowd.

More fire from the guards—and Han heard a faint yowl of pain! Checking the screen, he saw Muuurgh sag in his harness, clutching his side, though he still gripped his weapon. Mrrov reached him a second later and leaped to wrap her arms and legs around her mate, anchoring her to him.

Bria was firing steadily now, and Han saw a Gamorrean go down. The wire was ascending now, revolving slowly with its off-balance load. Mrrov grabbed Muuurgh's blaster out of his lax hand and fired over his shoulder. Han couldn't see whether she hit her target.

Han saw that most of the pilgrims had scattered, and only guards and priests remained near the Altar. Many of the guards had scattered in the crowd, but a few were still there, still firing. Han targeted the Altar of Promises, made sure his aim had pinpoint accuracy, and fired the laser cannon again.

The Altar went up with a *boom* Han could hear from inside the *Talisman*. Dust spurted up, and bits of stone rained down. The priests scattered, galloping away. Han was surprised by how fast and maneuverable their huge, four-footed bodies were. The guards had vanished.

Quiet suddenly reigned. Seconds ticked by, but outside, nothing was stirring. A few bodies, both guards and pilgrims, lay motionless where they'd been trampled in the panic.

From the nether regions of the ship, he heard Bria's voice. "I've got them! Let's go!"

Han checked that the bay doors were safely closed, then

took the *Talisman* up in a rush. The belly holocams showed a dizzying view of the amphitheater receding into the distance. Han flicked them off as he circled, checking the weather in relation to his closest escape vector.

Ironically, he'd have to angle back toward Colony One for the best "window" off Ylesia. Han gunned the *Talisman* and took her south and up . . . up . . .

We're almost there, he thought with a rush of excitement. *Almost free . . .*

Muuurgh repressed a moan as his shoulder banged against the side of the *Talisman*. He felt Bria's hands on him, then he heard Mrrov's voice say, in Basic: "Help me up. I can lift him."

He clung to the harness with his good hand and felt Mrrov's body brush against his as she was pulled into the hovering *Talisman*. The wound in his side was the fire-stab of a night-demon's talons. It was all he could do to breathe and make no sound. He was a hunter, and hunters knew how to be quiet.

The blaster shots had stopped. Muuurgh opened his eyes as the harness revolved slowly and saw that the Altar of Promises had been blown apart. Perhaps that had been the loud explosion he'd heard. At the time he'd thought it was inside his head.

The blaster wound was throbbing now, in waves. Muuurgh struggled to stay conscious as Bria and Mrrov grabbed his arms and hauled him, still in the harness, into the *Talisman*. Dimly, he was aware of the cargo airlock being sealed behind him.

Then he heard Bria's voice call out: "I've got them! Let's go!"

Muuurgh lay on the deck, breathing shallowly, but a little of his strength was returning. He could hear Mrrov talking to Bria. "Is there a medic kit aboard?"

"I'll check!" With a rustle, the human was gone, leaving him alone with Mrrov. With an effort, Muuurgh opened his eyes.

When she saw him looking up at her, Mrrov leaned over and lovingly rubbed his cheek with her own, exchanging scent, "My hunter," she murmured in their own language, licking his face tenderly. "You tracked me. You are the greatest hunter our people have ever known!"

"Mrrov . . ." Muuurgh managed to whisper.

"Quiet," she said. "Don't try to talk. Your wound is serious, though I believe it will heal, in time. Oh, Muuurgh! When I saw you come down from the belly of this ship, I could not believe that it was you! For all these days and weeks, I have wondered whether you would ever find me—and you did!"

"You knew I was here?" Muuurgh was confused. "If you knew, then why—"

Her lovely, orange-striped features were troubled as she gave him another cheek rub. Her whiskers entangled with his own, and Muuurgh sighed with pleasure, despite his pain.

"I had only been here a short while, when I realized that this entire place was a sham. I was searching for truths, but there are only lies, here. So I told the priests I wanted to leave. They showed me your picture, Muuurgh! They told me if I tried to leave, they would kill you!"

"So you stayed? You should have torn their throats out!" Muuurgh protested.

"At the cost of your life?" She shook her head, her eyes large and vividly golden. "No, my mate-to-be. I dared not take the chance. I only hoped that someday you would find me, and that you would have a ship. And . . . that day has finally come."

Muuurgh nodded weakly. "Thanks to . . . Vykk . . . Han . . ."

Bria came running back into the cargo compartment. "I found it!"

Moments later Muuurgh's pain was ebbing, and Mrrov and Bria were bandaging the wound in his side. "You're going to have an awful scar, Muuurgh," Bria said, sounding dismayed.

"Hunters show their scars proudly, on Togoria," Mrrov

said. "Muuurgh will heal, and he will have a scar everyone will envy."

Suddenly the ship shuddered. Bria shouted, "Han! What was that?"

"Someone's shooting at us!" he yelled from the bridge. "Someone get up here and man the weapons station! I need Muuurgh!"

Muuurgh struggled to get up. "No," Mrrov said. "I will do it. Among my people, females have the technical expertise. I am an engineer. I will do it."

Muuurgh opened his eyes, saw Bria's doubtful expression, and said, "Believe her. Muuurgh was not a very good shot, anyway. Ask Pilot . . ."

He closed his eyes, feeling blackness waiting behind the lids. He could resist it no longer . . . so, with a sigh, Muuurgh let himself slide under . . .

Han glanced at the tall Togorian form that slid into the copilot's seat beside him and started in surprise. "You're not Muuurgh!"

"I am Mrrov," the female Togorian introduced herself. She'd doffed her pilgrim's robe, and her glorious white and orange-striped coat blazed like fire. "I will handle the weapons for you. Acquaint me with what we have, please. You will find I am a far better weapons officer than Muuurgh. In our species, females are the technicians and experts with instruments." She glanced over at Han, and he saw that her slit-pupiled eyes were bright yellow. "Besides, Muuurgh is wounded, and in no shape for this."

"Is he gonna be okay?" Han felt a stab of concern.

"He should be. My people are very strong and hardy. Bria—is that her name?" Han nodded. "Your Bria is with him. He is resting."

"Okay," Han said. "This baby doesn't have a lot of weaponry, but it's got some concussion missiles and a light laser cannon. Right down there. Laser cannon to your right, missile launchers to your left. Targeting computer is straight in front of you."

"Very well." After spending a moment checking the board before her, she nodded. "I can do this. Who shot at us?"

"That's what I'm trying to find out," Han said tightly, studying his readouts. "I don't think the priests have surface-to-air stuff, but I'm hanged if I can see—"

He broke off with a whoop of laughter, just as the *Talisman* shuddered again. Mrrov looked at Han, who was still chuckling, as if he were crazy.

"It's okay," he said.

She pointed at the technical readout of their surrounding space. It showed several storm cells, safely removed in distance from their escape vector, but it also showed a small, teardrop-shaped craft rapidly gaining on the *Talisman*. "What do you mean, 'okay'? There is someone pursuing us and shooting at us, and they are gaining!"

"Aahhhh . . . it's just old Jalus Nebl in the *Ylesian Dream*," Han said, waving a dismissive hand. "The priests must've ordered him to come up here and shoot our asses down." He chuckled again.

Talisman lurched slightly. Han laughed again.

Mrrov was staring at him, obviously wondering if his mind had snapped from the strain. Han grinned at her cheerfully. "You don't understand," he said.

"No," agreed Mrrov. "Would you care to explain it to me?"

"Sure. Jalus Nebl and I are friends. He wouldn't shoot me down any more than I'd shoot him. So he's firing his laser cannon, just missing us by a hair each time, making it look good. We're gaining speed every minute, and soon, we're gonna be out of the atmosphere, and five minutes after *that*, we'll be out of the planet's gravity well. We're fine, Mrrov. Trust me."

Mrrov's whiskers twitched. "I believe I am beginning to understand. Your friend Jalus Nebl is putting on a show of attempting to shoot us down? So we have nothing to worry about?"

"Right," Han said cheerfully. "We're almost clear of the atmosphere, and if Nebl's got a grain of sense, he'll take the

Ylesian Dream and get his droopy-jowled little carcass off Ylesia, too. Or maybe he's decided to hang in with the priests and ask for a raise. They'll be desperate, with only one pilot left."

Another near-hit caused the *Talisman* to shiver. "That was close," Han muttered, checking his ship's hull and systems. "The little so-and-so's showing off."

He continued to track the *Ylesian Dream* as it followed them up through the last of the stratosphere, into the thin layer of ionosphere. Ahead lay the thinnest whisper of upper atmosphere—the exosphere.

As they burst upward, Han turned his attention to the navicomputer, checking on the programming for their jump to hyperspace. They wouldn't be clear of Ylesia's gravity well for several minutes yet, but he wanted to be ready.

"I see a vehicle on our sensors," Mrrov said. "Above us, in our path."

"That's just the space station. It orbits in a synchronous orbit with Colony One," Han said, not looking up. "That's where they off-load the pilgrims when the ships bring them in. You must've been there."

"No, Han." Mrrov's voice was suddenly urgent. "I remember it very well, but that's not it. That's no space station—it's a *spaceship*! A big one!"

Finally alarmed, Han looked up—and abruptly swore in six languages. "That's a Corellian corvette! What's it doing here?"

His hands flew over the controls as he began evasive maneuvers, increasing speed and sheering away from the huge vessel. With one part of his mind, Han noted the blip that was the *Dream* streaking off in the opposite direction.

Suddenly the *Talisman* jerked hard and bucked. The engine began to strain. "What's wrong?" Mrrov demanded, just as Bria burst into the cabin.

"Han . . . what happened?" she asked.

Han cut in the auxiliary power, felt the Ylesian yacht strain, but . . . it . . . wasn't . . . going . . . to . . . be . . . enough—

"No!" he yelled, frustrated, on the verge of panic. "No, we *can't* go back!"

His passengers stared at him, wide-eyed with fear, as Han began shutting down his engines to avoid burning them out.

As he did so, a voice erupted from the comm unit. "Attention, *Talisman*. This is Captain Ngyn Reeos in command of the Corellian corvette *Helot's Shackle* out of Kessel. We advise you to shut down your engines. You are caught in our tractor beam."

"I know!" Han yelled, not bothering to activate his comm unit. "Thanks for telling me!"

Captain Reeos went on, inexorably. "We have detained you because I have been advised by planetary authorities that you have taken the *Talisman* without authorization. These same planetary authorities have asked that we deliver you back to Ylesia to face charges there. Prepare to be boarded. Any attempt at resistance will be met with summary force."

Han stared at the narrow-waisted vessel with its eleven huge reactor tubes. The corvette was easily twenty times the size of his ship. He noted that the corvette had been modified so it had a docking bay.

"That's a huge ship," Bria whispered. "We're being pulled toward it, Han."

"There's nothing I can do, sweetheart," Han said dully. "They've got us caught—we can't break free."

"How many crew aboard that ship?" Mrrov asked, staring as if mesmerized at the slave ship—the ship that had come to fetch her and the other pilgrims to a grim fate in the mines.

"With a Navy crew aboard, the complement is 165. But this is a *modified* corvette. It's been altered to dock in space—probably to make it easier to take on cargo—or slaves. Crew size is probably forty or fifty."

"Too many to fight," Bria said, her voice ragged.

"They're not getting *me* without a fight," Han said. He drew his blaster and looked at them. "Who's with me?"

Bria just shook her head. "The three of us? Against forty? Han, you've got more courage than sense!"

He shook his head and, with a sudden, vicious gesture, holstered his blaster again. "You're right. But I don't have to like it."

Without warning, a sudden crackle of a different frequency filled the control cabin. A voice spoke in rapid-fire Sullustan. "Full throttle. Port turn. Seven seconds—Mark!"

"What the—" Han's fingers moved automatically as he throttled back up, using every bit of power he could squeeze out of the main and auxiliary engines. The sound of the straining engines was painful to hear as they revved, uselessly fighting the inexorable tractor beam.

By now the *Talisman* had been nearly drawn into the gaping maw of the ship's docking bay. Only a few hundred meters separated the two ships.

Han programmed his controls for a hard port turn, and his hand hovered, ready to implement the command. The engines strained and revved. In moments they'd burn out. "What's that crazy little—"

He broke off with a gasp as the *Ylesian Dream* came streaking toward them, moving at terrible speed.

Everyone in the *Talisman*'s control cabin ducked as the little freighter flashed by overhead, then banked hard to starboard. Jalus Nebl took the *Ylesian Dream* between the *Talisman* and *Helot's Shackle* at full throttle. The distance was so tight that the little Sullustan had to turn the *Dream* on her side to make it between the two closing vessels.

"Go!" cried Han. "Go, Nebl!" He activated the controls, turning the *Talisman* as hard to port as he could.

When the *Dream* rushed between the two ships, it broke the tractor beam for a few precious seconds. Han's suddenly released ship ricocheted away from the Corellian corvette like a blaster bolt, sheering off to the left, while Jalus Nebl sped away to the right.

"Yeeeeehah!" Han yelled in sheer exultation as he felt his ship soaring away from the *Helot's Shackle*. As he swooped by the huge vessel, just for good measure, Han fired two concussion missiles at the *Shackle*'s principle solar collector and stabilizer fin, which was located dorsally amidships.

He watched, openmouthed, as the first missile wiped out the minimal shield that had been all that was protecting the fin, allowing the second missile to explode with deadly force, destroying most of the fin. "They had their heavy shields down, those *idiots*!" he whooped. "They thought they had us, so they left that fin almost unshielded!"

He knew the corvette could still be a threat to them, so he didn't slow down. Neither did Jalus Nebl. The little Sullustan was still gaining speed when Han's sensors reported several minutes later that he'd successfully made the jump to hyperspace.

"And we're next," Han said, grinning at Bria. "Say goodbye to paradise, sweetheart . . ."

With a flourish, he stabbed down at the controls that would take them into hyperspace, and gloried in the sudden surge of power that thrust them out of realspace and into star-streaked brilliance.

"Home free," Han whispered, and slumped into his seat, only just now aware of how very, very tired he was.

Bria smiled at him and squeezed his hand. Mrrov gave him a cheek rub. "Thank you," they both whispered.

Han had never felt so good . . .

Chapter Twelve:

TOGORIA

Han awakened to the sound of soft, muffled sobbing. He had been sleeping on the floor in Teroenza's living area, on a pile of expensive carpets he'd dragged into place. He'd insisted that Bria take the one human-style bed. Since Mrrov had been the only one who'd gotten any rest the previous night, she'd volunteered to doze in the pilot's seat and keep an eye out for alarms—though now that they'd reached hyperspace, there wasn't much that could go wrong.

Han sat up with a groan, feeling stiff. Yesterday had been a hard day, and he now remembered, belatedly, that he hadn't eaten anything. Thirst was even worse than hunger. Climbing to his feet, he staggered over to the room's water dispenser and drank several cups.

As he did so, his hand brushed his face, and he frowned

as he touched his chin and felt thick, generous stubble. He had forgotten to shave since before they'd landed on Nal Hutta.

The sounds of human sobbing had stopped. Han grabbed his clothes and went into the luxurious refresher unit, glad that it contained appointments for almost all types of species. He even managed to find a shaver.

Minutes later, clothed and feeling considerably better, he went in search of Bria.

He found her in the tiny guard's room, sitting up on the little bunk, arms around her knees, her face pressed against them. "Hey . . ." Han whispered. "What's wrong? What's happened?"

She didn't raise her face, just waved him away. "No . . . please, just . . . let me . . . alone. I'll be . . . all right. I don't want you . . . to see me like this." She sniffled. "I look . . . terrible."

Han sat down beside her, but didn't touch her. "I look terrible, too," he said. "We could all do with a change of clothes. Hey . . ." he joked, trying to make her look at him, "at least I got rid of the beard. That's a big improvement."

She raised her head and gave him a watery smile. Her nose and eyes were red, but she still looked lovely to Han. "You did look kind of . . . scruffy . . . last night."

Han drew himself up, pretending to take umbrage. "*Scruffy? Me?* Never!" He slid an arm around her gently. "Bria, honey . . . what's wrong? Tell me."

She began to shudder. "It's the Exultation, Han. I woke up and realized that the pilgrims are gathering for devotions right now. And I realized I'll never have it again— never feel that good again!"

Han didn't know what to say. He realized that Bria was missing the physical and emotional sensations that accompanied the Exultation just as an addict would miss a dose of his or her drug of choice. The realization scared him. Would Bria be able to fight this dependency and win? Or would she go through life mourning what she'd lost?

"I think that's natural," he said cautiously, not wanting to frighten her by voicing his real thoughts. "Of course you'd miss it for a day or so, maybe a week. But we'll all help you through it, honey. You're a strong person. You'll get through it. And then"—he made an all-encompassing gesture with his hand—"it's a big galaxy, sweetheart. And it's all ours, now. We'll sell Teroenza's stuff, and sell the *Talisman*—"

"Sell the *Talisman*?" she broke in.

"Yeah, I'm afraid it's too recognizable. I'll take Muuurgh and Mrrov home, and then we'll look for a place to sell this ship. I think I know one. A used-ship dealer on Tralus, in the Corellian system. But we can easily book passage on a ship from there to Corellia."

He gave her shoulders a squeeze. "And there's one big advantage to that . . . I won't be busy piloting. You'll have my"—gently he kissed her cheek—"*undivided* attention."

She swallowed and looked flustered. Han started to lean toward her again, but she pulled back, slightly, and he took the hint.

She bit her lip, her blue-green eyes haunted. "Oh, Han . . . what if I can't get over this . . . this . . . *longing*? Han"—she twisted her hands together in a convulsive gesture—"it's worse than a longing! It's like a . . . a *craving*! My whole self is crying out to be Exulted! I feel like someone punched a big hole in me and *took* part of me away!"

She began to shiver violently. Han pulled her to him, held her tightly, and stroked her hair, murmuring words of comfort. Inside, though, his mind was racing, and he realized that *he* was scared, too. Scared of how much he felt for this woman. Han had had some pretty definite plans regarding Bria that had involved them spending copious amounts of time alone, in each other's arms.

But she's not ready for that, he realized with a sinking feeling. *She needs a friend, not a lover.*

How long would it take for Bria to regain herself?

Only time would tell.

.   .   .

"Coming up on Togoria," Han said, "where should I land us?"

"Our largest city is Caross," Mrrov told him, indicating an area on the schematic of the planet. "From Caross we can send a messenger to the Margrave of Togoria, the ruler of all the male hunters. There is a landing field just outside Caross. We do not have our own ships, yet, but traders and passenger ships from other worlds visit our planet."

"Okay, then, Caross it is," Han said. With great care he piloted the *Talisman* down to a perfect landing in the center of the field. At the moment, no other ships were present.

"Muuurgh," Han said as he updated his log, "are you two worried about reprisals from the t'landa Til or the Hutts?"

"Not greatly," Muuurgh said, ostentatiously flexing his claws. "When Mrrov and I have assembled our tribes, we will be wed. It is then traditional with our people for a newly married couple to spend a long—what do you call it?" He said a word in his own language to Mrrov, whose Basic was much better than his own.

"Honeymoon," she supplied.

"Yes, a long honeymoon together. Remember that on our world, males and females live separately for much of each year. Once we are past our honeymoon, Mrrov and I will see each other only once a year, for about a month. It is our way of life. But first"—the giant Togorian gave his mate-to-be a cheek rub—"we will spend a long time together, just the two of us, in the mountains. The Hutts and Ylesians will not find us, and our people will not tolerate their looking. Any pilot that lands on Togoria and asks questions about Mrrov or Muuurgh will be . . . dealt with."

Mrrov gave a feral smile that showed many needle-sharp teeth. "Not many species have the courage to intentionally anger Torgorians. I believe most bounty hunters would rather hunt . . . easier . . . prey."

"I can believe it," Han said sincerely. "Okay, then. We're here. Now what? Do you two just walk off, claw in claw?" He grinned at Bria, who gave him a wan smile. Food and rest had restored her somewhat, but he knew she was still battling her inner demons and longings.

"If Han must leave, Muuurgh and Mrrov will understand," said the giant male. "But if Han and Bria could stay for a day or two, they would be able to stand with us at our ceremony that will make us a mated couple. You would call it a 'wedding.' "

Han looked over at Bria. "So . . . we've just been invited to a wedding, sweetheart. Want to stay for a couple of days? I think we could both use a rest."

"Sure," she said, and smiled at the Togorians. "Nothing could please me more."

A contingent of Togorian females, with a small scattering of visiting males, was approaching the ship. Han and his party walked down the ramp. Mrrov and Muuurgh were immediately enfolded by the crowd, amid roars and yowls and vibrating purrs of happiness.

Still standing at the bottom of the ramp, Han took Bria's hand and looked around him at Togoria. "Nice planet," he said. "After Ylesia, *this* seems like a *real* paradise."

"It *is* beautiful," she agreed. "Just right."

It was, indeed, a beautiful world. Overhead arced a deep blue sky, with a few puffy white clouds. The sky held just a tint of green to it, so it was almost indigo around the horizon. Tall mountain peaks shone white and glistening in the distance. Dark forests made a backdrop for a blue lake surrounded by meadowlands. Exotic green-fringed white blooms with scarlet leaves waved in the gentle breeze.

Overhead, Han spotted a large flying creature, and realized it must be one of the mosgoths Muuurgh had told him were the principal means of travel on Togoria. Mosgoths were large flying lizards, very intelligent. Togorians had domesticated the mosgoths long ago. Each species worked together to protect each other against even larger winged reptiles, the deadly liphons who stole both Togorian cubs and mosgoth eggs.

As Han watched, the mosgoth circled the landing field, and then began to descend. Han saw the Togorian male perched on its back, guiding it by means of a nose-halter.

He was impressed by the rapport that appeared to exist between mount and rider.

Togorian air was some of the cleanest, most refreshing Han had ever breathed. Mrrov had told him earlier that all Togorian technology was based on solar power, for just this reason. Togorians revered their world and had no wish to despoil it or pollute it in the name of progress, as so many other species in the galaxy had done.

Han took an experimental step or two, then bounced on his heels. He felt light . . . almost buoyant. That fit, for Togoria's gravity was somewhat less than Corellian or Ylesian gravity.

Suddenly the crowd parted, and Muuurgh, still bandaged but walking with almost his old confident stride, emerged, with Mrrov at his side. "Our clans are being summoned for the mating ceremony, and the feast that will follow," he said. "You are our welcome guests. Please . . . follow us."

Han and Bria followed.

Caross proved to be a lovely city—white native stone was used to build terraced houses against the hillsides. Everywhere gardens abounded, and parks for strolling. Togorian females busied themselves with projects, or cared for rowdy cubs. Muuurgh explained that both female and male cubs remained with their mothers until they neared adulthood, then the males returned to the clan with their fathers to learn the ways of the hunter's life.

During the next two days, Han and Bria rested, ate delicious meals (though they insisted on their meat being cooked), and took long strolls together around the parks, through the gardens. Han also took flying lessons from a young male, Rrowv—lessons on how to ride and control a mosgoth. With his quick reflexes and daring, Han was soon soaring astride his mount far above the treetops, glorying in the feel of the sturdy ribbed wings pumping behind him as he sat in the small saddle mounted on the mosgoth's shoulders.

The mosgoths proved to be affectionate creatures that

enjoyed having their tiny ear flaps scratched and their chests rubbed.

All through the day following their arrival, mosgoths bearing male riders arrived from all over Togoria. The word had gone out that Muuurgh the hunter had returned, and all his clan-relatives were gathering to welcome him home and attend his and Mrrov's wedding.

Muuurgh and Mrrov were kept busy relating their adventures among the stars to audiences of their people. Mrrov never tired of repeating the story of what had happened to her, lest some other unwary female Togorian be sucked in by promises of a Ylesian "paradise."

The wedding "ceremony" took place at sunset of their third day on Togoria. Han and Bria stood beside Muuurgh and Mrrov as they solemnly faced their assembled clans. Their fur gleamed from hours of careful grooming. Only the small white bandage on Muuurgh's side marred his shining coat. On their native world, Togorians rarely wore clothing—their weather was so clement that it was seldom needed.

First the betrothed couple faced their clans, turning slowly so that all might see their faces. At Muuurgh's signal, Han and Bria then stepped back to stand with the crowd of onlookers.

Mrrov and Muuurgh turned to face each other. Han blinked in surprise as a low, growling yowl began emanating from their throats. Both bared their teeth and hissed. Their claws sprang out.

Then, so quickly that the eye could scarcely follow, they sprang at each other and went down on the ground, teeth locked in each other's throats. Growling, yowling, and snarling, they rolled over and over, slashing at each other with their front paw-hands. Their feet were busy, too, digging deep into each other's furred belly.

Han looked over at Bria, who was looking faintly alarmed. But no one in the crowd seemed to find anything amiss about what was happening. *It takes all kinds to make a galaxy* . . . Han thought.

Finally, panting and growling, the two combatants broke

apart. Despite the apparent ferocity of their attacks, no blood was visible on their coats. The two circled each other, and their yowls gradually died away into soft, gentle noises. They stood close together, rubbing their faces against each other for a long time. Han could hear their hoarse purring from where he was standing.

Then, suddenly, Mrrov hissed, spat, and lashed out at Muuurgh again. He leaped at her, and then they were down on the ground again, rolling and clawing and biting.

Han gave Bria's hand a squeeze. "Romantic, isn't it?" he whispered with a grin.

"Shhhhh!" she replied.

Moments later the nuptial pair were purring and rubbing against each other, eyes half-closed with pleasure.

The crowd was getting more excited. Han could hear a vibrating purr arising from all sides. Again Muuurgh and Mrrov went through their "fighting" act.

But this time, when they reached the cheek-rubbing stage, Muuurgh grabbed Mrrov by the loose folds of skin at the back of her neck. Clutching her in his teeth and powerful arms, he lifted her smaller form and carried her across the circle. The crowd parted before them, opening like a door.

Muuurgh vanished into the darkness, still carrying his mate. Moments later two loud, triumphantly ecstatic yowls broke the stillness—and then silence reigned.

The crowd murmured their approval of the completion of the rite. Han was nearly knocked over by Togorian relatives of Muuurgh's slapping his shoulders and assuring him that that had been one of the finest weddings they had ever been privileged to witness.

They feasted into the night. Han and Bria slipped away to take a walk in the park, beneath Togoria's two tiny moons. The stars blazed overhead. "So," Han said, "how did today go? Is it getting any easier?"

She nodded slightly. "A little. Sometimes I can go a whole hour without missing it, Han. Sometimes, though, I feel like the minutes are just crawling by, and I'm hanging on to my sanity by my fingernails."

"Well, tomorrow I've got something special planned," he said, smiling at her. "Get ready to have some fun. I've got everything arranged."

"What?" she asked. "What are we going to do?"

"That'd be telling," he teased. "Just prepare to get up with the birds, okay?"

"They don't have birds on Togoria," she reminded him. "Just teeny flying lizards."

"That's true," he said. "But get up early, okay?"

"Okay."

When Bria arose the next morning, she could not find Han anywhere in their suite of rooms. But she did find a basket of fruit, a jug of fruit juice, some strips of smoked meat, and a loaf of bread on a tray. On the tray was a strip of flimsy and written on it were the following words: "Dress, eat, and come outside. I'll be waiting—H."

Bria read the note, raised her eyebrows, then went off to do as it said. Her curiosity was so strong that it even muted the constant craving for the Exultation. Sometimes the longings came in waves so intense that she felt that she might go mad. But as the days passed, such occurrences were rarer.

Bria prayed to all the true gods of the universe that someday they would cease altogether.

When she reached the courtyard outside the building where they'd been quartered, Bria found Han waiting for her. He was sitting astride a mosgoth, with a pack and a blanket strapped behind the saddle. As she stood there uncertainly, he leaned down and held out a hand. "C'mon! Climb up!"

She stared from him to the mosgoth, to the open reaches of the Togorian sky. "You want me to fly with you on this . . . creature?" she asked. To fly in a spaceship, or aboard a landskimmer, was one thing. To climb aboard a huge reptile and soar off into the sky seemed quite another.

"Sure!" Han leaned over to pat the neck of his mount. "This is Kaydiss, and she's a real sweetie, aren't you, girl?"

The mosgoth arched her sinewy neck and flicked out a long, forked tongue, obviously enjoying the caress.

Bria took a deep breath. "Okay," she said. *After all*, she thought, *the worst that can happen is that we'll fall out of the sky and get killed. Then I wouldn't have to worry about the Exultation anymore, would I?*

Grasping his hand, she put a foot up onto the beast's leg, which it obligingly crooked to help her mount. With a pull and a scramble, she was up, sitting before Han. His arms were around her, as secure as a safety harness. Bria gasped, then shut her eyes as he clucked to Kaydiss and twitched the reins.

With two huge leaping strides and a thrust of the mosgoth's powerful wings, Han and Bria were airborne and climbing steadily. Bria opened her eyes to find herself high above the tops of the buildings. The wind rushed by her face, blowing her hair, bringing tears to her eyes.

"Oh!" she cried. "Han, this is *wonderful*!"

"Yep," he said, a pardonable note of smugness in his voice. "And just wait till you see where I'm taking you."

Bria held the front of the saddle (with the two of them squeezed together, she wasn't too worried about falling off) and exulted in the feeling of really *flying*.

Forests and rivers flowed by beneath them. Bria stared down at the fields, the towns, and the lakes, grinning ecstatically. She hadn't felt this good since . . . well, since her last Exultation.

But even the Exultation seemed to have lost its power over her, for the moment. Leaning forward, Bria opened her mouth, drinking in the wind of their passage. She wanted to wave her arms and whoop aloud, but she resisted, not wanting to chance unbalancing the mosgoth.

"Won't it tire her out, carrying double?" she shouted back at Han.

His voice came almost in her ear. She could feel the warmth of his breath. "She's used to carrying male Togorians. You and me together don't weigh as much as Muuurgh—or even some of the smaller males. Kaydiss is fine."

Half an hour later, the broad river they'd been following widened, until it branched into a large delta. Han turned the mosgoth north, and then, within a few more minutes, Bria saw the curling white breakers breaking over silvery-gold sand.

She turned to give Han an excited smile. "The beach!"

"I promised myself that someday we'd go to a real beach," he said. "One where we could swim, and not worry about getting eaten."

He was guiding the mosgoth lower and lower now, and finally, she came to a halt on the sand. Han slipped on her wing hobble, then left her to forage for herself in the nearby salt marsh. He returned, carrying the blanket and their lunch.

"Swim first," he asked, "or food first?"

Bria looked at the white surf and felt the tug of the water. Her family owned a beach house on Corellia, and she'd loved to swim ever since she'd been old enough to walk. "Swim," she said.

Glad that she'd worn a one-piece singlet beneath her shirt and trousers, Bria pulled off her outer clothes and raced into the water. Han, having stripped down to his shorts, followed her.

She soon found that, to her surprise, he couldn't swim.

"Never got the chance to learn," he admitted, a little embarrassed. "I was always working, and when I wasn't actually working, I was swoop racing or something. I told you, the beach on Ylesia was the first time I'd ever seen a lot of water all together."

"Well," said Bria firmly, "today you're going to learn. You're young and strong and you've got good balance and reflexes. You'll be fine."

Han proved an apt pupil. Bria was amazed at how hard he concentrated, how precisely he followed her instructions on how to move his arms, his legs, when to breathe, etc. She commented on it at one point. Han smiled sardonically. "Pilots learn to follow instructions," he said. "Or they wind up *dead* pilots."

Before they came out of the water to eat, he was paddling around fearlessly in the surf and had begun to be able to coordinate his breathing with his arm strokes and leg kicks.

"You're a very good pupil," Bria praised as they sat together on the blanket, gazing out to sea.

"Thanks," he said. "You're a good teacher."

They shared food from the provisions he'd brought, and then they walked hand in hand along the beach. At one point a tiny lizard flew overhead, winking in shades of green and gold. Bria put out a hand and held very, very still, and the tiny thing lighted on her fingers and clung there, its wings waving gently in the breeze. Han grinned at her. "You look . . . beautiful . . ." he said.

"I feel as though I own the world," she replied, half joking. "This day . . . I'll remember it always, Han."

"You own this beach," he said, smiling down at her. "I give it to you. It's yours, for today."

The lizard took wing, still quite unafraid, and flew away.

As they strolled through the breakers, Han told her more about his determination to get into the Imperial Academy. "People look up to an Imperial officer," he said. "Nobody's ever looked up to me for anything, before, but if I can get in, that's all going to change. I'll be able to turn my life around, Bria. I'll never have to steal or smuggle or cheat anyone again."

Bria's eyes filled with tears at the earnestness in his voice. She reached up and caressed his cheek gently. "My heart breaks for you, sometimes," she whispered. "You've known such cruelty, such betrayal . . ."

He touched her cheek in return, his brown eyes intent. The wind ruffled his hair. "But I also had one person who loved me," he said. "Let me tell you about Dewlanna . . ."

They walked slowly along, hand in hand, and Bria listened as he told her about his best friend during his childhood. By the time they'd reached the blanket again, they were walking in silence. "Garris Shrike sounds like he'd fit in perfectly on Ylesia," Bria said, finally.

"He'd probably wind up running the place," Han agreed, a bleak note in his voice. He lowered himself onto the blanket and sat, arms draped across the tops of his knees, looking out to sea, his expression troubled. "I should have killed him when I had the chance, Bria. But . . . I didn't."

She dropped down beside him. "That's because you're a decent person, Han," she said fiercely. "You think you're tough, and you are—but you're also *decent*. You're no cold-blooded killer like Shrike. If you'd shot him, you'd be no better than he is."

He turned to her, his face profoundly intent, very serious. "You're right," he said softly. "Sometimes when things seem so confused, you make them all come clear . . . with just a few words. You're a very . . . wise . . . woman . . ."

Bria sat perfectly still as he leaned forward and kissed her, gently, on the cheek. His lips were warm. As he started to pull away, she put her hand on his cheek. "Don't."

His head turned, and his lips found her mouth. He tasted of sea salt. Bria closed her eyes, and time seemed to stop.

After several long heartbeats, he drew back. Bria opened her eyes to find him searching her face. "How was that?" he asked softly, sounding a little breathless. "Okay?"

Bria was more than a little breathless. "Better than okay," she whispered, sliding her arms around his neck, feeling the sun-warmed skin of his bare shoulders. His arms went around her, holding her tightly. "Much, much better . . ."

She kissed him back, and it was a long, long time before they spoke again . . .

Chapter Thirteen:

Return to Corellia

The following day Mrrov and Muuurgh made ready to set off on their "honeymoon" and Bria and Han prepared to raise ship for the Corellian system.

At their final moment of parting, Muuurgh grasped Han by the shoulders and shook him, very gently. "I will miss you," he said in his halting—but much improved—Basic. "Must you go? You like Togoria, you said so. Without you, I would never have found Mrrov. The Margrave of all Togoria has asked me to tell you that you and Bria are welcome to stay forever. You can hunt with us, Han. Fly mosgoths. We would be happy."

Han smiled at the big alien. "And see Bria only once a year? I'm afraid that's not the way we humans do things, pal. But thanks for the invite, Muuurgh. Maybe I'll come back and see how you and Mrrov are doing someday."

"Han do that, and *soon*," Muuurgh said, his Basic disintegrating in the face of strong emotion. He grabbed the Corellian in a hug, scooping him clean off the ground. Han hugged him back.

Bria and Mrrov also exchanged a fond farewell. "You will conquer your need for the Exultation," Mrrov told Bria, earnestly. "I did. For a long while after I made myself resist it, I grieved for it. But after many days, the longing eased, and now I never feel it. I let my anger against those slavers help me wipe the longing from my spirit."

"I hope I can be as strong as you, Mrrov," Bria said.

"You already are," the Togorian female assured her. "You just don't realize it yet."

Once aboard the *Talisman*, Han lifted the Ylesian yacht into the clear skies of Togoria with a genuine feeling of regret. "This is a good world," he said to Bria, who was sitting beside him in the copilot's seat. "Good people, too."

"Yes," she agreed. "It was certainly good to *us*. I'll never forget yesterday, if I live to be a hundred."

Han smiled at her. "Me neither, sweetheart. All my life I wanted to go to the beach and just be able to act like a regular citizen—no scams, no security forces to worry about, no contraband burning a hole in my pocket. Thanks to you, I know what that's like, now."

She gave him such a tender smile that he leaned over and kissed her. "Bria . . . I . . ." Han hesitated, took a deep breath, and then shook his head.

Squaring his shoulders, he turned back to his controls and grew very busy with his piloting. Bria sat there watching him, never taking her eyes off him as he calculated their jump to hyperspace, and fed the coordinates he'd chosen into the navicomputer.

When the stars streaked by them, and they had safely made the jump, she swiveled her seat toward his and put a hand on his arm. "Yes?" she said. "Go on. You were saying?"

Han tried to look innocent, and failed. "Huh? What do you mean?"

"You were about to tell me something, when you got

busy piloting. Well, we're safely in hyperspace now, so there's no reason you can't tell me." She smiled slightly. "I'm waiting."

"Well, I was just thinking . . . that I'm hungry," he finished in a rush. "Really hungry. Let's go get some lunch."

"We ate before we left, barely an hour ago," she reminded him. Her expression gentle, she reached out and captured one of his hands and held it in both her own. "Tell me," she said.

"Well . . ." He shrugged. "I'm telling you I'm hungry again."

"Are you?" she asked quietly.

"I . . ." He shook his head, obviously ill at ease. "Uh, no. Hey . . . Bria, honey . . . I'm no good at this."

"You're good at *some* things," she said, smiling impishly.

"Like what?" he challenged, grinning back.

"Like . . . piloting. And fighting. And rescuing people."

"Yeah, I guess I am." He looked at her again, and all the sudden rush of bravado faded. "Bria . . . what I was trying to say was that I . . ." He cleared his throat. "This is not easy."

"I know," she said. "I know."

Raising his hand to her lips, she kissed it, then said, "Han . . . I love you, too."

He looked both pleased and surprised. "You do?"

"Yes. For a long time, now. I think I fell in love with you that day in the refectory, when you wouldn't go away, no matter how much I told you to."

"Really? I didn't know until . . . I don't know when I knew. But when I figured it out . . . it scared me, Bria. Never happened to me before."

"Loving someone? Or being loved?"

"Both. Except for Dewlanna. She loved me, I guess. But that was different."

"Yes." Her eyes were shining. "This is different. I just hope we can be together, Han."

Now it was his turn to take her hands in his. "Of course we'll be together," he said. "I won't let anything get in the way of that. Count on it, sweetheart."

. . .

Han set a course for the *Talisman* that took them far away from Hutt space and brought them in a leisurely three-day trip to the Corellian system. He was deliberately prolonging his and Bria's time alone together. Inwardly, he was dreading having to go back to Corellia and meet her family. He knew almost nothing about how "citizens" lived, and he was pretty sure he would have trouble fitting in.

He also knew that once they reached Tralus, he'd have to get busy. Han was all ready to change identities as soon as they landed on Corellia. But Bria would be wanted by the t'landa Til and the Hutts, too, and they knew *her* real name. The first thing Han planned to do as soon as he had credits available was to equip Bria with a fake ID.

Besides, he was trying to give her as much time as he could to heal. He knew she still pined for the Exultation, though she no longer broke down in panic attacks or fits of sobbing. But several times he'd awakened in the night to find her gone.

When he searched for her, he usually found her in the control cabin, sitting in the copilot's seat and staring out at the stars with such wistful longing in her eyes that Han felt a pang of jealousy.

Why can't I be enough for her? Why isn't our love enough? he wondered. He wanted to be enough for her, wanted her to be happy and content—but he could tell she wasn't. It grieved Han, and it made him angry, too.

Once he tried to talk to her about it. "It's been almost ten days! Why do you miss it so much, still?" he demanded, hearing the edge of anger in his voice and unable to stop it. "Tell me, Bria. Make me understand!"

She gazed at him, her blue-green eyes very sad, almost haunted. "I can't explain it, Han. It's like they took a piece of me . . . a piece of my spirit. It's not just missing the Exultation itself, the pleasure, the warmth. I'm getting past that. It's the . . ." she faltered, then fell silent.

He was sitting beside her in the pilot's seat, and he reached out and grasped her hands. They were cold, and he

warmed them gently in his. "Go on . . ." he said quietly.
"I'm here. I'm listening."

"Both Mrrov and Teroenza were wrong when they said
only weak-minded people fall into the trap of the Ylesian
religion," Bria said slowly, selecting her words with care.
"Oh, some of the pilgrims may be discontented people
who've never been successful in life and are looking for a
way to escape responsibility. But not most of them. I got to
know a lot of them, Han."

"Yeah, you did," he encouraged.

"Most of the Ylesian pilgrims were . . . idealists, I
guess you'd say. People who believed that there was something *better*, some *meaning* to life. They went looking in the
wrong places, they got fooled into believing the priest's
bilge about the One and the All . . . but that doesn't make
their goal—their *aspiration*—of believing in a higher power
stupid."

He nodded, and saw tears gather in her beautiful eyes
and spill over. Concerned, he burst out, "Bria . . . sweetheart. Don't tear yourself up like this! Just because this religion turned out to be a hokey fake doesn't mean life isn't
worth living. We have each other. We're gonna have money.
We'll be fine."

"Han . . ." Gently she touched his cheek, caressed his
face, and gave him a loving smile. "You're the ultimate
pragmatist, aren't you? If you're not getting shot at or
caught in a tractor beam, life is great, right?"

He shook his head, a little stung. "I'm a simple guy,
yeah, but that doesn't mean I can't understand what you're
talking about, Bria. It would be nice if there were some
higher power, maybe. I just don't happen to believe there
is. And it hurts me to see you hurt."

"Han . . . don't you realize that the only person you
can really take care of and protect is *you*—"

"And *you*, Bria," he broke in. "Don't forget that for one
second. We're a team, sweetheart."

"Yes," she said. "We are a team. But it's hard for me to
be content with not being shot at or having money. I want
more."

"You want some reason for everything that happens. You want to work to make your ideals real," he said.

"Yes," she agreed. "But I understand that you don't let questions like the meaning of life torment you. You're probably the smart one, Han."

"Smart?" Han frowned. "I ain't dumb, I know that, but I never pretended to be a philosopher or something."

"Right. You don't go around tearing yourself up over injustice and corruption and wrongdoing. You accept things as they are, and you figure out ways around them. Right?"

He thought about that, and finally nodded. "Yeah, I guess so. Maybe, a long time ago, I had some ideas about how I could become someone who righted wrongs and kicked the bad guys' butts, but"—he sighed and gave her a wry smile—"I think I got those ideas beaten out of me by the time I was just a little kid. When you lived under Garris Shrike's rule, you tumbled pretty quick to the fact that nobody was gonna look out for you except yourself—and that sticking your neck out for anyone else was a good way to get it whacked off."

"How about Dewlanna?" she asked.

"Yeah, I knew you'd bring her up." Han ran a hand through his hair and grimaced. "Dewlanna was different. We looked out for each other, yeah. But she was the only one, Bria. The *only* one who gave a vrelt's ass if I lived or died. Knowing that made me a . . . pragmatist, I guess."

"Of course it did," she said. "That's perfectly natural."

"But go on," he urged. "You were saying about how the pilgrims were . . . idealists. Are you one?"

She nodded. "I think so, Han. All my life I wanted to be *more,* to be *better*—to make the universe a better place because I was in it. When I found the Ylesian religion, I really, truly thought that was it. That I could somehow change the universe by believing and having faith." She smiled wryly and shrugged. "Obviously, I picked the wrong thing to believe in."

"Yeah," he said, turning over in his mind what she'd said. "But there are other things to believe in, Bria. Maybe some of 'em are real. Maybe you just have to find out what the real things are."

She stood up and came over to him, then bent down to kiss the top of his head. He stood up and slid his arms around her, held her tightly. "I know what one real thing is," she said. "You're *real*. You're the most *real* person I've ever met. The most alive."

He kissed her cheek, and she laid her head on his shoulder. They stood there like that for a minute, not speaking. Finally, he said, "Dewlanna told me about something she believes in. Some sort of life-strength shared by all creatures, all things. She believed in that. She swore to me it was real."

"Maybe I should go off to Kashyyyk," she said. "On a pilgrimage."

"Sure," he said. "Someday we'll go there. I'd like to see it. Dewlanna said it was a beautiful world. They live in the treetops."

"That would be nice," she said dreamily. "Just you and me in a treetop. What would we do with ourselves all day?"

"I can think of one thing," he said, and bent to kiss her with such passion that even the stars seemed to reel around her in long streaks, and her ears rang . . .

No, she realized, a moment later, it wasn't Han's kiss that had caused that reaction, it was the alarm beeping to tell them they were coming out of hyperspace. Han grimaced. "Talk about bad timing, sweetheart. But . . . later, okay?"

She smiled. "Later . . . I'll hold you to it."

He was already back in his seat as he checked their coordinates, but he spared a moment to give her a grin that made her heart turn over. "I can hardly wait . . ."

Han set the *Talisman* down in a privately owned landing field on Tralus. "What is this place?" Bria said, following him down the ramp and looking around her in bewilderment. Ships of all sizes and descriptions were clustered together. Some were little more than rusted-out hulks . . .

others looked almost brand-new. None had any identifying codes or names, however. Those markings had been scoured off by laser torches. "It's like . . . a ship's graveyard or something."

"Yeah. Old spaceships never die . . . they just wind up at Truthful Toryl's Used Spaceship Lot," Han said. "When you need a ship, or you want to get rid of a ship, and you don't want to leave a . . . trail . . . you come here."

Her eyes widened. "These ships are all . . . stolen?"

"Most of 'em," he said. "Ours is, too . . . remember?"

Bria grimaced. "I keep trying to forget."

Han glanced over at the small office set in the middle of the vast landing field. "And here comes Truthful Toryl himself," he said.

Truthful Toryl was a Duros, a tall, thin, blue-skinned humanoid. Completely bald, his face was quite human except for the absence of a nose—which gave him a mournful appearance. Han stepped forward, his hand held out. "Good day to you, Traveler Toryl," he said. Duros loved to travel so much that the word "traveler" was their preferred honorific. "I'm Keil d'Tana, and this is my associate, Kyloria m'Bal. Very pleased to meet you."

"And I you," Toryl said. "Greetings to two travelers. You have time for refreshment and sharing of stories?"

The Duros were famed for being wonderful storytellers throughout the galaxy. A Duros had a near-photographic memory for any story he or she heard. Most Duros "collected" stories, and apparently Toryl was no exception.

"I'm sorry," Han said. "We are in a bit of a rush. There's a passenger vessel we have to catch."

"I quite understand," the Duros said. "Since you are taking public transport, I gather you are here to sell, not buy, a ship."

"You're right, Traveler," Han said. "It's in prime condition, too. A lovely little pleasure yacht. Just needs a little refitting to be perfect for some rich Corellian family who wants to take the kids on the perfect vacation."

"Yacht?" Bria thought Toryl's voice sharpened on the

word, but couldn't be sure. "I will look and quote you a price, Traveler d'Tana."

Han led the way to where the *Talisman* rested. The Duros's normally mournful-appearing features lengthened even farther when he saw the Ylesian vessel. "Let me show you around," Han said, pointing at the ramp.

The Duros shook his bald blue head. "No need," he said. "I can offer you five thousand. Firm."

Han gaped at the alien, completely shaken out of his normal confident demeanor. "Huh?" he said blankly. "What? That's crazy! Five thousand for a ship like this? That's scrap price!"

The Duros bowed slightly in Han's direction. "Indeed it is, Traveler Draygo." He bowed in Bria's direction. "And Traveler Tharen." Waving a hand at the *Talisman*, Truthful Toryl said sadly, "I agree that it is a shame to reduce such a beautiful vessel to scrap. But that is all I could do with her. The Hutts are searching for this vessel . . . searching intensively. As they are searching for the resourceful pilot Vykk Draygo, who stole her."

Han turned away, and Bria saw his lips move in a scathing curse, but when he turned back to face Truthful Toryl, his composure was in place again. "I see," he said. "Five thousand . . . firm."

"Yes. I might be persuaded to raise that price slightly if you and your companion would tell me your stories . . ." Toryl added hopefully.

"Sorry, pal, no can do," Han said. He shrugged. "Okay, five thousand it is. Cash."

"Cash it is," Truthful Toryl said.

Later that same day, "Janil Andrus" and his wife, "Drea Andrus," boarded an intersystem shuttle bound for Corellia. Bria had worried about posing as husband and wife, but Han had assured her that the Hutt SECURITY ALERT bulletins listed them as being single. Privately, he was worried about whether the Hutts would try to trace them, since they knew Bria's last name, but he was also aware that the Hutts wouldn't want a scene or their scam on Ylesia revealed to the public. He had to hope that would keep them from openly trying to have them arrested. Han wasn't figuring on staying on Corellia long . . .

The pair arrived on their homeworld early in the evening and caught a transcontinental shuttle to the southern continent, where the Tharen home was located. When they arrived at the station, which Bria said was within walking distance of her home, they were tired and grubby, with no way to change clothes. Their only luggage was the backpack that held Teroenza's treasures.

"So . . ." Han said, shifting from one foot to the other and looking out of the station window into a soft, foggy drizzle, "now what? Find a place to hole up until morning? Or should we call 'em and warn 'em?"

"I think I had better call," Bria said, sounding uncertain herself. "Wait here." She headed off to borrow the station master's comlink. A few minutes later she was back.

Han saw how drawn and tired she looked and put an arm around her. "So . . . how'd it go?"

She smiled wanly. "My mother nearly fainted, then she started screaming at me." She sighed. "I know she loves me, but the ways she shows it make *me* want to scream sometimes. She wants the best for me—as long as it's *her* idea of what's best!"

Han nodded, thinking for the first time in his life that perhaps he'd been lucky, in a way, never having to deal with parents. "So do we start walking?"

She shook her head. "No. My father is coming for us in the speeder. He'll be here any minute."

Even as she spoke, an expensive speeder pulled up outside of the station. A handsome, distinguished-looking man with gray hair and a heavyset build was at the controls.

As Han and Bria approached the vehicle, the man leaped out of the speeder and, laughing and crying at the same time, embraced his daughter. Long moments later he turned to shake hands with Han. "I'm pleased to meet you," he said. "I understand from Bria that you saved her from . . . well, from terrible things. All I can say is . . . thank you. Thank you, er . . . ."

"Solo, sir," Han said. "Make it Han."

Tharen's grip was firm. "Please . . . call me Renn, Han."

"Yes, sir."

The ride to Bria's home was short. They passed through a reinforced set of security gates, then headed down a road that seemed to have no other houses on it. Han glanced to each side and saw high fences, the type he'd used to sneer at back during his days as a burglar. "Not many people live out here," he observed.

"Oh, this is our land," Renn Tharen said carelessly. "Bought it years ago as a cushion between ourselves and our neighbors. I'm a man who likes my privacy."

He turned the vehicle into a drive that was closed with a another, equally reinforced but more ornamental gate. Beyond it, Han saw the house and mumbled a virulent curse in Huttese under his breath. *Bria, baby . . .* he thought grimly, *why didn't you tell me your family was rich enough to buy and sell half of Corellia?*

The house was huge . . . wings and modified towers, and landscaping to match. The Tharen house made cousin Thrackan's place look like a cottage. Bria turned to Han and smiled tremulously. "Well, we're here."

"Yeah," Han said, deliberately keeping his voice noncommittal. He could tell that Bria was nearly sick with anxiety, and he didn't want to worry her more than she was. At least there was one advantage to Bria's parents being rich— the Hutts would never dare to try to grab her while she was in her parents' home. That would surely cause a major interstellar incident, and Hutts preferred to work clandestinely.

Before the party could reach the front door, Bria's mother came bursting out, dressed in a flowing gown that Han could only recognize as "rich."

"Darling!" she gasped, enfolding Bria in her arms. Han stood off to the side, glad to be out of the way until Bria and her parents were finished with their greetings.

Midway through the whole hubbub of greetings, recriminations, tears, embraces, and excited questions and answers, Bria's brother came home. Han recalled Bria saying her brother's name was "Pavik." Unlike his sister, Pavik Tharen took after his mother; short, slender, with dark hair and green eyes. He was a handsome youth, and seemed genuinely fond of his sister.

It was a long time before Bria could disengage herself from her family to introduce Han. Eyes shining, she took his hand and led him over to meet her mother, Sera Tharen, and her brother.

"Pleased to meet you, Lady Tharen," Han said, shaking hands and putting on his best manners. "And you, Pavik."

Bria's mother's handclasp was limp and unenthusiastic. She studied Han, and he gained the quick impression that she didn't much like what she saw. He sighed inwardly. *I've got a very bad feeling about this . . .*

"Well, please come in," Sera Tharen said. "Let's all sit down. I must say, this has been a shock. I never thought I'd see my baby again, I really didn't. Bria, darling, how could you do this to us?"

Still murmuring recriminations, Sera Tharen led the way inside.

When Han reached the parlor of the house, and they all sat down, he had to repress the urge to leap up and stride out. *I don't belong here*, he thought. *I know it, and they know it.*

The thought made him angry. Refusing to let his discomfort show, Han sat down and lounged back against the opulent cushions with a deliberate show of ease. He looked around, his professional eye automatically assessing the credit value the knickknacks and decorations would have to a fence. "Nice place," he said casually.

"Well, er—" Sera began.

"Han. Call me Han, Lady Tharen," Han said.

"Very well, Han," Bria's mother said stiffly, "I gather we have you to thank for Bria's return." Her eyes were fixed on Han's blaster, and he realized that, like most citizens, none of Bria's family went armed. *Tough, lady*, Han thought. *I don't take off my blaster for you or anybody. Live with it.*

"Well, I tried to be helpful, Lady Tharen," Han replied. "But I couldn't have managed without Bria. She's plenty tough when she wants to be. Good in a fight."

Lady Tharen stiffened, and Han realized that the woman would not regard what he'd said as a compliment. "Oh, dear . . ." she murmured. "Bria, darling, before you sit down, why don't you go and change? Really, dear, where *did* you get those *dreadful* clothes?"

"The tailor droid at the Ylesian Colony," Bria said quickly, and she cast an appealing glance at Han, as if to ask whether he'd be all right.

Han gave her a reassuring wave. "Run along, honey."

Lady Tharen stiffened again at the casual endearment. Bria smiled at Han, gave her mother and brother a doubtful glance, and went quickly from the room.

"So, Han," Pavik Tharen said, "what do you do?" He was staring closely at Han, his eyes assessing in a way that made the pilot uncomfortable.

"Oh, whatever it takes to get by," Han replied carelessly. "Mostly I'm a pilot."

"In the Navy?" Lady Tharen asked, brightening slightly. "Are you an officer?"

"Nope. Freighters, ma'am. I can fly most anything, anywhere. That's why I was on Ylesia, running—" Han broke off, remembering for the first time in a long while that the contraband spice trade was highly illegal, "That is, *hauling* cargo."

"Oh," murmured Lady Tharen, obviously not understanding, but uncomfortable with Han's answer. "How interesting."

"Yeah, it has its moments," Han said.

"I started out as a pilot, many years ago," Renn Tharen said, a note of approval in his voice. "When I was about your age, Han. Worked my way up until I owned the shipping company. That's how I made my first million."

Han thought of telling Renn Tharen that he was intending to enter the Imperial Academy, but the habit of not revealing any personal information was too ingrained. He just smiled and nodded at Bria's father. "Those were the exciting days, sir," he said. "Lots of pirates back then, right?"

Renn Tharen smiled. "I had a few run-ins. I imagine you have, too."

Han smiled back. "A few."

Sera Tharen looked from one to the other, vaguely disturbed. "Oh, dear. That sounds . . . dangerous."

"Comes with the job, Lady Tharen," Han said.

"But I'm forgetting my manners!" she said. "Captain Solo, can I get you something to drink or eat?"

"I wouldn't mind an Alderaanian ale," Han said. "And some flatbread with meat and cheese. We've been traveling all day."

"I'll tell the cook," Lady Tharen said. Han was astonished to realize that the "cook" was a living being, a female Selonian, instead of a droid. This further evidence of wealth impressed him more than anything he'd yet encountered.

By the time Bria reemerged, Han was sitting out in the dining room, eating. He saw her walk out and paused in midbite.

She wore a plain blue-green dress that matched her eyes. The soft fabric had a faint sheen and clung to her in all the right places. And, for the first time since he'd known her, Bria's hair was attractively styled, brushed out into a halo of soft red-gold curls. She looked so different from the blaster-toting thief of a few days ago that it was as though she'd stepped out of another universe.

It's a good thing Ganar Tos can't see her now, he thought wryly. "You look beautiful, honey," he said. "That's a pretty dress."

Han was sophisticated enough to realize that dress probably cost more credits than the average space pilot earned in a week. *She's been raised to have so much,* he thought uneasily. *How is she going to react to living on the salary of, first, an Imperial cadet, then an Imperial officer?*

Bria smiled and sat down beside him. "Mother, could I have something to eat, too? I'm starved!"

As Han and Bria munched their late-night snack, her family gathered around the table and sipped expensive vine-coffeine from fragile Levier-made porcelain cups, while the butler, another Selonian, waited on them.

"So, Captain Solo . . . you're Corellian?" Lady Tharen said, raising a delicate eyebrow to indicate that she was pretty sure he was. Han, still chewing, nodded, then swallowed. "Yes, ma'am."

"And your family?" she asked. "Are you one of the Sal-Solos?" There was a touch of hope in her voice. "They have a lovely old estate, I understand. I've met the son a few times, but Lady Sal-Solo is very reclusive. I understand her health is not robust."

"No, Lady Tharen," Han replied. "No relation."

"Oh," she said, visibly disappointed. "What branch of the family are you from, then?"

Bria was looking very uncomfortable, Han noticed, but he couldn't tell whether she was ill at ease *for* him, or *because* of him. "Don't know, Lady Tharen," he said honestly. "I'm an orphan, most likely. Traders found me wandering in an alley down by the waterfront near Capital Spaceport when I was a little kid. I was raised by 'em. Spent most of my time in space." Part of him took a perverse pleasure in watching her reaction to this information.

"That's odd," Pavik Tharen said. "You look so familiar. I know I've seen you somewhere before. Somewhere . . . at a barbecue, I think. I have a mental picture of seeing you at a barbecue that followed a swoop racing meet."

Han stiffened inwardly. Now that Pavik mentioned it, Han remembered him, too. Pavik was probably two or three years older than Han, and Bria's brother had been a frequent competitor at some of the swoop races. Due to the age difference, they'd never raced against each other, but Han remembered seeing him.

And, of course, every time he'd done major swoop racing, Han had been part of a "family unit" created by Garris Shrike to scam wealthy Corellians out of their money.

"Sorry, don't remember you," he said casually. "I've

been off-world for the past several years. Afraid I ain't been to a Corellian barbecue since I was a kid."

"But I remember it distinctly . . ." Pavik said, narrowing his eyes suspiciously. "You were leaning against a swoop, eating a plate of barbecued traladon ribs. The picture in my mind is very clear."

"Funny thing about that," Han said, leaning back in his seat with a smile. "People are always saying stuff like that to me. I must have one of those kinda faces—so ordinary that lots of people confuse me with other folks."

"I don't think you're ordinary-looking, Han," Bria said, not understanding what was going on, but trying to be loyal. "I don't think anyone who ever met you could forget you. You're . . . unique." She gave him a smile. "Handsome, too."

Han took a deep breath and managed to smile blandly at the assembled Tharens. "Thanks, honey," he said. "But I'm really just an ordinary kinda guy."

Bria finally caught the subtle hint and fell into silence. Pavik Tharen continued to study Han suspiciously.

"Well," Sera Tharen said too brightly, "I'm sure you're both tired. Captain Solo, I'll have Maronea prepare one of the guest rooms for you. Bria, obviously you'll want your room back, and, dear, I haven't changed a thing. I just *knew* that someday you'd come to your senses and return to us!"

"I really couldn't just *decide* to leave, Mother," Bria said quietly. "Once you go to Ylesia, they won't *let* you leave. There are no ships, and there are armed guards. If it hadn't been for Han . . . I would never have been able to escape."

"Oh, dear . . ." Lady Tharen said, distressed and looking as if she didn't know *what* to believe. Han had the impression that the woman's entire exposure to the seamier side of life probably occurred through the tri-dee action-adventure serials.

"I understand that, Bria," Renn Tharen said, holding Han's eyes with his own. "And I'll never forget it. Han is a hero, Sera, and we owe him more than we can ever repay.

If it hadn't been for him, we'd never have seen Bria again. He probably saved her life."

"Oh . . . oh, dear . . ." Lady Tharen was increasingly unnerved by these allusions to the danger her daughter had been in. Pavik Tharen was looking increasingly skeptical.

Han followed the Selonian maid, Maronea, to the room on the far side of the house. He was amused to note that his room was as far as it could possibly be from Bria's and that the master suite occupied by her parents lay between the two rooms. Bria's mother, it seemed, had decided to nip any chance of wee-hours assignations between her guest and her daughter in the bud.

Can't wait until we sell Teroenza's stuff and get outta here, he thought as he undressed and crawled into the bed. *Bria's dad ain't so bad, he seems like he used to be a regular guy, but her mom and her brother . . .*

Han sighed and closed his eyes. Tonight, at least, Lady Tharen need have no fears. He was so tired that the only thing on his mind was sleep. Funny thing about that . . . in some ways, spending two hours in the company of Bria's family had tired him out more than that whole escape from Ylesia . . .

Bria's mother came into her room to say good night and give her a last hug before she fell asleep. It was a tearful time for both mother and daughter. They hugged and cried a little, then hugged again. "I'm so glad to have my little girl back," Lady Tharen whispered.

"It's good to be back, Mother," Bria said, and at that moment she sincerely meant it. The evening had been a strain, no doubt. *But things will get better, they're bound to,* she thought, trying to comfort herself. *Han is so lovable. She's bound to fall for his charm and see how wonderful he is . . .*

"This young man you've brought home . . ." her mother said, almost as though she'd been reading her daughter's mind. "It's fairly obvious that you're not just . . . friends, dear. Exactly how . . . involved . . . are you two?"

Bria gazed at her mother unflinchingly. "I love Han, Mother, and he loves me. He wants me to stay with him. Nobody has mentioned marriage, yet, but I wouldn't be surprised if the subject came up."

Her mother took a quick, sharp breath, as though her worst fears had been confirmed. But something in Bria's choice of words alerted her, and like a hungry vrelt, she pounced. "I see. Well, he seems like a nice young man, though somewhat . . . rough around the edges, dear. But you say that *he* wants *you* to stay with *him*. Is that what *you* want?"

Bria nodded her head, then shook it, then had to fight back tears. She shrugged miserably. "Mother, I'm not sure. I know I love him, really love him, but . . . it's been hard for me. Leaving Ylesia, finding out that the religion I believed in and was devoting my whole life to was nothing but a lie. That hurt . . . a lot. I feel as though part of me is missing, Mother. And I also feel that I can't really promise to stay with Han when I'm not . . . whole."

"Does he know you have these doubts?" her mother asked, smoothing Bria's hair back tenderly. The young woman didn't miss the spark of happiness that had flared up in her mother's eyes when she'd spoken of her uncertainty about staying with Han.

She doesn't want me to stay with him, she realized with a dull ache of expectation fulfilled. *I knew she'd be like this. It's so unfair! The only reason I'm uncertain about staying with Han is because of ME, not how I feel about him! But she doesn't understand—she's incapable of understanding.*

"We've talked," Bria said, unwilling to confide in her mother any more than she'd already done. "And I can't imagine life without Han, so I'm going to do the best I can to stay with him and be a help to him."

Her mother looked troubled, but said no more. Bria lay down and tried to sleep. Being in her old bed was a luxury after sleeping on the hard Ylesian bunks, and in the ship. She missed Han's warmth, though. Her bed seemed cold.

Bria tossed and turned, thinking of Han, wondering what she should do.

He deserves someone better, she thought sadly. *Someone who can be there for him one hundred percent . . .*

Pounding her pillow in frustration, Bria felt tears well up again. *Why can't anything ever be EASY? I found a man I can love, who loves me—why can't that be enough?*

But it wasn't. Alone in the darkness of her childhood room, Bria acknowledged that.

She began to cry softly, aching with misery. After a long time, she cried herself to sleep . . .

The next day Han left the Tharen house shortly after breakfast and headed off to catch the shuttle to the nearest large city. He carried with him the backpack containing the items he and Bria had stolen from Teroenza. After the disappointing revenues received from the sale of the *Talisman,* Han knew he had to get top price for their small treasure trove.

He disembarked from the shuttle in the port city of Tyrena and went to a lockbox office, where he retrieved a few hundred credits and a set of "clean" IDs for one "Jenos Idanian." Then he went off to a branch of the Imperial Bank and opened an account, using the credits and ID.

When that errand was finished, he went in search of an antiquities and art store he recalled from past escapades. It had been several years since he'd visited it, and for all he knew, the little store might have closed.

But no, the place was still there. The sign above the door was picked out in subdued holographic lights, opalescent against the plain gray stone of the storefront. Han, toting the backpack, went inside. As he opened the door, he could hear a soft chime from deep within the store.

Han saw the clerk behind the counter, but he ignored the female Selonian. Instead, he walked as directly as possible through the labyrinthine paths between the displays of merchandise, until he reached a small door set inconspicuously at the back. It was covered with an ancient tapestry depicting the founding of the Republic, and only certain "customers" ever discovered the door was behind it.

Once there, he looked around to make sure he was alone and unobserved, then he knocked sharply, in a preordained pattern. He waited, and after another minute the sound of an electronic lock being released sounded from the other side of the door. Han raised the tapestry, slipped under it, and walked through, into the back room.

The proprietor was an old, old man, still spry despite his stooped body, wrinkled face, and wispy yellow-white hair. Galidon Okanor had looked exactly the same in the five years since Han had first met him. Now he looked up and smiled at Han. "Well, it's . . . um . . . who, today, son?"

Han smiled. "Jenos Idanian, sir. How are you?" He genuinely liked the little man, who was, at one and the same time, a genuinely respected art assessor and appraiser, and a very competent and trustworthy fence.

"Oh, can't complain, can't complain," said the little man. "Because if I did, what good would it do me?" he added, emitting a wheezing chuckle.

"You got a point," Han said.

Okanor sat down on a high stool before a table that was lit with a jeweler's and appraiser's light, specially angled and illumined to show flaws in gemstones and cracks or flaws in antiques. He waved to a seat opposite his. "Sit down, sit down, Jenos Idanian. What have you brought me today?"

"Lots of things," Han said. "I'd like a price for the lot, and I'd like the credits deposited immediately in the Imperial Bank on Coruscant."

"Fine, fine," said Okanor. He rubbed his aged, veiny hands together. "You usually have good taste, Jenos. Now let's see what you've brought me!"

"Okay," Han said, and began unloading the knapsack, placing each item on the table beneath the light. He held back his favorite treasure, though, a tiny golden statue of a long-extinct Corellian paledor. It was beautiful, and its eyes were flawless Keral fire-gems.

Okanor watched avidly, occasionally uttering a soft "oh"

or "ahhh," but he forbore to speak until Han was finished.
Then he carefully picked up each piece, studied it intently,
sometimes through a jeweler's glass, then placed it on the
table again and went on to the next.

"Remarkable, most remarkable," he said, finally. "I am
going to break a rule of mine and ask you where in the
name of the galaxy you found all of this? In a museum? I do
not approve of stealing from museums, you know."

Han shook his head. "Not a museum."

"A private collection?" Okanor pursed his lips. "I am
most impressed, lad. The collector in question is a sentient
of taste and discrimination. I will also tell you, young man,
that he is not very particular about his acquisition sources. I
recognize, from their description, that at least half of these
items have been reported stolen. Some have been on
WANTED lists for years."

"Doesn't surprise me," Han said. "And you, you'll sell
'em to museums, won't you?"

"Most of them, most of them," Okanor agreed.

"Okay, then, that's good," Han said, thinking that would
please Bria. "That's where they should be. So . . . how
much?"

Okanor named a figure.

Han gave the old man a look of withering contempt and
reached for his knapsack. "There's a guy over in Kolene
who will be thrilled to get a look at this stuff. I can see I
should have visited him *first,*" he said, reaching for the
scrimshawed bantha tusk from Tatooine.

Okanor named another, higher figure. Silently Han began stowing items in the backpack.

Okanor sighed as though he'd just breathed his last and
named another figure, considerably higher than the previous sum. "And that's final," he added.

Han shook his head. "It better not be, Okanor. I need at
least five thousand more than that."

Okanor clutched his chest and watched with anguished
eyes as Han continued to stow items away in the backpack.
Finally, as Han reached for the last, the tiny sculpture
carved from living ice, he squeaked, "No! Don't! You are

killing me! Impoverishing me! I shall be naked in the streets, Jenos, lad! Would you do that to an old man?"

Han gave him a feral grin. "In a heartbeat, Okanor. I know what I need to get out of this deal, I have a pretty good idea what it's worth, and I ain't taking less." He gave the old man an intent stare. "Frankly, Okanor, I can't *afford* to take less. I've got something important to spend these credits on. If what I've got in mind works, you won't see me again. I'll be outta all this for good."

Okanor nodded. "All right. You've broken me, Idanian. I'll meet your price."

"Good," Han said, and began taking the items out of the backpack again.

He left the store with a satisfied smile, and carefully stowed his "Jenos Idanian" IDs and the bank record into his credit pouch. He'd travel under different IDs and leave "Jenos Idanian" "clean," only using him for the bank withdrawal. He planned to store the golden paledor in a safe place he knew about. It never hurt to keep a little something in reserve for emergencies . . .

Knowing that Okanor's credits would be waiting for him on the capital world of the Empire, Han headed down the street toward the shuttle station, whistling.

When Han walked up to and through the gates of the Tharen estate, he noticed a small, very sporty landspeeder hovering in the paved courtyard. He approached the door and found a young man standing inside, in the parlor. Pavik Tharen and his mother were there, talking to him. When Sera Tharen saw Han, her face fell. *She was hoping I'd cut and run,* Han thought sourly.

"Hi, Lady Tharen," Han said. "Is Bria around?"

The young man turned to regard Han. He was a good-looking fellow, perhaps a year or so older than Han himself, and he was tastefully but fashionably dressed for an afternoon of net-ball.

"Hello," the young man said pleasantly, holding out his hand. "I'm Dael Levare, and you are—" His gaze sharpened, and before Han could speak up, he exclaimed, "Wait a minute! I *thought* you looked familiar! Tallus Bryne, right?"

Han could think of no curse profound enough. He smiled weakly and shook hands. "Hi, nice to meet you."

"Tallus Bryne?" Pavik Tharen said sharply.

"But he's—" Sera Tharen stopped abruptly when her son nudged her, none too gently.

Dael Levare was oblivious to the byplay as he wrung Han's hand. "What an honor this is! I still remember the day you set that record, and you did it by flying *through* the tunnel on Tabletop Mesa rather than *over* it! Everyone thought you were a goner, but you pulled it off!" He turned to Pavik. "You mean you didn't recognize him? Is *this* Bria's new suitor? The swoop racing champion of all Corellia! Your record still stands, Bryne. Or may I call you Tallus?"

"Tallus is fine," Han said with a mental shrug. *The vrelt's in the kitchen for sure, this time . . .*

Bria's entrance was a welcome interruption. Han tried to catch her eye and give her a "look sharp" high-sign, but all her attention was for the newcomer. "Dael! What are you doing here?"

"Your mother invited me over," Dael said. "You're looking wonderful, Bria. I'm so glad to see you back safely—and with such a distinguished escort! I've wanted to shake this man's hand ever since he won the swoop racing championship, last year!"

She looked at her mother. "You *invited* him over, Mother? How nice . . ." Han didn't miss the edge in her voice, and the flash of guilt in Sera Tharen's eyes. *I get it,* Han thought angrily. *Mama here wanted Bria to see me next to her rich-guy ex-fiancé, figuring I'd come out looking like some kind of low-life jerk.*

"Well, yes, dear . . . I knew Dael would be able to catch you up on all the news with the young crowd . . . much better than I could . . ." Sera Tharen twittered nervously. Bria's lip curled, and she turned away from her mother to smile at Dael.

"Well, Dael, it was lovely of you to drop by. Perhaps we

can all get together for lunch someday. Who are you seeing these days?" As she spoke, she moved toward Dael, and in one smooth motion took his arm and started him moving toward the door. Han smiled inwardly. *Slick, Bria, honey . . . nicely done.*

"Sulen Belos," Dael said. "She'd love to meet Tallus, too. She's quite a swoop racing fan."

"Tal—" Bria caught herself immediately, and laughed. "Well, she always was!" She cast a flirtatious glance at Han. "I'll have to watch you, won't I, *Tallus*? Sulen Belos is gorgeous, and she's never been able to resist a swoop racer."

Han smiled at her good-naturedly. *Great. Just great. From bad to worse.* "You gotta watch us swoop racers, too. We live for danger."

Half out the door, Dael Levare laughed, as though Han had said something clever. "Well, I'll call you. Nice meeting you, Tallus!"

"Nice meeting you, too," Han said.

"Don't forget to call," Bria urged, and then she shut the door behind Levare and leaned against it.

Silence ensued.

Han had never heard such a profound silence, even inside a spacesuit in vacuum. He glanced quickly from Bria, to Pavik, to Sera. All three were staring at him grimly. Han cleared his throat. "Think I'll take a little walk," he announced. "Get some air."

Not meeting anyone's eyes, he left.

Bria felt like screaming, then sobbing, but she struggled to control herself. The situation was bad enough without her dissolving into hysterics. She was pacing back and forth in her mother's dressing room. Pavik was sitting on the couch, waving his arms and raising his voice, and her mother was sitting in a pink brocade chair, alternating between gasped exclamations of "Oh, dear!" and "Bria, your brother is right, we must *do* something!"

"You heard him last night!" Pavik shouted. "He denied

having swoop-raced, and he gave us a fake name! Han Solo—right! Who knows what his real name is?"

"Stop it!" Bria cried. "Han Solo is his *real* name!"

"Then why is 'Tallus Bryne' listed as the swoop racing champion of Corellia last year?" Pavik said. "He can't be both, Bria. Face it, the guy's using an alias, and the only reason to do that is that he's got stuff to hide! And this is the guy you want us to accept with open arms, just because you say so?"

"Oh, dear!" Sera wrung her hands.

Bria bit her lip to keep from shrieking.

"And another thing," Pavik said. "My memory is starting to come back on this, and 'Tallus Bryne' wasn't Solo's only alias. The time I remembered was about three years earlier. He was just a kid, eating barbecue after a swoop race. That time, 'Solo' was 'Keil Garris,' the son of Venadar Garris. Remember him? That guy who went around one summer selling shares in that duralloy asteroid, and the whole thing turned out to be bogus? A scam?"

Bria *did* remember. "But even if this Garris man was a con artist, that doesn't mean that Han—"

Pavik threw up his arms in exasperation. "Sis, don't you remember how a couple of our friends' parents were nearly wiped *out* from buying worthless shares in that nonexistent asteroid?" He snorted. "That whole Garris family was nothing but a bunch of con artists—and that includes your new boyfriend, Bria!"

"This is terrible!" Sera Tharen said. "Perhaps we should *do* something!"

Both Bria and Pavik ignored their mother.

"But Han was just a kid then," she pointed out, fighting not to give in to tears. "You admitted that. He can't be held responsible for what you say his parents did."

"But he doesn't *have* any parents—or so he told us!"

Bria glared at him. "Well, maybe they were his parents, and he's disowned them because they were crooked," she said. "Pavik, Han is a good person! He's had a tough life and wound up having to do things he didn't like to survive, I already know that. But he's turned around now! He's trying to make something of himself, and you won't give him that chance!"

Pavik snorted derisively. "If they even *were* his parents," he said. "Sis . . . don't be blinded by good looks and the fact that he rescued you! Face it, this guy may have romanced you because he'd checked our family out and found that Dad has money!"

"Oh, dear!" Sera said. "Do you mean that the boy is a *thief*?"

"That's exactly what I'm saying, Mother," Pavik said.

"I should go and check to see whether anything is missing," Sera Tharen gasped. "Oh, dear, oh, dear, where shall I have him sleep tonight?"

"Mother, he's not going to *be* here, tonight," Pavik said. "I'm calling security. I'm sure this guy is wanted for all kinds of things."

"Don't you dare!" Bria cried. "If you call security I'll never speak to any of you again! You're wrong about Han! He had absolutely no idea my family was wealthy when we met. I never told him until we got here!"

"A guy like that has sources to check," Pavik pointed out. "He probably checked you out within days of knowing you, and found out everything he needed to know."

"No, he didn't!"

"Bria . . . I'm not trying to be an ogre!" Pavik said. "I'm just trying to make you see reason! I don't want you to be hurt, and I don't want you to get involved with someone who lives on the wrong side of the law!"

"Han isn't like that!" Bria cried, then taking a deep breath, she amended, "Okay, I admit that in the past he probably was. But he's different now. He's going to enter the Imperial Academy and become an officer. Can't you give him a chance? He's trying to change his life!"

"That's what he's told you, Bria, but guys like that lie for a living," Pavik said. "I'm calling security."

"Oh, dear!"

"No!" Bria stared wildly at her brother, for a moment wishing she were wearing a blaster. She couldn't let him do this!

Pavik's hand was actually on the CONNECT button on the comlink, when a voice from the doorway stopped him in his tracks. "Don't, Pavik. I forbid it."

All of them turned to see Renn Tharen standing there.

"But, Dad, you don't know—" Pavik began.

"Yes, I do," Tharen said. "I've been in my study, and the door was open. I've been listening to this entire disgraceful scene, and I'm telling you, Pavik, you're *not* calling security."

"But, Renn . . ." Sera Tharen began. Her husband turned to her, his glance scathing.

"Sera, I'm tired of you trying to use our daughter as a pawn to further your social ambitions. You're most of the reason she ran away last year. So *stop it*. Do you understand me?"

"Renn!" Sera Tharen gasped. "How *dare* you speak to me like that?"

"Because I'm angry, Sera, angry clear through," Bria's father snarled. "How can you be so blind? You don't understand the danger our daughter was in on Ylesia! Look!"

Seizing Bria's hand, her father dragged her over to stand before her mother. Taking her hands, he thrust them out before his wife's eyes. "Look, Sera! See her hands? See these scars? Those people *mistreated* Bria, they made her a *slave*. She might have died, Sera, if not for Han. I'm grateful to him, even if you don't have the common decency to realize that! He's a good kid, and I say that Bria could do far worse."

"But—" she whispered, wringing her hands and beginning to cry. "Oh, Bria, your poor hands, darling . . ."

"Not one more word, Sera. I forbid it."

Sera Tharen subsided into her chair, weeping softly.

Renn Tharen whirled around to confront his son. "Pavik, you've become as judgmental and class-conscious as your mother. I'm tired of you, too." Renn glared at the young man. "You're talking about a man who *risked his life* to save Bria from slavery. Bria's right about him applying to the Imperial Academy. Han Solo is a decent guy. He reminds me of myself when I was his age. There are some incidents in my past I'm not proud of, either. He deserves a chance, not jail. He deserves our thanks, not a call to CorSec."

When Renn Tharen stopped speaking, silence reigned. Then, with a sobbing gasp, Bria ran to her father and threw her arms around him. "Thank you, Dad!"

Han had walked the entire length of the Tharen estate, and was on his way back when he saw someone coming down the path toward him. It was Bria, and she carried a good-sized bag slung over her shoulder.

Han saw her expression and stopped. "What is it?"

"Come on," she said. "Before we're missed. We're getting out of here. I don't trust Pavik not to make that call to security behind Daddy's back."

Han turned back toward the transport station. "You sneaked out?"

"I left them a note," she said defensively. "Did you get the money transferred to Coruscant?"

"Yeah, we're fine," Han said.

They walked for a few minutes in silence, then Bria said, "Someday, I'd like to know all the truth. I hate surprises of this sort, Han."

He sighed. "I should have told you. I *will* tell you. Everything. I promise. I'm just not in the habit of trusting anyone."

"I can tell," she said grimly.

"Nice of your dad to stick up for me."

"Daddy says you remind him of himself, when he was a young pilot." She smiled faintly. "I gather he led a rather checkered existence for a few years, out on the Rim."

Han nodded and, cautiously, reached for her pack. "I'm really sorry about this. Let me carry it?"

She sighed and surrendered her bag. "Okay. It was probably a bad idea to come here, anyway." After a moment she reached over and took his hand. "Now it's just the two of us again."

Han nodded. "That's the way I like it, sweetheart."

Chapter Fourteen:
Down and Out on Coruscant

The trip to Coruscant was uneventful. True to his promise, Han related his history to Bria, in unvarnished detail. It bothered him to have to admit many of the things he'd done in the past, but he took his promise to her seriously, and he was as honest as he could be.

At first, Han worried that Bria might be repelled by all of the things he'd done during his checkered past, but she reassured him, saying that she loved him more, now that she knew the truth.

The five-day voyage to Coruscant was a long one. Han was beginning to suffer from boredom by the time the passenger liner docked at one of the massive space stations that serviced the huge Imperial city-world.

From the space station, the passengers were told, they'd be shuttled down to the spaceport in small ships. Han was surprised to discover that there was almost no place on the giant world where the natural ground could be seen or touched.

"Only in Monument Plaza," their steward told the assembled passengers who'd traveled on the liner *Radiance*. "There citizens may touch the top of the only mountain on the planet that still remains. About twenty meters of the peak extends into the air. The remainder is all hidden beneath buildings."

Coruscant, it seemed, was a warren of buildings, skyscrapers, towers, rooftops, and more buildings, all built one upon the other in a giant, labyrinthine hodgepodge. Han raised his hand when the steward asked whether there were any questions. "You say that the topmost rooftops are more than a kilometer above the lowest-level streets? What's down there?"

The *Radiance*'s steward shook his head warningly. "Sir, take my word for it. You do not want to know. The lowest levels never see the sun. They are so far beneath the clean air that they are fetid and damp and have their own weather systems. Foul rain drips down the sides of the buildings. The alleys are infested with granite slugs, duracrete worms, shadow-barnacles . . . and, worst of all, by the degenerate remnants of what once used to be human beings. These troglodytes are pale carrion and garbage eaters, disgusting in every way."

"Huh," Han whispered to Bria, "sounds like my kinda place."

"Stop it!" she hissed, smothering a grin. "You are such a smart-mouth . . ."

"I am, I really am." Han sat back in his seat, chuckling. "I'm impossible. I don't know how you put up with me."

"Neither do I," Bria said, smiling wryly.

The couple made their way over to one of the viewports on the station while they were waiting for a "surface" shuttle down. "It's like some beautiful golden gem," Bria whispered. "All those lighted buildings . . ."

"It looks like a corusca jewel," Han said, eyeing the

planet thoughtfully. "Must be where the world got its name."

They were standing in line, waiting to enter the shuttle, when an official stepped forward and pointed at Han's blaster. "Sorry, sir, you'll have to check your weapon. Guns aren't permitted on Coruscant."

Han stood there for a long moment; then with a shrug he unbuckled the tie-down strap from around his thigh, then released the big buckle that fastened his gunbelt. Wrapping the belt around the holster and weapon, Han handed it over to the official and received a numbered token in return. "Just give this to the official before boarding your return transport," the man said, "and you'll receive your weapon, sir."

Han and Bria got back into line. Han grimaced at how light his right leg felt without the customary weight against his thigh. "I feel naked," he mumbled to Bria. "Like I'm in one of those nightmares when you show up for something important and suddenly realize you forgot your pants."

She began to giggle at the idea. "I didn't know men had dreams like that, too."

"I don't have 'em often," Han said grimly.

"Well, if nobody's armed, then it's still even," she pointed out reasonably.

Han gave her a look as they started down the aisle of the surface shuttle. "Honey, don't be naive. There's an underworld on this planet, and you can bet your pretty eyes they're armed."

She glanced over at him as they fastened their seat restraints. "How do you know?"

"I took a look at the Imperial guards. *They* were all armed. I saw security guards on Alderaan, and none of the ones I saw were armed. So it's a good bet whoever they would be going up against wasn't either. But these Imperials are armed, and wearing armor, too. Gotta be a reason for it."

Bria shrugged. "I have to admit, your reasoning makes sense."

"I'm gonna feel strange walking into that bank tomorrow, with no blaster at my side," Han said, looking sadly at his empty thigh.

"Come *on*, Han," she whispered, "of all the places in the world, they wouldn't let you walk into a *bank* armed!"

"Why not?" Han asked. "It's not like a guy could swipe the credits. They don't keep hardly any credit disks there, or coins either. It's all electronic data entry onto personal IDs. Good system," he added thoughtfully. "Saves on guards."

"Well, it's a moot point, since you had to leave your blaster," she said, watching the city-world grow in the viewport. Soon they'd be entering the atmosphere.

"Yeah. Listen, Bria, I guess this is as good a time as any to discuss contingency plans," Han said.

"For what?" she demanded, alarmed. "Are you expecting trouble?"

"Keep your voice down," he cautioned. "Nope, I'm not expecting trouble. This should be a smooth operation, a piece of cake. 'Jenos Idanian' is clean, 'cause I only used him to open the account and deposit the money. He *should* be laser-proof. But, baby . . . I learned long ago to *always* plan for trouble."

"Okay," she said. "What do you want to plan for?"

"That's a big city, a big world," Han pointed out, just as the shuttle kissed the upper edges of the atmosphere. "If anything happens and we get separated, I want to set up a meeting place."

"Okay, that makes sense," she said. "Where?"

"The only address I know, 'cause I memorized the location a long time ago, is a bar called 'The Glow Spider.' That's where I'll be contacting Nici the Specialist," he said, keeping his voice very low, but not . . . quite . . . whispering. Whispers drew attention, Han had learned long ago, where low-voiced conversations did not.

"That's the guy who can get people IDs so perfect that even the Imperials can't detect them?"

"Yeah. He's got contacts with the people in the Imp offices who actually *make* the IDs. They're perfect, trust me.

Okay, so it's Nici the Specialist. He hangs out at The Glow Spider. Got that?"

"Nici the Specialist. Glow Spider," she repeated. "Where is it?"

"Level 132, megablock 17, block 5, subblock 12," Han recited. "Memorize that perfectly. This world is a maze, Bria."

Silently she repeated the location to herself over and over, until she could say confidently, "I've got it."

"Good."

When they reached the "surface"—the rooftop landing field where the shuttle landed—Han left Bria with their scanty luggage while he went over to an automated tourist center to get information and directions. He and Bria needed an inexpensive place to stay while he prepared for the entrance examinations for the Academy. Han planned to rent a cheap room for the duration.

When he came back to Bria, she saw that he had a palm-sized locator computer. "How much did *that* cost?" she asked, eyeing it worriedly. Their funds from the sale of the Ylesian yacht were running low.

"Only twenty," Han said. "This world's too easy to get lost on, I figure. All I gotta do is enter our destination, like this . . ." Squinting with concentration, he entered, "Level 86, megablock 4, block 2, subblock 13 . . ."

"What's that?"

"The place where I got us a room for tonight," Han answered, not looking up. "And . . . there!"

Directions from their present location appeared on the screen. "First, we take the turbolift down to level 16 . . ." Han muttered, looking around. "There!"

They headed for the sign marked TURBOLIFT.

Once aboard the lift, Bria gasped at the precipitous drop. They fell . . . and fell . . .

"Like being in space," Han said uneasily. "Almost free fall . . ."

"My stomach doesn't like this," Bria gulped.

Fortunately, the turbolift slowed as it reached its destination. Bria staggered off, looking slightly green.

"Now to find megablock 4 . . ." Han mumbled, still concentrating on his little gadget. "Then we'll go down again . . ."

Once out of the turbolift, Bria looked around her in wonder and growing claustrophobia. Everywhere buildings loomed over her, so high she had to crane her neck to see their tops. The tops of many of them supported another rooftop, probably like the one she was standing on.

Even though it had been bright (but chilly) daylight up on the landing pad, here it was dark and warm. No air seemed to move in the duracrete and transparisteel canyons between the buildings. She heard a distant rumble of thunder, but no rain reached her, and she had no way of telling whether the storm was *above* her or *below* her.

Occasional unbarricaded airshafts broke the permacrete on the rooftop, and about a hundred meters away, Bria could see the abrupt line of demarcation at the end of the pavement. Evidently a thoroughfare ran at the deepest levels.

She walked over to look down one of the airshafts and, after one brief glance, staggered back, head spinning and her palms crawling with vertigo. She glanced around, saw no one near her, then dropped to her hands and knees and crawled back to peek over again. As long as she wasn't standing, she thought that the dizziness might not be too bad.

Nearing the edge of the lip, she held on with both hands and peered down the airshaft.

The airshaft went down . . . and down . . . and down. It was amazing, frightening, to imagine her body falling down that seemingly bottomless expanse, helplessly turning and twisting in midair.

Bria stared down, shaking. If she were to lean a little farther, just a tiny bit farther, she'd fall down that shaft. It would be effortless. She wouldn't have to jump, no. Just . . . lean . . . and if she did that, she'd never have to feel the pangs of longing for the Exultation again. She'd be free from the pain, the craving. She'd be free . . .

Both drawn and repelled, Bria swayed, leaning farther toward the edge . . . farther . . .

"What are you *doing*?"

A hand grabbed her shoulder, yanking her back, away from that yawning drop into nothingness. Bria looked up dazedly, to see Han staring at her, his features twisted with worry. "Bria, honey! What were you *doing*?"

She put a hand to her head, shook it dizzily. "I . . . I don't know, Han. I felt . . . so strange." Gulping, black dots dancing before her eyes, she struggled not to faint or be sick.

Han pushed her head down between her knees, then knelt beside her as she trembled. He stroked her hair, hugged her tightly as her shudders intensified. She was shaking all over. "Easy . . . easy . . . just take it easy."

Finally, Bria looked up, feeling her shivers abate a little. "Han, I don't know what happened. I felt so strange for a moment there. I think I almost fell . . ."

"You did," he said grimly. "It's called vertigo, sweetheart. I've seen people get it before, out in space, when they look 'down' and lose their bearings. C'mon. I know which way to go, now. We're gonna take a horizontal tube for a ways."

In the tube, Bria huddled against Han, and he held her gently. Gradually, her shivering eased. "Doesn't it bother you?" she asked. "This world? It oppresses me. Fascinates me, but oppresses me, too."

"Don't forget, I grew up in space," Han reminded her. "Not much room for vertigo or claustrophobia there. I must've gotten adjusted long ago, because this place doesn't bother me. But you . . . you grew up on Corellia, with a *sky* above you all the time. No wonder you freaked."

"I'm not going to try looking down again," Bria said.

"Good idea."

After several more turbolift descents, they reached the little hostel where Han had reserved a room and paid for it in cash out of their dwindling funds. "When are you going to get our money at the Imperial Bank?" Bria asked, throwing herself down on the bed and stretching out with a tired sigh.

"I'll go first thing tomorrow morning," Han said. "Listen, honey, you look beat. I'll go get some food and bring it back here. We'll turn in early."

"But don't you want to see the sights?" Bria asked, thinking privately that his plan sounded like the best thing she'd heard all day.

"Plenty of time for that. I just want to eat and then sleep. Maybe watch the vid-unit, see what kind of propaganda Imperial City is putting out these days."

"Okay," Bria said, smothering an exhausted yawn. "I like your plan."

The next morning Han left Bria munching a pastry in their room and sipping stim-tea. "I'll be back in an hour or so," he told her. "Once I've got the money, we'll head over and find that bar I told you about. What's its name?"

"The Glow Spider," she repeated dutifully.

"And where is it?"

She recited the location.

"That's great," Han said approvingly. "If I get lost, you can get me there."

She chuckled. "Is this place harder to navigate than space?"

"In some ways," Han said. He gave Bria a kiss between the eyes. "I'll be right back."

"Okay, see you later."

With a cheerful wave, he was gone. Bria lay back on the bed with a sigh. *Maybe I'll just sleep late,* she thought, stretching luxuriously.

The Imperial Bank of Coruscant took up three levels in a monstrous, top-level skyscraper. Han walked up to the doors, and looked in. The lobby was enormous, all smoked glassine, black duracrete and marble, and dully shining transparisteel.

Taking a deep breath, and still missing the weight of his blaster, he walked in and up to the high, shining counter. The lobby was bustling with business types and citizens, and Han both looked and felt out of place in his old pilot's coverall, now stripped of all insignia, and his battered old jacket and boots.

The more uncomfortable he felt, the more arrogantly he held himself.

He had to wait in line for several minutes, but then found himself facing a woman clerk. She was young and pretty, but her gaze was impersonal—until Han gave her his best lopsided grin. Almost against her will, she smiled back. "Good morning," Han said. "I opened an account a little while ago, on Corellia, knowing I'd be comin' here. Like to withdraw the funds now."

"You wish to close out your account?"

"Yeah."

"Very well, sir, may I have your ID card? We will transfer the funds to that, and then they will be accessible from any credit port on Coruscant or any of the inner-system worlds. Will that be satisfactory, Master. . . ." Han slid the card beneath the glassine barrier to her. "Idanian?"

"That'll be okay," Han said, having to fight the urge to demand it all in credit vouchers and coin. If he did something that unusual, he'd be bound to appear suspicious.

The clerk scanned the card, and her eyebrows rose slightly as she took in the amount in the account. *Never expected a guy like me to have that kind of funds*, Han realized, grimly amused.

"Sir, this sum exceeds the amount I am authorized to disburse without approval from my supervisor. If you will wait just a moment, I will get that approval, then disburse the funds to your card."

There wasn't much Han could say except, "Okay."

Left standing at the desk, he suppressed the urge to fidget, and forcibly restrained himself from overtly scanning the huge lobby for guards or security.

Take it easy, he ordered himself. *You know that with a*

*withdrawal this big, they have to get it okayed. At least I
know for sure that Okanor transferred the funds the way I
told him to . . .*

Han saw the clerk speaking rapidly to a big, heavyset
man in a posh business suit. The man nodded, took Han's
ID card, and approached him on Han's side of the barrier.
"Jenos Idanian?" he asked courteously. He had a chubby,
pink face, pale blue eyes, and a balding pate with sparse
white hair.

"Yeah," Han said.

"I am Parq Yewgeen Plancke, the manager of this facility. I have authorized your withdrawal, sir, but before I can
give you back your card, I would like to see an additional
piece of ID, purely as a formality." The man smiled politely. "Financial institutions are subject to these rules, I'm
afraid. Will you step into my office?"

He waved at a glassine-enclosed cubicle. Han's hackles
rose, but he could see the entire office, and there was no
one else in there, no guards anywhere in evidence. "Okay,"
he said, "but I'm kinda in a hurry, so I hope it doesn't take
long."

"Only a second," Plancke assured him, waving Han on
ahead.

The Corellian walked into the office confidently, but
every sense was alert, every muscle coiled for action.
Plancke's office was blandly reassuring—an expensive black
marble-topped desk, with a stylus and styl-pad resting atop
it. An ultra-modern flower arrangement of black lorchads
graced the corner of the desk. There were two visitor
chairs, and Plancke's expensive cloned black leather chair.

"Have a seat, Master Idanian," Plancke said, gesturing to
a chair. Han sat down. "Now, if you will give me another
source of ID, I can scan it in and you will be on your way."

Han got the ID out without demur, but he didn't miss a
move Plancke made. *For two credits, I'd hightail it outta
here,* he thought. *I got a bad feeling about this . . .*

Plancke took the ID, scanned it in. "Oh, dear," he said,
not sounding at all surprised or regretful, "I'm afraid we

have a problem, sir. I have been ordered to place a freeze on your account. I cannot give you any of your money."

Han was up and out of his chair. "*What?* But I—what in the name of the galaxy is going *on* here?"

Plancke shook his head. "I only know that the Bank has been contacted by Inspector Hal Horn of CorSec. Your funds are suspected of being illegally accrued, and are frozen, pending a thorough investigation by Imperial and Corellian Security."

Han didn't waste his breath arguing, just headed for the door. His chest felt as though it were caught in a gee-vise. *No . . . it can't end like this . . .*

He was a meter from the thick, smoked-glassine door when he heard an electronic *click.* "I'm sorry, sir. I'm afraid I've been advised to hold you here for Imperial security forces," Plancke said, sounding as if he was enjoying his chance to be a hero. "Have a seat."

Han turned and looked back at the fat man. He was smiling blandly, his round little pink cheeks making him look like a jolly sprite out of a child's story. "I've also signaled for our guard. He should be here any moment. Please . . . have a seat while you wait to be arrested."

Rage filled Han with a strength he didn't know he possessed. "Over my dead *body!*" he snarled, bounding forward. He threw himself over the desk, grabbing the bank manager's writing stylus as he did so. Slamming into the astonished Plancke, he took him over backward in his expensive chair. In a second, he had the sharp point of the stylus positioned just behind Plancke's chubby pink earlobe. "One shove," he gritted, "and this slides between your jawbone and your skull, straight into your brain, Plancke. If you have one. You got a brain, Plancke?"

"Yes . . ."

"Good, then use it. I'm already mad . . . so don't push me any further, understand?"

Han could feel all the muscles of Plancke's throat contract as he swallowed. His voice was hoarse and shrill with fear. "Yes . . ."

"Good," Han said. "Now, I'm gonna get off you, and you're gonna get up and sit back down in your fancy chair. You're gonna let your guard in when he shows up, just like everything is fine . . . understand?"

"Yes . . ."

Moving precisely, Plancke did as he'd been told. Han crouched behind Plancke's chair, and now the hand holding the stylus sent the sharp instrument prodding into the man's back. "Trust me, Plancke," Han said, "one good thrust into the kidney will cause you more pain than you ever want to know. Might kill you. Want to take that chance?"

"No . . ."

"Good. Here comes your guard. Let him in."

"Yes . . ."

The door lock clicked, and the guard entered. In a second Han was on his feet, the point of the stylus digging into Plancke's throat again. "Tell him!"

"Don't move," Plancke said desperately. "He'll kill me!"

"He's right," Han said with a feral grin. "And I'll enjoy it, too. Now you," he said, "do exactly as you're told, if you want to see your next pay voucher. Place your blaster here on Plancke's desk. Move real slow, understand?"

"Yessir," the guard said. He was an elderly human, and looked terrified at the thought of actually having to do anything besides stand around, wearing his blaster.

Slowly, carefully, the guard removed the blaster from his holster, placing it on the black marble. Han reached over left-handed, and picked it up. "Now . . . under the desk. "Don't come out until I tell you to," he said.

"Yessir."

Han placed the muzzle of the blaster against Plancke's temple, still hugging the fat man to him. "Now we're leaving this bank," he said tightly. "We're walking outta here, slow and nice. We're heading for the turbolift. When I get there, if you've been a good little bank manager, I'm gonna let you go. Understand?"

"Yes . . ."

"Good."

They were halfway across the lobby before anyone noticed that something was amiss. A man yelled, another man squawked with fear, and a woman let out a shriek.

Han pointed the blaster at the ceiling and pulled the trigger. Flaming debris rained down. "Everybody down!" he shouted.

His command was unnecessary. Every citizen was already cowering on the expensive carpet. "Okay, Plancke . . . nice and easy now . . ."

Together they moved toward the doors, then out through them. Han relaxed his grip on Plancke slightly, ready to shove the big man down and then leap into the turbolift. He refused to think about what he was going to do afterwards! *One thing at a time,* he cautioned himself. *One thing at a time* . . .

He kept a sharp lookout as he and Plancke walked toward the turbolift, and so he spotted the squad of Imperial stormtroopers before they saw him. Han yanked Plancke tightly against him and placed the blaster to the man's head. "Don't shoot!" Plancke babbled as the troopers leveled their weapons. "I'm the one who called you! I'm the bank manager!"

Han backed toward the turbolift, dragging the heavy man with him. A glance at its lights reassured him that the lift was on its way to this level.

"He's getting away!" yelled one of the stormtroopers. Han stood before the door, tense, sweating, and ready to jump out of his skin. But he betrayed none of that, only waited, his body shielded behind the bank manager's trembling, corpulent form.

Han heard the turbolift doors slide open behind him. "Don't let him escape! Open fire!" yelled the stormtrooper officer.

"Noooooo!" screamed Plancke as the sizzle of blaster bolts filled the air.

Han jumped back, smelling burned flesh, dragging Plancke's falling body with him into the turbolift. He snapped off a shot, just as the turbolift doors closed, then slammed his fist against the lowest button on the bank of floors.

The high-speed turbolift dropped like a stone.

Gasping, Han managed to stagger to his feet. One look told him Plancke was dead. Too bad. He'd have let the man go, if those troopers hadn't started trouble . . .

Han's ears popped rapidly as the turbolift hurtled down. Quickly he pulled out his map-link and checked his location. If the link was correct, this lift would take him down about a hundred fifty stories, then he'd have to catch another.

The moment the lift doors opened, Han sprang out. The Corellian had dragged Plancke's body into the darkest corner of the lift, so it couldn't be seen from the front. Han had also shoved his blaster inside his leather jacket, but his hand rested lightly on its grip, ready to draw.

The scene that met his eyes was entirely peaceful. Citizens strolled along a passageway between buildings, and from somewhere not far away, music played.

Han glanced at his map-link as he strode along. *Turn right here . . .*

And there was the next turbolift. Han passed it up as being too obvious, and went on to take a horizontal tube into the next megablock. Then came another lift down. Two hundred stories, this time.

The streets were dirtier, now, as he searched for the next lift, making sure his turns were random. Down again. He was five hundred stories down, by now. The streets grew ever seedier.

One time, a gang of kids approached him as he hurried along. Han shook his head at them warningly. "Don't," he said.

" 'Don't'?" the leader, a huge, dark-skinned kid with a black fall of greasy hair, mocked. "Ooooooh, is big man afraid? Big man gonna be *real* afraid, when we get done with him . . ."

Six vibroblades flashed in the dim squalor of the alleys

the streets had come to resemble. Han sighed, rolled his eyes, and pulled out the blaster.

The gang evaporated so quickly they might have been snatched up by hawk-bats. Han stood there, blaster in hand, until he was certain the kids were gone.

A few startled passersby glanced at him, then quickly hurried on about their business, with a "Me? I didn't see *nothing*!" expression.

Shoving the blaster back into the front of his jacket, Han jogged down the shadowed street toward the next lift.

Another hundred stories, then another. He was seven hundred stories down. By now his map-link was useless. *How deep* is *this place?* he wondered, boarding another horizontal lift. The turbolift reeked of human and alien effluvia.

Eight hundred . . . eight hundred fifty.

By now Han was moving through streets lit only feebly by stray gleams from the airshafts, or by wan glow-lamps attached to the ramshackle buildings. The permacrete beneath his boots was often awash with foul-smelling, viscous liquid. Noxious rain spattered down, and fungi grew thick on the stonework.

No more citizens were in evidence—only darting forms that were too quick and furtive to identify. Han thought some of them might be aliens, and knowing Emperor Palpatine's poorly concealed dislike and distrust of nonhumans, Han wasn't surprised to find them lurking here, in the depths.

One thousand stories. Eleven hundred . . .

Han went in search of another lift, but couldn't find one. Instead he found a series of stairwells that took him down, and down . . .

He was now almost twelve hundred stories down. Approximately thirty-six hundred meters below where he'd started out at the top level at the Imperial Bank.

Han was panting, even though he was going downhill. The air down here was thick and humid, and smelled foul, as though he were at the bottom of a tunnel.

No sign of pursuit. *I've lost them,* Han thought, walking aimlessly along. He caught a flash of *something* scuttling along beside the front of one of the sagging, sunken buildings, something that moved hunched over, like an animal, but it walked on its hind legs. Tattered scraps of cloth barely concealed pallid skin, blotched with lesions and running sores. The creature snarled at Han from behind a mat of lank, filthy hair, revealing a mouth full of rotting stumps of teeth.

Han truly couldn't decide whether it was—or once had been—human.

The being scrambled away, hissing like a vrelt, half on its feet, half using all fours as it ran.

Shaken, Han took his blaster out of his jacket and stuck it into the front of his belt, wearing it openly, hoping its presence would deter any more creatures like the one he'd seen.

He passed the mouth of another alley, and there, in the ooze, several of the troglodytes crouched, tearing and ripping at something, cramming bits of it into their red-stained mouths. Revolted, Han drew his blaster, snapped off a shot over their heads, and watched them scatter.

He didn't go any closer to their prey, but swallowed uneasily when he saw that human-shaped ribs protruded from the mangled chest. *Minions of Xendor, what kind of place is this?*

His legs were growing very tired. He wasn't wearing a chrono, but when he passed beneath an airshaft, Han tilted his head far, far back and stared up at the dizzying height. A faint square of pallid light was visible at the very top. *Light's going. By the time I'll be able to reach the rendezvous, it'll be dark . . .* For the first time in hours, Han thought of Bria, and was very glad he hadn't taken her with him to the bank this morning.

She would be worried, he knew that. With a sigh, Han found another stairway and started the long, long climb upward.

By the time he'd reached a level that had such amenities

as parks, and park benches to sit on, Han's legs were cramped and he was shaky with exhausion. He slumped onto the bench, wondering, for the first time, what he'd do now.

He was so tired and disheartened that his mind spun like a creature trapped inside a barrel, rolling downhill. *Gotta think,* he told himself. *I can't go back to Bria like this . . .*

But, despite his best efforts, no solution to his present dilemma presented itself. Han got to his feet and shambled off toward the nearest turbolift, feeling like one of the troglodytes he'd seen—only marginally human.

When he checked his locator, he found that it was working again, and he began following it to the coordinates he'd told Bria about.

Level 132, megablock 17, block 5, subblock 12 . . . he kept repeating to himself. As he ascended the levels to ones that were, to his mind, livable, his stomach growled when he caught whiffs of enticing odors from cafés and restaurants he passed.

Finally, he saw a sign lighting up the night in a sleazy section that bordered the alien enclave. A huge, venom-dripping Devaronian fur-spider, picked out in garish greenish-black lights, dangled from an eye-searing scarlet web. *The Glow Spider. At last . . .*

Noise and bustle filled the streets, and many of the passersby were the worse for drink or drugs. Han passed the mouth of an alley and saw someone activate a light, then the blue flash and sizzle as a dose of glitterstim ignited.

Han paused in an alcove across the street from the cantina, wondering whether Bria was waiting outside or inside. He hoped she hadn't gone inside alone . . . or had she gone to try and make contact with Nici the Specialist? He sighed, wiped his sweaty face with his hand, and felt his head spin from exhaustion, thirst, and hunger.

As he hesitated, Han felt someone grab his arm. He spun on his heel, hand going to the front of his jacket where the blaster was hidden, and then stopped when he saw Bria. "Honey!" he gasped, grabbing her and holding her so tightly she began to struggle after a second. She felt—and smelled—so *good*!

"Han!" she gasped. "I can't breathe!"

He relaxed his grip slightly, stood swaying. She pushed his hair back from his brow, staring anxiously up into his eyes. "Oh, Han! What *happened*?"

Han felt his throat close up, and for a moment he was afraid he might disgrace himself and start bawling. But he took a deep breath, shook his head, and said, "Not here. Let's find a place to stay and some food. I'm done in."

Half an hour later, they were locked inside their room in a dingy flophouse. Han had been in worse, but it hurt him to see Bria's brave attempt to pretend she wasn't shocked by the dirt, the smells, and the scuttling insects. But the place was cheap and seemed secure.

The first thing Han did was wash up and drink several glasses of water. He still felt light-headed, but the smell of the carry-in food revived him somewhat. He sat down on the edge of the rickety bed, and he and Bria took turns eating out of the single container.

The food returned some energy to Han's exhausted body. He swallowed the last bite and sat back, staring hollow-eyed at Bria, wondering where to begin.

"Han, you have to tell me," she said. "I know from your expression that it's bad. You didn't get the money, did you?"

Han shook his head, then, slowly, haltingly, he told her what had happened. Tears filled Bria's eyes as she sat listening to him. Finally, he stopped . . . or ran down. "And I made it back here," he finished. "The rest . . . the rest you know. Honey"—he looked at her, feeling his throat close up—"this is it. There's no place left to turn. I can't think of anything to do except use the last of our credits to try and get off-world. Then . . . we can work. I can get a job piloting, I know I can." He sighed and buried his head in his hands.

"Baby . . . this is my fault. I should have realized the Hutts would run an all-system scan on my retinal patterns, and that they'd turn up all my aliases. I thought I'd been smart—but I was dumb as a box of rocks. Oh, Bria . . ."

He groaned, and turned to her, sliding his arms around her, putting his head on her shoulder. "Can you forgive me?"

She kissed his forehead and said softly, "There's nothing to forgive. It wasn't your fault. If you hadn't done what you did, I'd be in a pleasure-house being passed around from one stormtrooper to another. Never forget that, Han. You are a hero. You saved me, and I love you."

"I love you, too," he said, looking into her eyes. "I couldn't say it before . . . but . . . I want you to know. I love you, Bria."

She nodded, and a tear broke loose and coursed down her cheek. Han wiped it away with a fingertip. "Don't cry," he said. "I admit I came close to it myself, earlier, but I've been thinking. If we can just get off this blasted world, I know we can manage. We can work. We'll make a life . . . I know we can." He hesitated, then blurted, "We could even get married, sweetheart. If you want."

He could tell she was profoundly moved by his awkward proposal, but she shook her head. "Your dreams, Han. You can't give them up. We've gotten this close. We have to think of something. You're going to be an officer in the Imperial Navy, remember?"

It was his turn to shake his head. "Not anymore, Bria. That's over, now. I've gotta think of what else I'm gonna do with my life."

"Oh, Han!" she began to cry in earnest. "I can't bear to see you so hurt!"

"I'm okay," he insisted, though it was a lie.

Bria laid her head against his chest, then held him tightly. "We're okay for tonight," Han said. "Tomorrow we've gotta do some heavy-duty planning."

She was kissing him now, his cheek, his chin, his jaw . . . little, desperate, grazing kisses. Han held her tightly and captured her mouth, kissing her, touching her cheek, running his fingers through her hair, desperate to touch her, to be healed by her touch.

The dingy little room faded away, and all he could think about was how glad he was to be with her . . .

.   .   .

In the early hours before daylight, on this world where night and day meant very little to anyone who wasn't living a wealthy "top-level" existence, Bria Tharen sat huddled in the grubby, cramped refresher unit. In her hands was a stylus, and before her was a sheet of flimsy and a large stack of credits.

Faintly, from the bedroom, she could hear Han snoring lightly. He was so exhausted he'd never heard her get up and leave, never awakened when she'd returned, hours later.

Now she struggled with the flimsy and the stylus, stopping every so often to wipe away the tears that blurred her eyes, making it almost impossible to write. Six or seven times she'd voided the flimsy and started over, but time was ticking by, and she couldn't be here when Han awoke. If he awakened, Bria knew, she'd never, ever, be able to make herself go.

So she was taking the coward's way out, once again. Her sobs caught in her throat, and she pressed both hands against her chest. For a moment she wondered whether her heart might stop from the pain she felt, then she shook her head and told herself to stop delaying. *I'm so sorry*, she made herself write. *Please forgive me for doing this . . .*

Tonight, for the first time, she'd realized that Han might not achieve his lifelong dream if she stayed with him. She'd been dragging him down, holding him back, for weeks, but she hadn't wanted to admit it. But tonight . . . seeing the anguish in his eyes, hearing the catch in his voice—it had been too terrible to bear.

So she had slipped out, found a bar where the proprietor had let her pay him to borrow his comm unit, and called her father. Bria had appealed for help, both for herself and for Han. The pile of credit vouchers on the floor was the result. Renn Tharen was a man who knew how to get things done, and he had wasted no time. The money had been delivered to Bria by one of her father's Coruscant business associates, who had handed her the credits, refused thanks, then headed back out into the night, clearly glad to get away from the sleazy, all-night tavern.

During their brief conversation, Bria's father had warned her not to come home. Renn Tharen told her that inspectors from CorSec had come to the house shortly after Bria and Han escaped, asking about Bria's whereabouts. "I told them nothing," he said. "And your brother and mother aren't speaking to me, because I cut off their allowances for a month, even though they swore they hadn't called Cor-Sec. Be careful, dear . . ."

"I will, Dad," Bria promised. "I love you, Dad. Thanks . . ."

I've hurt him, too, Bria thought. *Why do I always hurt the people I love the most?*

Despair filled her, but she refused to let herself break down. All she could do for Han, if she loved him, was to leave him. *Be strong, Bria,* she commanded herself.

Gripping the stylus tightly, Bria wiped away her tears, then forced herself to finish the most difficult letter she would ever write . . .

Han knew something was wrong even before he opened his eyes. There was no sound, none at all. "Bria?" he called. *Where is she?* Sliding out of bed, he pulled on his clothes. "Bria, honey?"

No answer.

Han took a deep breath and told his wildly hammering heart to calm down. *She probably went out to get some stim-tea and pastry for breakfast,* he told himself. It was a reasonable guess, under the circumstances—but something told him that he was wrong.

He sealed the front of his coverall, then picked up his jacket. Only then did he notice that Bria's duffel was gone.

With a low moan of anguish, he saw something white protruding from the pocket of his jacket. Han pulled it out—and found himself holding a pouch filled with high-denomination credit vouchers. And there was something else, too . . .

A note. Written on creased and folded flimsy. Han shut his eyes, clutching it. It was nearly a full minute before he could force himself to open his eyes, force himself to read:

> Dearest Han:
> You don't deserve for this to happen, and all I can say is, I'm sorry. I love you, but I can't stay . . .

Chapter Fifteen:

OUT OF THE FIRE

She'll come back, was Han's first thought, and *I've lost her forever . . .* was his second. He stared wildly around the room, feeling as if it might explode if he didn't *DO* something. With a loud curse he hurled his jacket at the wall, then he yanked the pillows off the bed and flung them, too. Not enough—Han wondered frantically if he were going mad. His head felt too small to contain his mind, and he was filled with the need to howl his pain and anguish aloud, like a Wookiee.

"AAAAHHHHHHHHH!" he cried, and grabbing the battered chair that was one of the room's three pieces of furniture, Han swung it over his head and sent it crashing full-tilt into the door. A loud curse from his next-door neighbor followed. The chair lay there on the threadbare floor matting, unbroken. The door was still intact, too.

Han collapsed onto the bed and just lay there for several minutes, head buried in his arms. The pain came and went in waves. His chest ached, simply breathing *hurt*. His only relief came when he felt numb all over.

Somehow, the numbness was the worst of all.

After a long time, it occurred to Han that he had not finished Bria's letter. Except for the pile of credit vouchers, it was all he had left of her, so he dragged himself upright and squinted in the dim light to read the shaky words on the flimsy:

> *Dearest Han,*
>
> *You don't deserve for this to happen, and all I can say is, I'm sorry. I love you, but I can't stay . . .*
>
> *Every day I wonder if I'm going to snap and take the next ship back to Ylesia. I'm afraid I'm not strong enough to resist—but I must resist. I must face the fact that I am addicted to the Exultation, and that I must fight this addiction. I will need all my energy to do this and win, I'm afraid. I've been leaning on you for strength, but that's not good for either of us. You need all your strength and determination to pass those tests and make it through the Academy.*
>
> *Please don't abandon your dream of becoming an officer, Han. Don't be afraid to use the money I left. My father gave it to us freely, because he likes you and is grateful to you. Like me, he recognizes that you saved my life. Accept his gift, please. We both want you to succeed.*
>
> *I've learned so much from you. How to love, how to be loyal and brave. I've also learned how to find people who will help me change my identity, so don't bother looking for me. I'm going away, and I'm going to beat this addiction. I'm going to do it if it takes my last measure of strength and courage.*
>
> *You've been free all your life, Han. And strong. I envy you for that. I'm going to be free someday, too. And strong.*
>
> *Maybe then, we can meet again.*
>
> *Try not to hate me too much for what I'm doing. I*

*don't blame you if you do, though. Please know that, now
and forever, I love you . . .*

Yours,
Bria

Han made himself finish the letter all the way through.
Each word burned its way into his mind like a laser torch.
When he finished, he decided to go back and reread it,
because he was trying to put off the moment when he'd
have to start feeling and thinking again. While he was reading Bria's flimsy, it was as if she were still here. He could
almost hear her voice. Han knew that the moment he
stopped reading, she would be gone again.

But this time, although he squinted hard, he couldn't
make out the words. They were too blurred.

"Honey," he whispered to the letter, his throat so raw
that he could barely force the words out, "you shouldn't
have done this. We were a *team*, remember?"

Hearing himself use the past tense, Han shuddered, like
a man in the grip of a fever. He got up and began pacing
back and forth, back and forth. Moving seemed to be the
only thing that could help him bear this. Waves of anger
and frustration alternated with moments of grief so profound that he thought it might be easier to go mad.

*She lied. Never loved me. Rich girl, stuck-up, just having
a fling . . . used me to escape, used me till she got bored. I
hate her . . .*

Han groaned aloud, shaking his head. *No I don't. I love
her. How could she do this to me? She said she loved me.
Liar! Liar? No . . . she meant it. Face it, Han, she's been
suffering, you know it. Bria was troubled, in pain . . .*

Yes, she'd been in pain. Han remembered all those
nights he'd found her sobbing, and had held her, tried to
comfort her. *Baby . . . why? I tried so hard to help. You
shouldn't be alone. You should have stayed. We'd have
worked it out . . .*

He was terrified that her addiction might send her running back to Ylesia. Han had no illusions about Teroenza's
reaction if she did. The t'landa Til had no capacity to feel

pity or to be merciful. The High Priest would order Bria killed if he ever laid eyes on her again.

Han stared dazedly around the squalid little room. Had it only been last night that they'd been here, in each other's arms? Bria had held him tightly, fiercely. Now Han realized the reason for her passion. She'd known she was holding him for the last time . . .

He shook his head. How could things change so irrevocably in just a few hours?

Turn time back, some childish part of his mind said. *Make it be THEN, not NOW. I don't like NOW. I want it to be THEN* . . .

But of course that was stupid. Han caught his breath, and the sound was ragged, filled with pain. Almost a sob.

Suddenly he couldn't stand being here, seeing this dreadful little room, any longer. Stuffing his few belongings into his small bag, Han distributed handfuls of credit vouchers into his inside pockets, against his skin. Then he put on his ancient jacket and stuffed the blaster into the front of it.

He walked out, down the hall, past the sleazy-looking woman at the desk.

And kept walking . . .

All day he walked, moving like a droid through the unsavory crowds of this area, which was one of the "borderline" red-light districts that intersected with one of the nonhuman enclaves. He did not eat, could not face the idea of food.

He was always conscious of the stolen blaster in the front of his jacket. With part of his mind, Han rather hoped that someone *would* try to rob him. That would give him an excuse to lash out, to maim or kill—he wanted to *destroy* something. Or someone.

But nobody bothered him. Perhaps there was some aura he projected, some body language that warned others to keep "hands off."

His mind kept playing tug-of-war with his heart. He went over and over everything they'd ever said and done. Had he done something wrong? Was Bria a lovely, troubled, but decent girl fighting a deadly addiction? Or was she a spoiled, callous rich kid who'd been playing a cruel game? Had she ever *really* loved him?

At some point Han found himself on a street corner between two massive stone piles of rubble. In his hands was Bria's flimsy, and he was trying to read it by the flickering light of a brothel's sign. Han blinked. *Must be raining* . . . His face was wet . . .

He looked up at the sky, but of course, there was no sky, only a rooftop, high above. He held out a hand, palm up. No rain.

Folding the letter, Han put it away carefully. He resisted the momentary urge to shred it, or blast it into cinders. Something told him he'd regret it if he did.

Whatever she was, she's GONE, he decided, straightening his shoulders. *She's not coming back, and I've gotta pull myself together. First thing tomorrow, I go looking for Nici the Specialist at The Glow Spider* . . .

Han realized it was now late at night. He'd been wandering the streets for twelve or fifteen hours. Fortunately, in this district, some places never slept. The Corellian realized that he needed both food and sleep—he was so empty and exhausted that his head spun.

He began walking slowly back the way he'd come, realizing that every step felt as though he were treading on burning sand. His soles were abraded and blistered, and he limped.

The pain in his feet was a welcome distraction.

From now on, it's just me, Han Solo, he thought, stopping and peering up at the night sky, barely visible at the top of an airshaft. One star—or was it a space station?—winked against the blackness. Han's mental declaration had the conviction of a sworn oath. *Nobody else. I don't care about anybody else. Nobody gets close, from now on. I don't care how pretty she is, how smart, or how sweet. No friend, no lover* . . . *nobody is worth this kind of pain. From now on, it's just me* . . . *Solo*. With one part of his mind, he realized the grim irony of his inadvertent play on words, and he chuckled hollowly. From now on, his name *was* him. His name had come to stand for what he was, what was inside him.

Solo. From now on. Just me. The galaxy and everyone in it can go to blazes. I'm Solo, now and forever.

The last of the youthful softness had vanished from Han's features, and there was a new coldness, a new hardness in his eyes. He walked on into the night, and his boot heels sounded hard against the permacrete—as hard and unrelenting as the shell now sheathing his heart.

A week later Han Solo walked toward the Hall of Admissions of the Imperial Space Academy. The building was a huge, topmost-level structure, massive and quietly, solidly dignified in design.

The light from Coruscant's small white sun made him blink. It had been a long time since he'd seen sunlight, and his eyes were still sensitive, still easily irritated.

Having one's retinal patterns altered was possible, as Han had just proved, but it hadn't been a pleasant experience. He'd had the laser surgery and cell rearrangement, then he'd spent a day in a bacta tank, healing. He'd then worn a bacta visor for three more days, lying in a little back room at Nici's "clinic."

He'd put his forced inaction to good use, though, and had listened to hours of canned history and literature recordings, boning up for the examinations he hoped to begin. Han was under no illusions that the Academy testing would prove easy for him. His education had been spotty, at best.

Nici the Specialist had been worth every credit of his exorbitant fee. "Han Solo" now existed in the Imperial database, along with his retinal patterns, and other identifying marks. (Most of these scars were brand-new, carefully placed on his body by Nici's medical droids. Han had had most of his old scars erased.)

"Han Solo" now had IDs that were indistinguishable from those possessed by every loyal citizen of the Empire. For the first time in more than a decade, he was "clean"—

Han Solo wasn't wanted by anyone for anything. He no
longer had to glance guiltily behind him or try to grow eyes
in the back of his head. He didn't have to stay alert for the
betraying flash of light of a suddenly revealed blaster muzzle. He still tensed at loud noises, but that was just reflex.

Han Solo was a regular citizen, not a hunted fugitive.

He still had Vykk Draygo's and Jenos Idanian's IDs, buried deep in a credit case, but he was simply waiting for a
good chance to dispose of them. Han's face had never appeared on a WANTED poster or in a database, only his original retinal patterns. And they were gone, erased.

As he mounted the stone steps to the Hall of Admissions, Han's strides were sure and confident. He walked up
to the human recruiting officer sitting behind the desk and
smiled politely. "Hello," he said. "My name is Han Solo,
and I'd like to apply for admission into the Imperial Academy. I've always wanted to be a Naval officer."

The clerk did not smile back, but he was civil. "May I
see your identification, Mr. Solo?"

"Certainly," Han said, and laid it on the desk.

"This will take a moment. Please take a seat."

Han sat, feeling inner tension, but telling himself he had
nothing to be afraid of. Renn Tharen's credits had seen to
that . . .

Minutes later the clerk handed Han's IDs back to him
and offered a remote smile. "Everything checks out, Solo.
You can begin the application and testing process today.
Are you aware that over fifty percent of the candidates are
not accepted? And that fifty percent of those accepted
never complete their course at the Academy?"

"Yes, sir, I am," Han said. "But I'm determined to try.
I'm a good pilot."

"The Emperor needs good pilots," the man said, his
smile actually genuine for a moment. "Very well, let's get
you started . . ."

The next week was a calculated nightmare. The first step
was a thorough physical, more detailed than any Han had

experienced before. The medical droids poked and prodded places that made Han long to give them a swift kick in their circuitry, but he bore it all stoically.

He was very tense during the eye exam, but Nici's droid had been an expert. The Imperial medical droid found nothing wrong.

Han passed the physical with flying colors. His reaction time and reflexes were in the topmost percentile.

Then came the hard part . . .

Day after day, a steadily dwindling group of cadet candidates were ushered into private examination rooms. Each room came equipped with an examination droid, who posed the questions to the candidates, recorded their scores, and kept tabulations of their standing.

Each night Han went back to his tiny little cubicle in yet another flophouse and fell asleep, exhausted, only to dream all night of taking exams:

"Cadet Candidate Solo, I am going to show you four types of body armor. Which of these was used by the Mandalorian forces during the last century?"

And, *"Cadet Candidate Solo, in what year did our glorious Emperor become President of the Imperial Senate? What historical event preceded his election?"*

And, *"Cadet Candidate Solo, if a Victory-class Star Destroyer leaves Imperial Center at the displayed time, and carries the mass and weight of armament, cargo, and troops, as displayed on this screen, which course and approach vector to the Daedalon system will produce the most fuel efficiency? Which course and approach vector will produce the best speed? Be prepared to show the figures for your answer."*

And, *"Cadet Candidate Solo, which battle of the Noolian Crisis brought about the liberation of the Bothan Sector? On what date was it fought?"*

Worst of all, as far as Han was concerned, were the "cultural" questions. Each cadet was expected to be an officer and a gentleman (or woman), and a certain amount of cultural acumen was required. Han sweated his way through questions such as, "Cadet Candidate Solo, I am going to play music from three different worlds. Please identify the planet of origin of each piece of music."

Ironically, Han was much better at answering the art questions than the music ones. His background as a thief and burglar had given him at least a passing acquaintance with Art History and modern Galactic Art.

When, after three days of relentless examinations, Han found himself still listed among the CADET CANDIDATES on the vid-board in the giant Hall of Admissions, he was both surprised and ecstatic.

The piloting tests covered the last two days of the week-long testing period. During this portion, Han's experience stood him in good stead. The candidates were taken off-world in large transports and shipped to nearby Imperial bases. Only one section of the advanced-placement testing was conducted on Coruscant itself.

Every day, the candidates practiced piloting in a variety of different situations. Han did well, and knew he'd passed each test. Only one off-note was struck—one of Han's testing officers (human instructors were used during this portion) commented sourly to the other instructors that he felt that Han's "fastest time for assigned run" score should be stricken because it was highly irregular for a cadet candidate to fly a shuttle *through* Emperor Palpatine's Arch of Triumph on Imperial Center, rather than *above* it.

"He frightened several thousand Imperial citizens! We received hundreds of complaints!" the officer sputtered.

The head testing officer shrugged. "Nobody was injured, right?"

"Correct, sir."

"Then Cadet Candidate Solo's score stands. Those citizens could use a little excitement from time to time. Good for their circulation," the head testing officer decided.

Han was careful not to let on that he'd overheard the exchange.

The Corellian knew that while he'd done well on the piloting examinations, he'd passed several of the other subjects by the barest skin of his teeth.

Several times a "minus" sign appeared beside his name,

indicating that he would be slated for remedial studies in that area, should he pass and be accepted into the Academy.

Not surprisingly, "Music" was among those areas, as was "Ancient Pre-Republic History," "Interspatial Quantum Physics," and "Nonlinear Hyperspace Geometry."

Han studied every night and fell asleep to the sounds of "cram recordings" droning reams of information as he slumbered. Actually, Han didn't really mind dreaming endlessly about the examinations each night.

It beat dreaming of Bria.

Finally, the day came when he stood before the vidboard and looked for his name on the list of DISQUALIFIED CANDIDATES—and failed to find it.

Heart pounding, scarcely daring to hope, he went over to look at the other list across the Hall, the one labeled CADETS ACCEPTED.

Han Solo.

There it was, in glowing letters. Han stared at it, unable to think, hardly daring to believe it.

But there it was. He hung around the Hall for an hour, and went back three different times, and it was there every time. Finally, after the third time, Han allowed himself to whisper, *"Yes!"* and pump his fist into the air in triumph.

He walked down the steps and out into the massive top-level plaza, feeling the cold evening air of Coruscant, like a dash of cold, refreshing water.

This calls for a celebration, he thought exultantly.

Han treated himself to dinner at one of the posh upper-level restaurants, not too far from the Hall of Admissions. He ordered nerf medallions in tangy redor sauce, with a side order of fried tubers, and a salad of assorted greens. He also ordered an Alderaanian ale, which he sipped slowly, savoring it.

Once, during dinner, he glanced around at the beautiful decor, taking in the swanky metal and living ice sculpture, the muted jizz trio, and the *human* servers. Several high-ranking Imperial officers were there, escorting attractive women in beautiful evening gowns. Han raised his glass unobtrusively into the air and whispered, "Bria, I made it. I sure wish you were here to share this with me, sweetheart . . ."

After paying the exorbitant price for the meal without a single regret, Han walked out of the restaurant and strolled across the broad, elegant plaza. The weather deflector mounted high above the plaza kept off most of the wind, so he was almost warm enough as he walked. He sealed up his old jacket against the chill.

All around him, and above him, Han could see the topmost spires and roofs of the highest buildings. This plaza was located right below the highest level in this part of Coruscant. Long, corkscrewed ramps led up to the upper level, in addition to the ubiquitous turbolifts.

Once out of the brightest glare of the lights, Han leaned against a railing and tried to see the stars. He picked out one or two of the brightest, but the horizon completely overshadowed the heavens. Red and green auroras shimmered and flickered, seemingly painted against the blackness by some mad, gargantuan artist. It was a breathtaking view.

I made it!

Han smiled . . .

And then froze, as something hard and small and round jabbed into the small of his back. The muzzle of a blaster. A voice Han recognized, even though it had been nearly five months since he'd heard it, said jovially, "Hey, Han. Good to see you again, boy. I have to admit, you weren't easy to find."

This can't be happening, Han thought. *Not now! It's not fair!"*

The genial tones held a chuckle, now. "Han, why don't you turn around real slow and easy, and let's talk face-to-face."

Han turned, very slowly, and as he had known he would, found himself face-to-face with Garris Shrike. The captain of *Trader's Luck* had replaced his gaudy uniform with his old bounty hunter's garb of scarred leather vest, trousers, and snug-fitting Alderaanian nerf-wool tunic, but otherwise he looked exactly the same as he had the night Han had left him sprawled unconscious on the deckplates.

No . . . Han thought, *there's something different . . .*

After a moment he realized that he was looking slightly *down* at Shrike. *It's me that's different. I've grown a little. I'm taller . . .*

Shrike scrutinized him. "Well . . . ain't you handsome, boy," he said. "Too bad you can't come back with me to the *Luck* and let some of the ladies get a look at you. You'd be a real favorite, I'm sure."

Han finally found his voice. "What do you want, Garris?" he demanded coldly.

"Oh, so it's 'Garris' now, is it? Think you're my equal, do you?" The man backhanded Han viciously across the face. When Han started to react, the blaster dug threateningly into his midsection. Silently the younger man wiped blood from a split lower lip. "Well, you're *not* my equal, and don't you forget it. All you are to me is a pile of credits from the Hutts for bringing 'Vykk Draygo' back to them alive."

"The Hutts are looking for me?" Han asked, stalling for time.

"They're looking for Vykk Draygo, and Jenos Idanian, and all the rest of your aliases, boy. But you're 'Han Solo,' now, aren't you? And I'm the only one in the whole galaxy, practically, who knew that Han Solo was also Vykk Draygo and all those others. So when I saw the Hutt advert, I decided to come out of retirement just for you. Too many credits to pass up."

"I see," Han said.

Shrike rocked his head back with another hard slap. "No, you *don't* see, Han. You don't see that things ain't been going good for the *Luck* lately. You don't see that Larrad's never been the same since your Wookiee hag dislocated his arm. Those credits from the Hutts are gonna turn things around for all of us."

"Really?" Han asked. "I don't see how just capturing me is going to change your luck. You'd do better to pull some kind of scam on Gamorr. And I'm afraid . . . Garris . . . that I can't go along with this little scheme of yours . . ."

As he spoke, Han had begun lowering his voice, little by little, speaking more and more softly. Unconsciously, Shrike leaned forward slightly to hear—

—just as Han, with a wild scream, leaped straight at him. One arm swept up in a block, sweeping Shrike's arm, and almost at the same moment, Han brought his knee up into the man's groin. As Shrike doubled over with a grunt, Han punched him in the jaw, hard. The captain went down.

The blaster dropped out of Garris's hand, and Shrike grabbed for it. Han kicked it away, sending it skittering into the black, sharp-edged shadows. Then he leaped over Shrike's crouched form and bolted for the ramp leading up to the tallest roof. From there he could hide and catch a horizontal tube or a turbolift.

Han couldn't believe he'd actually managed to down Shrike in a fight. While he'd been growing up, he'd lived in terror of the captain's temper and his hard fists.

Han reached the ramp and went up the corkscrew with the rush of a ship using full thrusters. He reached the top of the ramp and hesitated, looking around. The rooftop looked otherworldly with its double-edged shadows from Coruscant's two small moons, edging everything into aching, sparkling white and bands of gray that plunged into impenetrable darkness.

As Han headed out across the rooftop, still scanning for a turbolift, a blue bolt shot out of the darkness at his right. The shot had come from the doorway of a turbolift. *Blaster on stun!* Han thought, running again, zigzagging frantically. *Shrike? How could he have got up here so fast?*

Another stun beam.

Han bolted across the rooftop like a vrelt running before a blaster ray, running as he'd never run before in his life. He passed another turbolift entrance, pulled up, and headed toward it. As he reached it, the door opened, and Shrike stood there, silhouetted in the doorway, blaster in hand.

Han skidded to a halt on the icy permacrete and reversed direction. *Shrike here? Who fired those other shots, then?*

But he was too busy racing across the rooftop to give the question much consideration.

Shrike's blaster spat, blue-green in the shadows. The uppermost level was mostly reserved for courting couples and was not well lit. Only the light of Coruscant's two small moons illumined the area.

Han's breath was visible in the darkness as he raced across the permacrete, leaping over curbs and exposed conduits. The uppermost spires of several buildings stuck up from the permacrete like grotesque stone evergreens. Han hurdled one and skidded on hoarfrost as he landed. It was *cold* up here, away from the protection of the weather deflector. His leather jacket offered little protection.

"Stop or I'll fry your ass!" Shrike yelled, and another stun beam split the night.

Han lengthened his strides, fleeing like a hunted animal, desperate to escape. Daring to look back over his shoulder, he saw Shrike's dark form light up faintly in the reflected glow from another stun beam.

Turning forward again, Han ran faster, harder—only to come to a screeching halt and stand teetering on the edge where the permacrete dead-ended!

Arms windmilling, Han threw himself backward. He had a brief glimpse of the gorgeously lit plaza, ten or more stories below him, including the elegant restaurant where he'd eaten dinner. Through the shimmer of the weather deflectors, he could see the elegant statues, the exotic flowers and greenery . . .

Dinner seemed a lifetime ago.

Han turned right, skidding a little, and headed the other way. Another stun beam lashed at him. His breath burned his chest as he gasped in the freezing air.

He hurdled another spire, felt it brush the inside of his trouser leg, but made it and ran on, dodging into a patch of shadow to escape another stun bolt.

The shadow suddenly gave way to complete and utter emptiness as an airshaft dropped away into nothingness!

Han was going too fast to stop. With a yell of terror, he leaped as hard as he could—

—and managed to clear the yawning gap. He landed heavily on the other side, fell, and rolled over, gasping, wind knocked out, trying to get to his feet again. He skidded on the icy permacrete, flailing, just as a stun beam *splatted* right beside him.

Han's entire right side went numb.

The Corellian crashed back to the permacrete with an agonized grunt. Letting himself go limp, he waited, hoping that he'd regain the use of his right side in time. Depending on the intensity level Shrike was using, it might take two minutes . . . or ten.

Breathing was torture, but Han gulped down every lungful, ignoring the pain. He needed to get his wind back, in case feeling returned to his right side.

Footsteps approached from his left. Shrike, going around the airshaft Han had hurdled. Han lay still. Only the white plume of his breath revealed that he still lived.

The footsteps paused beside him, circled him. Han could see Shrike's form dimly, through his eyelashes. Then a boot kicked him viciously in his right leg. Han gasped with the pain. "You low-life scum," Shrike spat. "For two credits I'd dump your worthless hide off the edge for what you did."

The fact that Han could feel pain in the place where Shrike's heavy boot had struck him was good. The stun paralysis was wearing off. But Han did not move, only lay limp as Shrike grabbed him by the collar of his jacket and dragged him over the permacrete, bumping and slithering, toward the nearest turbolift.

The trader captain was cursing steadily and, Han realized with a flare of satisfaction, walking with a distinct limp. The Corellian made himself the heaviest, deadest weight he could as he bumped along over the rooftop, feeling the icy scrape of the permacrete. His right hand tingled as it dragged, and that was good, too.

When Shrike reached the turbolift, he let go of Han's collar. It was hard to just let himself fall, but Han managed to make it look good, without banging his head too hard. Shrike's glittery-eyed countenance, a bruise darkening his jaw, appeared in his field of vision. "Now we're going down in this lift, and you're going to behave yourself, you little vrelt. We're going to be real chummy, you and me. I'm going to say you're my buddy who had too much to drink."

Han could hear the turbolift coming. He flexed the muscles of his right leg, his right arm. They responded, if sluggishly. He didn't have much time . . .

"So tell me, Han, did you make it into the Imperial Academy?" Shrike asked, just as though Han could speak. "Is that why you were out treating yourself good tonight, eh?"

He laughed. "The Imps must be real hard up if they'd take a loser like you." He spat, and warm spittle hit Han's face, just above his right eye. Han was careful not to react. The turbolift was very close. When those doors opened, Shrike would be distracted for a few precious seconds, and then . . . then he would make his move.

Imperceptibly, Han flexed his right fingers, and they answered the command of his brain. Shrike was still ranting. "Those Imperials . . . can't shoot straight, can't pilot, and can't fight worth a hoot. It's a wonder old Palpatine can get himself out of bed in the morning. All a bunch of losers . . ."

The turbolift doors opened. Shrike looked up, just as Han lunged up off the permacrete.

The element of surprise served him for a moment. Han managed to knock the blaster out of Shrike's hand again, but then Garris was on him. Iron-hard hands clamped around the younger man's throat. Han's eyes bulged as he hooked a leg behind Shrike's and sent the man over backward. Shrike didn't release his grip, so Han went down with him, and they landed in a kicking, punching sprawl.

Han slammed a fist into Shrike's midsection, heard the man grunt in pain. The fingers around his throat loosened for a second—then Shrike released his grip and tried to gouge Han's eye.

His *right* eye. The viciously gouging thumb skidded in Shrike's own saliva, and Han turned his head and snapped like an animal. His teeth closed on Shrike's thumb, clamped down. Shrike screamed as Han tore his flesh. The Corellian tasted blood.

Han took advantage of the man's momentary distraction to bring his knee up into Shrike's midsection. The older man's breath whooshed out in a stinking rush of white, into the cold night air.

Han heaved upward, throwing Shrike off him. The man lost his grip and went sprawling backward. Han scrambled for where he'd heard the blaster land—and his fingers found it.

Shrike was already up and heading purposefully for the younger man, when Han came up onto his knees, the blaster pointed directly at him. Han ostentatiously thumbed the intensity level up to its highest setting. "Your turn to freeze, Shrike," he said. Speaking brought on a spasm of coughing and searing pain in Han's abused throat, but he managed to get Shrike in his sights.

Shrike laughed, and slowed, but didn't stop. He was perhaps six meters away. "Now, Han, son," he said coaxingly, "old Captain Shrike was just having a little fun with you, is all. I wasn't going to turn you over to those Hutts, no indeed. Did you know you *killed* one of them, boy? Hutts don't like that, no they don't. They're never going to stop searching for old 'Vykk Draygo,' you know?"

"Stop right there," Han said, and was terrified to hear the quaver in his own voice. He'd never shot anyone down in cold blood before. Especially someone he *knew*. Could he do it?

Shrike grinned as if he could read Han's mind. "C'mon, Han. You know you ain't going to shoot me. You can't. I'm like your daddy, almost."

Han shook his head and replied with a Huttese obscenity so blistering that Shrike raised his eyebrows. "Oh, my, you've developed such a dirty mouth while you were gone, ain't you, kid?"

He was still moving. Only about four meters separated them now. Han tightened his grip on the blaster, but he was horrified to realize the muzzle was wavering.

"Let's go down below and talk about this, Han," Shrike

said, his voice low and soothing. "I won't hurt you, you've got my word on it."

"Your word?" Han laughed, then coughed. "That's a laugh. Your word isn't worth spit."

"Sure, my word. Besides . . . if you shoot me, boy, you'll never find out about your parents. Who they were . . . why you wound up being dumped into those alleys where I found you."

Han stared at Shrike. "You know who they were? You know why I was abandoned?" He swallowed, and it was searing pain. "Tell me, and I may let you live."

Shrike was almost within grabbing distance of the blaster now. Only a meter or so away. Han knew he should shoot him, *knew* Shrike couldn't be trusted—but still he hesitated. "Tell me, Shrike!"

"I'll tell you everything when you give me the blaster," Shrike said. "Everything. You have my word."

Shoot him! Now! Han's mind screamed.

With a wash of red light, a blaster bolt struck Garris Shrike directly in the chest. The captain threw up his hands, a look of terror and pain contorting his features. He fell backward like a stone, dead before he hit the permacrete.

Han stared wildly at his hand. His finger was on the trigger of the blaster, but he hadn't moved it . . . had he?

The shot, he realized, a second later, had come from *behind* him.

Han whirled, still on his knees, to find himself facing another man. He was human, young, medium tall, slender build. Darkish hair frosted by moonlight. He held a drawn blaster, and every line of him screamed "bounty hunter."

"Okay, kid, it's over," he said, removing a pair of wrist-binders from his belt. "Stand up. You're coming with me."

Those first two shots! Han thought. *It must have been him. He followed me up here, and just waited for Shrike to take me down, so he could step in and get me.*

As if he'd sensed what Han was thinking, the bounty hunter added, "I knew old Shrike would find you. The Hutts don't have a picture of you, so I followed Shrike, 'cause he practically raised you, didn't he, Vykk? I knew he'd pick you out for me."

No! Han's mind screamed. *Not now! Not* again!"

He was still stiff from the paralysis, exhausted and hurt from the fight with Shrike. Every muscle screamed with pain and weariness.

The bounty hunter gestured with the blaster. "Drop your blaster, kid, or I'll stun you right in the head and scramble your brains good. The Hutts want you *alive,* but they didn't say nothing about in your right mind. Drop it."

Shaking, Han dropped the blaster from his nerveless fingers. With a grunt of effort, he tried to get up, but his right leg buckled beneath him.

"My leg . . ." he mumbled. "Right leg won't take my weight . . . Shrike kicked me."

"Yeah, I saw him. Not very professional of him, but old Shrike always was hot-tempered," the bounty hunter said. Moving forward, he added, "Now I'm going to give you a hand up. Don't try—"

With a demented howl, Han hurled himself headfirst into the bounty hunter's midsection.

This man was younger than Shrike, stronger and faster. But Han was fighting like a madman, with the strength borne of utter desperation. He had nothing to lose, and he knew it.

The bounty hunter went over backward with a yell of surprise. Han threw himself after him, pummeling the man. Recovering himself, the bounty hunter slammed Han across the temple with the muzzle of his blaster.

Blood spurted, ran into Han's left eye, but the Corellian didn't let it slow him down. He clawed his way up the other's body as though it were a jungle vine and head-butted the bounty hunter, slamming his forehead into the man's nose. Han heard and felt cartilage break against the bone of his skull. The man's shrill scream rang through the night.

Cursing, the bounty hunter grappled with Han, slamming him on the back and in the kidneys with the blaster. Han grabbed his arm and slammed his hand against the permacrete, *wham* . . . *WHAM!* The blaster dropped from the man's fingers. Han butted the bounty hunter in the face again, ignoring the splitting of his own skin.

"You're NOT taking me!" the Corellian yelled, slamming his head into the man's face repeatedly. With a yell of terror, the bounty hunter heaved upward with all his strength and sent Han flying.

The Corellian hit, tried to roll, and slammed up against the structure that housed the turbolift. The bounty hunter, his face a gory mask from his broken nose and split lips, rushed for Han, murder in his eyes.

Han waited until the last possible second, then dodged. As the man went by, Han slammed his full weight into the other's shoulder.

The bounty hunter's head impacted with the stone structure with a *crack* that seemed to echo throughout the icy night.

The man jerked, went limp, then slid down the wall, to lie motionless on the permacrete.

Weaving, biting his lip, and swallowing bile, Han lurched to his feet and stumbled over to the man. Two fingers against his throat assured the Corellian that the bounty hunter was now as dead as Garris Shrike, who was lying sprawled a few meters away, staring up at the twin moons with blank, sightless eyes.

Han slid down the wall in his own turn and just sat there, his head whirling, sick and exhausted. He began to shake all over, and the bout lasted for nearly a minute.

Gotta get hold of myself, he thought dully. *Gotta think. Think . . .*

Climbing back to his feet, Han staggered over to the bounty hunter again and stood eyeing him. The man was about his own size, and he, too, had brown hair. Darker than Han's own, but that might not be noticed . . .

Han's breath puffed white as he yanked on the man's boots, pulling them off. Slowly, methodically, he set about stripping the bounty hunter.

Five minutes later, Han stood swaying, dressed now in the bounty hunter's clothing. Grimly, he began putting his own clothes onto the corpse . . . his worn gray pilot's jumpsuit, his battered lizard-skin jacket, his boots. He replaced the bounty hunter's blaster in his holster. Lastly, he took a handful of credits, and all of his faked IDs, and placed them in the man's inside pocket, sealing the pocket shut. Then he sealed the jacket closed, too.

Stumbling and limping, Han went looking for Shrike's blaster. He found it, finally, and went back to the body. Wincing, he adjusted it to its highest setting, aimed the weapon, then, turning his head to the side, he fired directly into the corpse's face. When he forced himself to look, the dead man no longer *had* a face—or eyes.

Or retinas.

Han staggered away a few feet and was thoroughly, wretchedly, sick. The thought of what that meal had cost him made him even sicker . . .

With a groan of effort, he grabbed the body beneath the arms and dragged the bounty hunter across the icy permacrete, just as Shrike had dragged him. He went backward slowly, carefully, until he was once again beside that deep, deep airshaft that he'd jumped.

Han peered down, then looked away quickly, fighting dizziness. The shaft went down a long, long way.

He rolled the body to the edge, then, with a hard push of both hands, sent the bounty hunter over the edge, tumbling out into empty air.

Han didn't watch the body fall. With dragging, limping steps, he lurched back to Shrike's body and placed the captain's blaster in the dead fingers. Then he pressed the button to summon the turbolift.

When the doors opened, he nearly fell into the lighted interior.

The turbolift started down, and Han stood swaying, bracing himself with both hands. He had to work at not passing out.

It had been a long night . . .

EPILOGUE:

REBIRTH

Han Solo stood alone amid the teeming mass of cadets gathered at the rooftop landing field on Coruscant. The tight collar of his new uniform chafed his neck, but he resisted the urge to tug at it. Doing so might wrinkle it, and Han wanted to look his best.

All around him, cadets were being hugged and kissed farewell by their families. Only a few cadets were alone, as he was. Han scanned the crowd and noticed a dark-skinned boy a few meters away, who didn't seem to have anybody. And there was a young woman with military-short hair standing across the landing field who was also alone.

But most of the cadets had fathers, and mothers, brothers and sisters and grandparents, uncles and aunts and cousins, who'd come to see them off in their hour of triumph. Han felt a wave of loneliness. He was older than the other cadets, and that, too, set him apart.

But hey . . . I'm here. I made it.

The transport *Imperator* lay waiting for them on the landing field. Soon, the cadets would be boarding it for their trip to Carida, the Imperial military training world. Han smiled a little as he studied its lines, its oversized dorsal fin. A Corellian corvette. How fitting . . .

He gazed at the crowd again, searchingly, and suddenly realized that he'd been hoping to see a certain red-gold head among the well-wishers. *Dumb, Solo. Really dumb. You didn't really expect her to show up, did you? She's long gone!*

No, Han decided, he really hadn't *expected* Bria to show up. But maybe, deep down, he'd *hoped* she would . . .

He sighed. Dewlanna had used to quote an old Wookiee proverb at him, something that translated into Basic as, roughly: "Joy unmixed with sorrow is suspect."

Dewlanna . . .

If only she could see him now. Han imagined her, her tall, shaggy form, her snubbed black nose, her little, twinkling eyes nearly hidden beneath tufts of graying tan Wookiee hair. She would be very proud today, he knew that. For a moment she was so real that he could almost imagine her, could almost hear her growls and moans as she told him how proud he'd made her. She'd ruffle up his hair so he'd look attractively "scruffy."

Han smiled faintly at the idea. *I made it, Dewlanna,* he told her image silently. *Look at me. You're my family, my only family, so it's right that you be here today, even if you're only in my memory . . .*

And Bria . . .

Face it, Solo, you still care. You still watch for her, and listen for the sound of her step, her voice. You need to get over this, man . . .

Han shook his head, as though he could dismiss Bria's image as easily as he'd summoned Dewlanna's. But he was taking Bria aboard the *Imperator,* as surely as if she were here, walking beside him. No matter how he tried, he couldn't forget her.

Another of Dewlanna's old Wookiee proverbs surfaced in his mind: "To have a good memory is to be both blessed and cursed . . ."

How right you are, Dewlanna, Han thought.

He shifted his weight, and stabbing pain in his right leg reminded him of the fight the night before last. Han blew out his breath. *He's dead, Dewlanna,* he thought. *Your killer is dead. You can rest easier, knowing that, I'll bet . . .*

An Imperial officer was making his way through the crowd, now. As he passed Han, the Lieutenant paused and looked at him sharply. "Your name, Cadet?"

Han snapped to attention. "Cadet Han Solo, sir!"

"You forget how to salute, Cadet Solo?"

"No, sir!" Han said, and gave the man his best salute.

The officer gazed at Han's face. "Cadet Solo, what happened to your face?"

For a moment Han was tempted to say he walked into a door, but he decided that the truth was probably the best answer. "Sir, I got in a fight."

"Really? I could never have told," the lieutenant said, a tinge of sarcasm in his voice. "What was the fight about, Cadet Solo?"

Han thought fast. "My opponent insulted the Imperial Navy, sir."

After all, it was true.

The lieutenant raised an eyebrow. "Really, Cadet? That was most . . . unwise . . . of him. Did you give him a good thrashing for his disrespect, Cadet Solo?"

Han remembered just in time not to nod. "I did, sir. I assure the lieutenant that he will never say anything insulting about the Imperial forces again, sir."

"Very good, Cadet Solo." The lieutenant smiled faintly and walked on, to the head of the group.

Han breathed a long, slow sigh of relief. *Made it through that one!*

An amplified voice echoed across the landing fields. A

noncommissioned officer was standing beside the lieutenant, giving orders. "Imperial cadets! Assemble in ranks!"

There was general confusion for a second, then the lines of cadets formed into ranks. "We will board the transport ship in rows. No talking, and pick up your feet."

Silence fell. Han was in Row 4. He stood as straight as he could, looking neither left nor right, waiting for his orders to move. From somewhere, the martial theme of the Imperial Navy began playing in the background.

"Row one! March!"

"Row two! March!"

"Row three! March!"

Excitement coursed through Han, singing in his blood. *This is it. What I've waited for all my life* . . .

"Row four! March!" bawled the noncom.

Han right-faced smartly and followed the man ahead of him toward the *Imperator*. As he marched, he allowed himself a faint smile.

Today it begins, he thought. *My real life begins.*

He imagined Dewlanna's and Bria's faces. They were smiling, too.

His feet were on the ramp. Han took a deep breath, the kind of breath that a newborn might draw in order to give its first cry, its first shout of, *I'm here! Listen to me, I'm ALIVE!*

Han Solo *felt* new, as though he'd just been born. The dark past tumbled off his shoulders, and only the bright future lay ahead.

He marched forward into it eagerly, and did not look back.

ABOUT THE AUTHOR

Ann C. Crispin is the bestselling author of over 16 books, including four *Star Trek* novels and her original *StarBridge* science fiction series.

Her first appearance in the Star Wars universe came when her friend Kevin Anderson asked her to write two short stories for the Star Wars anthologies, "Tales From the Mos Eisley Cantina" and "Tales From Jabba's Palace."

Ann has been a full-time writer since 1983, and currently serves as Eastern Regional Director of the Science Fiction and Fantasy Writers of America. She is a frequent guest at science fiction conventions, where she often teaches writers' workshops.

She lives in Maryland, with her son, Jason, five cats, a German Shepherd, two Appaloosas, and Michael Capobianco, a writer of hard s.f. In her spare time (what's that?) she enjoys horseback riding, sailing, camping, and reading books she didn't write.

Her forthcoming works include the seventh novel in her *StarBridge* Series, *Voices of Chaos* (co-authored with Ru Emerson), and *The Exiles of Boq'urain*, a fantasy trilogy from Avon Books.

The World of
STAR WARS Novels

In May 1991, *Star Wars* caused a sensation in the publishing industry with the Bantam release of Timothy Zahn's novel *Heir to the Empire*. For the first time, Lucasfilm Ltd. had authorized new novels that *continued* the famous story told in George Lucas's three blockbuster motion pictures: *Star Wars*, *The Empire Strikes Back* and *Return of the Jedi*. Reader reaction was immediate and tumultuous: *Heir* reached No. 1 on the *New York Times* bestseller list and demonstrated that *Star Wars* lovers were eager for exciting new stories set in this universe, written by leading science fiction authors who shared their passion. Since then, each Bantam *Star Wars* novel has been an instant national bestseller.

Lucasfilm and Bantam decided that future novels in the series would be interconnected: That is, events in one novel would have consequences in the others. You might say that each Bantam *Star Wars* novel, enjoyable on its own, is also part of a much larger tale.

Here is a special look at Bantam's *Star Wars* books, along with excerpts from the more recent novels. Each one is available now wherever Bantam Books are sold.

The Han Solo Trilogy:
THE PARADISE SNARE
and coming soon,
THE HUTT GAMBIT
REBEL DAWN
by A. C. Crispin
Setting before *Star Wars: A New Hope*

What was Han Solo like before we met him in the first STAR WARS movie? This trilogy answers that tantalizing question, filling in lots of historical lore about our favourite swashbuckling hero and thrilling us with adventures of the brash young pilot that we never knew he'd experienced. As the trilogy begins, the young Han makes a life-changing decision: to escape from the clutches of Garris Shrike, head of the trading "clan" who has brutalized Han while taking advantage of his piloting abilities. Here's a tense early scene from The Paradise Snare featuring Han, Shrike, and Dewlanna, a Wookiee who is Han's only friend in this horrible situation:

"I've had it with you, Solo. I've been lenient with you so far, because you're a blasted good swoop pilot and all that prize money came in handy, but my patience is ended." Shrike ceremoniously pushed up the sleeves of his bedizened uniform, then balled his hands into fists. The galley's artificial lighting made the blood-jewel ring glitter dull silver. "Let's see what a few days of fighting off Devaronian blood-poisoning does for your attitude—along with maybe a few broken bones. I'm doing this for your own good, boy. Someday you'll thank me."

Han gulped with terror as Shrike started toward him. He'd lashed out at the trader captain once before, two years ago, when he'd been feeling cocky after winning the gladiatorial Free-For-All on Jubilar—and had been instantly sorry. The speed and strength of Garris's returning blow had snapped his head back and split both lips so thoroughly that Dewlanna had had to feed him mush for a week until they healed.

With a snarl, Dewlanna stepped forward. Shrike's hand dropped to his blaster. "You stay out of this, old Wookiee," he snapped in a voice nearly as harsh as Dewlanna's. "Your cooking isn't *that* good."

Han had already grabbed his friend's furry arm and was forcibly holding her back. "Dewlanna, no!"

She shook off his hold as easily as she would have waved off an annoying insect and roared at Shrike. The captain drew his blaster, and chaos erupted.

"Noooo!" Han screamed, and leaped forward, his foot lashing out in an old street-fighting technique. His instep impacted solidly with Shrike's breastbone. The captain's breath went out in a great *houf!* and he went over backward. Han hit the deck and rolled. A tingler bolt sizzled past his ear.

"Larrad!" wheezed the captain as Dewlanna started toward him.

Shrike's brother drew his blaster and pointed it at the Wookiee. "Stop, Dewlanna!"

His words had no more effect than Han's. Dewlanna's blood was up—she was in full Wookiee battle rage. With a roar that deafened the combatants, she grabbed Larrad's wrist and yanked, spinning him around and snapping him in a terrible parody of a child's "snap the whip" game. Han heard a *crunch,* mixed with several *pops* as tendons and ligaments gave way. Larrad Shrike shrieked, a high, shrill noise that carried such pain that the Corellian youth's arm ached in sympathy.

Grabbing the blaster from his belt, Han snapped off a shot at the Elomin who was leaping forward, tingler ready and aimed at Dewlanna's midsection. Brafid howled, dropping his weapon. Han was amazed that he'd managed to hit him, but he didn't have long to wonder about the accuracy of his aim.

Shrike was staggering to his feet, blaster in hand, aimed squarely at Han's head. "Larrad?" he yelled at the writhing heap of agony that was his brother. Larrad did not reply.

Shrike cocked the blaster and stepped even closer to Han. "Stop it, Dewlanna!" the captain snarled at the Wookiee. "Or your buddy Solo dies!"

Han dropped his blaster and put his hands up in a gesture of surrender.

Dewlanna stopped in her tracks, growling softly.

Shrike leveled the blaster, and his finger tightened on the trigger. Pure malevolent hatred was etched upon his features, and then he smiled, pale blue eyes glittering with ruthless joy. "For insubordination and striking your captain," he announced, "I sentence you to death, Solo. May you rot in all the hells there ever were."

SHADOWS OF THE EMPIRE
by Steve Perry
Setting: Between *The Empire Strikes Back* and *Return of the Jedi*

Here is a very special STAR WARS story dealing with Black Sun, a galaxy-spanning criminal organization that is masterminded by one of the most interesting villains in the STAR WARS universe: Xizor, dark prince of the Falleen. Xizor's chief rival for the favor of Emperor Palpatine is none other than Darth Vader himself—alive and well, and a major character in this story, since it is set during the events of the STAR WARS film trilogy.

In the opening prologue, we revisit a familiar scene from The Empire Strikes Back, *and are introduced to our marvelous new bad guy:*

He looks like a walking corpse, Xizor thought. *Like a mummified body dead a thousand years. Amazing he is still alive, much less the most powerful man in the galaxy. He isn't even that old; it is more as if something is slowly eating him.*

Xizor stood four meters away from the Emperor, watching as the man who had long ago been Senator Palpatine moved to stand in the holocam field. He imagined he could smell the decay in the Emperor's worn body. Likely that was just some trick of the recycled air, run through dozens of filters to ensure that there was no chance of any poison gas being introduced into it. Filtered the life out of it, perhaps, giving it that dead smell.

The viewer on the other end of the holo-link would see a close-up of the Emperor's head and shoulders, of an age-ravaged face shrouded in the cowl of his dark zeyd-cloth robe. The man on the other end of the transmission, light-years away, would not see Xizor, though Xizor would be able to see him. It was a measure of the Emperor's trust that Xizor was allowed to be here while the conversation took place.

The man on the other end of the transmission—if he could still be called that—

The air swirled inside the Imperial chamber in front of the Emperor, coalesced, and blossomed into the image of a figure down on one knee. A caped humanoid biped dressed in jet black, face hidden under a full helmet and breathing mask:

Darth Vader.

Vader spoke: "What is thy bidding, my master?"

If Xizor could have hurled a power bolt through time and space to strike Vader dead, he would have done it without blinking. Wishful thinking: Vader was too powerful to attack directly.

"There is a great disturbance in the Force," the Emperor said.

"I have felt it," Vader said.

"We have a new enemy. Luke Skywalker."

Skywalker? That had been Vader's name, a long time ago. Who was this person with the same name, someone so powerful as to be worth a conversation between the Emperor and his most loathsome creation? More importantly, why had Xizor's agents not uncovered this before now? Xizor's ire was instant—but cold. No sign of his surprise or anger would show on his imperturbable features. The Falleen did not allow their emotions to burst forth as did many of the inferior species; no, the Falleen ancestry was not fur but scales, not mammalian but reptilian. Not wild but coolly calculating. Such was much better. Much safer.

"Yes, my master," Vader continued.

"He could destroy us," the Emperor said.

Xizor's attention was riveted upon the Emperor and the holographic image of Vader kneeling on the deck of a ship far away. Here was interesting news indeed. Something the Emperor perceived as a danger to himself? Something the Emperor feared?

"He's just a boy," Vader said. "Obi-Wan can no longer help him."

Obi-Wan. That name Xizor knew. He was among the last of the Jedi Knights, a general. But he'd been dead for decades, hadn't he?

Apparently Xizor's information was wrong if Obi-Wan had been helping someone who was still a boy. His agents were going to be sorry.

Even as Xizor took in the distant image of Vader and the nearness of the Emperor, even as he was aware of the luxury of the Emperor's private and protected chamber at the core of the giant pyramidal palace, he was also able to make a mental note to himself: Somebody's head would roll for the failure to make him aware of all this. Knowledge was power; lack of knowledge was weakness. This was something he could not permit.

The Emperor continued. "The Force is strong with him. The son of Skywalker must not become a Jedi."

Son of Skywalker?

Vader's son! Amazing!

"If he could be turned he would become a powerful ally," Vader said.

There was something in Vader's voice when he said this, something Xizor could not quite put his finger on. Longing? Worry?

Hope?

"Yes . . . yes. He would be a great asset," the Emperor said. "Can it be done?"

There was the briefest of pauses. "He will join us or die, master."

Xizor felt the smile, though he did not allow it to show any more than he had allowed his anger play. Ah. Vader wanted Skywalker alive, *that* was what had been in his tone. Yes, he had said that the boy would join them or die, but this latter part was obviously meant only to placate the Emperor. Vader had no intention of killing Skywalker, his own son; that was obvious to one as skilled in reading voices as was Xizor. He had not gotten to be the Dark Prince, Underlord of Black Sun, the largest criminal organization in the galaxy, merely on his formidable good looks. Xizor didn't truly understand the Force that sustained the Emperor and made him and Vader so powerful, save to know that it certainly worked somehow. But he did know that it was something the extinct Jedi had supposedly mastered. And now, apparently, this new player had tapped into it. Vader wanted Skywalker alive, had practically promised the Emperor that he would deliver him alive—and converted.

This was most interesting.

Most interesting indeed.

The Emperor finished his communication and turned back to face him. "Now, where were we, Prince Xizor?"

The Dark Prince smiled. He would attend to the business at hand, but he would not forget the name of Luke Skywalker.

THE TRUCE AT BAKURA by Kathy Tyers
Setting: Immediately after *Return of the Jedi*

The day after his climactic battle with Emperor Palpatine and the sacrifice of his father, Darth Vader, who died saving his life, Luke Skywalker helps recover an Imperial drone ship bearing a startling message intended for the Emperor. It is a distress signal from the far-off Imperial outpost of Bakura, which is under attack by an alien invasion force, the Ssi-ruuk. Leia sees a rescue mission as an opportunity to achieve a diplomatic victory for the Rebel Alliance, even if it means fighting alongside former Imperials. But Luke receives a vision from Obi-Wan Kenobi revealing that the stakes are even higher: the invasion at Bakura threatens everything the Rebels have won at such great cost.

STAR WARS: X-WING
by Michael A. Stackpole
ROGUE SQUADRON
WEDGE'S GAMBLE
THE KRYTOS TRAP
THE BACTA WAR
Setting: Three years after *Return of the Jedi*

Inspired by X-wing, *the bestselling computer game from LucasArts Entertainment Co., this exciting series chronicles the further adventures of the most feared and fearless fighting force in the galaxy. A new generation of X-wing pilots, led by Commander Wedge Antilles, is combating the remnants of the Empire still left after the events of the STAR WARS movies. Here are novels full of explosive space action, nonstop adventure, and the special brand of wonder known as STAR WARS.*

In this very early scene, young Corellian pilot Corran Horn faces a tough challenge fast enough to get his heart pounding—and this is only a simulation! [P.S.: ''Whistler'' is Corran's R2 astromech droid]:

The Corellian brought his proton torpedo targeting program up and locked on to the TIE. It tried to break the lock, but turbolaser fire from the *Korolev* boxed it in. Corran's heads-up display went red and he triggered the torpedo. ''Scratch one eyeball.''

The missile shot straight in at the fighter, but the pilot broke hard to port and away, causing the missile to overshoot the target. *Nice flying!* Corran brought his X-wing over and started down to loop in behind the TIE, but as he did so, the TIE vanished from his forward screen and reappeared in his aft arc. Yanking the stick hard to the right and pulling it back, Corran wrestled the X-wing up and to starboard, then inverted and rolled out to the left.

A laser shot jolted a tremor through the simulator's couch. *Lucky thing I had all shields aft!* Corran reinforced them with energy from his lasers, then evened them out fore and aft. Jinking the fighter right and left, he avoided laser shots coming in from behind, but they all came in far closer than he liked.

He knew Jace had been in the bomber, and Jace was the only pilot in the unit who could have stayed with him. *Except for our leader.* Corran smiled broadly. *Coming to see how good I really am, Commander Antilles? Let me give you a clinic.* ''Make sure you're in there solid, Whistler, because we're going for a little ride.''

Corran refused to let the R2's moan slow him down. A snap-roll brought the X-wing up on its port wing. Pulling back on the stick yanked the fighter's nose up away from the original line of flight. The TIE stayed with him, then tightened up on the arc to close distance. Corran then rolled another ninety degrees and continued the turn into a dive. Throttling back, Corran hung in the dive for three seconds, then hauled back hard on the stick and cruised up into the TIE fighter's aft.

The X-wing's laser fire missed wide to the right as the TIE cut to the left. Corran kicked his speed up to full and broke with the TIE. He let the X-wing rise above the plane of the break, then put the fighter through a twisting roll that ate up enough time to bring him again into the TIE's rear. The TIE snapped to the right and Corran looped out left.

He watched the tracking display as the distance between them grew to be a kilometer and a half, then slowed. *Fine, you want to go nose to nose? I've got shields and you don't.* If Commander Antilles wanted to commit virtual suicide, Corran was happy to oblige him. He tugged the stick back to his sternum and rolled out in an inversion loop. *Coming at you!*

The two starfighters closed swiftly. Corran centered his foe in the crosshairs and waited for a dead shot. Without shields the TIE fighter would die with one burst, and Corran wanted the kill to be clean. His HUD flicked green as the TIE juked in and out of the center, then locked green as they closed.

The TIE started firing at maximum range and scored hits. At that distance the lasers did no real damage against the shields, prompting Corran to wonder why Wedge was wasting the energy. Then, as the HUD's green color started to flicker, realization dawned. *The bright bursts on the shields are a distraction to my targeting! I better kill him now!*

Corran tightened down on the trigger button, sending red laser needles stabbing out at the closing TIE fighter. He couldn't tell if he had hit anything. Lights flashed in the cockpit and Whistler started screeching furiously. Corran's main monitor went black, his shields were down, and his weapons controls were dead.

The pilot looked left and right. "Where is he, Whistler?"

The monitor in front of him flickered to life and a diagnostic report began to scroll by. Bloodred bordered the damage reports. "Scanners, out; lasers, out; shields, out; engine, out! I'm a wallowing Hutt just hanging here in space."

THE COURTSHIP OF PRINCESS LEIA
by Dave Wolverton
Setting: Four years after *Return of the Jedi*

One of the most interesting developments in Bantam's STAR WARS novels is that in their storyline, Han Solo and Princess Leia start a family. This tale reveals how the couple originally got together. Wishing to strengthen the fledgling New Republic by bringing in powerful allies, Leia opens talks with the Hapes consortium of more than sixty worlds. But the consortium is ruled by the Queen Mother, who, to Han's dismay, wants Leia to marry her son, Prince Isolder. Before this action-packed story is over, Luke will join forces with Isolder against a group of Force-trained "witches" and face a deadly foe.

HEIR TO THE EMPIRE
DARK FORCE RISING
THE LAST COMMAND
by Timothy Zahn
Setting: Five years after *Return of the Jedi*

This #1 bestselling trilogy introduces two legendary forces of evil into the STAR WARS literary pantheon. Grand Admiral Thrawn has taken control of the Imperial fleet in the years since the destruction of the Death Star, and the mysterious Joruus C'baoth is a fearsome Jedi Master who has been seduced by the dark side. Han and Leia have

*now been married for about a year, and as the story begins, she is
pregnant with twins. Thrawn's plan is to crush the Rebellion and
resurrect the Empire's New Order with C'baoth's help—and in return,
the Dark Master will get Han and Leia's Jedi children to mold as he
wishes. For as readers of this magnificent trilogy will see, Luke
Skywalker is not the last of the old Jedi. He is the first of the new.*

The Jedi Academy Trilogy:
JEDI SEARCH
DARK APPRENTICE
CHAMPIONS OF THE FORCE
by Kevin J. Anderson
Setting: Seven years after *Return of the Jedi*

*In order to assure the continuation of the Jedi Knights, Luke
Skywalker has decided to start a training facility: a Jedi Academy. He
will gather Force-sensitive students who show potential as prospective
Jedi and serve as their mentor, as Jedi Masters Obi-Wan Kenobi and
Yoda did for him. Han and Leia's twins are now toddlers, and there is
a third Jedi child: the infant Anakin, named after Luke and Leia's
father. In this trilogy, we discover the existence of a powerful Imperial
doomsday weapon, the horrifying Sun Crusher—which will soon become the centerpiece of a titanic struggle between Luke Skywalker
and his most brilliant Jedi Academy student, who is delving danger-
ously into the dark side.*

CHILDREN OF THE JEDI
by Barbara Hambly
Setting: Eight years after *Return of the Jedi*

*The STAR WARS characters face a menace from the glory days of the
Empire when a thirty-year-old automated Imperial Dreadnaught
comes to life and begins its grim mission: to gather forces and annihi-
late a long-forgotten stronghold of Jedi children. When Luke is
whisked onboard, he begins to communicate with the brave Jedi
Knight who paralyzed the ship decades ago, and gave her life in the
process. Now she is part of the vessel, existing in its artificial intelligence core, and guiding Luke through one of the most unusual adventures he has ever had.*

DARKSABER by Kevin J. Anderson
Setting: Immediately thereafter

Not long after Children of the Jedi, *Luke and Han learn that evil Hutts are building a reconstruction of the original Death Star—and that the Empire is still alive, in the form of Daala, who has joined forces with Pellaeon, former second in command to the feared Grand Admiral Thrawn. In this early scene, Luke has returned to the home of Obi-Wan Kenobi on Tatooine to try and consult a long-gone mentor:*

He stood anxious and alone, feeling like a prodigal son outside the ramshackle, collapsed hut that had once been the home of Obi-Wan Kenobi.

Luke swallowed and stepped forward, his footsteps crunching in the silence. He had not been here in many years. The door had fallen off its hinges; part of the clay front wall had fallen in. Boulders and crumbled adobe jammed the entrance. A pair of small, screeching desert rodents snapped at him and fled for cover; Luke ignored them.

Gingerly, he ducked low and stepped into the home of his first mentor.

Luke stood in the middle of the room breathing deeply, turning around, trying to sense the presence he desperately needed to see. This was the place where Obi-Wan Kenobi had told Luke of the Force. Here, the old man had first given Luke his lightsaber and hinted at the truth about his father, "from a certain point of view," dispelling the diversionary story that Uncle Owen had told, at the same time planting seeds of his own deceptions.

"Ben," he said and closed his eyes, calling out with his mind as well as his voice. He tried to penetrate the invisible walls of the Force and reach to the luminous being of Obi-Wan Kenobi who had visited him numerous times, before saying he could never speak with Luke again.

"Ben, I need you," Luke said. Circumstances had changed. He could think of no other way past the obstacles he faced. Obi-Wan had to answer. It wouldn't take long, but it could give him the key he needed with all his heart.

Luke paused and listened and sensed—

But felt nothing. If he could not summon Obi-Wan's spirit here in the empty dwelling where the old man had lived in exile for so many years, Luke didn't believe he could find his former teacher ever again.

He echoed the words Leia had used more than a decade earlier, beseeching him, "Help me, Obi-Wan Kenobi," Luke whispered, "you're my only hope."

THE CRYSTAL STAR
by Vonda N. McIntyre
Setting: Ten years after *Return of the Jedi*

Leia's three children have been kidnapped. That horrible fact is made worse by Leia's realization that she can no longer sense her children through the Force! While she, Artoo-Detoo, and Chewbacca trail the kidnappers, Luke and Han discover a planet that is suffering strange quantum effects from a nearby star. Slowly freezing into a perfect crystal and disrupting the Force, the star is blunting Luke's power and crippling the Millennium Falcon. *These strands converge in an apocalyptic threat not only to the fate of the New Republic, but to the universe itself.*

The Black Fleet Crisis
BEFORE THE STORM
SHIELD OF LIES
TYRANT'S TEST
by Michael P. Kube-McDowell
Setting: Twelve years after *Return of the Jedi*

Long after setting up the hard-won New Republic, yesterday's Rebels have become today's administrators and diplomats. But the peace is not to last for long. A restless Luke must journey to his mother's homeworld in a desperate quest to find her people; Lando seizes a mysterious spacecraft with unimaginable weapons of destruction; and waiting in the wings is an horrific battle fleet under the control of a ruthless leader bent on a genocidal war.

Here is an opening scene from Before the Storm:

In the pristine silence of space, the Fifth Battle Group of the New Republic Defense Fleet blossomed over the planet Bessimir like a beautiful, deadly flower.

The formation of capital ships sprang into view with startling suddenness, trailing fire-white wakes of twisted space and bristling with weapons. Angular Star Destroyers guarded fat-hulled fleet carriers, while the assault cruisers, their mirror finishes gleaming, took the point.

A halo of smaller ships appeared at the same time. The fighters among them quickly deployed in a spherical defensive screen. As the Star Destroyers firmed up their formation, their flight decks quickly spawned scores of additional fighters.

At the same time, the carriers and cruisers began to disgorge the bombers, transports, and gunboats they had ferried to the battle. There was no reason to risk the loss of one fully loaded—a lesson the Republic had learned in pain. At Orinda, the commander of the fleet carrier *Endurance* had kept his pilots waiting in the launch bays, to protect the smaller craft from Imperial fire as long as possible. They were still there when *Endurance* took the brunt of a Super Star Destroyer attack and vanished in a ball of metal fire.

Before long more than two hundred warships, large and small, were bearing down on Bessimir and its twin moons. But the terrible, restless power of the armada could be heard and felt only by the ships' crews. The silence of the approach was broken only on the fleet comm channels, which had crackled to life in the first moments with encoded bursts of noise and cryptic ship-to-ship chatter.

At the center of the formation of great vessels was the flagship of the Fifth Battle Group, the fleet carrier *Intrepid*. She was so new from the yards at Hakassi that her corridors still reeked of sealing compound and cleaning solvent. Her huge realspace thruster engines still sang with the high-pitched squeal that the engine crews called "the baby's cry."

It would take more than a year for the mingled scents of the crew to displace the chemical smells from the first impressions of visitors. But after a hundred more hours under way, her engines' vibrations would drop two octaves, to the reassuring thrum of a seasoned thruster bank.

On *Intrepid*'s bridge, a tall Dornean in general's uniform paced along an arc of command stations equipped with large monitors. His eye-folds were swollen and fanned by an unconscious Dornean defensive reflex, and his leathery face was flushed purple by concern. Before the deployment was even a minute old, Etahn A'baht's first command had been bloodied.

The fleet tender *Ahazi* had overshot its jump, coming out of hyperspace too close to Bessimir and too late for its crew to recover from the error. Etahn A'baht watched the bright flare of light in the upper atmosphere from *Intrepid*'s forward viewstation, knowing that it meant six young men were dead.

THE NEW REBELLION
by Kristine Kathryn Rusch
Setting: Thirteen years after *Return of the Jedi*

*Victorious though the New Republic may be, there is still no end to the
threats to its continuing existence—this novel explores the price of
keeping the peace. First, somewhere in the galaxy, millions suddenly
perish in a blinding instant of pain. Then, as Leia prepares to address
the Senate on Coruscant, a horrifying event changes the governmental
equation in a flash.*

Here is that latter calamity, in an early scene from The New Rebellion:

An explosion rocked the Chamber, flinging Leia into the air. She
flew backward and slammed onto a desk, her entire body shuddering
with the power of her hit. Blood and shrapnel rained around her.
Smoke and dust rose, filling the room with a grainy darkness. She
could hear nothing. With a shaking hand, she touched the side of her
face. Warmth stained her cheeks and her earlobes. The ringing would
start soon. The explosion was loud enough to affect her eardrums.

Emergency glow panels seared the gloom. She could feel rather
than hear pieces of the crystal ceiling fall to the ground. A guard had
landed beside her, his head tilted at an unnatural angle. She grabbed
his blaster. She had to get out. She wasn't certain if the attack had
come from within or from without. Wherever it had come from, she
had to make certain no other bombs would go off.

The force of the explosion had affected her balance. She crawled
over bodies, some still moving, as she made her way to the stairs. The
slightest movement made her dizzy and nauseous, but she ignored the
feelings. She had to.

A face loomed before hers. Streaked with dirt and blood, helmet
askew, she recognized him as one of the guards who had been with
her since Alderaan. *Your Highness*, he mouthed, and she couldn't read
the rest. She shook her head at him, gasping at the increased dizziness,
and kept going.

Finally she reached the stairs. She used the remains of a desk to get
to her feet. Her gown was soaked in blood, sticky, and clinging to her
legs. She held the blaster in front of her, wishing that she could hear.
If she could hear, she could defend herself.

A hand reached out of the rubble beside her. She whirled, faced it,
watched as Meido pulled himself out. His slender features were covered with dirt, but he appeared unharmed. He saw her blaster and

cringed. She nodded once to acknowledge him, and kept moving. The guard was flanking her.

More rubble dropped from the ceiling. She crouched, hands over her head to protect herself. Small pebbles pelted her, and the floor shivered as large chunks of tile fell. Dust rose, choking her. She coughed, feeling it, but not able to hear it. Within an instant, the Hall had gone from a place of ceremonial comfort to a place of death.

The image of the death's-head mask rose in front of her again, this time from memory. She had known this was going to happen. Somewhere, from some part of her Force-sensitive brain, she had seen this. Luke said that Jedi were sometimes able to see the future. But she had never completed her training. She wasn't a Jedi.

But she was close enough.

The Corellian Trilogy:
AMBUSH AT CORELLIA
ASSAULT AT SELONIA
SHOWDOWN AT CENTERPOINT
by Roger MacBride Allen
Setting: Fourteen years after *Return of the Jedi*

This trilogy takes us to Corellia, Han Solo's homeworld, which Han has not visited in quite some time. A trade summit brings Han, Leia, and the children—now developing their own clear personalities and instinctively learning more about their innate skills in the Force—into the middle of a situation that most closely resembles a burning fuse. The Corellian system is on the brink of civil war, there are New Republic intelligence agents on a mysterious mission which even Han does not understand, and worst of all, a fanatical rebel leader has his hands on a superweapon of unimaginable power—and just wait until you find out who that leader is!

Here is an early scene from Ambush *that gives you a wonderful look at the growing Solo children (the twins are Jacen and Jaina, and their little brother is Anakin):*

Anakin plugged the board into the innards of the droid and pressed a button. The droid's black, boxy body shuddered awake, it drew in its wheels to stand up a bit taller, its status lights lit, and it made a sort of triple beep. "That's good," he said, and pushed the button again. The droid's status lights went out, and its body slumped down again. Anakin picked up the next piece, a motivation actuator. He frowned at it as he turned it over in his hands. He shook his head. "That's *not* good," he announced.

"What's not good?" Jaina asked.

"This thing," Anakin said, handing her the actuator. "Can't you *tell*? The insides part is all melty."

Jaina and Jacen exchanged a look. "The outside looks okay," Jaina said, giving the part to her brother. "How can he tell what the *inside* of it looks like? It's sealed shut when they make it."

Anakin, still sitting on the floor, took the device from his brother and frowned at it again. He turned it over and over in his hands, and then held it over his head and looked at it as if he were holding it up to the light. "There," he said, pointing a chubby finger at one point on the unmarked surface. "In there is the bad part." He rearranged himself to sit cross-legged, put the actuator in his lap, and put his right index finger over the "bad" part. "Fix," he said. "Fix." The dark brown outer case of the actuator seemed to glow for a second with an odd blue-red light, but then the glow sputtered out and Anakin pulled his finger away quickly and stuck it in his mouth, as if he had burned it on something.

"Better now?" Jaina asked.

"*Some* better," Anakin said, pulling his finger out of his mouth. "Not *all* better." He took the actuator in his hand and stood up. He opened the access panel on the broken droid and plugged in the actuator. He closed the door and looked expectantly at his older brother and sister.

"Done?" Jaina asked.

"Done," Anakin agreed. "But *I'm* not going to push the button." He backed well away from the droid, sat down on the floor, and folded his arms.

Jacen looked at his sister.

"Not me," she said. "This was your idea."

Jacen stepped forward to the droid, reached out to push the power button from as far away as he could, and then stepped hurriedly back.

Once again, the droid shuddered awake, rattling a bit this time as it did so. It pulled its wheels in, lit its panel lights, and made the same triple beep. But then its holocam eye viewlens wobbled back and forth, and its panel lights dimmed and flared. It rolled backward just a bit, and then recovered itself.

"Good morning, young mistress and masters," it said. "How may I surge you?"

Well, one word wrong, but so what? Jacen grinned and clapped his hands and rubbed them together eagerly. "Good day, droid," he said. They had done it! But what to ask for first? "First tidy up this room," he said. A simple task, and one that ought to serve as a good test of what this droid could do.

Suddenly the droid's overhead access door blew off and there was a flash of light from its interior. A thin plume of smoke drifted out of the droid. Its panel lights flared again, and then the work arm sagged downward. The droid's body, softened by heat, sagged in on itself and drooped to the floor. The floor and walls and ceiling of the playroom were supposed to be fireproof, but nonetheless the floor under the droid darkened a bit, and the ceiling turned black. The ventilators kicked on high automatically, and drew the smoke out of the room. After a moment they shut themselves off, and the room was silent.

The three children stood, every bit as frozen to the spot as the droid was, absolutely stunned. It was Anakin who recovered first. He walked cautiously toward the droid and looked at it carefully, being sure not to get too close or touch it. "*Really* melty now," he announced, and then wandered off to the other side of the room to play with his blocks.

The twins looked at the droid, and then at each other.

"We're dead," Jacen announced, surveying the wreckage.

STAR WARS: THE CANTINA TRILOGY
Edited by Kevin J. Anderson

Tales from the Mos Eisley Cantina

In a far corner of the universe, on the small desert planet of Tatooine, there is a dark, nic-i-tain-filled cantina where you can down your favorite intoxicant while listening to the best jizz riffs in the universe. But beware your fellow denizens of this pangalactic watering hole, for they are cut-throats and cutpurses, assassins and troopers, humans and aliens, gangsters and thieves . . .

0 553 40971 9

Tales from Jabba's Palace

In the dusty heat of twin-sunned Tatooine lives the wealthiest gangster in a hundred worlds, master of a vast crime empire and keeper of a vicious, flesh-eating monster for entertainment (and disposal of his enemies). Bloated and sinister, Jabba the Hutt might have made a good joke – if he weren't so dangerous. A cast of soldiers, spies, assassins, scoundrels, bounty hunters, and pleasure seekers have come to his palace, and every visitor to Jabba's grand abode has a story. Some of them may even live to tell it . . .

0 553 50413 4

Tales of the Bounty Hunters

In a wild and battle-scarred galaxy, assassins, pirates, smugglers, and cut-throats of every description roam at will, fearing only the professional bounty hunters – amoral adventurers who track down the scum of the universe . . . for a fee. When Darth Vader seeks to strike at the heart of the Rebellion by targeting Han Solo and the Millennium Falcon, he calls upon six of the most successful – and feared – hunters, including the merciless Boba Fett. They all have two things in common: lust for profit and contempt for life . . .

0 553 50471 1

A SELECTION OF SCIENCE FICTION
AND FANTASY TITLES
AVAILABLE FROM BANTAM BOOKS

THE PRICES SHOWN BELOW WERE CORRECT AT THE TIME OF GOING
TO PRESS. HOWEVER TRANSWORLD PUBLISHERS RESERVE THE RIGHT
TO SHOW NEW RETAIL PRICES ON COVERS WHICH MAY DIFFER FROM
THOSE PREVIOUSLY ADVERTISED IN THE TEXT OR ELSEWHERE.

☐ 40808 9	**STAR WARS: Jedi Search**	*Kevin J. Anderson*	£3.99
☐ 40809 7	**STAR WARS: Dark Apprentice**	*Kevin J. Anderson*	£3.99
☐ 40810 0	**STAR WARS: Champions of the Force**	*Kevin J. Anderson*	£3.99
☐ 40971 9	**STAR WARS: Tales from the Mos Eisley Cantina**	*Kevin J. Anderson (ed.)*	£4.99
☐ 50413 4	**STAR WARS: Tales from Jabba's Palace**	*Kevin J. Anderson (ed.)*	£4.99
☐ 50471 1	**STAR WARS: Tales of the Bounty Hunters**	*Kevin J. Anderson (ed.)*	£4.99
☐ 40880 1	**STAR WARS: Darksaber**	*Kevin J. Anderson*	£5.99
☐ 29138 6	**STAR TREK 1**	*James Blish*	£4.99
☐ 29139 4	**STAR TREK 2**	*James Blish*	£4.99
☐ 29140 8	**STAR TREK 3**	*James Blish*	£4.99
☐ 40879 8	**STAR WARS: Children of the Jedi**	*Barbara Hambly*	£4.99
☐ 40501 2	**STAINLESS STEEL RAT SINGS THE BLUES**	*Harry Harrison*	£4.99
☐ 50431 2	**STAR WARS: Before the Storm**	*Michael P. Kube-McDowell*	£4.99
☐ 50479 7	**STAR WARS: Shield of Lies·**	*Michael P. Kube-McDowell*	£4.99
☐ 50480 0	**STAR WARS: Tyrant's Test**	*Michael P. Kube-McDowell*	£4.99
☐ 50426 6	**SHADOW MOON**	*George Lucas & Chris Claremont*	£4.99
☐ 40881 X	**STAR WARS: Ambush at Corellia**	*Roger MacBride Allen*	£4.99
☐ 40882 8	**STAR WARS: Assault at Selonia**	*Roger MacBride Allen*	£4.99
☐ 40883 6	**STAR WARS: Showdown at Centerpoint**	*Roger MacBride Allen*	£4.99
☐ 40878 X	**STAR WARS: The Crystal Star**	*Vonda McIntyre*	£4.99
☐ 40926 3	**STAR WARS X-Wing 1: Rogue Squadron**	*Michael A. Stackpole*	£4.99
☐ 40923 9	**STAR WARS X-Wing 2: Wedge's Gamble**	*Michael A. Stackpole*	£4.99
☐ 40925 5	**STAR WARS X-Wing 3: The Krytos Trap**	*Michael A. Stackpole*	£4.99
☐ 40924 7	**STAR WARS X-Wing 4: The Bacta War**	*Michael A. Stackpole*	£4.99
☐ 40758 9	**STAR WARS: The Truce at Bakura**	*Kathy Tyers*	£4.99
☐ 50492 4	**HONOR AMONG ENEMIES**	*David Weber*	£4.99
☐ 40807 0	**STAR WARS: The Courtship of Princess Leia**	*Dave Wolverton*	£4.99
☐ 40471 7	**STAR WARS: Heir to the Empire**	*Timothy Zahn*	£4.99
☐ 40442 5	**STAR WARS: Dark Force Rising**	*Timothy Zahn*	£4.99
☐ 40443 1	**STAR WARS: The Last Command**	*Timothy Zahn*	£4.99
☐ 40853 4	**CONQUERORS' PRIDE**	*Timothy Zahn*	£4.99
☐ 40854 2	**CONQUERORS' HERITAGE**	*Timothy Zahn*	£4.99
☐ 40855 0	**CONQUERORS' LEGACY**	*Timothy Zahn*	£4.99

All Transworld titles are available by post from:

Book Service By Post, P.O. Box 29, Douglas, Isle of Man IM99 1BQ

Credit cards accepted. Please telephone 01624 675137,
fax 01624 670923, Internet http://www.bookpost.co.uk or
e-mail: bookshop@enterprise.net for details.

Free postage and packing in the UK. Overseas customers allow
£1 per book (paperbacks) and £3 per book (hardbacks).